DREAMS AND DESIRES

BOOK TWO

BY

PAUL BLADES

Dark Visions Publications
darkvisionspub@gmail.com

All characters and events portrayed in this work are
fictitious

Other books by Paul Blades:

The Maddy Saga:

PART ONE: PREPARATIONS

CHAPTER ONE

Kelly awoke on her third day of captivity to the delicious sensation of her dream man running his power laden hand down the soft curve of her hip and along her thigh. A wave of happiness infused her as she saw the face of her lover and lord gazing into her eyes. She had dreamt the mist dreams again, seemingly all night long, and she felt her body bursting with energy to convey to him. When he removed her gag and kissed her, spreading her lips with his and filling her mouth with his tongue, her whole body became charged with need. The man released her bonds and after affixing her hands to the headboard, rolled her to her back and entered her. During her body and mind wrenching climaxes, she could feel her night's accumulation of other worldly substance passing to the impassioned man through her fevered sex and mouth. In return, he granted her two of his long, soothing discharges.

Ramón rose from the bed rejuvenated. His pretty familiar needed to recover from her taxing release of the essences she had brought to him from across the dimensional divide. It was early yet and, after checking on the still sleeping Adele, he went outside to re-experience the wondrous sensations, both visual and physical, of the new day.

It was colder than it had been on the first morning he had made this excursion. The sky was overcast and grey, impending, he sensed, the release of moisture from the air to the ground. Two deer stood watching him warily on the edge of the woods as he made his way to the noisy brook. He was tempted to bring them to him, to examine them more closely and to run his hands through their appealing looking fur, but he had a busy, important morning ahead of him. He did take the time, however, to again drench his body in the pool of frigid water where the brook slowed and curved to change direction. The stimulation to his flesh was exquisite, but his body quickly reacted unpleasantly to the bitter cold of the air when he emerged and he hurried back into the house to dry himself and achieve a resumption of a more tolerable temperature.

Before getting dressed, he awoke his blond acolyte from her sleep. He sensed there was still a part of her brain disturbed by her new mindset and he spent some time calming her. It would have been easy to drive all thoughts other than obedience from her, but he wanted to maintain a more sophisticated, delicate control. He respected her as an intelligent life form and his codes forbade him from disturbing her more than necessary.

The shapely blond stirred dreamily from her sleep. He disconnected her bonds and eased her gag from her mouth. After stretching her soft, nude body luxuriantly, she looked up at him expectantly and taking hold of his hand, drew him towards her.

Adele's flesh was comfortably warm to his still chilled skin. Her bountiful breasts pressed pleasantly against his chest and her legs slid around his thighs as he entered her. She moaned into his mouth her gratitude for his filling of her hungry space.

Their lovemaking was long and tender. He let the radiance of his cock suffuse her with soft, comforting, pleasure. Her hands pulled him into her as her hips ground slowly back into his, relishing each prolonged stroke of his manhood. When her orgasm approached, she let out a long, pleased moan and her hands and legs gripped him tightly. "Ohhhhhhhhhhhhh!" she murmured happily as her crevasse began its throbs. As it mounted into heavy, ecstatic pulses, her moans became louder, almost desperate. Ramón could feel her pussy's walls clench tightly around him and he came with a deep, throaty groan, his mind reveling in each spasm of his cock as it jetted his entrancing sperm deep into the frantic blond woman's womb.

The couple took a few minutes to let the echoes of their orgasms calm their bodies. Adele rubbed her hand through Ramón's flowing, black hair as she tightened her pussy's muscles to give him one last, pleasurable squeeze. "You can wake me like that every day, honey," she told him, an affectionate, adoring smile on her lips. "But I've got lot's to do and so, unless you want to spend the day in bed, not that I'd mind, you better let me up."

Ramón drew himself up of off his appreciative servant. He went into the living room to turn on the TV while Adele removed her bindings and went into the kitchen. He was watching the news when she emerged and went into the bathroom. "The coffee'll be ready in a few minutes, honey," she said. "I've got to take a shower or the dog catcher will be after me."

He could hear the percolation of the coffee maker in the kitchen and the drum of the water from the shower as he watched the reporter relating the news about the most recent disaster, a train wreck outside of Tuscaloosa. Four people were killed. It reminded him of the hazards of this world he had entered. In turn, the dangers of his quest rose into his mind. Five years was a long time for the renegade to be able to prepare. He wouldn't even have the element of surprise since he would have been long expecting him. He had many things to do. First he had to secure his base. He would start that this morning with a visit to the female's laboratory. Then he would need to take steps to develop substances and technology that would protect and preserve his familiar and advance his quest. He needed an identity and to learn to drive one of their primitive vehicles. He required access to information and materials and that meant he needed to accumulate large quantities of the medium of exchange these beings referred to as money. Only then could he begin his search for the deviant jumper.

Adele finished her shower and, after bringing Ramón a nice hot cup of coffee, milk, no sugar, she went into the bedroom. She crawled up onto the bed and lay next to her friend. Kelly was sprawled out full length and lying on her right side, her hands reaching out above her to the headboard. Adele stroked her lightly on her cheek until she saw her eyes flutter to wakefulness. Kelly smiled at the warm welcome to her return to consciousness. The blond woman placed her lips on Kelly's and gave her a deep soulful kiss, mingling their tongues and pressing their flesh together.

When they broke apart, Adele leaned aback and caressed Kelly's breasts and tummy softly. "I can feel his energy in you, you know," she said, watching her hand as it slid over Kelly's smooth skin. "It makes me want to eat you up." She gave Kelly another kiss, this time, just bussing their lips together. "But we've got to get up. I've got to get you ready for work and get you some breakfast. I bought some nice cranberry banana muffins yesterday."

Adele unfastened Kelly's wrists from the bed and, after helping her to a sitting position, refastened them behind her back. The lead was on the nightstand and she snapped it on Kelly's collar. She led her into the bathroom where she washed her face, helped her use the toilet and brushed her hair. She then bought her to the kitchen and knelt her down on the little orange rug. "I'd put your gag in but we're going to eat in a minute so just sit tight here and don't say anything, okay?" She was stroking Kelly's smooth, brushed out auburn hair. Kelly gave a little nod and Adele went about her business.

The captive woman watched as her friend scurried nude around the kitchen. While the muffins were toasting, she put two placemats and knives on the table, butter, marmalade, two glasses of orange juice and three coffee cups. She filled the cups with hot brew, poured milk into two and two scoops of sugar into one. She turned to Kelly. "I know you don't take sugar, sweetie, so I gave you your own cup." The toaster dinged and Adele called out to the dream man. "Breakfast is ready, Ramón! Get it while it's hot!"

The three ranged around the table consuming their repast. Adele fed the kneeling, bound Kelly bits of butter laden muffin and let her drink some orange juice from her glass. The coffee felt good going down, its warmth spreading from her esophagus to her tummy. Kelly was conscious of and humiliated by the leash hanging loosely between her breasts as she ate. It swung from her body each time she leaned over to take a large crumb of muffin from her oblivious blond friend's hand. It reminded her of her demeaned status as a creature not permitted a will of her own. As if reading her mind, Ramón would, from time to time, give her breast a gentle squeeze or caress her head, sending messages of comfort.

For once, Adele had nothing to say. There was a palpable nervousness in the room. All thoughts were on the upcoming day. The 800 pound gorilla was how Kelly would take to being in public during the length of the workday. And there were things she needed to do. The grant application was due Wednesday. There were research protocols to set up. Friday's experiments were blown and would have to be repeated. Kelly's mother called usually a couple times a week and she had friends who checked in once and a while from all over the country. There were business details to attend to and the miscellaneous interruptions we all experience. She would have to deal with the girls, Chandra, Melissa and Felicity.

And then there was the fact that although Kelly had responded well to Ramón's bonding with her, she was, much more than technically, a prisoner. She had not been permitted a volitional movement for two days. She was forbidden to speak and she was kept in close bondage for most of the time, even when her captor was fucking her. She had not been converted to Ramón's will like Adele had, who would probably throw herself in front of a bus rather than disobey the dream man. The difference between them was that Kelly was aware there was something wrong about having been reduced to a creature of lust. She knew she should be rebelling against the dream man's control over her. She just did not want to.

The thing that was uppermost in Kelly's mind was how she would survive the day without continuously satisfying the compelling, overwhelming need she had developed for the man's flesh, his touch and the pleasure he brought her. Just watching him eat while she knelt subserviently a little more than two feet away from him made her loins burn. Her stomach turned as she thought of being separated from him.

Adele finished first and she got up to clear away the dishes and put away the butter and milk. She let Kelly drink down the now cooled remnants of her coffee and put the cup in the dishwasher. Ramón had finished and had turned his chair to Kelly expectantly. Without ceremony, Adele lifted Kelly from her knees by her leash, moved the rug in front of Ramón and guided the bound woman back to the floor. She patted her head and said, "Don't take too long, Kelly. I'm going to put my face on and then I'll do yours."

The effusions of radiant pleasure that flowed from Ramón's stiff cock through her mouth made all of Kelly's concerns disappear. The dream man would take care of everything, she thought. She languidly ran her lips down the dream man's stiff pole, licking and kissing the bulbous head at the terminus of each upstroke. He passed his lust through to her with his hand as het stroked her head. When the pleasurable pulses of the man's orgasm began to thrill her lips, her pussy responded in kind. As her orgasm coursed through her, Kelly sensed her friend standing next to her, stroking her head soothingly. She became conscious of the picture she must be making, on her knees, her lips pursed around the dream man's cock, her eyes closed in fulfillment, her bare breasts swaying as she moved her head to bring pleasure to the hard meat. Her nipples were taut with her arousal and her bound hands writhed behind her, displaying her fevered excitement at receiving his discharge.

"Oh, you're so pretty, Kelly," Adele said wistfully when Kelly's orgasm had wound down and she bashfully let Ramón's cock slip from her mouth. The kind words were all it took to dispel Kelly's embarrassment. She felt pretty. No, more than pretty. She felt beautiful, desired. Yesterday, Adele had called her lucky. Yes, she was lucky. Of the millions of women in the world he could have chosen, many of them far prettier and alluring, he had chosen her, Kelly. She did not know or care why. For her wild, obsessive infatuation with the man, his presence, his flesh, could not stand introspection. It was more than something out of a love story. What love story had ever posited the weird relationship she had with her dream man?

Kelly was woozy with the dream man's energies when Adele pulled her from her knees. There was a small dollop of the man's fluid on her lip and Adele scooped it up with a finger and placed it in her mouth. Her body shuddered. "Mmmmmmmm!" she said dreamily.

Adele sat Kelly on the closed toilet while she applied the light powder Kelly used to give her cheeks just a touch of color. She applied a pale red lipstick and outlined her eyelashes and under her eyes with a thin line of black. When she brought Kelly to the mirror, Kelly decided that her friend had got it just right.

When Adele brought Kelly to the bedroom, she had her sit on the edge of the foot of the bed while she rummaged through her stocking drawer for something appropriate. She chose a pair of dark, sheer, self supporting stockings which had a four inch wide band of black lace at the tops. This was not what Kelly usually wore to work. Although she really didn't care for pantyhose much, it was her habit to wear a pair that was light beige, barely announcing that she was wearing stockings at all. Kelly didn't like to call attention to her femininity at work. Work was all about being professional, getting the job done. But Kelly knew she had no right to protest and, what would happen to her if she did. It was just one more reminder she had no control over herself any more.

Adele's hands were warm and sensual as she drew the stockings up Kelly's legs. Kneeling between them, she paused to appreciate the alluring look of Kelly's thighs, her pale skin so clearly set off from the pretty, black lacework. Suddenly, Kelly became aware of the lasciviousness of the bare flesh between her stockinged legs. She remembered her hairlessness and blanched. Adele seemed to have the same thought and she spread Kelly's thighs a little wider and gave her pudenda a gentle stroke. "Oh," she said as she ran her fingers over the soft flesh. "You've gotten a little stubbly, honey. I'll have to fix that up. I'll have to remember to shave you twice a day."

Adele got to her feet, ran into the kitchen to get one of Kelly's aluminum mixing bowls, ran into the bathroom to get some hot water, soap and lotion and returned. She guided Kelly to her back on the bed and pushed up her thighs so her feet were on the mattress on either side of her. Kelly's bound hands were underneath her and her bottom was lifted just enough so Adele could complete her chore. She carefully scraped the sensitive skin with the razor after applying a thin screen of warm soap. Kelly closed her eyes, feeling her passion growing at the handling of her mons despite her shame at the woman's view of her bare love lips. When Adele finished applying the lotion, Kelly's slit had lubricated and she was not displeased when she felt Adele's tongue sliding along its sensitive length.

The prisoner moaned as Adele's lush tongue inflamed her. She bit her lower lip when it massaged her stiffened love button. Through her fog of passion, Kelly remembered Adele's promise to her the night before that she would make her come with her mouth in the morning. She wondered idly as she absorbed the undeniable pleasures of the blond woman's lips, how many mornings they would repeat this ritual, and how many nights. How often she would be displayed so obscenely on the bed, or on her bathroom floor, her knees spread wide lasciviously, Adele's mouth driving her to pleasure?

She sensed another presence in the room and saw through her fog her captor standing at the bedroom door watching. He had dressed and was wearing a dark blue t-shirt and his brand new jeans. What had seemed barely acceptable in private seemed lewd and deviant with the man present, especially now that he wore the raiment of an ordinary man. Her face grimaced and she whined in dismay. She weakly tried to close her legs. Adele placed her hands on them firmly, keeping them apart. Kelly looked at the man and had an image of herself in some porno gallery, putting on a display for the prurient passions of strange, feverishly lustful men. Suddenly, the man sent to her mind a wave of approval and acceptance and Kelly's objections succumbed almost instantly to the pleasure being brought to her by the blond woman's mouth and lips. As she felt her climax rising, she wondered at her newfound sexual voraciousness. She had already come four times today, three when the man had drained her of the mist she had received in her dreams and once when he had come in her mouth, less than ten minutes ago. This would be her fifth. And how many times had she come yesterday, and the day before? She had lost count. These thoughts took place in an instant and were followed by a surge of intense lust and then by the fierce, pleasure inducing contractions of her sex. Her body arched as she received them.

When Adele got up to put away her tools, the dream man approached Kelly and stood before her. She shuddered as his eyes focused on her bare, well pleasured slit. Not having been given permission to move, she kept her widespread thighs in place. Something in her wanted him to look at her denuded gash, to appreciate the proffer of her loins to him. At the same time, the image in her mind of what he was so intently looking at made her blush with shame.

Ramón sensed the woman's conflict. While he had not created her unhappiness at her hairless sex, he had stoked it and, at the same time created a need in her to display it to him. By forcing her to overcome her intense inner reticence to please him in this way, she would be reminded starkly of her submission to his control. The fact that the enticing love lips she displayed to him so wantonly were forbidden to her touch would deepen her need to proffer them to him to seek his. The female had raised her hips slightly and was peering at him hopefully with her clear, blue eyes. He took a finger and placed it lightly between her pale, smooth labia, sending his power through it and drawing it slowly upwards until it reached the nub at its apex. The female sighed with passion and he sensed her joy that he had brought contact between them there, that her display had brought the desired reward.

The perky, young blond woman came rushing back in and gave Ramón a gentle shove. "If you start her up all over again, we'll never get to the lab on time," she said playfully.

Ramón stepped away so Kelly's adornment could continue. As he did so, he noted the pleasure he had received from seeing the woman's thighs and legs decorated with the sheer, black material. The delicate lace at the top was particularly enticing, calling for caresses to her soft inner thighs. This additional function of clothing was something he had not thought about. And he made note that the visual satisfaction he had received was one more sensual experience that had delighted him.

Adele had picked out Kelly's shortest skirt. It was pleated and was a red and black plaid. Kelly was usually too shy to wear something so revealing and, having purchased it in a moment of impetuousness, had only worn it once. Although it violated her self imposed, strictly conservative work dress code, Kelly, still dazed from her orgasm and the man's teasing of her still glowing slit, stepped into it obediently. She was confused that Adele had not selected a pair of panties for her first and then realized, to her mortification, she was expected to go throughout the day without them. She wanted to protest. The man was still watching and so she bit her tongue. In spite of her overwhelming need and lust for the man, she still feared him and his ability to bring instant, mind jarring, inner pain to her.

The dream man was watching his familiar carefully. He sensed her distress at the revealing nature of her skirt. To him, she looked enticing. Somehow, the presence of the adornments to her lower body invited the eye to drink of the gracefulness of her thighs, the roundness of her hips, and the mind to speculate about what lay further above the skirt's hem. Knowing there was nothing that would block his access to her sweet sex should he reach his hand under it, stirred his male, human lust. She looked at him almost fearfully, her mouth formed into a small frown, her eyes soft and watery. Her naked breasts remained pleasantly within his view, pushed out slightly by the force of her bound arms behind her. The collar around her neck and the leash that dangled from it between her shimmering breasts advertised her submissiveness, her bondage to his will. Her silky, long, reddish brown hair flowed alluringly over her shoulders. The red hues of her hair and her skirt highlighted the darker, almost maroon shade of her areolas. It was a shame her pretty, soft, round globes had to be hidden away. They accentuated the softness of her body, were reminiscent of the pleasure he felt in stroking it, having her flesh rub against his.

Bringing over two of Kelly's pullover, turtle necked shirts, Adele showed them to her. "This way you can still wear your collar and no one will be able to see it," she said happily. She held them up one at a time to the skirt and rejected the black one in favor of the dark beige. She undid Kelly's braceleted arms from behind her back, and after removing the leash from her collar, slid it over her head. As she did so, Kelly realized she would be going braless too, something she never did, and her unhappiness intensified. She would look like a tart with her exposed upper thighs and her swaying breasts every time she moved. And the shirt was just a little too tight for her. She would have returned it except that she bought it back in Jersey the last time she was home.

Adele picked out a pair of black high heels Kelly often wore. She was thankful she didn't own any real spikes or she was sure Adele would have chosen them instead.

The blond dressier stood back to consider her decoration of Kelly's body. She smiled with satisfaction. "You look terrific, honey," she said. "You should dress like this all the time. You know, if ya got it, flaunt it."

She led Kelly over to the full length mirror on the door to the closet so Kelly could see herself. The turtlenecked shirt pulled tightly over her breasts, clearly demarking their separation and form, the hard points of her nipples readily discernable. The red and black, pleated skirt lay loosely across her thighs, revealing six inches of the dark, sheer stockings above her knees. "I look like some slutty high school kid looking to score," she thought miserably. She put her hand up to the neck of the shirt and felt her collar underneath it. She would be wearing it all day, a reminder of her captivity. But that was the idea, wasn't it? Her bracelets were lumps at the ends of her long-sleeved pullover. She wondered whether she would be forced to wear them all day too. Adele was standing behind Kelly in the mirror smiling impishly. She was still naked and to Kelly she looked like some sprite that had magically appeared in her bedroom, full of fun and mischief. She experienced a more accurate sense of her role when she gently took hold of her arms and, after sliding up the sleeves, connected her wrists behind her back.

"I've got to get dressed, honey, so why don't you have a seat in the living room for a little while till we're ready to go?" Adele said as she led Kelly from the bedroom by her arm. She sat Kelly in the chair that had a view of the outside door. Kelly had to lean forwards so she wouldn't place her weight on her bound arms. Adele went back to the bedroom for a moment and returned carrying her gag and the ankle bracelets, which she had removed when putting on her stockings. She placed the bracelets over the stockings on each leg and then bound them together. She then presented the gag to Kelly's mouth. "Be careful not to muss your lipstick," she said as she carefully guided it into place. After she locked the straps in place behind Kelly's head, she ran off to the spare room to put on her clothes.

It was about another fifteen minutes until they were ready to leave. Kelly, was unable to do anything but wait. Sitting alone and bound, she stared at the door to the outside. Her safe, secure, regular life had been turned upside down since she had last crossed the portal. She pulled slightly on the bonds behind her back and on her legs as if to make sure they were real, that she was really sitting in a chair in her own home bound and gagged. The funny thing was it felt almost natural. At first, she had rebelled at the thought of being so thoroughly confined. Now the encircling bands of softly lined leather seemed comforting, as if she did not have to chide herself for failing to physically resist the man and his will for her and could, instead, absolve herself of guilt for her joyous surrender.

As her eyes focused on the door, she wondered what would have happened if she had been able to get it shut before the dream man came back into the house after his early morning frolic on Saturday. Would he have mesmerized her into opening it again? Could his powers flow through walls? Even though she was a confined prisoner, had lost all rights of personal integrity, and was apparently being used for some ulterior purpose of the man's, she wondered if she would have tried to close the door if she knew then what she knew now. If someone had offered her the conscious choice between the almost intolerable bliss she had experienced over the last two days and her freedom, what would she have chosen? She knew she would have chosen freedom, because there would have been no way to convey the inexpressible joy she felt at the man's presence, the ecstasy she felt at his touch. And still now, she wondered, if somehow the man's control over her lapsed, if she got the chance to run away today, would she take it? Probably not. What was freedom after all compared to bliss?

Kelly was also afraid of being someplace other than here, in the comfortable, warm environment of her house, where her mystical transformation had taken place. Here, she did not have to be confronted by the real world, deal with the fact that no one could ever understand what she had been through, never mind approve of what she had become. And what if, being confronted by the realities of her outside existence, somehow the spell was broken? She would lose the feeling of utter contentment she felt whenever the man put his hands on her. She would lose the burning need she felt for him, a need that made her feel more alive than she had ever felt before. She would lose the orgasmic bliss he brought to her whenever he placed his hard cock inside her body and discharged himself there. Just the thought of it made her need for him rise.

The man came and sat down opposite her. He was drinking his second cup of coffee. He saw she was nervous and noted her growing lust. It was good to feel it flow across the small room to him. His eyes surveyed the picture of his pretty familiar. The blond woman had done her job well, and the female was a delectable sight. Her bound hands behind her curved her shoulders back, proffering her covered, clearly distinguishable breasts. Her legs looked long and sensual. Her helpless confinement and doleful look made her even more appealing to his male, human mind.

Kelly shifted uncomfortably as the man's eyes scanned her body. His gaze made her more conscious of her bonds, her defenselessness. She could not help thinking of her naked breasts beneath her knitted top, breasts he could caress or kiss merely by the raising of the bottom of her shirt. She was reminded of her bare pussy that lurked under her short, revealing skirt, open to his possession by the simple expedient of lifting her hem. Her body shivered as her lust began to grow. "How will I ever make it through the day?" she asked herself fearfully.

Adele came storming into the living room. She was dressed in one of her standard miniskirts and a tight, flowered blouse. "I'm ready. I'm ready," she announced merrily. She knelt down before Kelly and released and removed her ankle bindings. Standing up, she disconnected the bracelets around her wrists and eased the gag from her mouth. She put the ankle bracelets and gag in her big, red purse. She retrieved Kelly's fall jacket from the closet and helped her put it on. When Kelly looked up, the man was standing in front of her. He was wearing a supple, form fitting, black leather jacket with a bright brass zipper that looked very good on him. He placed his hands on either side of her auburn head and sent her a strong signal of the need to obey his will combined with a surge of pleasure. Kelly felt her knees weaken as she absorbed it. When the man released her, Adele put her arms around her and gave her a long, passionate kiss. Kelly hugged her back and returned the kiss happily. They were best friends, lovers now, she thought. Adele would take care of her. As if reading her mind, Adele told her when they broke their kiss, "Don't worry, Kelly, everything will be all right. And tonight, I'll have a really nice surprise for you." She then locked Kelly's wrists together in front of her.

It was a twenty minute drive to the lab from Kelly's house except when the usually light traffic got snarled where Route 246 crosses Becker Farm Road. Today, of all days, traffic was heavy. Kelly's composure about the upcoming day lasted only a few miles. At the first signs of the otherwise normalcy of the day, the cars breezing up and down the country road, the telephone poles whizzing by, the stores and coffee shops, Kelly's heart sank into a deep funk. Like a condemned woman tired of waiting for her doom, Kelly sat in the back seat behind Ramón and counted each long minute of their trip. They had taken her car and Kelly was driving. A light drizzle was making everything worse.

How could the world be the same, she thought miserably, when she had changed so much? Although her wrists were bound in front of her, they were clearly meant only as something symbolic since she could still release her seat belt by pressing the little button to her left and operate the door handle to her right. It was her own will that kept her a prisoner, her decision to succumb to her need for the man sitting in the passenger seat in front of her.

"And why does he want to go to my lab?" she wondered, looking at the long, black hair at the back of his head. Does he need it for some reason? Is this what this is all about? Was that why she was selected?

The fact that the man might have chosen her for purely utilitarian purposes rather than as a result of an infatuation or obsession with her was disconcerting. It struck at her self respect and pride. She still had no real answer to how he had appeared so suddenly in her bed, locked in a passionate embrace with her. It was clear he had chosen her. Was he merely trading on the emotional barrenness of her life, counting on her desperate need for intimate companionship? Did he really care for her?

Ramón, otherwise entranced by the strange new world he was traveling through, turned from time to time to check up on his familiar. When they had come out of the house, Ramón had stood still for a moment, his face upturned as the rainwater caressed it. Adele had stopped walking to the car when she discovered he was not right behind her, and said jokingly, "It's just rain, baby. You'll get to see a lot of that around here this time of year."

When he looked back to where his familiar was sitting in the car, he could sense her distraught state. He sent soothing, comforting messages to her, signals that would, temporarily cause her to relax her tense body, ease the conflicts within her. When he looked back a few minutes later, he would see the same, tense, nervous look on her face.

Twice, Kelly had the urge to jump out of the car. The first was when they stopped at the red light about three miles from her house. She knew the owner of the gas station there and imagined herself running inside and begging him to call the police. The second time was when they stopped at the light at Meyer's Junction. There, an actual police car pulled up right beside them in the right hand turn lane. The young officer peered into their car with feigned nonchalance. Kelly looked back. It would take only a look, a mouthing of the word 'help' to summon assistance, start in motion a chain of events that would lead to her liberation. A wave of misery flooded her when she thought of being separated from her dream lover and she let the police cruiser pull away.

She was filled with dread when they finally pulled into the driveway for the lab a little before 8 o'clock. Ramón got out first and opened her door. When she stepped out, he took her arm. A thin curtain of light rain was still falling. As luck would have it, Mr. Hardings, her landlord was arriving just at the same time. He was broadchested and about 5'8" tall. He was wearing a heavy, plaid winter jacket that, coincidentally, matched Kelly's skirt, and a red and yellow Washington Redskins knitted pullover cap. Kelly, distressed that he would see her bound wrists, tried to pull them up into the sleeves of her jacket.

"Morning, Dr. Jameson," he said to her amiably.

"That's right," Kelly said to herself. "I'm Dr. Jameson." She was about to return the greeting when she was hit by a wall of panic. If she didn't speak, Hardings would think there was something weird going on. If she did speak, her captor might punish her. She looked anxiously at Ramón. He sent her a message of reassurance.

Ramón, of all people, saved the day.

"Hi," he said, holding out his hand. "I'm Ramón Vasquez, Mr. Hardings. Nice to meet you. I'm going to be working with Dr. Jameson for a while. We've brought in a few new grants and are going to be very busy."

"Well, that's great," Hardings replied shaking Ramón's hand back heartily. That his tenant was prospering was good news indeed!

Kelly looked at Ramón as if he was a manikin that had just recited the Gettysburg Address. The dream man had a voice after all! And it was perfect, slightly accented English. She was about to say something when Adele broke in. "Hi,

I'm Adele. I'm the office manager. I've seen you around a lot but we've never met." She extended her hand to formalize the greeting. "We've got a conference call with some of the money people in a few minutes so we can't chat. Ramón'll come over later and talk to you about some plans we've been working on."

"Okay, Okay," Hardings said merrily. And to Ramón, "Come over any time. Anything I can do for Dr. Jameson, I'd be happy."

Adele unlocked the door to the lab and the trio entered. Ramón immediately began to look around the place. Adele escorted Kelly to her office and, after unlocking her bracelets and removing her coat, locked them back together before her and sat her in her chair behind her desk.

Kelly's beautiful, large, dark oak desk had been a present from her family when she had opened the lab. Its shiny top was covered by a clean, black bordered, green felt pad, had a picture of Kelly, her mom and dad and her younger brother and sister in it sitting in a frame, an old fashioned green tinted desk lamp and the usual assortment of office conveniences: a stapler, Scotch tape, a round container for pens, etc. There was a small stack of papers on the front right of the desk in a little bin and her thin computer screen on the left in front of which sat her keyboard. The telephone was on the right, just far enough to be out of the way, but within easy reach.

After sitting Kelly in her chair, Adele pulled the cord from the telephone base. She then unplugged the computer and closed the blinds on the outside windows. There was a set of blinds which Kelly never used which covered the interior windows that looked over the lab area. Adele closed them too.

Kelly watched sadly as she was cut off from contact with the outside world. She felt like a little girl in her grandmother's parlor with her hands graciously and respectfully folded in her lap. It was about another hour before the lab techs would arrive. She thought nervously about how they would react if they saw her bound hands and her skimpy dress, not to mention all the drawn blinds. Adele had even lowered the shade over the window on the door. And how would she communicate with anybody? Were they going to make her sit in her chair all day with nothing to do?

Kelly felt a tear roll down her cheek. Was the dream man going to take everything away from her? Adele had taken the dark wooden chair with the padded seat to the left in front of her desk. She just sat there, smiling and waiting.

Kelly's office was warmly decorated. The lab area had once been a large warehouse and the manager's office had been carved out of the storage area and was constructed of concrete block. It rose about ten feet high under the 20' high roof. It been modeled in late early industrial decor when she took over the lab. The torn, sheetrocked walls were a faded, dirty white, the ceiling consisted of the bare underside of the concrete overhead. The floor had been painted gray over what had once been painted red, and scuff marks and gouges made the older, red paint stand out like wounds.

Using a small amount of money from her first year's grant, and with the help of reduced price workmen Mr. Hardings had sent her, Kelly had the walls repaired and painted a light, pastel green. The floors were covered with a dark green and cream colored oriental style carpet over a thick pad. She had had a drop ceiling installed and a large, round light fixture put in to replace the banged up fluorescent ones. The walls were covered with her mementos, diplomas, awards, letters of commendation. She had several of her favorite prints matted and framed in dark, brown wood. Across from her desk was her favorite Degas, a picture of several, young, pretty, student ballerinas in flowing, chimerical ballet dresses, flexing their legs, taking practice adagios against a backdrop of a long, tall mirror. Their delicate hands floated in the air or swept towards the ground as they anchored themselves to the long wooden bar that ran across it. The painting was suffused with pleasant reds, blues, yellows and whites and clearly showed the painter's affection for the delicate, young girls.

Looking at it now, Kelly felt fear for the pretty, young girls who worked for her. Ramón would corrupt them, she just knew it. They were all over eighteen and probably had active sex lives of their own. They also had boyfriends and family and Chandra, whose family had emigrated from New Delhi, went to night classes. Were they all to become his servants? To what purpose? Didn't she have some responsibility to warn them, to protect them? They looked up to her as a kind of surrogate mother, sometimes coming in to her office to cry over this and that. And they treated Adele like a favored older sister, the same Adele who would happily facilitate their betrayal.

While the women waited for him in Kelly's office, Ramón took his time examining the facilities of the lab. It had been an interesting ride from the house. He was surprised at how much these beings had marred the natural beauty of their environment, with large, garish billboards here and there, the ubiquitous power and telephone lines, the interminable stores. Why they needed so many he couldn't figure out. And the amount of resources the devoted to their means of locomotion was astounding. He counted two new car dealers and three used ones on the 15 mile ride from the female's house to here. There had been four gas stations and two parts stores too. And that didn't include the vast spaces devoted to parking the vehicles at all the different commercial establishments.

His servant had popped on the radio while they drove and while some of the sounds were jarring, the melodies of others were interesting and the beat was compelling. The noise of what he recognized as selling messages were the worst. He wondered if these beings could recognize the falsity in the voices of the pitch men and women.

The strangest part of the ride had been his search for the computer guidance mechanism he presumed gave the drivers of the cars the confidence to travel so fast and so close to one another. The vehicles coming in the opposite direction often made him flinch as they looked to be coming right at them. Although he had courageously made five dimensional jumps, he had never felt the apprehension he felt during that ride. It had distracted him for caring for his familiar who, he realized, was suffering bouts of intense apprehension in the back seat. He gave her what assurances he could before pinning his eyes again on the fearsome traffic approaching them.

The feel of the light drizzle of rain on his face had been wondrous. It felt like a thousand tiny kisses on his skin. The woman, Adele, had been amused at his enjoyment of this new, pleasurable sensation. It was a shame, he thought, that these beings had been so inured to the pleasures around them they were barely noticed.

He examined the laboratory equipment and recognized most of its uses. He went to the rear of the building and took stock of the steel emergency door. Adele had informed him about the vacant space which was located next to the lab. He would speak to Hardings about that today. The meeting in the parking lot had been fortuitous, obviating the need for an introduction later. He had taken from his familiar's mind what little she knew about his operations on the other side of the concrete wall that divided them. It seemed he might have had a stroke of luck. If Hardings had government contracts for military applications, he would probably have access to strategic materials Ramón would need. And he was sure he could produce innovations to Hardings' products that would bring very quick financial rewards. Until then, he would need to live off of the foundation money the female had access to. He would have her add him as a signatory to those accounts today.

He took his time, looking in cabinets and drawers, examining tools and the stock room. Some of the raw materials would be useful. He needed to study some more to know for sure. He had already identified, in his research, several compounds and types of biological materials he would need. Adele would make sure orders were placed before the day was out.

It was about 8:30 when he walked into Kelly's office. He knew the three young laboratory assistants would be showing up in a half hour or so and he wanted to be ready for them. Also, he needed to acclimatize his familiar to his dominance of her here and he wanted to complete that process before the others arrived.

Kelly had been sitting quietly in her office, sullenly staring at her assistant and friend. Adele just smiled back. "I could get up and run," she thought. She might be able to surprise Adele, knock her down or something, and dash out of her office door. If the man was in the back of the lab, she might be able to get to the main door before he could do anything about it. There were security men watching on the cameras that were mounted on the roof and they might see her frantically fleeing the building before the man caught her. They would investigate. She could save the girls, get her lab back. She kept on trying to will her body into motion with no success. Her stomach would cringe with the thought of being disobedient to her captor, her lord and master. She would get a vision of his face, his body and she would recoil from the idea of being parted from them.

He had spoken! What a trip that was! His voice was deep and comforting. She wished she could hear more of it, but for some reason he didn't deign to use it in her presence unless he had to. He communicated to Adele psychically, apparently, since she always seemed to know what he wanted without any conversation passing between them. She had secured Kelly's office without any words being exchanged, unless they had planned out what she should do on arrival before Kelly awoke. Adele had picked up quickly on Ramón's lie to Mr. Hardings and followed it up with a convenient and consistent lie of her own.

Then Kelly had a brainstorm. Mr. Hardings worked on all kinds of secret government stuff. Was that the purpose of the dream man's capture of her? Was she the cat's paw by which he would gain access to Mr. Hardings' secrets and steal them away? Or maybe he was sent here by some superior race of beings and meant to sabotage them to prevent earthlings from advancing into space, or developing super weapons with which we would destroy ourselves. It occurred to Kelly she had seen movies and TV shows with themes like that. Was that it? Was she being ridiculous? Melodramatic? Well, it was as possible as anything else that had happened since she met the powerful, entrancing man. Maybe they used dreams as some kind of travel between their worlds or galaxies. It was not something science would deem possible, yet neither was his ability to control people, to enter her mind, to regulate her body. She couldn't discount it just because it seemed outlandish.

What obligation did that impose on her? Was she to be the Judas of her race, betraying it for the physical and mental joy he brought her? Was her blissful lust the equivalent of thirty pieces of silver? She just had to get away. The entire human civilization might depend on it.

At that moment, Ramón opened the door to Kelly's office and stepped in. Kelly felt a surge of lust for him as soon as he appeared. Her rambling internal discourse on the future of the human race faded right away. Her need for him became paramount once more. Ramón shut the door behind him and started taking off his clothes, beginning with his dark blue t-shirt. As soon as Kelly saw his muscular naked chest, she felt her pussy begin to tingle with excitement. "Oh, my god," she thought, panicked. "He's going to do me right here in my office!"

Whatever objection Kelly had to his use of her in her private, almost sacred, chamber, it withered quickly away. She watched him with lustful anticipation as he removed the rest of his clothes. She shifted her gaze momentarily to Adele as if to see whether she, too, was affected by the man's mere presence. She was watching him wistfully. Suddenly, the dream man stood right before her. He offered her his hand. Slowly, as if in a dream herself, Kelly lifted her joined hands to him and let him pull her to her feet from the chair.

The strong, naked man put his arms around the trembling woman and offered her his lips. Kelly raised hers and when they met, she felt a surge of passion in her loins. He kissed her long and hard, bringing her lusts to a boil. Her bound hands were crushed between them, resting on his hardening prick. She circled it automatically and reveled in its feel, wanting it inside her. His tongue was hot in her mouth, and she commingled it with hers, relishing the flow of warmth to her body.

Kelly felt the man's hands lifting her tight, turtle neck shirt until it slipped above her breasts, baring them. His hands seized her globes, sending his energies through them, causing her to moan with pleasure. His lips parted from hers and he pulled the shirt up over her head and slid it down her arms. It could not pass her bound hands and he left it there, bunched up and intertwined with her wrists. Stepping behind her, he pressed his cock against her rear, his bare back against hers and circled her torso with his strong arms, reclaiming her breasts, massaging them gently, luxuriously, pinching at her taut nipples. The feel of the man's fingers teasing her stiffened teats sent charges of fierce need through the half naked women's body. She pressed her rear back towards him, loving the feel of his hard manhood against her.

Kelly expected the man to lift her skirt to gain access to her sex, but the man had other ideas. One of his hands left her breasts and he leaned away from her. Kelly, through her impassioned haze, felt him undo the clasp at the back of her skirt and the zipper slowly descending. The garment loosened about her waist and the man lowered it, crouching down to assist her in pulling it over her black, high heeled shoes.

She was nude now, but for the sheer, luxurious black stockings that ended in bands of fine, sexy lace at the tops of her thighs. "I'm naked in my office," Kelly thought as the cool air caressed her bare skin. She didn't know whether to be happy or sad. Whatever sense of safety she had felt from the man by being in her own special place was shattered. With the ability to shield their activities from the world by lowering the blinds, he could take her here anytime he wanted. Now, when she sat at her desk she would remember being naked here, having his hands run over her body and soon, very soon, taking possession of her by feeding his thick cock into her hungry cleft.

Ramón stood and gently urged Kelly's body forward, until her bare hips met the edge of her desk. Adele stood up and cooperatively moved the desk lamp aside to give Kelly room to stretch her upper body over it. He then pressed at her back until she bent her torso down. She placed her elbows and forearms on the desk, staring down at the green felt of her desk mat as he nudged her thighs apart with his knees. He ran his stiff cock along her labial lips, bringing a surge of passion to her. "Ohhhhhhh," she moaned as the contact between his cock and her skin electrified her. When he slid himself home into her already moistened pussy, her whole body rejoiced.

Kelly could think of nothing else except the thick manhood delving deep into her womb and back again. Each long, slow stroke sent a wave of heavenly sensation through her. His hot hands were on her back, caressing her skin. It was not long before she felt her orgasm rising, the surge of blood to her loins, the tightness in her stiff nipples. She looked up and arched her back, readying herself for the fierce contractions she knew she would soon feel. She saw her friend Adele watching her performance, lust across her face. The sight of her friend, dressed and comfortably sitting in her office chair, observing her rut like an animal on her desk, disconcerted her for only a moment. Her lusts overflowed their banks and her body began to shudder with her climax. "Oh! Oh! Oh! Oh!" she called out as each stroke of the man's cock sent a wave of pleasure through her. She could feel her breasts swaying and jerking beneath her at each thrust of the man's hips against her rear. She put her head down, resting it on the pillow made by her shirt on her joined hands and let her orgasm take its course.

She realized when her spasms began to fade that the man had not come and that he was not through with her. She felt his long, hard shaft withdraw from her still shuddering channel. His hot hands took hold of her firm rear cheeks and separated them and she understood immediately that he intended to use the smaller, tighter portal there. "Not here! Not like this!" her mind screamed. "Not with Adele watching!" But her revolt lasted only until she felt the tip of his cock pierce the small opening. The passionate energies it emitted radiated all around the taut circle that guarded her bowels.

The slippery moisture from her pussy's discharge during her climax clung to the hard cock and it passed easily through the small star of her rear. As the shaft rasped across the sensitive tissue, Kelly moaned again. He had done this to her, she knew that. He had made her love the feel of his cock inside her most private place, made the sensation of his prick crossing the portal send a sharp, electrical burst of pleasure through her body. But what difference did it make whether he had created this lustful response or found it buried deeply within her and brought it to the fore? What was important was to revel in each moment of his possession of her. She knew what he was doing. By fucking her there, making her submit to him in spite of her shame at the pleasure she experienced at this use, he was reminding her of his mastery of her. Here, in what had been her inner sanctum, a place she had infused with her personality, made her own, he was lord, not her.

The man had her hips pinned to the desk and was thrusting himself back and forth in her rear almost brutally. He was leaning over her and she could feel the heat of his chest on her back. Kelly felt that her whole body was going to explode with lust. She moaned deeply as the fire of passion spread from her electrified anal ring to her loins. When she felt his cock jerk and spasm, flooding her bowels with his essence, she came again, shuddering and shaking, letting the ecstasy of her completion thunder through her.

After the man came, he remained inside her. He was still stiff and Kelly could feel his energies from his cock seeping deep into her. He leaned back and caressed her spine and shoulders with his hard but gentle hands and she felt strong signals of approval and comfort flowing into her from them. Yes, he was her lord and master. He could take possession of her any time and in any way he wanted. He could be intent on world conquest and Kelly would not care. She couldn't live without him. She knew that.

As his semen diffused in the female's depths, Ramón savored the feel of her small ring of flesh around his pleasured cock. He had drunk well from the flow of lusts she had given off. He could sense her submission to him. But he would not leave her yet. He wanted her sated and dazed when he dealt with the young lab assistants. She would watch silently while he claimed them one by one. He wanted her to confess her own lasciviousness, her physical dependence on him, her wantonness. He eased the pressure on her hips until there was a small gap between his hips and her soft but firm rear globes. He passed a surge of lust to her through his cock. He wanted her to initiate the resumption of their coupling, to push back against him in need, to facilitate her own impalement by him.

The naked, auburn haired woman felt the man deliver to her a forceful pulse of passion through his lodged manhood. She cursed herself as damned as she realized she desperately wanted his climax inside her again and that the man was forcing her to confess it. Her body yearned to feel the resumption of the drag of his meat along her delicate rear tissue. She wanted to come again, to feel her body quake with passion. Slowly, she pressed her rear upwards, her mind begging the man to resume his stroking of her. When he did not respond, she brought her hips down and then pressed against him again. She groaned with need and she did it again and then again. Before she knew it, she was feverishly milking the hard cock that filled her rear. "Oh, please, please, fuck me, please!" her mind screamed. And then he finally gave into her psychic entreaties, pushing his cock deep into her, seizing her hips with his hands and guiding her back and forth on his thick rod.

Kelly came again as he did. She writhed underneath him as her passions ran wildly through her. When she was done shuddering and moaning, her pussy finally coming to rest, she pushed her bound hands forward and placed her face on her soft, green felt pad. Her breasts pressed against the hard surface of her desk. She could feel his fluids merging with her. She was dazed, satisfied. She was pleased the man had claimed her. She wanted nothing but union with him. Nothing else mattered.

Ramón slipped his cock from the female's body. He stood back, appreciating her naked, limp form. Her rear was lifted up from the desk and he could see her twin, satisfied portals. Her stockings made her body look alluring and emphasized the pale, nude, soft flesh above them. Adele ran out of the office and came back with a bowl of hot water, soap and a washcloth. She knelt before him and performed ablutions on his softened meat, soaping it up thoroughly and then rinsing it clean. He could feel her desire for him. When she was done, she leaned forward and captured the bulbous head of his cock in her mouth and suckled it gently until it stirred and began to rise to hardness again. Ramón pushed her head back gently. Her eyes were glassy and her mouth remained open for a few moments, pursed to receive him.

"Ohhhhh," Adele sighed. And then, gathering herself, she announced she would get them all some hot tea.

Kelly lay still on her desk, not wanting to disturb her reverie. She didn't want the girls to see her like this, naked and spent, but she hadn't the energy to rise. Ramón took a seat in a chair by the door. Adele came back with three mugs of steaming tea and set them on the desk.

"We've got to get you up," she told Kelly sweetly. She stood behind the bare skinned, drained woman and, taking her by the arms, brought her to her feet. Kelly felt her exhausted body sway for balance. Adele quickly restored her shirt to her body, pulling it up her arms, over her head and then down her torso. She then had her step back into her skirt, zipping it up behind her. Kelly was amazed at how quickly she was transformed from a naked harlot to the enticingly dressed teenager. It was if her escapade on her desk had been a fleeting fantasy.

Adele had thoughtfully placed an abosorbant pad on Kelly's chair and she hiked the skirt up around her hips and sat her down on it. She caressed Kelly's face softly and kissed her on the lips. The dazed woman smiled at the gesture of kindness. "Adele understands," she thought. "She's my friend and she understands."

Adele dashed out of the office and returned immediately with a hair brush and stroked Kelly's locks until they were strait and untangled. She then handed her a cup of tea and resumed her seat on the other side of the desk to wait.

CHAPTER TWO

Melissa and Felicity arrived together at five to nine in Melissa's beat up, old Volkswagen Beetle. They were both drinking medium sized cups of Dunkin' Donuts' coffee. Felicity was tall, with long, straight, dirty blond hair that went down to her waist. Her face was pleasant and long, with pouty lips and a thin, graceful nose. Her blue eyes were starry and flashed with interest whenever she spoke to you. Melissa was shorter, short, actually, about 5'2", pixie like. She wore her chestnut colored hair long, like Felicity. Her eyes were large and brown and her eyebrows were dark and thick. Her pert nose was offset by large, plump lips. Her face was round and pleasing.

The girls had known each other almost all of their lives and had graduated Jacksonville High School last June. Melissa was a little older, having crested nineteen in September. Felicity's 19th birthday would be in March. They had both worked as interns at Dr. Jameson's lab during their senior year, moving up to full time positions in May when they had completed all of their courses. They liked Dr. Jameson and her assistant, Ms. Somers. Dr. Jameson seemed to them the model of what a woman should be, intelligent, educated, and successful. All except her personal life. Neither of them wanted to ever be 27 years old and without a boyfriend, lover or, better yet, a husband. Not that they couldn't wait for the bonds of matrimony. Like Adele, they were wise enough about the world around them to know what a mistake tying themselves down this young would be. Small town rumors of Ms. Somers' escapades had reached them and they envied the older woman her exuberant life.

"Why aren't we going in?" Melissa asked her friend. "It's almost 9 o'clock."

"I want to wait until Chandra gets here," Felicity replied.

"How come?"

"Adele usually has some dirty job to be done first thing on Mondays and I don't want to have to do it," Felicity answered.

"How do you know she's not already there?" Melissa asked.

Felicity took a long sip of her hot coffee before answering. "I saw her mother's car still in the driveway when we passed her house."

"Oh," was all Melissa could reply. It wasn't that the two pretty, white girls didn't like Chandra. She was, well, just kinda weird as far as they were concerned. All of the girls lived at home, there was nothing wrong with that. But Chandra's family was very strict and ran almost all aspects of her life. Melissa and Felicity had had the average American female high school graduate's experience with boys, but they knew for a fact that Chandra was kept on a very tight rein. She had taken her cousin, a big eared, pudgy kid with zits, to the Senior Prom. Her dress had been something out of the Fifties.

"So, did you go out with Billy on Saturday?" Felicity asked her diminutive friend. She wondered sometimes how the small girl saw over the steering wheel.

"Nah," she answered. "I dumped him."

"You dumped him?"

"Yeah. He was a creep. A few weeks ago we went up to his dad's hunting cabin and he's been bugging the shit out of me ever since."

Felicity giggled. "Did you let him fuck you?"

Melissa giggled back. "Yessssss," she said in pretended exasperation. "As a matter of fact, we fucked all day. At least, you could call it fucking. He's a point and shoot kind of guy. Every time he got near my pussy, he dumped his load."

Felicity gave out a huge, snarfy laugh. She had been taking a sip of her coffee and some of it ran down her nose. "Don't do that when I'm drinking!" she said.

"Sor-ry!" Melissa replied, amused. "Anyway, he's been trying to get me to go back ever since. Friday night I saw him at the Burger King and he started up all over again. I got pissed and so I dumped him." She took a sip of coffee and then asked Felicity, "What about you? What'd you do?"

"Ohhh, Tommy Hughes and I went out to a movie."

"Tommy Hughes! You've got to be kidding! Since when!"

"Since last week."

"And what about Jasmine? Aren't they still going out?"

"She was away," Felicity answered.

Melissa leaned over to her friend and asked her conspiratorially in a low whisper, "Did you do it?"

Felicity giggled again. "No, we didn't do it!" she answered, putting a large emphasis on the word 'it'.

"Well, if you didn't do 'it', what did you do?"

Felicity just smiled and put her coffee cup to her lips.

"Oh you sucked him off, didn't you?" Melissa shouted, amused and admiring.

"Mmm hmmmm," Felicity hummed in confirmation.

"And?" Melissa insisted.

"And what?" Felicity asked.

"What was it like?"

"It was green with big purple bumps on it and when he came it sang Yankee Doodle Dandy, what do you think?" Both girls erupted in laughter at the visualization.

"What was his car like?"

"It was cool," Felicity replied enthusiastically. "When he took off down the street you could feel the vibration of the engine all through your body. It made me kind of hot."

The girls fell silent for a minute, finishing off their coffees.

Finally Melissa asked Felicity, "Are you going to see him again?"

"Nah," Felicity responded. "He's a jerk. In fact, all the guys around here are jerks. I keep telling you, we gotta to get out of this stupid assed town. I'm sick of it."

"Me too," Melissa answered. "Maybe in the spring we can go to Florida or something. This place is so dull. Nothing ever happens here and if you don't put out, you'd never get a date." She smiled at a secret thought and looked at her friend. "I'll bet you get a lot of calls after Tommy talks to his friends," she said. Both girls laughed.

"Well, they better have hot cars or no blow job," Felicity retorted. They laughed heartily again.

Chandra's mother's car pulled into the lot. Felicity and Melissa sank down in their seats to make themselves inconspicuous. Chandra hopped out of the front passenger seat and slammed the door. She was wearing a large, dark brown overcoat. Her long black hair was in a braid behind her. Without saying goodbye to her mother or thanking her for the lift, she strode quickly and determinedly into the building.

It had been another lousy morning for Chandra. She was sick and tired of her mother and her interference in her life. Chandra had wanted to wear this cute little skirt she had bought on Saturday at the mall in Slayton. It was short and somewhat tight around her hips. Felicity and Melissa always looked so hot and she was tired of looking like a schoolmarm when she went to work. She was thin and shapely enough, and big breasted for an Asian girl. Her face was pretty. But every day when she left the house she felt as if she was a drudge no boy would ever want to date, never mind kiss.

She had worn the skirt under her long, dowdy overcoat and had hoped her mother wouldn't notice. But just before they left, her mother had forced her to open her coat and there it was.

A huge fight ensued. Chandra had stormed off to her room and slammed the door shut, vowing never to leave it again. Her father had come upstairs and pounded on the door prefatory to a lecture on respect for one's mother. Eventually, after a long cry, she had donned the calf length, purple skirt her mother had instructed her to put on and the light green, round necked top she usually wore with it. Its neckline had a little frill of lace around it and showed about an inch or two of her bare chest, about as close as her mother would ever let her get to advertising the pleasing femininity of her breasts. She came back down the stairs, morose and contrite. There was no use struggling. Until she saved up enough money to get her own place she would have to live by her parent's rules. No boys, no sexy clothes, no fun. Half her money they took and sent back to India. Almost all the other half went to her tuition at the county college. But she was determined she would get out someday. She wanted to be a scientist like Dr. Jameson.

Chandra had spotted her coworkers in the parking lot scrunched down in the front seat of Melissa's orange VW. She knew why and she didn't care. She didn't mind if Ms. Somers gave her the tough, dirty jobs. She figured it was the best way to let her and Dr. Jameson know that she was the best, most reliable worker. And the fact that the American girls would be later than she was was ok too.

Chandra didn't get along with the two "native" American girls, although she was born here too and was as American as anybody. They were sometimes haughty and cool to her. Born and bred in the South, they naturally carried some of the prejudices of their forefathers. Her skin was dark, like some of the African American girls she had known at high school. But they didn't really accept her either. She was not, in fact, black, and shared little of their love of hip hop or dancing or 'gangsta' culture. She was the only Indian girl in the school. Even the two Japanese descended girls stayed away from her. But she didn't care. She would make it on her own. She would be successful and pretty and have lovers. She would!

Kelly was startled when she heard the door to the lab shut with a loud 'clang!' The three of them had been sitting there silently for about ten minutes. The girls were late as they often were on Mondays, all except Chandra who usually was early. She had been holding onto her hot cup of tea with both hands and letting the warmth comfort her. It was the first thing she had been allowed to feed to herself in two days and she enjoyed the ability to decide for herself when she would take sips. It was strange to see the naked man sitting in her office drinking tea while she and Adele sat in the same chairs they had often sat in to discuss the upcoming business of the day.

Adele put her cup of tea down on Kelly's desk and rose to go out to the lab area. Kelly's heart sank as she realized the time for the enslavement of the three sweet girls had come. What would he do with them? It hurt her to think that she had a role in their despoilment. But one stern look from her naked captor as he sat in readiness for them was enough to keep her silent. There was nothing that she could do.

"Good morning, Chandra," Adele greeted the Indian-American girl.

Chandra returned the greeting. She had placed her coat in the closet and was putting on her lab coat when she saw the blinds had been drawn shut on Dr. Jameson's office. They had never been closed before. "Is something the matter?" she asked Adele, nervously. She knew money was always an issue for the lab, but she hoped it had not closed down. What would she do?

"No, no, Chandra," Adele reassured her. "Nothing's wrong. We're just having a conference, that's all. A meeting.

Don't put your lab coat on yet. Dr. Jameson wants to talk to each of you one at a time to explain some changes that are going to take place here."

A look of unhappiness spread across Chandra's pretty face. Her dark skin was clear and smooth. Her eyes, more black than brown, were exotic, with thick, dark eyebrows above them. Her lips were slim and delicate. They formed a small frown now. "Is the lab closing down?" she asked, fearfully.

Adele laughed. "Certainly not. In fact we're going to be busier than ever. It's just that there will be some new rules and procedures and we want everyone to have a good understanding of them. So we're going to talk to you one at a time. Okay?"

Chandra nodded, not quite convinced. She was about to ask another question when the other girls came in. They were still giggling about Felicity's joke.

Melissa saw Ms. Somers and Chandra standing by the work bench. "Shit!" she thought. "We're all gonna catch hell for being late!"

Adele made the same explanations she had made to Chandra to Felicity and Melissa. All the girls remained nervous. Nothing like this had ever happened at the lab and change was always difficult. If it was up to the girls, things would remain just as they were.

"Felicity, why don't we go in first? You girls make your self some tea or coffee. It won't take long."

The tall, lanky blond girl was unhappy at being selected first. Wasn't that the whole point of waiting for Chandra?

Kelly watched the door expectantly. Ramón was seated so that when the door swung open, he would be behind it. He wouldn't be seen until the girl was well into the room and had shut the door. He looked at her and sent her a signal of warning, a mere taste of what disobedience would bring. Kelly had a momentary surge of illness in her body which was followed by a warm message of contentment and pleasure the dream man sent her afterwards. The meaning was clear, she could choose punishment or pleasure. But what was going to be done, would be done nonetheless.

The door opened and Adele came in leading the young, long haired blond girl by the hand. She was wearing a pretty, dark orange blouse with a dark beige miniskirt. She had not yet doffed her high heels for the sneakers she wore while working. Her eyes lit up when she saw Kelly behind the desk. Adele swung the door closed.

"Hiya, Dr. J…" was all she got out. She had picked up the figure of Ramón in the corner of her eyes. Her face seemed to say, "Is there really a naked Mexican guy in Dr. Jamison's office?" She turned to look at him and Ramón captured her vision with his dark, piercing eyes. Felicity opened her mouth and then closed it, swallowing deeply. She looked back at Kelly and then back at Ramón and her eyes seemed to roll back in her head and her eyes fluttered. Kelly thought the poor girl was going to faint. Her body swayed for a few moments and then a look of satisfaction and happiness crossed her face. Her hands, which she had been holding out in front of her, sank to the fronts of her thighs where she rubbed them like she was straightening out her skirt. Her eyes were focused on Ramón's loins and the stiff prick he was holding out to her in his right hand. She looked at Kelly and then Adele, licking her lower lip. She looked back at Ramón, leaning towards him as if she was stuck in place. And then she walked the two steps over to him, fell to her knees and subsumed his rampant, thick cock between her lips.

There was nothing shy or hesitant about Felicity's treatment of Ramón's cock. She gripped it firmly in her right hand and slurped her mouth over it energetically. Her left hand sneaked under her short dress and was stroking the hidden treasure between her thighs. Ramón's head was tilted back and his eyes were closed as he absorbed the girl's pleasurable attentions. His hands were on her head, sending rewards for the girl's lustful exhibition and reinforcing her desire to please him.

Kelly watched the young girl in lustful action, mesmerized by her alacrity in pleasuring her captor. Effusions of Ramón's lust was passing through the room and she closed her thighs and pressed her knees together in need. Adele was standing there behind the girl, watching with her own lustful approval.

Felicity moaned and whimpered as she hungrily sucked Ramón's rigid meat. It did not take long for her to reach her first climax, her body shuddering and her head remaining motionless and impaled as her orgasm ripped through her. When it had crested, she eagerly resumed her task. Ramón's body stiffened and he groaned from deep inside his throat. His thighs quivered as his first lust laden ejaculation poured his essence into the young girl's accepting mouth.

"Ohhhhhhhhhhh!" Felicity moaned as she received it. Her free hand was still pumping wildly between her thighs and she shook and shuddered again as her pussy exploded with pleasure.

Felicity made sure she excised every drop of Ramón's intoxicating cum before she released him. Adele helped her regain her feet.

"Come on, Felicity," she said, "we've got to talk to the other girls too, you know."

It was like a light had gone on in Felicity's head. She stared at the dream man intently. She had discovered a purpose in life. She had never met anyone who inspired her as did the man. He had filled her brain with caring and affection, teaching her her worth, her path. She turned to look at Dr. Jameson. She saw her importance to the man, Ramón, as he called himself. Her boss had never looked so pretty, so radiant. She would do anything for her. She felt Adele's soft hand on her shoulder. "Are you okay, Felicity," she asked kindly.

Felicity shook her head in affirmation and then giggled. It was so nice what had happened. Tommy's dick was nothing like Ramón's. She wanted to suck on it again, have its radiance inside her. Adele opened the door to the office and took her by the hand. "Come on Felicity," she said softly. The girl looked at Kelly and smiled affectionately and then let herself be escorted from the room.

When Melissa came in and her eyes met Ramón's for the first time, she stood for almost a minute staring back at him. Her body shuddered several times. And then, without ceremony, she reached her hands under her short, fluffy, pink and white, flowered skirt and pulled her thong down her slim, dainty thighs, over her knees and off of her feet all without taking her eyes off of her new master. She tossed the bright pink garment aside and stepped up close to Ramón between his legs. Taking hold of his stiff manhood with her left hand, she reached under her skirt and stroked her labia, probing herself until she was moist. She then climbed on his lap facing him and, guiding his tall, rigid pole to her slit, slowly lowered herself over it, moaning lowly, her head tilted forwards, her eyes closed in ecstasy.

Melissa looked like a little doll as she crouched in Ramón's lap. His large, muscular body loomed over her. She pumped herself up and down slowly, her hands wrapped around his strong neck, her forehead buried into his chest. The point of contact of their loins was hidden under her small, flouncy skirt. Ramón's large hands circled her head, adjusting her and sending his approval to her. When she came, she jammed her pussy hard down on Ramón's long cock, wanting it all inside her. Ramón came then too, causing the girl's tiny body to spasm sharply and then to go limp as her womb was suffused with his essence.

Chandra was waiting impatiently for her turn. Why was the dirty, brown skinned girl always the last, she thought miserably. She was going to be fired, she knew it. Even Dr. Jameson, who had seemed so nice and encouraging to her, apparently preferred the light skin of people similar to herself. It didn't help that Felicity was all giggly and smiles when she emerged from the office. Chandra asked her what had happened in the office and she just giggled some more.

When Melissa came out, Chandra was ready to walk out the door. The small statured girl had a smirk on her face. "So everyone is in on the joke except Chandra," the Indian girl thought.

Ramón sat in his chair, the reverberations of his orgasms flowing through him. He had converted the girls as quickly and as delicately as he could. They would need some more work. As to their sexual acts, he had left it up to them, merely exciting their minds beyond their control. Felicity had been surprisingly skilled at giving oral pleasure. She truly loved cock sucking and had developed the fetish as a way to gain acceptance with boys, who she was extremely nervous around. Melissa, he learned by probing her, loved the close contact of skin to skin and craved the strength and security she found in the arms of the opposite sex. Their lusts were young and untrammeled, giving off a sweet taste as he fed on them. The passions of his familiar and her friend were heavier, more complex and flavored, like the wine his blond servant had fed him the day before for lunch. He anxiously awaited the next girl, looking forward to the pleasure she would give him.

Kelly's guilt about what was happening to her charges was rising rapidly. She saw how Ramón had struck them with his will, altered them with a thought. She had never seen the side of them they displayed when they voraciously satisfied their sexual appetites on his body. Chandra was next, dear, sweet

Chandra. Her dismay began to grow critical, competing with her passionate response to the radiation of lust throughout the small, warmly decorated room.

"Come on, Chandra, you're next," Adele said pleasantly after returning Melissa to the lab. Chandra looked at her supervisor suspiciously. Something was going on here and she didn't like it. Felicity and Melissa were huddled together, giggling. Were they preparing some huge practical joke on her?

But it was Adele's pleasant smile, her outstretched hand and her resident need for obedience that finally got her to move. When she turned the corner of the door to the office and saw Dr. Jameson's distressed face, she halted. Adele took the edge of the door and swung it closed. Her heart stopped when she saw the naked, dark skinned man.

But Chandra's concern only lasted a moment. Her brain was quickly awash with feelings of pleasure and tranquility. She saw who the man was, a great man, someone she should follow. She had been looking for some way to transfer her loyalties away from her suffocating family. This man was offering her everything she wanted. She would do anything for him.

Kelly watched the glow of happiness spread across Chandra's face. She envied her her joy but, at the same time, wondered fearfully at the man's powers. On Saturday, he had needed to stroke and caress Adele in order to convert her to his will. Was he getting stronger? More dangerous? What did that impend for her?

Suddenly, the tranquil Chandra began to cry. Her body had been sending her irresistible signals of lust for the man. Her hands rubbed against her belly and her lips opened passionately. But then she broke into tears.

"Oh, Chandra," Adele said concernedly. "What's the matter?"

"I don't know what to do!" the grieved teenager cried out. She looked at Adele miserably. "I never have...I mean I haven't..." and then she became unable to speak due to her sobs.

Adele stepped towards her and put her arms around her, hugging her. "It's all right, Chandra," she told the forlorn girl. "I'll help you."

The tall, blond woman led Chandra to the awaiting dream man and guided her to her knees, taking a place beside her. She lifted the girl's delicate chin until it was level with Ramón's cock. The girl stared at it with a mixture of desire and alarm. Adele took her hand from her side and led it to Ramón's manhood. "Just hold it for a minute, honey," she said gently. "See what it feels like."

Chandra put her hand to Ramón's tool and circled it with her fingers and palm. Her eyes widened a she felt its radiance flow into her hand, up her arm and into her body. "Ohhh!" she said. She looked up at the dark haired man. He had a peaceful, comforting look on his face and she felt these emotions pass into her.

"Now stroke it, Chandra, softly." Adele instructed her. Chandra returned her gaze to the source of her amazement and pulled gently on the tube of meat. Her lust was visibly growing higher and higher. "Ohhhhhh," she moaned again. "It's so....I don't know."

"Now give the end a little kiss, Chandra, feel Ramón's cock give your lips a bit of his energy."

Chandra pursed her lips and hesitatingly connected them to the very tip of Ramón's prick. She moaned as its power was transferred to her. Adele let her languor in the flow of pleasure through her body for a few moments. "Now open your lips and circle them around the head until the fat part is in your mouth," she told the girl. Chandra parted her lips and as the head of Ramón's cock entered her mouth, her eyes closed to slits and she sighed deeply. Her hand was still languidly stroking the long, thick shaft. She closed her lips around the helmet to Ramón's prick, her thin cheeks bulging with its presence.

Kelly was overwhelmed with lust at the display. Chandra was a beautiful, sweet girl and she looked intensely erotic as she knelt to service the dream man. She yearned to place her hands between her thighs and stroke herself, caress her breasts, do something to alleviate and satisfy her growing need but she knew she dared not. Even if he did not see it, he would read it in her mind and punish her later.

Chandra's body was more than exotic. It seemed out of some ancient, Indian painting, a temple girl pleasuring one of their many gods. Her long, black braided hair lay down her sinuous back. Her face was a mask of ecstasy. Her thin, graceful arm extended from her body, terminating in long, delicate fingers circling the manhood of her deity. Kelly could feel the exuberant flow of her captor's energies, making her yearn for him, wishing it was her mouth and lips circling the pleasure giving prick.

She heard Adele give more kindly, affectionate instructions to the dark skinned girl. "Now suck on it like you would the top of an ice cream cone," she told her. "Do it soft and gentle like you were savoring its taste." And then, "Move your head back and forth. Don't worry about getting it all in just now, just give pleasure to the head."

Chandra's jaws began to work as she suckled the bulbous end of Ramón's cock. She looked like she was entranced, which she certainly was. Adele reached her hands under Chandra's long, purple skirt which draped onto the floor like a flower around her. Kelly could see her hands tugging Chandra's underwear down off of her hips. She gently lifted first one knee and then the other and pulled them down her shins to her ankles and then free. She tossed aside the clean, white cotton panties. Chandra didn't miss a stroke. "Spread your legs, honey," she told her.

Obediently, Chandra spread her thighs and Adele placed her hands between them under her skirt. The young girl's body stiffened and then seemed to melt as it recorded Adele's gentle stokes to her sex. Her suckling at the tip of Ramón's wand became more energetic, more needy. Adele continued to coax her, whispering encouragement into her ear. She must have sensed Ramón's approaching climax, since Kelly heard her tell the girl, "Take it all in, honey, drink it all down. Let it inside you."

Ramón stiffened and groaned and Chandra let out a wild, muffled cry. Her body began to jerk and shake. "Mmmmmm! Mmmmmmm! Mmmmmmmmm!" she called out as her own, first, true orgasm flooded through her. Her throat flexed and contracted as she drank down the man's gift to her. Ramón's hands were on her head, lying there softly, transferring his will and his blessing to her.

When Chandra's orgasm was done, she released her mouth and hand from Ramón's organ and threw her arms around Adele. She was crying and sobbing. "Oh, thank you!" she said, her joy brimming over. "Thank you! Thank you!" Adele held her tightly in her arms, stroking the side of her head. After a few moments, Chandra struggled to her feet and threw herself into Ramón's arms. He hugged her tightly and her hands held his head to her shoulder. "Oh, thank you!" she cried again. Ramón put his hands on the side of her head and placed his lips on hers. He parted them with his tongue and probed her mouth. Chandra kissed him back as fervently as any lover ever did. Gradually, he pulled his mouth back and eased her off of his body. Adele was standing there, waiting.

"Come on, Chandra," she said affectionately. "You can do it again, later. Ramón has things he needs to do and you have to get to work." Chandra reluctantly came back to her feet.

Her hand lingered on Ramón's face for a moment and then, after giving a tender adoring glance at Kelly, she let Adele lead her away. She left her panties behind on the floor.

CHAPTER THREE

The day, although eventful, went quickly. After Chandra left, Adele came back and silently stroked Ramón on his head. Kelly saw something pass between them and Adele stepped back smiling gratefully. She reached beneath her short skirt, much like Melissa had done before her, and pulled her panties to her ankles and then stepped out of them. She turned and sank to her knees, spreading her legs, her head and forearms on the rug. Ramón knelt down behind her, running his hands over her back, and then pushed her skirt up around her hips, displaying her round rear cheeks. He angled her hips for his penetration and then eased inside as she gave a long, languid sigh.

Ramón stroked the groaning blond woman to orgasm twice before spending himself in her. He wanted to reward her for her execution of his will. When he rose to his feet, he saw his familiar's need for him was exquisite. Seeing that, he approached her chair and proffered himself to her. She cupped her bound hands reverently under his soft stones while she dank from his lust radiating cock, coming forcefully when he did.

Afterwards, the female leaned back in her chair, an expression of dazed satisfaction across her face. Ramón dressed quickly. His mind felt powerful and energized from the absorption of the women's passions, but his human body was tired from the expenditure of so much energy and fluids. He would need to rest it. All of the women should be happy for a while. One of his projects was to try and find ways to extend their satisfactions without needing to divert his attentions to them. And he would need to acclimate them to service of his familiar and she to them. He left the office, the female's eyes dreamily staring at him. Adele left right behind him.

Adele soon came back to Kelly's office and announced that Kelly's computer was restored, telling her, "Ramón fixed it. You can access all of the files, but not the Internet. I'll bring your emails by later. If your mother calls, I'll tell her you'll call her back."

It took a while for Kelly's haze to clear. She was able to open the Edelman grant application file and complete significant portions of it. It felt odd to be at her workaday job when so much had happened to her. Since her hands were bound, she had to hunt and peck on the keyboard. Her office was still cut off from the lab by the drawn blinds so she had no idea what the girls were doing. Every once in a while, one would enter, smile happily at her, and place a lab sheet in her box on her desk. Twice, Adele came and got her so she could use the bathroom.

When Chandra had emerged from Kelly's office, Felicity and Melissa gave her a big hug. Tears flowed from all eyes. Felicity uncharacteristically volunteered to clean out the ruined experiments from over the weekend, a tedious, tiresome job since all the discarded raw materials had to be specially bagged and the petrie dishes double cleaned.

Ramón worked Adele's computer. He still had a lot of learning to do. He had enough information to set up some preliminary experiments and Chandra was assigned the task of preparing them.

The girls ate their lunch at the lab benches. Adele ran out and got large containers of vegetarian chili and toasted foccacia bread with butter and she and Ramón and Kelly ate at Kelly's desk. Kelly was both glad and disappointed she was not brought to her knees to feed at Ramón's cock as she had after every meal at her house. She was desperately afraid one of the girls would come in and see her. But her hunger for the man's essence was growing inside her and she unconsciously gave a little whine when he finished his lunch and left the room.

Ramón had decided that after lunch would be a good time to go visit Mr. Hardings. He was escorted to his office by a cute, little, filing clerk. Hardings' secretary was a handsome African American woman, 40ish, who had maintained a fine figure. He made a point of shaking her hand when he introduced himself and sent her an instruction to follow later.

Hardings was glad to discuss the empty space and he promised to have an amended lease to Ramón by tomorrow afternoon. Ramón made pleasant, nonchalant inquiries as to the type of work Hardings did, just enough so as not to be suspicious, and Hardings gave appropriately evasive answers.

Kelly had grown too needy to be able to work by midafternoon. Ramón I't been in her office since lunch and her mind kept drifting off to him, wondering where he was, when he would come back. Adele kept bringing her papers to sign and she complied dreamily. She had typed out answers to the email Adele had brought her in the morning and Adele printed them and sent them off on her computer. She had brought her more this afternoon. Kelly had tried three times to go through them, but she couldn't make head or tails of what was in them.

Her lust for the dream man grew so strong she had twice lowered her joined hands to the hem of her skirt to get some self relief, but her hands recoiled each time in fear of his retribution. Finally, her need for him became so intense she decided she had to act. She got up from her chair and walked to her office door. She turned the knob with her joined hands and walked outside into the lab area. The girls were all hard at work dressed in their long, white lab coats and did not notice her. Adele was working at her desk, and when Kelly approached, looked up from her computer screen.

"Oh, you poor dear," Adele cried out. "Ramón'll be back

soon. Here, let me take you back to your office."

Reluctantly, Kelly followed Adele's grasp on her arm and retreated to the small office where she had sat all day. The girls had heard Adele's exclamation and they followed her with their eyes as she walked haltingly the 30' or so. Adele released her bound hands only to bind them again behind her and sat her back down on her chair. Then, saying, "I'll be right back," she ran out. She came back carrying her big red leather handbag. She withdrew Kelly's gag from it and presented it to the unhappy woman.

Kelly started to cry when her hands were fastened behind her back. This wasn't what she wanted. When Adele proffered the gag to her, she held her head down, away from it. She didn't want to be gagged. Especially here, right in her office where the girls would see it if they came in. But Adele was insistent. She held Kelly by the chin and lifted it up. "Honey, it'll do you good, I promise," she said, her voice filled with concern. "Just let me put it in and see, okay?"

Kelly, reminded of the totemic quality of the gag, reluctantly opened her mouth. It would remind her of him, succor her for a while until he returned. Adele hooked the gag up behind her head and then crouched down before her. She affixed her ankle bracelets to her legs and wrapped a chain around the stem of her chair connecting them and binding Kelly in place. "He'll be back soon, sweetheart. We can't have you wandering off. I'll send him here as soon as he walks in the door."

Adele walked out, closing the door behind her. Kelly leaned back on her bound hands and closed her eyes. She let the feel of the faux penis comfort her. He would be back soon. Adele had promised. Her need for him was like a virus that was eating away at her. She squeezed her thighs together in an effort to assuage her lust, her mind focused on the smooth, hairless mons between them.

Ramón went to Kelly's office as soon as he returned from Hardings'. His conversation with the man had gone on longer than he wanted, but there were details of the lease for the new space that needed to be worked out. He had taken the time to read as much of the human male's mind as he could. It was the first male he had encountered and he needed to know what his abilities were in that area. He had had some success, seeing the man's mind troubled at some difficulties he was having completing some of the important and secret government projects he was responsible for. He also detected the man's underlying loneliness and unhappiness. It was disconcerting to him to feel such psychic pain, but he realized this was a possible avenue to his use of the man. He would need to explore it more thoroughly.

When he returned, he went directly to his familiar's office. He saw the pretty woman leaning back in her chair, her eyes peering up at him forlornly, full of anguish. He chided himself for being so long from her. She was his responsibility. He had created this need, stoked it, developed it, and it was improper of him to let her be wracked with agony for lack of its satisfaction.

After undressing, the man bent over and released the chain that bound her ankles to the chair and then stood next to her, awaiting the proper response. He would not move or act to alleviate her distress until he saw it.

Kelly saw the man staring at her. Her eyes pleaded with him for relief. Why doesn't he comfort me, she thought, madly. "Why doesn't he put his hands on me and make it right?" But then, after a few moments, she realized why. She knew what he wanted. Shamed at her need, but desperate for the man's touch, Kelly turned her chair to him and then leaned back as far as she could, slowly raising her feet from the floor. She kept raising them, spreading her legs, until they were lodged on the chair on either side of her. Her raised thighs pushed her skirt up to her lap. She pushed up her hips and thrust her loins out at the man hopefully.

Ramón looked down at the displayed woman. Her hairless slit was proffered to him obediently. He reached a hand down and stroked a finger along its length causing the woman to tremor with lust. He sent a strong, warm message of comfort and approval to her and her eyes rolled back with relief. His cock had stiffened quickly at the vision of the female's pale thighs above the bands of lace that encircled them, the gleaming of her arousal on the edges of her nether lips. He took the bottom of her dark beige shirt and lifted it up over her breasts, exposing them for his visual delight. Circling his arms under her thighs, he lifted them, pushing them up over his shoulders. Then, taking his cock in his hand, he placed it at the center of her engorged labia and pushed himself inside.

Kelly gasped as the man entered her. As he stroked himself along the fevered walls of her crevasse, waves of bliss ran through her. She came almost at once, and then again as he continued to plow her with his thick cock. When he discharged himself into her, her mind exploded with relief and pleasure.

The dream man rose from his satisfied familiar. He let her legs fall to the floor and pulled her up from her chair. Releasing her gag and easing it from her mouth, he circled her with his arms and kissed her, pressing her body firmly into his.

Kelly treasured the expression of affection from her lord. Now that he had sated her, all was well again. His essence flowed within her, calming her, bringing a haze of fulfillment to her body and mind.

Ramón spent the rest of the afternoon reading a series of texts he had Adele download to Kelly's computer. After fucking her, he had remained disrobed, feeling more comfortable in the nude. The girls tittered and giggled when they dropped off lab reports into Kelly's bin. Kelly occupied the rest of her day sitting in the chair nearest him, savoring the feelings of warmth and comfort she received from being near him. He had rebound her arms in front of her and reconnected the chain to her ankles.

At 4:45, a shy, embarrassed Chandra appeared at the door to the office. Ramón invited her to him and she sat in his lap kissing him while he stroked her under her skirt. Her hand stroked his stiffened wand tentatively. When she came, she clasped her arms about him and moaned. As she left, she bent down and kissed Kelly on her lips, a sweet, brief brush of flesh, and left. Her mother would pick her up exactly at 5:01.

Melissa and Felicity came in together. The smaller girl waited anxiously, biting her nails as she watched her friend repeat her service of the morning to the dream man. When she was finished, Melissa reached under her skirt and lowered her slim, pink panties again. Ramón sat her on the desk and pushed her back down onto it. He raised her knees and fucked her there, her long brown hair splayed around her head, her hands caressing his strong, hairless chest. When he had come inside her and she had cried out her pleasures, she and Felicity joined hands and left, both stating, almost in unison, "Good night, Dr. Jameson. See you tomorrow."

Adele came into the office when the girls had left the building. She crouched down in front of Kelly and stroked her hair. "How ya doin, honey," she asked tenderly. "You've had a rough day, I know. It'll get better. I promise." She then gave Kelly a deep, soulful kiss that both comforted and impassioned her.

Ramón was finishing up some notes for experiments in the morning. Adele stood there, watching him as she idly stroked Kelly's head. "I made it," Kelly thought. "I made it through the day." She was proud of herself, proud she had pleased the dream man, happy the girls seemed to be so comfortable and free in their bondage to him. Adele's soft strokes to her hair made her feel warm and comfortable.

The dream man shut down the computer and rose from his chair. After Adele had released Kelly's ankles from their bonds, he took her hands and urged her up. He led her over to the rug in front of her desk and, while Adele shifted the chairs to give her room, he guided her to the floor. Kelly stretched out her body so she was lying on her side beside him and he placed his hands on her head and kissed her. He sent a wave of approval through her, making her heart race with happiness. After rolling her to her back, he pulled her red and black plaid skirt up to her hips and spread her legs. He returned his lips to hers and, while filling her mouth with his tongue, slid his hand over the insides of her thighs, caressing them softly. He found her smooth, bare cleft and teased and probed it until Kelly gave a deep moan into his mouth.

Kelly was in heaven. She knew he was rewarding her, reinforcing her need to please him. She wanted nothing more. With his free hand, he was holding her bound wrists above her, pinned to the floor. She spread her legs wider as his finger slowly and softly massaged her stiffened clit. When his legs crossed over so he was between hers, she raised her hips, offering herself to him.

He took her slowly, languidly. He had raised her shirt and he took her teats between his lips, suckling them, alternating between them, biting them with his teeth just hard enough so the tiny impulses of pain blended with her arousal. She thrust her hips back at him madly until the onset of her climax sent a spasm of pleasure through her body. Her fierce contractions triggered his crises and he spilled his radiant essence into her womb.

They lay there intertwined like lovers for a long time. Kelly circled her bound arms around his head and neck and drew him into her. Her mind floated on a sea of bliss. She relished the feel on the man's heavy body on hers, his hot skin. It was the perfect ending to her day and all her tension and nervousness had gone. Suddenly, the absurdity of the whole situation came home to her. The space man who had come to conquer earth had just fucked her on the rug in her office while her best friend watched with lustful encouragement. Her lovely, sweet natured employees had become, if not zombies, then sort of like Moonies, their whole beings turned to devotion to the visitor from another planet. Her home had become a tinder box of sexual arousal for her. Her whole life had been taken over. And yet she was happier than she had ever been in her life!

It started out as a little hiccup, a small sound that emerged from her throat. Then it became a giggle, low first, then loud and constant. And then she started to laugh. Not a chuckle or a guffaw, but a full throttled belly laugh. She hugged the man's body to hers and laughed louder and longer than she had in a very long time. The dream man, or alien, or invader from mars, what ever he was, pulled his head back and looked at her gravely as if trying to parse the nature of her sudden affliction. Kelly stopped her laugh long enough to pull his head back down and give him an intense, soulful kiss. And then she started to laugh again.

Ramón was concerned at the physical and mental reaction his familiar was undergoing. His mind probed hers and found it full of concepts like absurdity, irony, humor, that he could not comprehend. He was about to send her a strong, calming wave from his psyche when he sensed the flow of comfort, pleasure and well being her brain was sending to itself. He felt something strange inside him as his mind received her messages of glee. Suddenly, he was effused with merriment. Her laughter was contagious. A strange sound came from his throat, and then another. And then he started to laugh too. He felt his brain flood with happiness and he found he could not control the outpouring of its effects.

Adele was stunned by the sudden outbreak of hilarity. She got up from her chair and, starting to chuckle herself, knelt down by Kelly and the man and asked "What's so funny?" Kelly looked at her and her laughing became louder and more raucous. The man's laughter accelerated too, as if the fact that they were laughing was the funniest thing in the world. Finally, Adele began to join in the fun. She laughed and lay down and hugged the merry couple.

Their laughter continued for about ten minutes. It would wind down slowly until there was silence between them and then one or the other would give out a little titter and then they would be off to the races again. When they were finally able to calm themselves, the dream man, overcome by the delightful emotions, rolled off of his familiar and was lying on his back beside her, trying to catch his breath. Adele put her hand to Kelly's cheek, her own face aglow and gave her a brief, affectionate kiss on the lips. Their eyes met. A powerful blast of emotion passed between the two women. Adele leaned over and kissed her friend again, this time parting her lips and inhaling her sweet breath. Kelly looped her bound arms around her blond friend's neck and pulled her down to her. The two women pressed their lips together passionately. Kelly rose to her knees, pushing the younger, blond woman back, their lips and tongues united.

Both women were seized with a frantic passion. Kelly began to fumble at the buttons to Adele's blouse. Something had come over her and she wanted desperately to taste of her friend's flesh. When she had the third button free, Adele put her own hands on the two sides of the blouse and tore it open, sending the remaining buttons flying. Kelly's bound hands seized her right breast, pulling the delicate bra that held it in place up over it. Adele struggled to get her blouse the rest of the way off of her body, but was satisfied to have it dangling at the end of one arm as she reached behind her back and freed her bra's clasp.

Adele moaned as Kelly placed her lips on her teat and began to suck at it fervently. The mop haired blonde freed her bra straps from her arms and tore her bra away from her chest, throwing it aside. Kelly pushed her back to the floor and lay atop her, kissing and licking at her large, heavy breasts. Adele was frantic for her lover's touch and took Kelly's bound hands and freed them She drew the beige shirt up over her head and down her arms and then flung it across the small room. As soon as her hands were liberated, the auburn haired older woman seized both of Adele's breasts, squeezing them harshly while moving her mouth from teat to teat, sucking and biting on her nipples.

Desperate for full body contact with the moaning, blond girl, Kelly grabbed the waist of her Adele's miniskirt and began tugging it down. Adele's hands moved to assist her and within a few moments, Kelly had drawn the skirt and her matching thong over her friend's knees and ankles and then removed her own. She pressed her body forward until she felt their bellies match, their breasts intermingle and she found the writhing blond woman's lips again.

Ramón was taken aback by the women's sudden outbreak of lust. He could feel their burning passion for each other's flesh flowing from them like a stream. It excited him to watch them meld their bodies together. He approved of his familiar's outpouring of uncontrollable desire. His cock was hard and he began to stroke it almost unconsciously.

Kelly insinuated her legs between Adele's and pushed her thighs apart until their pelvises were married. Her bare pussy rubbed up against Adele's golden haired one and she pressed down against it, rubbing their labial lips together. The urge to pleasure her friend as she had pleasured her now twice, overcame her. She was energized with love for her, thankful for her affectionate role in making her suitable for the desires of the star man. She shifted her body down Adele's thin, curvaceous torso, stopping to lap at her stiffened nipples, running her tongue down her taut belly, kissing her skin, her hands stroking her sides. She brought herself to her knees and slid her energized hands over the soft, pale insides of Adele's widespread thighs and, after hesitating for a moment to take in the view of the moist, engorged object of her lust, delved her head downwards and ran her tongue deeply inside Adele's crevasse. She licked slowly upwards until she reached its apex and then, seizing the hardened bud atop it between her lips, sucked gently but firmly on it, making the blond haired woman writhe and moan with pleasure.

The sensation of supping at her friend's sex was intoxicating. Kelly had smelled her own discharge on her fingers before, sniffing lazily at them after a session of self administered pleasure. But she had not been prepared for the overwhelming sensation of breathing in the pungent, musky aroma directly from its source. And the taste was strange but delicious. Her lips and tongue lapped up her friend's juices hungrily.

The dream man's lusts began to overpower him. He rose to his knees and took a position behind the pale, round rear haunches of his familiar. He placed his hands on her hips, sending a wave of intense passion through her. When she moaned and spread her thighs, offering herself to his penetration, he placed his hot cock between her hairless, blood filled love lips and pushed himself between them.

Kelly groaned when she felt the man's cock sink home in her womb. She could feel the radiance of his cock effuse through her body. Suddenly, she felt as if it was passing through her, enflaming every cell of her body on the way, until it emerged from her mouth and tongue and was transmitted to her friend's fevered cunt.

Sensing his passion traveling through the intermediary of Kelly's writhing flesh to the blond woman's, Ramón increased its flow. It had been his plan for the two women to become enraptured with each other's flesh and he wanted to stoke his familiar's compulsion. He leaned over and gently took her arms in his hands and connected her wrists behind her back, so that her sole contact with her friend's flesh was between her mouth and Adele's flowered, juicing pussy.

Kelly felt the surge of her captor's lust pass through her. When he bound her arms, her mind burst with ecstasy at the confirmation of her submission to him and his approval of her desire for her friend's flesh. She ground her lips and mouth on Adele's gash, making the woman moan loudly and twist her hips beneath her. Adele's body tensed as her climax began. She seized Kelly's head with her hands and pressed it hard into her loins. "Oh, god!" she yelled. "Oh, god! Oh, god!"

The blond woman's screams of passion set Kelly's crises in motion. When she felt the relentless, driving cock in her womb begin to throb, her pussy sent a hard, wrenching pulse of pleasure through her. She moaned into her lover's flooded gash, lapping her tongue deep inside it and then, seizing the pleasure bud at its apex , sucked at it feverishly.

When their orgasms subsided, the trio of lovers lay for a long time, intertwined and relishing the aftershocks of their exertions. Adele recovered first. Kelly's head had come to rest on her belly and she lifted it gently and wriggled out from under her. "Whew!" she said in her pleasing, Southern drawl. "What was that?"

She lifted Kelly's chin and gave her a peck on the lips. "That was great, baby. I love you." She gave her another buss and went to look for her clothes. Kelly's dream lover slowly extricated his softened manhood from her glowing cleft and did the same.

* * * * * * * * * * * * * *

Ramón puzzled over his outbreak of human emotion all the way home. What had come over him? He had let the exquisite sensual experiences of this world distract him before, but he had never lost control over himself. It was a strange, experience. But his mind felt warm and contented when he thought of the epidemic of mirth that had struck the three. He feared, though, that he was being seduced from his true nature, that the human side of him was beginning to predominate. He could not let that happen. It was the way of the renegade. Although he was possessed of warm, affectionate feelings for his female wards, especially his familiar, he had a mission to perform and the female beings he had enthralled were but a means to that end, even expendable if need be. The renegade must be brought in at all costs.

The technicians of the Whole were unable to make much sense of the millions of signals that came through the barrier from this dimension every day. Their essence was of emotion, not information. So they could not 'view' the events here as they unfolded, not even to identify with any certainty the identity of the being whose emotional trail they ultimately selected to use for the jump. They had identified it as female, as the females of this species tended, by far, to be the more emotional of the sexes. The source was young, at least relatively, at a part of her life where emotional issues still predominated. But she had to be old enough to have developed a strong, disciplined intellect. For it was the combination of strength of emotion and intellect that made the ephemeral strand identifiable and pure.

The strand emanating from the renegade's familiar had been, like his female's, particularly strong. They were able to continue to trace it after the renegade's jump, although they could not specify its location. What they had found was not pretty. The signals of passion and desire that crossed the divide were mixed with equally strong messages of fear and pain. It was a sign that the renegade was violating the laws of the Whole, bringing psychic torment to his familiar for the purposes of making stronger her ability to draw essence from the other side. And if the renegade had cast away his ethical responsibilities to his familiar, it was a logical assumption that he was doing the same to other sentient creatures as well. He had probably interfered with the lives of hundreds, if not thousands, of sentient females over the last five years, making their lives living hells. To the Whole, this damage to sentient beings, no matter how low along the scale of intelligence that they were, was more than unacceptable. It caused a great disturbance to the Whole's sense of being, of purpose. For its intrusions into other universes were benignly conceived.

Ramón could see how the temptation to devote one's considerable, almost god-like, powers to the aggrandizement of one's senses would be hard to resist. When he had gone to visit Hardings, he had been tempted by the sinewy, enticing body of the young woman who had led him to his office. She had short, brown hair and delicious eyes. She had flitted them at him invitingly, no doubt affected by the glow of sexual power he emitted and the comely form his familiar's dreams had given him. But that would have served no purpose legitimate to his mission and so he had subdued the emanations from his psyche and let her go.

The good looking, black skinned secretary outside of Hardings' office was another story. He would have a use for her. And so he claimed her, passing his control to her lightly but firmly through the contact of their skin when they shook hands.

Ramón turned in his seat and looked at his familiar. It was dark inside the automobile, but he could see her face clearly each time a vehicle passed them going the other way, their headlights illuminating it briefly. She was smiling contentedly. Her eyes seemed to be looking deeply into the ether, not focused on anything in the car. He could feel the flow of happiness as it leaked from her. Whatever had happened this afternoon, he decided, was good. She had been tense and fraught with conflict all day. The epic episode of hilarity and the madly impassioned attack she had mounted on the other female had drawn all of that out of her.

There would be harder times ahead for the pretty, auburn haired woman. It was good to see her resiliency. She would need it.

Kelly had been lost in a trance like state the whole ride home. The only time she had been conscious of the world around her was when Adele had stopped for Mexican take out. She had phoned ahead and was in and out of the little store in the Hadley strip mall in a minute. Kelly watched the other people entering and exiting, going about their business. "Earthlings," she thought lazily. They talked and laughed and argued with each other, oblivious to the danger in their midst. But what did she care? She had cast her lot with the invader.

When the car pulled to a stop at her homestead, Kelly had a pang of disquietude. The house was the crucible of the man's control over her, a hothouse of passion. She had had moments of relative freedom and clearness of mind during the day. But here, the man would be again unrestricted in his control over her. She would again become the helpless, obsessed prisoner upon whom everything was imposed and nothing was asked. She had had several chances to escape today. She had taken none of them. Now, as she was confronted with the prospect of the renewal of her continuous state of sexual stimulation, driving out all rational thought, she was not so sure she had made the right decision.

Ramón took her by the arm and led her from the car to

the porch. They both waited while Adele unlocked the door. Ramón entered first, followed by Kelly and then Adele. Ramón turned to Kelly once they had crossed the threshold and, holding her cheeks in his hands, gave her a long, comforting kiss, sending a wave or reassurance and caring into her. Kelly's mind fogged at the reception of his message. She stood there listlessly, at the entrance to her home, while Adele unfastened her wrists and helped her take off her coat. Kelly stood and watched as she put it into the closet, unsure of what she should do. When Adele returned, she gave her confused friend a kiss and proceeded to undress her completely, including her stockings and shoes. She locked her hands behind her back and readorned her with her ankle bracelets, and gag. She had left the leash by the door and she clipped it onto Kelly's collar. As Adele was reestablishing her status as a totally controlled being, Kelly looked dolefully at her friend. She was so affectionate and concerned over her it was easy to forget, as she had at the lab before they left, that she was first and foremost the servant of her captor.

"Come on, honey, it's time for your surprise," she said.

Kelly had forgotten about Adele's promise of a surprise this morning when they left. Her heart darkened as to what it might be. Her gifts to her to date had not been of a nature to reassure her.

She followed, with trepidation, the blond woman's lead into the bedroom and lay down on the bed obediently. Adele scurried from the room and returned in a moment with the plastic shopping bag from the adult store. She pulled from it a bright pink, translucent vibrator molded in the form of a penis and a tube of lubrication. The vibrator was attached to a belt that went around the waist and thighs. Kelly looked at it unhappily. She had never used a vibrator and considered them a weird fetishism. She was chagrined at the new indignity her friend was imposing on her. She knew its purpose. While she had been a prisoner here over the weekend, she had existed in an almost constant sate of sexual arousal and bliss. Her day at the lab had broken that spell. The purpose of the sex toy was to reestablish it. And she could writhe and twist in pleasure while her tormentors went about their other business. She was going to be put on automatic.

When Adele presented the lubed device to her, Kelly shook her head and closed her legs. She didn't want that thing inside her. "Come on, Kelly," Adele said. "It'll only be for a little while, until I get dinner ready. It's what Ramón wants."

As if on signal, the dream man appeared in the doorway. He had stripped down and his physical presence sent a wave of lust through her. She saw him frown and she knew he was upset at her reluctance to comply with Adele's demand. With a tear in her eye, she spread her legs, exposing her hairless mons to the man and his acolyte. Her hips were raised by her bound hands underneath her and Adele had no trouble gaining access to her sex. She felt the tip of the device probe at her slit. Adele began to stroke her pleasure bud gently. That and the wave of passion the man sent her caused her gash quickly to moisten with desire.

The plastic penis split her labia and entered her. Adele pushed it in slowly until it was fully lodged in her crevasse. It was cool and hard, but it filled her exquisitely. Adele wrapped the straps around her and then, after connecting her ankles directly to each other, wrapped a black belt around her thighs, forcing them together. The belt fastened with Velcro and Adele was able to pull it very tight. She then urged her gently to her side. She connected her ankles to her wrists with the chain that had previously connected her ankles together. And there was one last thing. Adele retrieved from the bag a black mask that fitted over the eyes. The sockets were rounded and when she put it around Kelly's head, it shut out all light.

"That'll help you concentrate better, honey," Adele said.

"Just relax and enjoy it. Dinner'll be ready in a little while. I want to make some veggies and change my clothes. I'll set the control to medium."

The beast within Kelly's loins sprang to life. The end of it had a little attachment that sat directly over her hooded clit and Kelly began to experience a steady vibration that flowed through the walls of her pussy and sent a strange tingle across her love button. She felt the bed move as her friend got up to leave. She whined a protest from her darkness. And then she felt the man's hand run over her hip and down her naked thigh. He sent her an intense signal of passion and warmth. Her nervousness and mental discomfort at being filled with the sex toy passed away. By the time the delicious hand left her, her filled tunnel had begun to burn with lust.

Ramón left the female to enjoy her passions. He and Adele had an assignation tonight and it was important she be fully mesmerized with sexual bliss before they left. She would not like being left alone, but there was nothing he could do. It was bad enough to have to transport her daily back and forth from the lab, but to have her out in the world more than necessary was a hazard. Although leaving her alone in the house was also dangerous, it was the lesser of two evils. He went back to the living room and booted up Kelly's laptop. There were some formulas he had been going over at the lab before they left and he wanted to finish working on them while they were still on his mind.

The buzzing in her sex soon had Kelly writhing with desire. The man had closed the bedroom door when he left and the only sound she could hear were her own soft moans as her lusts began to build and the feint sound of the toy buried in her depths. The denial of her sight make the feelings in her body more intense, as of there was nothing else in the world but her impassioned body. When she felt her first orgasm coming, she tried to fight it off. She didn't want to come this way. In fact, it made her yearn for the presence of her captor's thick prick in her body, his hands on her flesh. Her breasts ached, breasts that were forbidden to her touch even if she could have somehow have freed her bound hands. She clamped her teeth on the faux penis in her mouth lustfully.

Kelly's pussy teetered on the edge of climax for a long time. Each time it threatened to explode into mind wrenching pleasure, she fought it back. And then it came. Anguished at her inability to control her own body, she clamped her bound thighs together tightly. She pulled at the chain that fixed her ankles and wrists to each other, writhing and moaning into the darkness that blanketed her. Her orgasm never really subsided completely. It faded into soft spasms in her pussy and then the relentless vibrations started her passions rising again. It was as if someone had turned on the lust button in her brain and had neglected to turn it off. Her second orgasm was harder, more forceful than her first. To her dismay, the vibrations continued.

It was just after her third, wrenching climax that she heard the door to her room open. She sensed the presence of her dream man. She had no idea how long she had been lost in the darkness, deep in passion's throes, but she welcomed the arrival of another being into her solitary universe. She felt his eyes roaming over her naked, abjectly bound form. The bed lowered behind her and she felt his hands on her rear globes and the probing of a finger at her private place. The man was lubing her small, rear aperture.

"Oh, no!" Kelly's mind screamed. "I couldn't stand it! Please don't!"

The chain that connected her limbs had some play in it and Kelly felt her hands pushed to the side, close to her hip. She felt the tip of the man's hard cock probe against her rear entrance. Her passions soared as it slowly and easily entered her. When it started to stroke across the tender tissues, it sent a rapturous wave though her body. His strong, warm chest pressed against her back. Kelly pulled futilely at her confined wrists and ankles. She strained to open her encircled thighs. But she could not escape the man's excruciating administration of pleasure to her. She was totally bound to his will, denied movement, sight and sound. All there was was him. All that had been done to her was at his behest, for his pleasure or purpose, as they case may be. His heavy hand seized her breasts, massaging each one in turn, sending heavy pulses of his lust through her body. She heard him groan as he pleasured himself in her bowels. The sensation of her vibrating pussy and clit and the fullness at being doubly penetrated was overwhelming. Her impassioned cleft resumed its contractions of passion and her body shook as it received them. She cried out when she felt the man's cock begin to pulse and throb across the sensitive membranes of her rear entrance and the warmth of the spread of his radiant seed inside her.

When the man's passion was spent, he turned off the vibrator in her pussy with the remote Adele had left beside her on the bed. Kelly gave a long, grateful sigh. Her body was limp with its exertions and her mind was filled with bliss. It felt like it had been stuffed with soft cotton that muffled everything else but the residues of her bout of lust. She lay there quietly, a bound prisoner, while the man went to the bathroom to clean himself. When he returned, he released the connection between her limbs and tenderly rolled her to her back. He pulled the blindfold off of her eyes and released her gag. She peered into his steely eyes with adoration for him, grateful for the life of bliss he had bought her. Taking hold of her breasts, he gave her a long, soothing, approving kiss.

Kelly knelt mesmerized by the table during dinner. Adele had reheated the cheese and bean burritos and made some fresh green beans and salad. She was dressed in her blue jeans and a pink top with a low, scoop neck bordered by frilly, white lace. Kelly wondered why she had not stripped herself naked as she had on Sunday. But the combination of her mesmerized state from her long session of passion, the good, warm food and the occasional pleasure giving caresses of her dream man, negated any real concern she had for an answer to that question. Adele had reopened her unfinished bottle of merlot, and the sensuous feeling the tart, fruity beverage gave as it went down her throat made her feel happy and content.

While Adele cleaned up, she pleased her captor as she had after every other meal in her home since he had arrived. She was surprised but content when he had her continue past his first ejaculation until he had sent her mouth a second, effusive, radiant discharge of his essence, triggering yet another series of pleasurable spasms in her sex.

Adele had finished the dishes and she lifted Kelly to her feet. She guided her entranced friend to the hallway where she placed the orange rug on the floor and had Kelly kneel. Kelly barely registered it when she bound her ankles together with a short chain and fastened her wrists tightly to them. Her friend affixed a chain around the exposed pipe that ran up the wall and fastened her in place. The black mask had been dangling around her neck since the end of her session with the vibrator. Adele lifted it until it covered her eyes again.

The enraptured young woman tried to focus on the significance of being restrained as she had been Sunday when she and Ramón were waiting to Adele to appear. She sensed her dream man kneeling in front of her and then his hands held the sides of her head while he gave her an impassioned kiss, sending his messages of affection and warmth to her. When his hands and lips left her, she felt her gag probe at her lips and she dutifully parted them to accept it.

Adele spoke to her while caressing her breasts and belly tenderly. "Ramón and I have to go out now, Kelly. I'm sorry that we have to leave you alone, but we'll be back as soon as we can, I promise. We can't take you with us or we would. But like I said, we'll be back just as soon as we can."

Through the haze of her mind and body's reverie from her use by the dream man, Kelly heard Adele's words. "Going out?" she questioned. "What? Where?" She heard the sharp report of Adele's hard soled boots on the kitchen floor, the jangling of keys and then sensed her passing by her. Ramón's footsteps followed her to the front door. It opened and closed and a moment later, she heard her car engine start and the sound of it pulling away from the house. And then, there was silence.

Kelly had been deprived of sight, but also, as a result, of all sense of time. The darkness in which she had been left made the glow of her body and the stupefaction of her mind more intense. For a long time, she knelt in place, relishing the feeling of the man's essence suffusing through her. But eventually, little by little, the reality of her confinement and abandonment started to creep into her consciousness.

The sounds of the house, unnoticeable when people were present or when her mind was able to concentrate on what had been her regular, daily tasks, reading, watching TV, surfing the net, even sitting back in her chair drinking tea and thinking about her day, became loud and ominous, emphasizing her solitude. Her dream man had left her. Where had he gone? Why had he left? She began to feel her separation from him in her belly, a slow, gnawing need for his reassuring presence. As time went on, dragging slowly by, her questioning of herself became more intense as did her physical symptoms as a result of their separation. How could he leave her like this? Was he really coming back? Why couldn't she go with him?

And then her hunger for the man started to grow in her loins. Her breasts started to yearn for his touch. She cursed herself for it. It was like a drug she had become addicted to. She pressed her thighs together and leaned her torso forward as far as it would go, stretching her bound arms, straining her shoulders. She tried to fight off her tears of loneliness and despair. Why had she let herself become his slave, she fretted. What did the man want with her? Why hand't she run away when she had the chance? The whole thing was like a continuous, extended psychotic episode. She had been entranced into becoming some kind of weird plaything for the man, had cast away everything important to her. Why was he treating her this way? Had she done something wrong? Was she now less than a person? At this self suggestion, the miserable young woman began to cry.

* * * * * * * * * * * * *

It had been about 7:30 when Ramón and Adele had left the house. It was now about 9:45. Ramón was sitting naked at a small, polished wooden table, pouring over a sheaf of documents, in room 512 of the Starlite Motel out on Route 246, the very place where Adele's 'date' on Friday night had tried to tempt her to. He was not alone. Lying naked on the bed, face down, asleep, her arms scrunched under the cheap motel pillow, was Mr. Hardings' personal secretary, Hannah Greene.

Mrs. Greene had showed up at the motel room sharply at 8 P.M. as per instructions Adele had given her over the telephone shortly after Ramón had returned from his meeting with Hardings. Ramón had been sitting on the bed, naked, waiting for her. She tapped timidly on the door and he walked over and opened it. She was still wearing the turquoise, long sleeved, shirtwaist, knee length dress she had worn earlier that day. It had a modest 'v' neck that revealed a chaste portion of the dark brown skin of her chest and just the beginnings of the interior curves of her full breasts. Her face was startled and her eyes widened when she saw the nude, coffee colored man at the door, but she took his hand when he offered it and stepped inside.

Hannah was carrying a large, brown imitation leather handbag. The edge of a 9x12" manila envelope peeked from the top. She placed the bag down just inside the door and followed Ramón's lead until she was well inside. Ramón had been sending her intent messages of passion through his hand and when he let go of hers, the handsome, fortyish woman stared at him for a moment as if trying to decipher his instructions. Then, licking her broad lips, she reached behind her and began to unbutton her dress, staring at him in wonderment. When it was unbuttoned and she had pulled the bodice down to reveal her sturdy, white cotton bra and had slid her graceful arms free, she kicked off her shiny, black, thick heeled shoes and then stepped out of it. She was wearing sheer, black tinted pantyhose over a pair of blue and white flowered panties and she pulled them off, revealing thick, but trim thighs and a wide, black, hairy bush. She released the covering over her full, round breasts and dropped her bra to the floor.

The black woman's face was showing the signs of a developing lust. It still had an aspect of puzzlement to it, as if she was finding it hard to believe she was in a motel room stripping in front of a man she had just met today and had spoken maybe five or six words to. But her concerned look faded when Ramón retook her hand, transmitting strong messages of assurance to her along with a stoking of her passions, and guided her to the bed.

They made love for the better part of an hour. The woman's flesh was soft and full, luxuriant. Ramón took pleasure in exploring the deeply shaded skin, darker even than his, finding its hue rich and exciting. When the dream man penetrated her, she sighed deeply with passion and gripped his body tightly to her. When she came, she thrust her hips at him urgently, crying out a deep, throaty moan.

Ramón probed her mind while they rested after he had delivered a second, satisfying orgasm to her and flooded her womb with his entrancing essence. The dream man reveled in the deep, rich textured of the woman's emotions. They were complex and flavorful, not unlike the tart, rich wine he had consumed with dinner. He found inside her a desperate loneliness, a permeating sorrow. Her inner nature was passionate, giving. He was amazed at the font of love and affection the woman's psyche harbored. Her heart contained a wellspring of caring that for a long time had no one to drink of it.

Ramón learned Hannah had lost her husband three years before. He was a supervisor for the Virginia Highway Department and had been struck and killed by a tractor trailer while on a maintenance job on Highway 15 in Petersville. They had been married twenty two years. Gaylord had worked his way up from a laborer to supervisor. They had raised three kids together, all of whom were now pursuing successful careers. Taylor and Lincoln, the twins, had graduated from state college by now and were working as store managers with the beginnings of families of their own. Lawanda was a senior at Gartersburg State College and was looking at business schools. They would never have made it without the help of Mr. Hardings. The State pension was not enough to finish the financing of the kids' secondary educations. Harding had paid the tuitions and supplemented Hannah's salary.

The 44 year old widow had more than gratitude in her heart for the older, white man. She had watched him mourn at the loss of his own wife of 35 years three years before Gaylord had died. He was still mourning and Hannah's heart went out to him. She saw his inner goodness and need, but the barriers of race and Harding's inbred reserve had prevented her from reaching out to him. That and the fact she was afraid Hardings would see her expression of love for him as mere repayment for his charity.

Ramón could see the intense conflict he had caused the woman in compelling her to produce printouts of Hardings' files. He eased her concerns, bringing her to believe in the greater good it would serve. He spent a long time with her, delicately redirecting her mind to an intense belief in him without disturbing her primary loyalties and beliefs.

It had been years since Hannah had experienced the pleasure her body could give her and Ramón gave her a full measure of it now. She eagerly and gratefully pleasured him in return, her soft lips scouring his body before lustfully encompassing his manhood. Her body shuddered and shook with delight each time he emptied himself into it, firmly fixing the bond between them.

As the woman slept peacefully, Ramón was going over the computer printouts selecting a list of files for the woman to download and turn over to him for review the next day. He had no need to write them down, he would transfer the list psychically to the black woman before she left. She would be eager to cooperate. He was matching the names on the files with information he had drawn from her during their union. He was going over the last page when there was a faint tapping at the door.

One of the several errands Adele had run while he had been making love to Hannah was to obtain jump drives Hannah could use to deliver Hardings' confidential computer files to Ramón. He would use the information to develop changes and improvements to Hardings' products and processes. He was confident he could produce innovations that would be immediately profitable to the entrepreneur. The problem was how to approach the man, how to win his confidence and cooperation. Hardings, because of his government projects, would have access to many of the strategic materials Ramón would need. The financial benefits Hardings would receive would pay for them. But he was a hard nut to crack. He was scrupulously honest and a straight arrow morally and ethically. He was strongly religious. W.C. Fields said you can't cheat an honest man and Hardings was a good example of that. Not that Ramón would cheat him, but the aphorism applied equally to the inability to corrupt an honest man. Hardings would not be prey to the allure of wealth and power Ramón could easily offer him. He could make Hannah his slave, or any other woman for that matter, not to mention the desirable file clerk Ramón had met earlier that day. But, from what Ramón had read from the man's mind during their meeting and what he could glean from Hannah's mind, he would not bite at that bait.

Adele came into the motel room carrying a little bag from Radio Shack. It held five jump drives to be given to Hannah to take with her. Ramón put the papers back in the envelope and walked to the bed to awaken the slumbering woman. She stirred slowly and smiled at him. Adele knelt next to the bed and leaned over and kissed her, stroking her curly, shoulder length black hair. Hannah took no umbrage at the young, blond woman's gesture of friendship, and kissed her back. Ramón had placed in her an affinity for his servant and he was happy to see that the two women were able to share affection.

Hannah dressed quietly, unembarrassed at her nakedness before the young white girl. She kissed Ramón passionately when she was done, receiving from him reinforcement of her commitment to him and assurances of the propriety of serving him. She took the plastic bag with the jump drives in it from Adele and left.

* * * * * * * * * * * * *

When Kelly heard the car pull up her driveway, her heart
leapt. She had been crying on an off for the longest time. Her
physical need for release was tearing at her. In her agony, she
had cursed the dream man and her friend, promising herself
she would escape from them somehow, that she would not
give in to her need for the man, succumb to his rapture. But
when the door opened and his familiar footsteps approached
her, all other thoughts than her need for him passed away. He
placed his hand on her head, removing her blindfold and
peered into her desperate eyes. She felt joy and relief he was
back.

Adele knelt next to her as well and released her bonds as
the dream man disrobed before her. "I'm so sorry, Kelly. I'm
sorry it took so long. We won't leave you alone ever again, I
promise," she told her remorsefully.

Kelly threw herself into Ramón's arms as soon as she was
free. He removed her gag and they kissed fervently. He could
feel the pain that had been stored up in his familiar and he
was touched by it, remonstrating with himself at his fault in
producing it. He passed a warm flow of soothing energy to
the auburn haired woman as she pressed her body against him
hungrily. Her need for him was intense and she clenched her
hands against his back, drawing him into her. He was sitting
cross legged on the floor and she was atop of his lap. Her
hands ran wildly over his shoulders and arms while she drank
at his lips.

Kelly was frantic at her need for the man. She absorbed
his essence through her hands and her mouth, but it was her
sex that needed him most. She reached under herself and took
his hardened cock in her hand, stroking it with desire. She
lifted her body up and poised the hard rod at her already
moistened portal and enveloped it, taking it inside, giving a

deep, satisfied sigh as it filled her.

"Oh, yes, yes, yes," Kelly's mind called out as she felt the thick meat push her inner walls aside. She had thought she had been abandoned, had begged God to release her from her bondage to the dream man, the visitor, the invader, whatever he was. But as she felt his manhood inside her, felt the energies of his psyche pouring into her, she forgave him for his cruel treatment, wanting nothing more than to be wholly and totally devoted to him.

Her orgasm, which came quickly, was like an explosion inside her. She felt the man's essence flooding her canal as he came too, and welcomed it. The man lifted her up from the floor, still engaged on his cock, and brought her into the bedroom where he laid her on her back and made her come again.

Afterwards, Ramón let the female explore him, use him as her need dictated. He rolled to his back and the woman washed his body with her kisses, stroked his manhood, engulfed it with her lips. She touched every inch of his body, free for the first time since Saturday night to experience the tactile pleasure of his flesh with her fingers and palms. He filled her with his essence three times before they were done. When she had exhausted her passions, she laid nestled into his shoulder, her hand rubbing over his chest and belly, softly sobbing her gratitude for his use. He sent her his sorrow for her pain and his deep, caring affection for her. When he sensed her calm acceptance, he turned his head and kissed her smiling lips as she caressed his face.

Adele was waiting for Kelly, kneeling naked at the foot of the bed when her dream man rose from his familiar's embrace. She took Kelly gently by the hand and brought her to the bathroom where she bathed her and took care of her other needs. She shaved away the slight stubble that had risen on her mons during the course of the day and gave loving release with her mouth afterwards on the bathroom rug. As she had promised the day before, she applied a bright red polish to her finger and toe nails. When Adele presented her to the dream man, bound and chained as she had been the night before, Kelly was pleased to have been decorated for his pleasure.

CHAPTER FOUR

Their days soon settled into a regular routine. In the mornings, after the man had drained her of the mists she had gathered for him during her dreams, Adele would give them all breakfast. Kelly would feed on her lord's cock while Adele made her face ready for the day and then the blond woman would shave her loins as she lay on the bed and mouth her to pleasure, often while the dream man watched appreciatively. She would then adorn and dress her. She had purchased a few more short, revealing skirts for her while Ramón had been busy at the motel and some more pullover shirts. She would not let her wear anything that buttoned since it would interfere with Ramón's access to her breasts during the day. Except for when Kelly was taken from the car into the lab, there was no more need to hide her leather collar and so there was no necessity for turtlenecks. Instead, when they left the house, Adele covered the accepting woman's neck with a scarf, which concealed the collar until they got inside the lab.

When they arrived at the office, Ramón would reinforce his bond to her and her obedience to his will by bringing her to orgasm and filling her with his warm essence in her office, either on her desk or on the soft, cushioned rug. The girls would all greet the dream man as they had the first day, although by Thursday, Felicity was offering her pussy to the man and Melissa had, on Wednesday night before the girls went home, knelt between his thighs and pleasured him with her mouth. Chandra was still embarrassed at her lack of sexual experience, but needed no more coaching to bring pleasure to the man with her lips.

Every evening, when they returned home, Kelly would undergo a prolonged session with her vibrator, during which her sexual delirium would be reestablished. Ramón would make love to her afterwards, opting for the orifice of his choice before they assembled around the dinner table for their supper. Adele had bought a couple of vegetarian cookbooks and tried her hand at making interesting meals, proudly announcing each night the name and contents of the recipe.

Kelly's fear that the lab girls would discover her in the midst of sexual union with the dream man was realized Tuesday afternoon when Felicity came into Kelly's office to drop off a lab slip. Kelly was on her knees, her hands bound behind her, gratefully pleasuring the dream man's cock when the door opened. Adele had dressed her in a soft, pale blue sweater that morning and Ramón had pulled it up over her head and down her arms behind her. She felt a surge of shame at the revelation of her subservience to the man, her bared breasts, the confinement of her wrists. But Ramón, who was naked, merely sent her a reassuring wave of pleasure through his hands on her head and it quickly passed.

That evening, any doubt Kelly had that the lab assistants were fully aware of the nature of her enthrallment to the man was dispelled. After dinner, she had been bound in place in the hallway as they prepared to leave. Kelly was frantic she would be abandoned again, unhappy that Adele's promise of the night before was going to be broken. Her mind and body were filled with the mesmerizing effects of the man's discharges into her, but she was able to understand the import of her confinements and began to whine and cry behind her gag. To her surprise, she heard a car pull up the driveway, the sound of feet on the porch and a light knock on the door.

Adele opened the door and escorted Melissa and Felicity into the house. She took their coats and led them into the hallway. They were dressed in jeans and t-shirts and smiled sweetly at their grotesquely bound employer.

Kelly whined and moaned through her gag at being displayed naked and bound to the pretty young girls. Every time she thought she had reached the nadir of shame and humiliation at being made into the dream man's fuck toy, she only had to wait to discover a new low. Adele ignored her protestations. "The girls are going to keep you company and take care of you while we're out," Adele said to Kelly softly as she knelt next to her and stroked her breasts. She motioned for the girls to approach. "Dr. Jameson will need to be comforted while Ramón is away. We'll be back around ten. Make sure she gets release about every half an hour or so. Otherwise, she'll suffer. Can you do that?"

The young girls, who had taken kneeling positions in front of the bound woman, nodded sheepishly. Their friendship had intensified as a result of their enthrallment by Ramón and they were holding hands. Kelly, through her mind fogging mist as a result of Ramón's after dinner attentions, tried to muster a protest at being displayed so obscenely before the young girls. But the dream man sent her such an intense wave of pleasure and reassurance through his hands as Adele waited for him by the door, that her revulsion at the exposure of her abasement was temporarily subsumed by her bliss.

After Ramón and Adele left, the girls knelt on their haunches silently before the bound woman for a long while. Kelly's mind was clearing and she was already beginning to feel the distress of being separated from her captor. The looks in the girls' eyes was adoring and respectful of their ostensive employer, ostensive because it was clear Ramón was the one who controlled their actions now. Kelly thought they looked like they were as uncomfortable and unsure of themselves as she was, having been charged with what was certainly in their minds a huge and strange responsibility. While she was sad at being left behind by Ramón and Adele and dismayed at the display of her naked and bound body to the young girls, she appreciated the fact that at least she was not alone and blindfolded, forced to endure her separation from the man in the lonely quietude of the small farmhouse.

Neither Melissa nor Felicity had harbored any inclination to lesbianism prior to their enthrallment by Ramón. Their affection for each other had grown and they had taken to kissing each other when they met in the morning and separated in the evenings. And throughout the past two days, they had increased their physical contact with each other, holding hands as they were now, or stroking or caressing each others' arms or shoulders when they talked. But to be responsible for the 'comfort' of another woman was something they were not fully prepared for. They both revered Dr. Jameson as the especial thrall of their new found lord. However, kissing and touching the intimate flesh of another female was offputting, to say the least.

Felicity was the one to take the bull by the horns. After gazing appreciatively at Kelly's exposed, delectable form, she broke the contact between her and her friend's hands and unceremoniously pulled her t-shirt up over her head. She was braless and her breasts swayed gently on her chest as she tossed the top aside. Melissa looked at her wide eyed. She had never seen Felicity's boobs before, not naked anyway. She stared as her girlfriend got to her feet and began to unbuckle her jeans.

"Come on, Liss," Felicity told her. "If Dr. Jameson has to be naked, then it's only fair we are too."

"I, I don't know," Melissa replied. "I'm not sure that I want to."

Felicity had kicked off her boots and was pulling her pants down over her hips, underwear and all. "Well, I'm going to. Dr. Jameson needs us to help her and we really can't do that if we're wearing clothes. It just wouldn't seem right."

Melissa watched as Felicity drew her jeans over her feet and dropped them on the floor behind her. Felicity had graceful hips and long legs. Her slit was covered with a thin layer of soft, curly blond hair. Her belly was flat. "Wow," Melissa said to her friend in admiration and amazement. "You're really pretty, Fel." And then she giggled. "At least I know now for sure you're a natural blond."

Felicity laughed. "It's funny," she said. "I've let maybe a dozen boys see my cunny, a couple that I hardly even knew. And yet you're my best friend and you've never seen it." She stroked her hand the length of it, from the bottom to the top. "How do you like it?" she asked, smiling.

Melissa looked uncomfortable at her friend's interrogatory. She didn't want her to get the wrong idea. "Oh, it's pretty," she said finally. "Like the rest of you."

The taller blond girl, satisfied with her friend's answer, knelt down again next to her. "I'm not sure what to do next," she announced.

Bother girls stared at the older, bound woman for several minutes. Kelly tried to fight off the feelings of lust that were rising within her. The idea that the young girl's lips and hands might soon be on her were driving her passions. "What has Ramón done to me?" she thought miserably. She knew she would not be able to last long without exhibiting signs of her desire. Her pussy began to tingle and she pressed her thighs together. Her breasts were becoming tight and her nipples had hardened. She was unable to suppress a sigh.

"See," Felicity told her friend, "she needs us." Tentatively, the naked blond girl crept closer to the bound woman on her knees. She placed a small hand on the woman's shoulder and stroked it softly, her touch light as a feather.

Kelly felt her skin tingle as the gentle fingers drew across her flesh. She wanted this and yet didn't. She was about to cross yet another boundary. She had made love to Adele, enjoyed and relished her caresses, moaned and writhed as her friend pleasured her. But this was something else entirely. It would confirm her transformation into an engine of undifferentiated lust, a being willing to couple with anyone who would bring her pleasure, she thought, miserably. But would it really? These young girls were the servants of her master. Their touch was his touch. Their lips were his lips. And her desire for them was a corollary of her desire for the man who had enthralled her. And there was no sign of exploitation or derision in the young girls' eyes. Their affection and caring for her were clear on their unpretentious, young faces. And her need was real, would become stronger, almost intolerable as the night grew on.

Kelly felt a wave of affection for the two girls. The goodness and benevolence of the man who had converted them to his use shown through them. Why shouldn't she love them? And why shouldn't she accept their caresses, their warmth?

Felicity had been encouraged by the sensation of touching the older woman's warm flesh. She crept a little closer and put both of her hands on her shoulders, caressing them. She was kneeling straight up and she leaned forward and placed a kiss on the captive woman's forehead. Kelley's burnt orange hair was loose and free about her shoulders and back. Their naked breasts touched gently, sending both women a thrill. Felicity leaned over and planted a soothing, impassioned kiss on Kelly's neck, just under her leather collar, at the joinder with her shoulder. She slid her hands down and took possession of the woman's stiff nipples, delicately stroking them, teasing them until the woman moaned with pleasure. Leaning back, the thin, blond girl cupped her hands under the woman's left breast and lifted it to her mouth, suckling on the tip lovingly, running her tongue around the hardened teat until the bound woman moaned again. She repeated her oral adoration to the other breast, giving it long, loving attention. She looked up into the eyes of her master's precious thrall. "Oh, Dr.

Jameson," she said. "I'm so happy. You're so beautiful, I, I...."
A tear formed in her eye and she placed her hands around the older woman's neck and hugged her tightly, pressing their chests firmly together, rubbing her belly and breasts against her. Kelly revered the warmth that flowed between them, the genuineness of the girl's affectionate gesture. Felicity then let her hands fall down the woman's shoulders and arms, down along her shapely torso and over her hips. Moving slightly to the side, she placed one hand on her lower back and pressed the other between her thighs.

Kelly had tightened her knees when she had been trying to fight off her lust and shame at her display before the two young girls. They were still pressed together firmly now. "Please spread you legs, Dr. Jameson," Felicity whispered into her ear, her hand stroking her thighs. "I want to make you come."

A surge of lust flowed through Kelly at the young girl's brazen statement. She closed her eyes and widened her knees, admitting the pleasing hand to her loins. A tender, probing finger traced its way along the length of her bare slit and then down again, sending a thrill of pleasure through her. The finger repeated its trek, more firmly and with more confidence. The third time, it nestled against her bud of pleasure and stroked it gently making Kelly's body shudder with delight.

Melissa watched her friend make love to their bound boss with lustful fascination. Her palms had become sweaty and her pussy began to burn. Unconsciously, her hand rose to her breasts and began to stroke them through her thin t-shirt. Her lips parted and her tongue darted around them. She could not believe what she was seeing. If someone had asked her a few hours ago how she would feel about watching two women make love, she would have made a yucky face and put her finger down her throat. But now, she wasn't so sure. The rapture on Dr. Jameson's face was unmistakable. And the vision of her friend suckling her breasts and fingering her cleft made her own pussy tingle with excitement.

Felicity's hand began to stroke and caress Kelly's fevered canal more intently. Kelly could feel her lust rising higher and higher. She clamped her teeth down on the intruder in her mouth and moaned as the first, pleasurable spasm rocked her. Felicity's fingers probed deep inside her while her thumb massaged her clit. "Mmmmmmmpf! Mmmmmmmpf!" Kelly called out from her filled mouth as her body shuddered with her release. Mmmmmmmmpf!" she exclaimed at each intensely pleasurable spasm, "Mmmmmmpf!" A river of ecstasy flowed through her as the young girl's hand relentlessly massaged her electrified pussy.

As her convulsions of pleasure waned, the young, blond girl held Kelly tightly in her arms. "Oh, Dr. Jameson, that was so nice," she said to her sweetly. Her hand was still gently stroking the bound, auburn haired woman's mons, encouraging the aftershocks of Kelly's orgasm. She turned to her mesmerized friend. "It's so soft and smooth," she said to her. "It's really nice to touch."

Melissa screwed up her courage. "Let me feel it," she responded, hopefully.

"Not unless you take your clothes off, Liss," Felicity told her. "It wouldn't be fair to Dr. Jameson."

The chestnut haired, diminutive girl licked her lips while she hesitated. The allure of her employer's pleasured body was too much to resist. She pulled up her t-shirt and removed it. She was wearing a lacy, revealing bra underneath and she reached behind her back and freed it, allowing her pretty, youthful breasts to drop free. After she tossed it aside, she loosened the belt and the snaps to her tight blue jeans and, sitting down on her rump, pulled it over her hips and down to her ankles. In her rush, she had neglected to remove her pink and white Reeboks and had to lean forward and pop them off before drawing her jeans and socks over her feet and off. She was wearing a light pastel green thong.

"Come on, Liss," Felicity said. "You have to take everything off."

Melissa paused to give some thought to the exposure of her love lips and the fine, thick bush of chestnut colored hair that surrounded it. But, in for a penny, in for a pound, she finally eased it from her hips and over her legs. She then knelt up and looked at her friend for her approval.

"Liss, you're really hairy down there," Felicity remarked, a touch of amusement in her voice.

"Soooo!" her friend returned, embarrassed.

"So, nothing," Felicity said. "I just didn't know, that's all."

"Can I touch her now?" Melissa asked.

"Sure," Felicity answered. "Come closer. But you have to kiss her first."

The pixie-like girl edged her way over to the two naked women on her knees. Her full breasts swayed gracefully as she approached. She was nervous, being naked and all next to her friend and the older woman. She clamped her thighs tightly together and kept her left arm crossed over her torso, hiding her tight, bold nipples.

"Come on, Liss," Felicity said softly. "Give Dr. Jameson a kiss. Show her that you love her."

"I do love her," Melissa answered. She looked over the body of the confined woman. Of course she loved her master's familiar. Who wouldn't? The man had impressed on both young girls her importance to him and his affection for her. And she was so brave to serve him with everything she had to go through. Dr. Jameson was a figure of great respect and awe to her. And now she was going to be allowed to touch her private place! A kiss was a small price to pay.

Melissa leaned over and, making herself as tall as she

could on her knees, placed a tender kiss on Kelly's forehead. Kelly's breasts pressed against her taut, youthful belly. She leaned back and caressed Kelly's face.

"Oh, Dr. Jameson," she said, "I'm so happy for you. You're so nice."

Kelly was awash in tender sentiment for the two girls who had been left as caretakers for her in her lord and master's absence. Her body still reverberated from her bout of passion at the hands of the young, blond woman. She felt oddly proud they saw her as a kind of shrine to the dream man. Part of her mind knew she should be offended and disconcerted at her callous treatment, being bound and gagged in her own house and left as a plaything for the two young women. But their affection for her was so genuine and their innocence so compelling she pushed those thoughts aside.

Melissa hesitatingly put her hand down near Kelly's exposed, hairless sex. Her friend withdrew hers and made room for the smaller, brown haired girl. Melissa's fingers made tentative contact with the smooth skin and then, gaining confidence, she cupped the older woman's pudenda with her palm, rubbing it tenderly.

"Ohhhh!" Melissa exclaimed. "It's so soft and smooth!" She looked at her blond friend and smiled. "I like it!"

Felicity smiled back and put her own hand over her friend's "Put your finger inside," she said conspiratorially. "It's really soft and warm."

Melissa giggled slightly and extended a finger from her hand and slipped it between Kelly's smooth love lips, making the woman sigh. "Ohhhh!" she repeated. "It feels good! It's like its mine, but it somebody else's. It feels, well, different."

Felicity took her arm and put it over her friend's naked shoulder. She whispered in her ear. Melissa's body shuddered as she felt the close contact of her friend's body, the press of her breast against her arm. She suppressed another giggle at

Felicity's suggestion.

"Oh, I don't know," she said, bashfully.

"Come on," Felicity continued, louder this time. "Ramón'll like it."

This was the key expression. Melissa, smirking, nodded her agreement. "Ok," she said. "I'll do it if you do."

Felicity leaned over and planted a small kiss on Kelly's right nipple. "We'll be back in a little while, Dr. Jameson."

The girls both rose to their feet. "I'll go in the bathroom. You look in the kitchen for a bowl or something and put some hot water in it," the taller blond girl instructed her friend.

Kelly watched the girls run off. For a moment she panicked. They weren't going to leave her, were they? Felicity returned first, holding Kelly's razor in one hand and a can of shaving cream in the other. Melissa appeared next, holding one of her mixing bowls full of hot water.

The girls looked at each other like school girls intent on playing some prank. "Let's do it in the bedroom," Felicity suggested.

From her perch in the hallway, Kelly had a clear view of the bedroom through the mirror on the wall. The girls hesitated for a moment, standing by its foot, and she heard Felicity tell Melissa she would do her first. Melissa crawled up on the bed, her ass at its end and opened her legs widely, just as Kelly did each morning when Adele removed her nightlong pubic growth. "Be careful, okay?" she heard her tell her friend, her voice tentative and unsure.

Kelly watched intently as she saw Felicity lay a thick layer of foam over Melissa's loins and work it into the thick hair. She swirled the razor around in the hot water and then went to work.

Melissa kept telling her friend to be 'careful' and writhed her hands nervously on her belly. "You've got to hold still, Liss!" Felicity warned her.

"Okay, okay," the pretty girl responded dolefully.

Within a few minutes, Melissa's slit was hairless and smooth. Before they changed places, Felicity came running out and got a bowl of fresh, hot water and scurried back. Melissa was sitting on the bed, her legs dangling over the end. She was rubbing her naked mound. "It feels so funny," she said. "It's neat."

"Come on and do me," Felicity instructed her. She put the hot bowl of water on the floor and the girls exchanged places. Her pubic hair was thinner and sparser than her friend's and Melissa's job was over quickly. The brown haired girl rubbed her hand over the smooth surfaces of Felicity's now hairless pussy. Felicity had raised her body up on her elbows and Melissa's eyes locked with her friend's, a guilty, embarrassed look crossing over her face. There was a moment of pregnant silence between them.

Felicity broke the spell. "Let me put some lotion on you, Liss. It'll make it feel real nice."

Without waiting for her friend's approval, the blond girl hopped off the bed and hurried into the bathroom. She smiled at Kelly as she passed her. She returned in a moment with a tube of skin cream.

"Come on, Liss," she told her friend. "Get up on the bed."

Melissa hesitated at first, but then climbed onto the mattress. The blond girl lay on her back next to her, her body fully extended. "Do me first," she told her. "And then I'll do you."

Felicity was lying to Melissa's left as she faced her, farthest away from the mirror. Kelly watched the brown haired girl take a dollop of cream from the tube and begin to smear it on Felicity's proffered loins. The blond girl had her knees bent and her legs spread wide.

"Ohhhh, Liss," she moaned as the smaller girl worked the lotion into her tender skin, "that feels so good. Don't stop.

Put on some more."

Melissa took another squeeze of lotion and, after letting it warm in her hand for a moment, gently placed her palm and fingers on her friend's love lips and caressed them softly.

"Ohhhh, yea, Liss," Felicity moaned. "That feels so nice." She luxuriated in her friend's delicate touch for several minutes. Then she placed her hand on Melissa's wrist and announced in a soft, husky, impassioned voice, "Now let me do you."

Felicity rose from her back and guided her friend to hers. When Melissa had been applying the lotion to her blond friend's shaved loins, Kelly had only been able to see the smaller girl's back and the movements of her arm between her friend's legs. But now that the girls had shifted positions, she could see Melissa's extended torso, her soft round breasts as they lay peacefully on her chest, her pretty, mesmerized face. She could also see the impassioned glow in the blond girl's as she looked over her friend's recumbent form, her pretty breasts as they swayed softly, the stiffened nipples evidencing her arousal.

Felicity took some lotion in her right palm and let it warm for a second. Melissa was lying with her legs flat and together. "Spread your legs, Liss, and lift your knees so I can get at your pussy," Felicity instructed her softly. Melissa looked up at her friend, momentarily undecided. Her brown eyes were large and watery. "Oh, Felicity," she murmured, placing her hand on her arm. "I'm scared."

"Don't be scared, Liss. I'm not going to hurt you. We're friend's right?"

Melissa nodded dolefully.

"Then lift you legs for me so I can put some lotion on you. You'll see, it'll feel really good."

The small brown haired girl slowly lifted her knees. Felicity gently nudged them apart and took a position kneeling next to her friend's small, beauteous form. She placed her hand between her thighs and began to rub it over the timid girl's love lips. Kelly watched the hand work slowly and rhythmically between the supine girl's legs. The blond girl's attentions divided between an intense gaze at the workings of her hand and her friend's face. Melissa's eyes were closed as she absorbed the feel of her friend's gentle fingers on the plump mound of her sex. Kelly could see the signs of her nascent passion. Her lips were parted and her tongue flitted over them. Her breathing was becoming deep and heavy. The nipples on her breasts were standing firm and tall.

As Kelly watched he unfolding tableau, her own passions began to rise. Her breasts began to get tight and her pussy tingled. She tried to shift her position, but her bound hands and tied off ankles gave her little room for maneuver. In the mirror in her room, Felicity had moved her body down onto the bed, lying next to her friend, making full contact with her. She took one of the small, brown haired girl's nipples in her mouth and began to suck on it gently. Melissa moaned and her hips shifted. Her right arm was trapped between their two bodies, but her left hand was free and she placed it on the blond girl's head, stroking her hair. Felicity looked up at her and, raising her torso, gently placed her lips on Melissa's. The girls exchanged a warm, luxuriant kiss. Melissa's free hand drifted to Felicity's breast and squeezed it gently. The blond girl broke their kiss and Kelly heard her whisper quietly to her friend, "Put your hand on my pussy, Liss, play with me until I come," before she took the baby faced, young girl's lips once again.

Kelly's arousal began to become intense as she stared at the image of the two love making young girls in the mirror. It was like she was there with them and she was not. She could hear their moans and cries of lust as if they were right next to her. But at the same time, their reflected images as they feverishly worked each other's young, nubile bodies made them seem distant, unreal.

Melissa had turned her back to the mirror, the better to face her friend and Felicity's right arm had snaked under her neck and was holding onto her head from behind, forcing their lips together. Her upper leg was raised and her foot was flat down on the bed so as to give her friend better access to her now hairless pussy.

It was Melissa who came first. She gave a long, low moan and her body began to shake. She broke their kiss and cried out, "Oh, Fel! Oh Fel! Oh! Oh!" as her orgasm overtook her. Kelly could see Felicity's hand working feverishly between her thighs. She must have, in post orgasmic bliss, slowed her efforts at her friend's pussy since Felicity began to exclaim, "Oh, don't stop, Lissa! Don't stop! Oh, fuck me! Fuck my cunt! Make me come! Oh God! Yes! Yes!"

Kelly saw her arm pull Melissa's lips back to hers fiercely as her other hand continued its relentless delivery of pleasure to her friend's puss. The small girl's body stiffened again and she resumed her moaning and shaking. They were exclaiming their pleasures in unison, loud, staccato cries of pleasure muffled by each other's lips, until finally, as their efforts slowed, their moans became whimpers and then long, languorous sighs while their bodies came to rest.

Kelly's own lust was on the burn from watching the lascivious display of the naked, young bodies in heat. The man had done this to her, she knew that. She had never been this way, never lusted for the feel and taste of female flesh. But the fact that her passion was induced did not make it any less real. She squeezed her thighs in frustration as her eyes begged for the return of the two young girls to their duties. She pressed her teeth down on the thick gag in her mouth, receiving a flow of dizzying lust from it. She at once despised herself for her need and rejoiced in it, her body being electrified with sensation.

The two young women lay pressed against each other, holding their bodies tight. "I'm so glad you're my friend, Liss," Felicity whispered softly.

"I love you, Fel," the smaller girl answered.

"Me too, Liss. I love you too." They kissed, opening their mouths and exchanging their tongues. Then, suddenly, Felicity broke it off. "Oh shit! We forgot about Dr. Jameson!" she exclaimed.

The two young women slid off the bed and rushed out into the hall. They knelt in front of the naked and bound scientist, their employer and, now, their goddess. "I'm so sorry, Dr, Jameson," Felicity said, her hand caressing the anxious older woman's long, wavy auburn hair while staring into her distressed face. She turned to Melissa. "See, she needs us. It's your turn to make her come."

Melissa looked at the nude, proffered form of the woman and licked her lips. "I, I don't know what I should do," she said plaintively.

"Just kiss her and rub your body against her for starts. Do what you would want her to do to you."

The small, chestnut haired girl looked lustfully at Kelly's body. She shifted her knees so she was closer and directly in front of her and she leaned forward and put her arms around the older woman's neck. She pressed her breasts against Kelly's and began a slow, rhythmic motion, sliding the front of her torso against the bound woman's. She then circled her dainty arms under Kelly's and pulled against her naked back, forcing their bodies tightly together.

Kelly reveled in the heat of the young woman's soft, girlish flesh. She closed her eyes and let the pleasure of their contact flow through her, the vision of her recently impassioned face in her mind. Felicity just knelt there watching, admiring her friend's efforts to please the older woman.

After a short while, Melissa pulled herself back and looked at Felicity. Her face was livid with desire. "Can I kiss her?" she asked, timidly.

"I guess it's okay," Felicity answered, and she leaned over and released the belt that held Kelly's gag firmly between her lips. She slowly eased it out until the woman's mouth was free.

Melissa stroked Kelly's cheek softly while gazing lovingly into her eyes. "You're so nice, Dr. Jameson," she said. Her eyes were watering with tears, overcome by emotion. She closed them, one hand holding the back of the bound woman's head, and pressed her lips against Kelly's, sliding her tongue inside her mouth.

Kelly moaned as the younger woman's tongue enflamed her. Her body was afire from where their flesh had met. Her pussy burned with need. As the young girl kissed her, she slid her hands down her sides and over her hips. One hand continued down across her sensitive belly and found her clean smooth mons, while the other rose up and seized a breast. Kelly sucked hungrily at the young woman's tongue as her hands enflamed her. She groaned with pleasure as Melissa's small fingers delicately opened her slit and delved inside. Her body shook with anticipation of her climax when she felt a finger stroke her hard bud of pleasure softly.

The enraptured girl engaged in a long, determined inflammation of Kelly's cunt, making the older woman writhe and moan. When she sensed the immanency of the captive woman's orgasm, she intensified her efforts at pleasing her. Her hand began to franticly stroke her pussy, her mouth pressed firmly against the older woman's lips. She squeezed her breasts hard, pulling at her stiff nipples. When Kelly came, her body convulsed with pleasure.

Melissa was pleased she had brought to bound woman to

climax. As Kelly's orgasm faded, she kissed her face and hugged her. She turned and looked at her friend. "That was outrageous!" she said excitedly. Felicity nodded her excited agreement and then gave her a kiss and hugged her.

"We have to put her gag back in," she said. She had been holding it like a treasure while her friend had pleasured the bound woman. She pressed it against her lips and, in her post orgasmic fog, Kelly opened her mouth and accepted it.

Across town, Ramón was reading Hardings' computer programs on Kelly's laptop at the Starlite Motel. Hannah Greene and Adele were making love to each other in the large king sized bed. Their slurps and moans were more than moderately distracting. Ramón had pleasured the dark skinned woman first, rewarding her for her service and binding her more strongly to him. Hannah had not objected when Adele had disrobed and joined them. He had watched them twist and turn frantically against each other for a while, his lusts stirred by the sight of the delightful contrast between their brown and white skins in feverish contact. But he wanted to review the files and get back to the house as soon as he could and so he restrained his impulses to provide himself with more pleasure.

The files were very helpful. He had already singled out several projects where he could be of great assistance to the businessman. He would need to get hold of some of the actual engineering drawings and some additional files. That meant he would have to meet Mrs. Greene again. But he didn't want to arouse any suspicions of her activities and so he would wait at least a week. Also, he would need to obtain the services of an engineer capable of putting his innovations down on paper, someone skilled at technical drawings. He could do it, but it would be time consuming to learn the physical skills inherent in drawing and to accomplish the tedious task of making drawings himself.

He made a note for his servant to scour the engineering firms in the area for a female qualified to do the work. It would mean converting another woman to his will, but it couldn't be helped. With the limited funds of his familiar's grant, he couldn't afford to pay an engineering firm to do it and, even if he could, he could not be assured of the confidentiality his work required. Especially when it came to designs he would have to author with regard to the equipment he needed to build for his own purposes. The technology would be far too advanced for this culture and would amount to a significant interference in its development, something that, as a dimensional jumper, he was bound by the ethics of the Whole not to do.

Ramón wondered how far the renegade had gone in introducing new technology to this dimension. It was another reason he had to be stopped. The renegade might think he could control any inventions he made, but leaks were inevitable. Moreover, to paraphrase one of the poets he had read during a break from his research, if you cut him, he would bleed. A bullet or a knife would end his existence as readily as it would any actual human person. An ambitious subordinate could assassinate him and try to achieve local or even world domination through the weapons that could easily be made possible. Planetwide conflagration would be the eventual result. No, the renegade must be stopped. All other considerations, even the diversion of sentients from the normal pathways of their lives, either temporarily or permanently, had to give way to that goal.

After about an hour, he was finished. The women were sleeping, having exhausted themselves. He called to them from their slumber and gave Hannah a long drink from his cock before he let her dress. He watched her blissful, dark face as she suckled him, admiring the deep, rich tones of her skin as he received his pleasure and absorbed her psychic emanations of lust. Through his passionate haze, he pondered at the oddity that the sentients with the most pleasing and warm tones of skin were considered inferior by so many of the white skinned humans. He would have thought it the other way around, that the interesting, variated tones of their skin would have made them a sort of nobility among their fellow creatures, but he was no sociologist and he had other, more compelling issues to solve.

When Hannah had brought him to orgasm and received his discharge and another wrenching climax of her own in exchange, he kissed her and passed on a new set of instructions. She received them gratefully and hugged him and his servant warmly before she dressed and left. Twenty minutes later, he and the blond woman arrived back at the farmhouse.

The girls' eyes widened when they heard the car pull up the driveway. Having exhausted their own lusts and Kelly's, they had spent the last twenty minutes or so kneeling in front of her, holding hands, admiring the bound woman as if she were some kind of idol to worship, reaching out occasionally, to stroke or caress her. Kelly had spent a long time looking back at them. Her eyes kept drifting down to their newly shaved love lips which they proudly displayed between their widened thighs. Each time she saw them, she was reminded of her own hairlessness. Adele had been right about how it made her pussy look. It was like an invitation to fuck.

And the freedom with which they had explored her body made more stark the fact that the areas of her body that brought her pleasure were beyond her reach. The girls had marveled at how soft and smooth her pussy was, but she had not touched it even once since Adele had first shaved her. Melissa and Felicity had both suckled at her breasts, massaged them with their hands, pulled and teased at her nipples, actions that were denied her. Her own desires to sample the alluring flesh of the pretty, lustful girls was frustrated by her bound hands. She had longed to run them across their soft, youthful skins, measure the heft of their breasts, caress their loins, bring them pleasure as they had brought it to her. But what she wanted was of no importance while she was under the dream man's tutelage. His will ruled everything, even access to the pleasing flesh of his young acolytes.

In spite of the girls' efforts, Kelly's need for the presence and touch of the dream man had grown steadily through the night. It had become a burning within her. When she heard the sound of the car's engine and the crunch of its tires on the gravel, she rejoiced. When the door opened and the compelling form of her captor walked in, she felt her need surge within her.

"Hello everybody, we're back," Adele announced gaily as she removed her coat. Melissa and Felicity had turned their bodies to the couple when they entered. Their eyes were pinned on Ramón while he undressed. Adele walked up to them. "Oh!" she exclaimed when she got a good look at their bare sexes. "You've shaved. Look how pretty they are Ramón! Well, if everybody's going to go commando, I guess I'll have to too!" she said, laughing, her hands affectionately patting the young women's heads.

The blond woman stepped over to her friend. "We're home, Kelly," she said, stroking her hair. "I'll bet you had a better time than you did last night. Let me get you unhooked and Ramón will see to you right away."

The blond woman unfastened Kelly's bindings to the pipe behind her and loosened her ankles. She eased her to her feet and led her a short distance into the living room and brought her back to her knees. Kelly was looking up at the naked form of her dream man lustfully. He knelt before her and, after removing her gag, gave her a deep, soulful kiss. He caressed her breasts, exciting her and then moved behind her and spread her legs. She bent her torso down, her forehead to the floor, in anticipation of his use.

Kelly had felt a rush of desire as the man placed his hands and lips on her. Her need was so great she quickly overcame her shame at being fucked in front of the young lab assistants. The man caressed her flanks and her rear with his pleasure giving hands, sending waves of lust through her. She gasped when she felt his cock press between her labia and sighed deeply when he entered her from behind.

She came noisily, conscious of the other three women watching her. She received the dream man's essence happily nonetheless. When he had let his manhood finally slide from her, Adele raised her torso to a vertical position and all of them kissed her. "Come on, honey," Adele said to her sweetly. "You've got to have your bath." And to the pretty young girls, she said. "Ramón is going to thank you for taking care of Dr. Jameson. Now don't wear him out, he's got some work to do."

The dream man took the two smiling girls into the bedroom as Adele led Kelly to her bath. After Adele bathed her, Kelly lay sedated in the hot bath water, soaking in the luxuriant bath oil, her wrists confined to the towel rack above her. She could not stop thinking of her dream man servicing the pretty, young girls in her bed. Although it was closed, she heard a long, repeated series of youthful moans through the bathroom door. From the tone, it sounded like Felicity celebrating a powerful climax. It made her pussy burn and she tightened her thighs together and sucked on her gag in a futile attempt to suppress her lust.

By the time she emerged from the bathroom in her chains, shaved and pleasured by Adele's adept tongue and lips, the girls had left. Ramón gave her the benefit of his attentions for close to an hour before she was led off to bed.

* * * * * * * * * * * * *

After Tuesday, the week went on fairly uneventfully for Kelly. She spent her mornings reviewing emails and was even permitted to take a few telephone calls. Under the watchful eye of her captor, she assured her mother she was fine and had just been busy. She spoke to her grant administrator twice and once to an old friend from medical school who had called repeatedly. After each call, the dream man gave her to drink from of his mind numbing essence and she spent the next several hours blindfolded, gagged and bound to her chair, as if to erase her memory of her brief resumption of verbal, oral communication.

Once her usefulness for the day was finished, Ramón would make a concerted effort to return her to a state of hazy consciousness, befuddled by her desires. Adele gave her many papers to sign and fielded all of the calls. The girls would come in and out of her office at will, often coming upon her in the midst of union with the visitor, or shortly thereafter, dazed, lying on the floor or sitting in her chair with her skirt raised and her shirt up around her chest.

There were things going on around the lab Kelly couldn't fathom. She was kept mostly in her office with all the blinds drawn, but occasionally during the day, for instance when Adele or one of the girls escorted her to the bathroom, she would be out in the lab proper. She had heard the sounds of construction work, but was surprised when she saw workmen coming and going and that a door had been broken through to another part of the building. Her concern at the strange goings on would last only until Ramón caressed her breast or stroked her head, sending yet another wave of comfort and warmth to her, making all of the dissonance at what was happening go away.

The girls were kind and solicitous towards her, especially Felicity and Melissa, kissing her and giving her warm caresses whenever they had the opportunity. They stayed mostly in the lab though, except when they received their daily doses of Ramón's essence at the beginning and end of each day. On Thursday night, they had come over to mind her again while Adele and Ramón went out. This time, they were allowed to free her from her disconcerting mounting to the pipe in the hallway with the understanding she should remain otherwise bound at all times. They took her to the bedroom and affixed her wrists to the headboard of the bed, alternating between making love to each other and to her. Their sexual activities had become more daring and they each took a turn mouthing her to pleasure while the other kissed her and caressed her breasts.

When Ramón returned, Kelly saw that Adele had taken him on another shopping spree and that he was wearing a rather sharp off the rack suit, a dress shirt and a colorful silk tie. After he undressed, the girls lay on either side of her while he plowed her burning furrow and then, to the captive woman's shame, raised her knees to her chest and spilled himself in her rear while she moaned and shuddered with pleasure. Felicity had begged him to take them that way too and, as Adele was escorting Kelly to her bath, she saw the blond girl lubricating Melissa's back passage. The tiny, brown haired girl knelt on the bed, her breasts crushed on her knees, an unsure and apprehensive look on her face as she turned to watch what was going on behind her.

On Saturday, the girls came around again while Adele took the dream man out for driving lessons. They came back around four o'clock and Adele announced to Kelly that they were having a little party for Chandra that evening. Melissa and Felicity seemed to already know about it and they helped Adele prepare some dishes and appetizers in the kitchen.

It was just after 7 P.M. when Chandra's mother dropped her off. Kelly was just emerging dazed and sated from her daily solo session with her vibrator and the follow-up love making with her dream man. The house immediately took on an aspect of gaiety, with all the females kissing and hugging the young Indian girl. She was dressed as she was when she came to work, a plain, colored top and a long, heavy skirt. But she looked to Kelly happier than she had seen her all week. Twice, she had come into Kelly's office while Adele was there and cried while the blond woman held her in her lap, caressing her and whispering consolingly in her ear.

Kelly was way past any concern for her appearance, and she knelt peacefully, naked and bound by the table, while the other women and Ramón happily ate the dinner Adele, Felicity and Melissa had prepared. Everyone except Kelly had dressed for dinner, an unusual circumstance since most of the time everyone went around the house naked. The solicitous women took turns feeding Kelly with a little bite of this or that, caressing and kissing her when she took it in her mouth. Chandra seemed shy and reserved, nervous about something.

After the main course had been completed, Melissa and Felicity, giggling like school girls, escorted Chandra in to the bedroom. Kelly knelt, gratefully receiving her lord's discharge while Adele cleaned up. Through her sex induced fog, Kelly could hear the girls running out of the bedroom and into the bathroom and back again. She was resting on her knees, her head in her captor's lap, receiving blissful strokes of his hand on her hair when the three girls finally emerged together. The two white girls were dressed in short, lacy, white negligees. Each of them had in their possession one of Chandra's hands and they were leading her into the kitchen.

When Kelly looked up and saw her she was amazed. The girls had worked a marvelous transformation of the Indian girl. She was wearing a dark red, lacey babydoll held up by straps which ascended her chest from her breasts and tied off behind her graceful, bare neck. The hem came down about one third of the way down her thighs. The lacework mingled with the sheer, dark red background, giving a hint of the bare, brown flesh beneath. The hem and neckline were bordered by black satin with a small black bow tied off in the deep 'v' of the bodice. Her graceful thighs were encased in sheer, red, self supporting stockings that had a four inch wide band of lace at the tops. Her thick, jet black hair had been loosened from her seemingly permanent braid and was flowing all around her body, down to just above her round, pronounced hips. The girls had painted her fingernails and plump lips bright red and had accentuated her dark, sultry eyes.

The Indian girl was smiling nervously as she followed the lead of her two white friends. Her feet were adorned with bright red, high heels and Chandra's gait was a little unsure as she balanced herself as she walked. They brought her right up to Ramón and presented her long, delicate hands to him. He turned his chair to face her and took them in his. Kelly sensed the surge of lust and comfort the dream man sent to the young, dark skinned woman who shuddered as she received it, leaning over and presenting her parted lips to him.

Ramón had known, of course, that the young Indian girl was to be presented to him tonight for deflowerment. But he did not expect her to be presented so alluringly. The girls had adorned her with perfume and a musky, flowered scent emanated from her body. He received the offer of her lips and he felt his lust grow as their tongues intertwined. He could sense her apprehension but also her pride in her impending womanhood. When their lips parted, she eagerly drew him from his chair.

"Isn't she pretty?" Felicity asked Adele, happy and proud of her and her friend's accomplishment.

"She's as pretty as any girl I've ever seen," Adele answered her wistfully.

Kelly just stared at the apparition. Chandra had undergone a transformation. Gone was the awkward, prim youth she had hired almost a year ago. Instead, Chandra had the appearance of a sultry Rani, an Indian princess. She felt the lust emanating from her dream man and felt a surge of her own. What was the strange man doing, she thought. Was he creating some kind of harem for himself? But she knew his purposes went far beyond the sexual enthrallment of beautiful women. Somehow, he fed off of their lusts, drew power from them. She was concerned for the young woman, who had seemed to her, until now, childlike. She had a moment's tug of jealousy. He was her dream man, after all. But watching the girl's happy face as Ramón caressed her cheek, Kelly could not gainsay the girl's eminent happiness, her eagerness for union with the dream man, could not begrudge her her opportunity for ecstasy with him.

Ramón took the young girl by the hand and led her into the bedroom, shutting the door behind him. The room was lit by two large, flickering candles on each side of the bed, creating a dream like atmosphere. The girls had turned down the bed and strewn it with rose petals. The excited girl tossed off her shoes and climbed onto it eagerly. She knelt there, her legs folded under her, her delicate hands poised on her thighs, watching lustfully as he drew off his clothes. Her chest was heaving slowly with her growing passion, her firm breasts trembling beneath the exotic garment. Her eyes were wide with expectancy and her red glossed lips were wet and parted.

"What passions these creatures have," Ramón thought approvingly as he climbed on the bed. "And what depth of emotion and feeling." He could sense the girl's adoration of him, a mindset that had grown of its own accord from the seed he had planted. She saw in him the redemption of her years of pining for beauty, love and acceptance. Her belief in his goodness was unquestioning. And he saw what a special moment this was for the girl. These humans invested so much in the performance of the sexual act. It was odd they shrouded it with so much mystery, and yet it permeated their thoughts all throughout the day. He hadn't compelled the other women to frenetic sexual activity, he had merely released the gates that bound in their libidos and strengthened their affection for each other. They had done the rest.

Kneeling in front of her, Ramón took the girl's head in his hands and encouraged her lusts while he kissed her again. Her lithe arms circled around him, drawing him to her. Her firm breasts were squeezed against his chest. He felt his cock, grown to hardness, pressing against her belly. He took his hands and untied the straps of the negligee from behind the girl's neck and pulled the bodice down, revealing her round, dark brown orbs. Her nipples were succulently long and fat and were surrounded by the wide, flat circles of her areolas. He placed his hands on her virgin breasts and caressed them lovingly. He knew this introduction into the world of adult passion was a special moment for the girl and he intended to give her all the affection and warmth he could. It was an appropriate exchange for the gift the girl was making of herself to him.

Chandra moaned with pleasure when he put his lips to her teats, sucking on them softly, running his tongue over and around them. He eased her to her back and drew the lacey, red garment over her hips, down her thighs and off of her legs. She was wearing a pair of dainty, matching panties consisting of a triangle of red silk held around her waist by a gossamer thin band of ribbon. He kissed her belly, letting his tongue wash her skin, absorbing her salty taste, the smoothness and firmness of her young body. When he pulled the panties from her loins, the impassioned girl lifted her hips and knees, facilitating the exposure of her secret place to his pleasures.

The young girl's eyes were soft and wet with tears of happiness when Ramón took his place between her opened thighs. He had stroked her sex to fullness, teasing the sensitive lips, tenderly massaging the bud of pleasure above them until her pussy opened like a blossoming flower. She was ready for him, eager for his possession of her. She sighed when he presented his stiff cock to her lush gates, probing the interior with its bulbous head. He entered her slowly while she moaned with bliss, her thighs pressing against his, her arms draped around his back.

The dream man could easily have spared the girl the pain puncturing her hymen would bring. But he sensed the tearing of the membrane and the brief spasm of pain it brought was like a rite of passage for the girl he did not wish to deny her. When he felt his cock push against it, he pressed his lips down upon hers, intertwining their feverish tongues, stoking the girl's lusts. He gave a strong thrust with his hips. The thin barrier held for a single, timeless moment and then he was through. Chandra moaned with pain, her hands and arms squeezing him tightly, her hips retreating, her thighs shuddering. "Ohhhhhhh!" she moaned softly. He was deep within her and he broke their kiss, pausing to let the girl recover from her pain. Looking into the beauty of her strained face, he emitted a surge of radiance, rewarding her for her bravery, granting her a vision of the lustful pleasures that awaited her.

The girl lay still for a moment. He felt her absorbing his energies, reveling in her fullness. Her eyes had been clamped shut as he penetrated her. They opened now, full of wonderment at the feel of his thick cock within her and of pride at her accomplishment. Tears started to flow from her dark, alluring eyes as she stared back at him. "Oh, Ramón," she moaned. "I love you so much."

Sensing the girl was ready, the dream man began a long, slow, luxurious stroke within her. "Ohhhhhhh!" she moaned again, this time not with pain, but with pleasure. "Oh, god!"

she called out.   "That feels so good! Ohhhhhhh! Ohhhhhhhh!"

Ramón slowly but surely increased the rhythm of his strokes within her tight, hot canal. The girl's body responded lustfully, meeting his thrusts with her hips, clenching his body onto hers. When she came, she cried out loudly, calling his name and her love for him. He waited until she came again, scratching his back with her fingernails, biting into his neck, wrapping her legs around his thighs, before discharging his essence into her, flooding her chamber with his enrapturing fluids.

They made love for about an hour, resting deliciously between bouts. She took his manhood between her lips, gratefully and lovingly drawing out his essence, her long, jet black hair arrayed around her body like a fabulous, beautifying mantilla. He supped between her thighs, bringing her to a new height in ecstasy.

The girls had brought Kelly into the living room. All of the women were overcome with lust at the thought of the dream man fucking the happy Indian girl in the next room. They had all cast off their clothes. Adele sat back in one of the easy chairs, her pale thighs ajar, while Melissa knelt between them, stroking and pleasuring her agitated pussy with her tongue and lips while massaging her own sex to climax. Felicity had stretched Kelly out on the floor and brought her off twice with her hand before falling to her back and guiding her goddess's head to her sex. Kelly, her hands bound behind her, her auburn hair spread out over the girl's belly and thighs, eagerly drank at the girl's lush gash.

When Chandra emerged from the bedroom, her face aglow with pride and satisfaction, the other women were lolling in each other's arms, blissfully enjoying the warmth of each other's flesh. Melissa and Felicity jumped up to kiss and hug her, squealing their delight at their friend's happiness.

The slender, naked Indian girl, the pale red traces of her deflowerment dried on her thighs, went over to Adele, who was still sitting in her chair, and threw her arms around her, hugging her tightly.

"Oh Ms. Somers, it was wonderful! I love him so much! I love all of you!" she cried.

"We all love you too, Chandra," Adele returned sweetly, stroking her long, dark colored back with her pale, white hand.

Chandra kissed her passionately while Felicity and Melissa stood by smiling and holding hands. Seeing the newly made woman triggered Kelly's lust for her dream man. She had risen to a sitting position, her hands still bound behind her. Felicity had dutifully regagged her when she had finished worshiping her pussy and she bit down on it unconsciously, seeking reassurance.

When the Indian girl broke her kiss with Adele, she turned to Kelly. She knelt down in front of her and hugged her too. "Dr. Jameson, you're so wonderful!" she told her tearfully. "Without you, none of this would ever have happened! I want to take care of you!"

Chandra began to kiss Kelly all around her face and then down her neck and to her shoulders. Their breasts rubbed together, sending a wave of lust through the bound woman. "Oh, God," Kelly exclaimed to herself, "I'm on fire!" She longed to hug and return the kisses of the beautiful, young girl. Chandra caressed her breasts lightly, pulling gently at her hardened nipples before leaning back and then guiding her to her feet by her arms. Kelly's leash hung between her breasts and Chandra took hold of it. Smiling sweetly at her, she urged her forward.

Kelly was shamed at the girl's use of the infernal instrument that hung from her collar. Her mind protested at her debasement, but her body followed the happy, young girl docilely. When they turned the corner to her bedroom, she saw the naked form of the dream man on her bed. He was lying on his side, his head up, leaning on his left hand, elbow on the bed, looking at her expectantly. His right hand was languidly stroking his stiffened cock.

A surge of passion went through her. Chandra closed the door behind them and led her to the bed, helping her mount it. After freeing her mouth and lips from the gag, she loosened her bound wrists from behind her and, laying her down, fastened them to the headboard. As the dream man moved between her thighs, Chandra, lying next to her, turned Kelly's head and took possession of her lips, parting them with her tongue and then filling her mouth. When Ramón's hard cock slid into her belly, Kelly raised her knees and moaned with pleasure.

CHAPTER FIVE

Two weeks later, Ramón was sitting in the small conference room next to Hardings' office. The heavyset man was looking over several technical memos Ramón had prepared which pointed out improvements to his processes and products that would greatly improve productivity and quality. Included was a proposal for an innovation that would be a certain cash cow were it manufactured. Hardings did not look happy.

"Who the fuck are you?" Hardings eventually said, looking up at him accusingly.

"You know who I am Mr. Hardings," Ramón replied.

"You know what I mean. How'd you get your hands on my privileged files? Who gave them to you?"

"I'd rather not say, Mr. Hardings."

"Why shouldn't I just call the police right now? What is it you want?"

Ramón knew he was taking a risk in making such a direct approach to the businessman. If he called the police, well, there was no amount of explaining that would get him out of it. His cover would last all of about ten minutes, but it was a chance he had to take. The renegade had to be dealt with as soon as possible. He would be very strong now and getting stronger every day. Every day the misery and harm he was doing was compounding. Adele had his familiar ready to make a quick getaway if his gambit to the older man failed. They would have to start again somewhere else. Ramón had the technical ability to shut down all electronic communications within a 25 mile radius. He had set that up before he came to see Hardings. It was simple, really, a modification to a powerful transmitter he had mounted on the roof. The button to initiate the powerful pulse of disabling electronic waves was right in his pocket. Even with that, he would become a fugitive and if he was caught and separated from his familiar, it was a veritable death sentence. He had some powers to influence male humans, but not enough to make a jail break.

On the other hand, Ramón had made a thorough scan of the factory owner. He was honest, moral and trustworthy. He would reveal the nature of his mission to him and hope for the best. He had sensed a deep spirituality in the man, a belief in the war between good and evil.

"I want you to help me," Ramón answered the man.

"Help you? How?"

"There are materials I need, technical assistance. Money."

"Money? For what?"

"I don't think you would believe me if I told you, Mr. Hardings," Ramón said. "Let's just say I've been sent here to rid your world of a great danger."

"Sent? Sent by who?"

"That's not important. What is important is that another being, someone just like me has come to your world with immense powers. Right now he's out there using those powers to destroy people's lives and building an immoral empire that could affect the destiny of the human race."

Hardings looked at him for a few moments intently. He then broke out into a laugh. "Where's the Candid Camera?" he asked. "You expect me to believe this? You don't look like a creature from another planet to me. You look like a man on the make, someone who'd invade someone else's computer files and try and scam them. I've never seen formulas like you've proposed in these documents. The equipment you describe doesn't exist. The technology to make them doesn't exist."

"Suppose I could prove to you I have powers beyond your comprehension, Mr. Hardings? Would you believe me then?"

"What are you going to do, levitate the building or

something?" Hardings threw back at him sarcastically.

"Given the right equipment and some time, I could do that if you wanted, but I don't think you would want your building floating around in the air. People would notice. No, I mean a simpler, more immediate demonstration. I can control the minds of human females. Make them succumb to my will, do anything I ask, things they wouldn't do in a hundred years for love or money."

"That'd be a good trick," Hardings responded. "But what would that prove?"

"It would prove I'm not a normal human being, for starters. And it will give you an idea of what I could do if I wanted, something that the being I'm pursuing probably does every day."

"Okay, okay," Hardings answered him. "How are you going to do this?"

"Call in any one of your female employees. Bring her here and I'll have her declare her undying love for you, strip for you, offer herself to you."

"And suppose I don't want a love slave, Mr. Spaceman? And suppose I don't want a lawsuit for sexual harassment?"

"I'll go slow. You can stop me at any time. And when it's over, I'll make her forget the whole thing."

Ramón could sense the man mulling things over in his mind. He gave him a mental nudge to accept the challenge.

"Okay, okay," the man said finally. "I must be crazy to even consider something like this. I'm not a teenager or one of those space nuts. And I don't believe in Santa Claus. But there's something about you that makes me want to make sure I'm wrong. The second I think you've gotten out of line I'm going to throw you out of my office and call the cops."

Hardings punched the intercom. A familiar voice answered.

"Yes, Mr. Hardings?"

"Hannah, call Lucy Douglas in here for a moment. I want to talk to her."

"Right away, Mr. Hardings," Hannah answered.

Ramón had not given the enthralled black woman any hint of the reason for his meeting with Hardings. He didn't want her to get all nervous about it. At their last meeting, she had delivered the blueprints to him and stayed in the motel with him while Adele went out and had them copied. Before she left, he had suppressed her memories of what she had done for him. She was now a dormant tool, ready to be reactivated when the need arose.

The men waited about ten minutes before the young woman Hardings had summoned appeared at the door to the conference room. Hardings had taken the time to again go through a couple of Ramón's memos. His face recorded his interest and amazement at the proposals, despite his huge misgivings.

The woman who entered was the young file clerk who had escorted Ramón in to see Hardings the first day. She was pretty, about 22 years old, with dark brown, hair that ended in a little flip. She was wearing a short skirt and a stylish, short sleeved blouse. She had fine, graceful hips and a sweet smile, although she looked a little nervous. Being called in to see the boss was not always a good thing. "You wanted to see me, Mr. Hardings?" Lucy said demurely.

"Close the door, Lucy," Hardings told her. The girl took a deep swallow and complied with Hardings' request.

"This is Mr. Vasquez, Lucy. He wants to ask you a question. And if it's not the right question, I'm going to throw him out on his ass."

"Yes, Mr. Hardings," Lucy replied, somewhat puzzled. She turned to look at the dark and handsome man she had met the other day. He was cute, she thought. He was looking back at her kind of funny. And then, she realized something she had apparently been hiding from herself for a long, long time. She looked back at Mr. Hardings. She had always thought of him as nice, but now she realized he was much more than that. He was powerful and wise and kind. But most of all, he was very, very sexy.

Hardings had noticed the change in the young woman's face. He hadn't seen a look like that for many years. About 40 years to be exact. He noticed the pretty young women who worked for him and on the streets, in stores and everywhere else. He was a man after all, and couldn't help looking, even though he usually felt uncomfortable when he found himself staring and broke off his gaze as soon as he could. But the young women he looked at never, never looked back. He wasn't even on their radar screen. He was old and overweight and dressed like a hick. Hell, he was a hick! But he remembered the look all right. He had been young once, and a bit of a hellraiser. Until he met Emily, his wife. That had been the end of his roaming for 35 years.

The look the girl was giving him was one he knew well. It was unmistakable. Her eyes had softened and her lips had parted. She was standing just a little bit straighter and had taken one of her hands from behind her back and was fiddling with the top button of her blouse.

Ramón spoke to her, his voice low, slightly accented, "It's all right, Lucy. Why don't you tell Mr. Hardings what you want to say to him."

The pretty, young woman looked back at Ramón as if to confirm his permission. He had sent her a surge of passion and encouragement. She looked back at her boss.

"I, I,..." she stuttered. She was having difficulty finding the words. After all, what if she said the wrong thing and Mr. Hardings rejected her? What would she do then?

"Do you think I'm pretty, Mr. Hardings?" Lucy finally got out.

Hardings was taken aback by the interrogatory. "Y-yes, Lucy," he answered her.

"I think you're handsome, Mr. Hardings," she continued. "I mean, like, you're really cool and everything."

"Thank you, Lucy," Hardings said back. He did what every man in his situation would do, he sucked in his gut a little bit and tried to sit straighter. He stole a glance at the "spaceman" as he had called him. "What is going on?" he thought.

Lucy took a step closer to him. She had unbuttoned the top button of her blouse. "I'd like to get to know you a lot better, Mr. Hardings," she said, her voice a little over a whisper. "If that's okay with you."

"Well, I don't know, Lucy," Hardings stammered out. "You work for me and…"

"I'd be really good to you, Mr. Hardings," Lucy continued, somewhat desperately. She had unbuttoned a few more buttons of her blouse and her lacy bra was showing. Her face was flushed.

Hardings looked over at Ramón. "Okay, you've proved your point. Make her stop."

A look of intense disappointment came over Lucy's face. Tears formed in her eyes. "Don't you like me, Mr. Hardings?" she asked.

Ramón called her over to him and took her hand. "Listen, Lucy," he said aloud so Hardings could hear him give her instructions, "Mr. Hardings likes you very much. You like him too. He's like an uncle to you, a kind, friendly uncle. You like to make him happy, but he doesn't appeal to you sexually. You will forget about what happened here. Mr. Hardings wanted to let you know he was happy with your work. Okay?"

A wide smile came over Lucy's face. "Okay," she said happily. She turned to Hardings. "Thank you Mr. Hardings. I like working for you a lot. Is there anything else you need me for?"

"N-no, Lucy," Hardings replied, trying to compose himself. "But your blouse has become unbuttoned. Why don't you fix it before you go back to your desk?"

Lucy looked down at her unbuttoned blouse and covered it up quickly, laughing, her face turning a little red. "I'm sorry, Mr. Hardings. I don't know how that happened." She turned away from him and quickly buttoned up.

"Don't worry about that Lucy," Ramón told her. "Go back to work now."

Lucy made a gesture of compliance and made to walk out of the room. "Do you want the door open or closed, Mr. Hardings?" she asked.

"Definitely closed," Hardings replied.

When the door was shut, Hardings looked intently at the strange man who sat opposite him. "I'll be damned," he said.

There was a long silence in the small, but comfortable room. Like Hardings himself, it was simple, straightforwardly decorated. On the wall were various plaques and awards he and his company had won, several pictures of the company softball team kneeling and standing behind trophies, a picture of Hardings and his deceased wife at some formal function shaking the hands of the Governor, a large picture of the building taken years ago, sometime in the spring. A lone wolf like Hardings didn't have much need of a fancy conference room. He had no board of directors, no stockholders but himself. He met here with his engineers and supervisors, customers, on occasion, and once a quarter with his accountant.

Hardings finally spoke again. "What does Dr. Jameson think about all of this?"

"You'll have to leave Dr. Jameson to me," Ramón responded.

"Did you hypnotize her too? Is she your love slave now?"

Hardings was a man who could put two and two together pretty quickly. It was natural for him to get to the bottom of things and he always put people first. He liked Dr. Jameson and wouldn't want anything bad to happen to her.

"I mean no harm to Dr. Jameson. Or to anyone else. Let's just say she and her staff are committed to me and my purposes."

"So your answer is, 'Yes, she's my sex slave but that's none of my business.' Is that right?"

"I can't answer that in any way that will be acceptable to you. Dr. Jameson is essential to my existence here. She performs a 'function', if you want to call it that, that allows me to stay here and pursue my mission."

"How do I know your intentions are so benign, as you've said? How do I know you're not controlling my mind? That when I've helped you, you won't make me your slave? How do I know, assuming I believe any of this, that you're not the bad guy?"

"The only answer I can give you is that you'll have to have faith in me. You won't know for sure until it's all over. In the meantime, I think there's something I can do for you that will help you make up your mind."

"And what's that?"

"You have a daughter, Natalie, I believe."

"My daughter? What's she got to do with this?" Hardings was visibly upset at the mention of Natalie.

"Nothing, really," Ramón responded. "But I can help you with her."

"My daughter is none of your business, Mr. Vasquez, or whatever your real name is. She and I haven't spoken since before my wife died."

"Yes, and I can help you with that."

"How do you even know about her? No one here knows anything about her except...." A light went off in Hardings' head. "Except Hannah," he continued. "You've hypnotized Hannah, my secretary. That's how you got all this information, isn't it?"

"Hypnotized is the wrong word, Mr. Hardings. And you shouldn't blame Mrs. Greene. She had no choice."

"She had no choice because you stole her brain!" Hardings was visibly upset at the prospect of the dream man's interference with his secretary. He had a special feeling for her, an affection, even if it was apparently unrequited. "If you've hurt her in any way, I'll fix your wagon good!" Hardings threatened, his voice bordering on ferocious.

"I haven't harmed Mrs. Greene. You should know, though, that she is in love with you."

"In love with me? How would you know that?"

"I can read her mind, her feelings, her emotions. She loves you very much."

Hardings sat back in his chair. Today was a day for revelations.

"And yes, she helped me. I needed to be able to show you I can help your business very much, make you a millionaire many times over, if that's what you want. And I can, to some extent, read your mind too. I can feel your love for Hannah. I can help bring you together."

"I told you, I don't want a love slave, especially someone I care about."

"That wouldn't be necessary, Mr. Hardings. All she really needs is a sign from you."

Ramón let his information about the middle aged, black secretary sink in. When he saw Hardings was over his initial, protective rage, he continued.

"But back to your daughter, Mr. Hardings. I can bring her home to you." The dream man knew Hardings considered his daughter a lost cause. From what he learned from Hannah and had drawn from Hardings' mind, he realized the man had good reason for his abandonment of hope for her.

Natalie had started out as a normal, sweet, little girl, born quite a few years into his and his wife's marriage. She had gone away to college and, once there, had fallen into bad company. She dropped out after her sophomore year and held a series of low paying, menial jobs while her drug addiction was blossoming. She had shown up at her mother's funeral, gaunt and strung out. He had not seen her since. From a private investigator about two years ago, he had learned she had turned to prostitution to support her heroin habit and was a fixture on the "Strip' as they called it, near the airport in Richmond, a four laned roadway lined with hot sheet motels and strip joints. Natalie had descended into a roadside whore, not fit even to work as a call girl. He had the P.I. check up on her from time to time and he knew she was still there.

Hardings stared at the star man. There was nothing more he wanted than his sweet Natalie back again, and nothing less. He didn't know how he could ever see past what she had done to herself, think past the vision of the countless men who had used her body. And how was she to cure her heroin addiction? The last thing he wanted was to have her back only to lose her again.

"You're playing with fire, Mr. Spaceman," Harding said to him tensely. "I ought to throw you out of here right now."

"Mr. Hardings, if I could bring Natalie back to you, cure her heroin addiction, make her a free and healthy woman again, would that convince you to help me?"   A   tear   had formed in Hardings' eye. His face was a mask of anguish. After a moment's pause, he replied.

"If you could restore Natalie to me, take her away permanently from her awful life, I wouldn't care if you were Beelzebub himself," the man told him, a fierce determination in his eyes. "I would give you anything and everything that I own. I swear that on my wife's grave."

"I will hold you to that, Mr. Hardings. I will do what you want. But, if I do, I cannot have you questioning anything I do. I don't need all of your wealth and property. I just need your cooperation. And I swear to you on everything that's sacred to me, everything I've told you is the truth. I mean no one any harm beyond what is necessary for my mission."

Hardings stood up and proffered Ramón his trembling hand. As they shook, Hardings told him, "If you're fucking with me, I'll kill you."

Three days later, Ramón was cruising Kelly's Sentra down Route 227 outside of Richmond Municipal Airport. It was a lonely, desolate road, except for the gaudy neon lights of the sin palaces. This was his third time cruising down the Strip, slowing long enough to allow the bevy of former beauties to call out to him, offering various services. In spite of the late December cold, the girls were all dressed scantily, showing off their naked legs, proffering their breasts to him through the light, revealing tops they wore. He was appalled at the sorrow and unhappiness he detected in them, lives brutalized by drugs, alcohol, the cruelties of men. He could easily have turned their minds, eased their pain. But that was not what he was here for. His was not a crusade to fix everything wrong with this planet's culture. In any event, someone, somewhere would notice if the 20 or so whores who were trawling this desolate lane for johns all decided to quit the life all at once, all on the same night.

On the third cruise down the highway, he finally saw the girl he was looking for. She had just gotten out of a long, metallic blue, late model Cadillac. Two other girls got out of the car with her. They were all dressed in short skirts that hiked up their thighs as they stepped out. The rear license plate of the car, registered in Washington D.C., said 'SHABAZZ GIRLZ', all in capital letters, and was surrounded by a trim of small lights. He could not see the driver's face, but he wore a large, oversized, heavy fur coat and a broad rimmed hat. While the whores were getting out of the car, a cigarette end flew out the driver's window and landed on the roadway in an explosion of orange sparks. When they were all out of the car, it sped away.

Ramón waited a few minutes for the new girls to get settled. He let three cars cruise the Strip before he made his move. There seemed to be some kind of a system among the women and three of them approached each car, giving the john a limited choice. There were conversations, some ribald exchanges and finally, the front passenger door opened and one of the girls, the lucky one selected, got in. The car drove away.

Natalie, who was wearing a short, tight, red skirt and long, black leather boots, was huddled by one of the steel drums the whores had set alight for warmth. She had on a waist length, white, imitation fur jacket. Her black hair was long and stringy, her face pale and drawn. He had seen pictures of the girl from when she had started college, and if he had not also seen the pictures taken by the P.I. a year ago, he would not have recognized her. He was sitting by the side of the road opposite from where the prostitutes congregated, about 40 yards away. He could just detect Natalie's psychic emanations from that distance, faint and barely distinguishable from that of the other women. All of their emotional discharges were blunted and flat, as if deliberately truncated. Who could blame them? What future could they have? They were already near the bottom of the barrel, street whores in such a god forsaken place. It was hard to imagine where the next stop along their descent into death would be.

Before he could move his car, a police patrol car came cruising slowly down the street. It stopped just in front of a congregation of the shivering, scantily dressed girls. They tried to ignore it, but the car put on its overheads and it beeped its siren twice. Three of the girls reluctantly approached it. One of them was Natalie. There was a brief conversation and two of the girls wandered away. Natalie got in.

Between the choice of following the cop car and waiting for it to return, Ramón chose the latter course. It seemed unlikely Natalie had been arrested and, even if she had, she would probably make bail in the morning and be back tomorrow night. What seemed more probable was Natalie had been selected to pay a 'duty' on behalf of the other girls in exchange for not getting rousted this cold, December night. Ramón was sure the cop would bring Natalie back quickly since he was supposed to be on patrol and could not afford a long, unexplained absence from his duties.

Sure enough, about twenty minutes later, the patrol car reappeared and Natalie came bouncing out. When the cop car pulled away, she surreptitiously raised her middle finger at him in what Ramón understood as a near universal sign of disparagement.

As soon as Natalie got settled, Ramón started his car and slowly cruised up to the bevy of what might have been at one time, beauties. Two women approached his car from the passenger side and he powered the window down. A large black skinned whore shoved her face in, her large, droopy breasts hanging over the bottom of the window opening. She smelled of cheap perfume and was wearing a light, pink, fuzzy jacket that she opened so Ramón could get a better look at her attributes.

"Lookin' for a party, honey?" she asked with a false sweetness. "How about a nice blow job? Fifty bucks."

"Come on, Ilona," a scratchy female voice behind her called out. "Let the man see a real set of tits." A tall white girl with even larger breasts than Ilona squeezed into the window frame next to the black woman. She had discarded her jacket and was wearing a halter top. She flipped it up, revealing her breasts. "How'd ya like to suck on these, Jose," she said, referring to Ramón's obvious Hispanic background.

A third girl, skinny, about 5'2" tall stepped up to the driver's side window. Ramón lowered his window and looked at her. She looked like she could pass for 15 years old, although he could read her mind and saw she was, in fact, 24. She was high on heroin and her eyes were all watery and her face sagged. "Want a blow job, mister?" she said, her words slow and slurred.

"My friend told me to look up a girl named Natalie," Ramón responded. "Is she here?" he asked. The black woman answered him, "What do you want that scraggly bitch for? I tell you what, I'll suck you off for 40 bucks. Just cause you're so handsome." She laughed.

Ramón had had enough. He sent all the girls a message of obedience, slight enough so they wouldn't be startled, but strong enough to make them comply with his command. The black whore took herself out of the window. "Hey Natalie!" she yelled. "Some spic's got the hots for you!"

He watched as the white jacketed whore approached the car. Having just been required to give away a freebie, she was anxious to start earning. She stuck her head in the window. "Hey good looking," she said. "You looking for me?"

"You Natalie?" Ramón asked. He would have to play the charade of a john so the other girls wouldn't get suspicious. He didn't want any of them to have reason to remember his license plate number. Natalie would not be coming back.

"If you want me to be," the girl answered coyly. "Whatja lookin for?"

"My friend says you give a real hot blowjob," Ramón said, staying in character. "Twenty bucks."

"For twenty bucks you can blow yourself," the girl replied. She too was high. She had opened her white imitation fur jacket and had pulled aside her thin, 'v' necked blouse to show him her tits. "Fifty bucks," she stated. "I'll roll your eyeballs back in their sockets."

"My friend says twenty five," Ramón rejoined.

"Forty," was Natalie's answer.

"Thirty, or I'll party with one of your friends instead," Ramón insisted.

"Have you got a big, fat dick?" the girl asked, a salacious grin on her face.

"Sure," Ramón answered. "Big enough."

"Then, okay," the girl agreed, "thirty it is." She opened the door and stepped inside. When she closed the door, Ramón eased the car away.

"First thing I gotta ask you is if you're a cop," Natalie said. Her voice was businesslike.

"No, I'm not a cop," Ramón answered.

"Sorry," she said. "You don't look like a cop, but I gotta ask. Rules is rules."

"Sure," Ramón answered.

"Pull up at the next road and make a left," Natalie instructed him. "There's a bunch of trees about 50 yards down the way. Pull over there."

Ramón pulled the car over where Natalie indicated and turned out the lights. He kept the engine running. The other girls would be watching, a kind of citizens' committee of self protection. If he tried to pull anything nasty on the black haired whore, they would all come screaming over.

Ramón didn't waste any time. Before the girl could ask for her money, he sent her a strong signal of obedience. She looked at him wide eyed and succumbed immediately. He sent her another psychic message to relax and be calm. Her eyes returned to normal and she looked to him for instructions.

He gave her none as pulled the car slowly down the lane.

He waited to turn on his lights until he was about a half mile down the road. There was a motel about another half mile further on the right hand side called, imaginatively, the Airport Inn. It sat on the corner of another main roadway. He pulled into the lot in case any of the whores from the pick up place were watching and he drove around to the other side. He exited the parking lot and made a right hand turn. In front of one of the rooms on the first floor in the back was the Caddy with the license plate "SHABAZZ GIRLZ".

Ramón had rented a room on the other side of the city, closer to the Interstate that would take him back to Jacksonville. He would need some time to work on the girls' mind. She had a wondering look on her face as he led her into the room. It was a typical motel room, with a large, hard, double bed, a TV, a cheap green rug and a small, ash wood bedside stand with a small lamp on it. The walls were standard motel white. Ramón didn't require luxurious accommodations for his task. They would not be there long.

He sent the girl a command to disrobe and he stripped himself while she was doing so. Her body was skinny and he could see her ribs. Her arms carried the evidence of her addiction with fierce track marks up and down them. Her sex had been shaved except for a sparse beard of black just above her slit. Her pimp had had tattooed in large, bright blue, cursive letters on her belly, just above the thin rectangle of pubic hair the words, "Property of Shabazz."

She was a sad, pitiable sight. Her death wish was strong, almost as strong as her need for the white powder she shot up six or seven times a day. He could sense her fear of him, natural under the circumstances. But her mind was resigned to whatever fate he had in store for her.

Ramón commanded her to go to her knees between his thighs and she obeyed without hesitation. He scanned her body for disease and was happy to learn she had, luckily, not yet been infected. When her lips seized his still flaccid cock, he put his hands on her head and began to delve deeply into her mind, while sending her a strong signal of lust.

She was well skilled and quickly had him hard. Her whore's mentality drove her to suck at him with quick, hard strokes of her lips. He commanded her to slow her efforts to enable him to prolong his enjoyment and to give him time to rearrange her destructive and perverted mental patterns. While the warmth of her mouth and her agile tongue sent waves of pleasure to him, he sought the source of her unhappiness.

Natalie had been a shy, reserved girl. She had had difficulty in high school, rejected by her friends and all of the good looking boys because of her awkward looks and bright mind. She had always felt alone and isolated, even at home where her parents were mystified at the source of her unhappiness. She had blossomed by her senior year, but her self doubts by then had been so deeply ingrained that when her first love affair in college ended badly, she had sought refuge in alcohol and recreational drugs. It had been a small step to heroin and coke. She had quickly lost interest in school and when a boyfriend who had dropped out asked her to come live with him, she had accepted. It was all downhill from there.

Slowly, Ramón eased the sources of her unhappiness, showed her her self worth. He relieved that part of her mind dependant on the fog and bliss the heroin gave her and freed her body from its need for it. He showed her her love for her father and sent her a strong message of her father's love while at the same time he stoked her passion, bringing her mind into sync with her body for the first time in many years.

The black haired girl was moaning with pleasure as Ramón's lust approached its crest. When he came, he groaned as he flooded her with his captivating essence. The girl came too, her body shuddering, moans of ecstasy emerging from her throat.

When he throbbing cock began to still, Natalie slowly raised her head from Ramón's loins and looked at him, a mixture of extreme sorrow and joy etched on her face.

"Oh my god!" she murmured. "What did you do to me? Oh my god! I can't believe it? I, I...." The woeful girl broke down into sobs. She lowered her head to his lap and circled her arms around him. "Oh, god! Thank you! Thank you! Oh god! I can't believe it! Ohhhhhh!"

The dream man let the girl release the flood of her years of misery. He rubbed her hair on her head and sent her soothing, calming messages of reassurance. She cried for at least fifteen minutes. When she raised her head again, her eyes swollen from her sobbing, her cheeks awash with her tears of pain and joy, she thanked him again and again. Finally, she gained a modicum of control over herself and asked him tentatively, "Who are you?"

"That doesn't matter," he answered her.

The information sparked another round of tears. Ramón could have driven all of her sorrow away in a moment, but he calculated it was best she experience the catharsis her sobbing brought her. She had earned the right to cry.

Several minutes later, she raised her head again. "Please don't make me go back, please. I'll do anything you want, but please don't send me back there, please," she begged.

"You never have to go back," Ramón answered her. He sent her a strong message of reassurance.

"He's an animal. That man, Shabazz. He'll come after me. He owns me."

"Don't worry about him," Ramón told her. "I can deal with him."

"But where will you take me? I've got to hide."

"I'm taking you home," Ramón told her. "To your father."

Natalie started to cry again. "He'll find me there! He knows where I lived. He knows everything about me!"

Ramón sent the girl a warm, mesmerizing flow of his psychic energy. The girl's eyes rolled back and her body relaxed. He stroked her head several times, reinforcing his assurances to her and fully binding her to his will.

When she had calmed enough, he gave her a command to get dressed. He had anticipated her being attired in scandalous, revealing clothes and so, on Adele's advice, he had brought her a clean pair of panties, a pair of jeans, sneakers, a heavy sweatshirt and a winter jacket. They were a little big on her and she had to pull the belt on the jeans to the last hole and roll up the cuffs. She swam in the oversized jacket, looking even more frail and wounded than before.

After he dressed, he looked at the girl. Her eyes were all red, but she had a smile on her face. "Thank you," she said earnestly and put her arms around him, hugging him tightly. And then she sensed a surge of sorrow go through her. She stared to cry again. He pushed her back from him, holding her arms tightly as he scanned her for the source of her misery.

Cindy, a 19 year old runaway from Eastern Illinois was Natalie's best and only friend. She had followed a similar downward spiral as Natalie in the three years since she had left home. She was back at the motel with the pimp who, he learned, often kept one of the girls with him on slow nights for his own use and delight while the others worked. Tonight was Cindy's turn. Natalie was frantic at the thought of leaving her behind.

Ramón could feel the deep well of sorrow inside Natalie at the thought of abandoning her. Shabazz would be furious at her disappearance and all the girls would suffer for it, especially Cindy since she was Natalie's friend. He could erase her concern in an instant, but something about the young woman's strong affection for the other girl made him pause. He couldn't save all the whores in the world. Some of them maybe wouldn't want to be saved. But he could sense Cindy would. It would be a risk, but he decided, for Natalie's sake, to take it.

It was a little after one o'clock in the morning. From Natalie he learned Shabazz usually picked up the girls from the Strip a little after three. He would leave Cindy in the motel room while he drove the mile or so to get the other girls who had been working. All of the girls would need a fix before they headed back to D.C. and it was better they get it in the room than in the car. It was their reward for their hard work. But if they hadn't earned, they would have to make the drive strung out and aching from their need. It would only take a few minutes for Shabazz to drive up to the Strip and get the girls and return. They would have to act fast.

Ramón parked the Sentra in the motel lot in a spot where he could keep an eye on Shabazz's car. Like clockwork, at 3 A.M., the door to his room opened and he strode out confidently to his car. He was wearing his heavy fur coat and his broad brimmed, pimp hat. He got into the Caddy, fired up the engine, backed out of the spot and pulled away.

Ramón had parked tail in in his spot and left the car running. He quickly ran it up to the parking space Shabazz had vacated. He and Natalie got out of the car and hurried up to the door. Natalie banged on it loudly. "Cindy! Cindy!" she yelled. "Open the door!"

There was no answer. "Cindy!" she yelled again. "It's me, Natalie! Open up! Hurry!"

After long, tense moments, the handle turned and a blitzed out, naked, blond haired girl opened the door. She was swaying on her feet and her eyes were barely open. She had small, coffee cup sized, pointed breasts and short hair. Her torso was long and thin. She bore several black and blue marks on her as if she had been recently beaten. Ramón saw Shabazz's tattoo on her belly. He sent her a strong command of obedience.

While he pulled the drugged and almost comatose Cindy outside to the car, Natalie ran in the room and seized a blanket from the bed. Ramón placed them both in the back seat, where Natalie could give her friend some comfort and he backed up quickly and pulled from the lot. He watched carefully in his rear view mirror to make sure they were not followed. In fifteen minutes, they were on the Interstate and heading south.

It took about two and a half hours to get back to the farmhouse. It was still dark, but the tendrils of the dawn were reaching over the mountains in the distance. The dream man was concerned about his familiar, who had spent more than ten hours without him, longer than he had anticipated. Although he was loathe to do it, he agreed to Adele's proposal that they sedate the enthralled woman to make it easier on her. The problem was that while she was sedated, she would not be drawing the essence he needed from his native dimension. Soon, he would have a better solution to the prolonged separations that would be necessary as he hunted for the renegade. But for now, this would have to do.

He entered the house quietly, not wanting to disturb the female if she was sleeping. Natalie followed, assisting the still virtually comatose and as yet unconverted Cindy. He had them take seats on the living room couch while he went into the bedroom.

Adele and the female were both asleep on the bed, intertwined in each other's arms. His familiar was moaning quietly in her sleep, her body shuddering. He would need to comfort her shortly, but first he had to see to the young, blond whore.

He took some time in repairing Cindy's mind and binding

her to his service. Like Natalie, she cried and cried when she felt her captivity to her hellish lifestyle lifted. The two young women hugged each other fervently and sobbed in each other's arms after expressing their thanks to him again and again. After Cindy had recovered from her bout of tears, he brought them both back to Adele's room where he instructed them to lay down. Adele had liberated the room from Kelly's odds and ends and now had a large double bed there. Natalie threw off her clothes and joined Cindy on the bed and they were both very quickly asleep.

Ramón showered and then walked quietly into Kelly's bedroom. He sent a message to Adele to rise and filled her in on the night's success and the presence of the young blond girl. Adele smiled at him and kissed him before leaving, going out to sleep on the couch. He settled down on the bed and stroked the auburn haired woman's face until she woke. Her face beamed with joy at his return. He made long, languorous love to her, serving her need for him.

The next day was Christmas Eve. In anticipation of the long night before and because of the holiday, Adele had told the girls not to come in to work. Ramón and Kelly slept for a long time. He had freed her mind from the effects of the sedative and when they both awoke, he drew from her the mists she had gathered in her dreams. Not wanting to leave her yet, he remained by her side while she dozed off, recovering from the mesmerizing effects of transferring her night's harvest to him.

It had been a hard night for Kelly. Even through her doped state, her need for the presence of the dream man had eaten at her. She was overjoyed at his return and was happy when she was able to dream and draw from the other world her captor's vital substance. Adele had not told her about the man's mission and she was surprised and disturbed, later that morning, a little before noon, when she was led by Ramón into the kitchen, naked and bound, to see the two young girls there. They were nude and obviously had recently showered, their hair still moist and their skin pink and clean. The black haired one looked oddly familiar, as if she had seen a picture of her somewhere.

Adele quickly introduced them and told her what Ramón had done. When the story was finished, Kelly had a surge of affection and pride for her dream man. Although her commitment to his will had never flagged, she had had recurring doubts as to the beneficence of his purposes. Now, she felt relieved that he had proven himself. She was kneeling next to Ramón, who was sitting naked at the kitchen table, and she felt him send her a surge of his energies, rewarding her for her thoughts of him. The two young girls, who had become teary eyed at the retelling of their tales, came to her and hugged and kissed her, warmly expressing their gratitude and their admiration for her.

"If it wasn't for you," Natalie told her, "none of this would have happened. Ramón told us all about you and how important you are to him. We want to help anyway we can. We'll do anything for you."

Kelly was overwhelmed with the girls' sincere, heartfelt emotions. She could sense the presence of her master in them and when they hugged her again, their warm, young bodies sent a thrill of lust through her.

"Now, girls," Adele said. "Kelly and Ramón have got to eat breakfast and then we've got to call Natalie's dad and let him know how everything worked out. We're all going over there later for a big family dinner. And we've got to get you some clothes. I'll drive you both over to the mall in a little while."

The two former whores gleefully fed Kelly bits of buttered toast and banana all the while caressing her breasts and the inside of her thighs. Kelly was dizzy with passion when they brought her over to Ramón so she could drink of his essence. The enthralled woman marveled at how easily she accepted their affections and caresses as she drew her lips around the dream man's rigid cock. When he filled her mouth with his discharge, she came hard and long, encouraged by the girls' nimble fingers and lips.

Adele made the telephone call to Hardings. Natalie stood next to her biting her fingernails and stepping from foot to foot in anticipation. When she was handed the phone, she began to cry again. She told him how much she loved him and how sorry she was for everything she had done. She grinned from ear to ear when she put the hand piece back in the cradle. Cindy was crying too and Adele came over and hugged them both.

"Come on girls, let find you some clothes so we can go shopping. We're due at Natalie's dad's by three o'clock. I'm sure you want to look nice when you see him. And I think we need to give Kelly some time alone with Ramón. She's earned it."

Natalie dressed in the clothes Ramón had provided her with the night before. Adele went through Kelly's clothes and found the young, blond girl something presentable. Cindy was approximately Kelly's size, but she was so thin that the blouse and skirt Adele selected just hung on her.

When the three women left, Ramón got up and guided Kelly back to the bedroom. He freed her hands and allowed her to caress him. She came sitting in his lap, facing him, welcoming the warmth in her belly as his essence spread within her. Afterwards, they remained in place and she wrapped her arms around him lovingly, absorbing the warmth of his body. She could not remember ever being so happy.

Hardings had invited all of the girls from the lab to the dinner party. He lived in a large, expansive house hidden behind a large grove of tall evergreen trees. There was a broad swath of grass surrounding the structure. It was opulent, but not ostentatious, the living place of a man who had met with great success in his life, but who had not let it go to his head.

Hannah was already there. She was wearing a festive, bright green dress with a red silk scarf tied around her neck. She was also adorned with a frilly apron, having apparently taken over the duties of managing the feast. Ramón could see the evidence of their blossoming relationship as they gazed at each other from time to time, pleasure in their eyes.

Melissa, Felicity and Chandra were there already too, as well as Hannah's sons, their wives and her daughter.

Natalie's reunion with her father was heartbreaking. The tall, broad shouldered, normally stoical man broke into tears when he saw her. He kept repeating, "I can't believe it; I can't believe it," as he hugged her tightly. Natalie hugged him back as if holding onto him for dear life. Everyone started to cry at the happy scene. Even Ramón had the beginnings of tears in his eyes.

When Hardings let go of his daughter, she introduced Cindy. He caressed her short blond hair and welcomed her. He said, "A week ago I was all alone. Now I have two daughters." This, of course initiated another round of tears from everyone. He hugged both young women and then took Hannah in his arms and hugged her too. "And you, too, Hannah." She put her arms around him and gave him a deep soulful kiss to everyone's applause.

Finally, Hannah announced, wiping her eyes, "We can either stand around all afternoon crying or we can have dinner. I say, let's eat!"

Hardings' dining room was long and wide with a commensurate table that easily fit everyone. Hardings sat at one end with Hannah and Natalie sitting next to him. Kelly sat at the opposite end with Ramón and Adele to her right and left. The dinner was scrumptious. There was a large turkey Hannah had cooked with all the fixings. She had made several vegetarian dishes for Ramón, Adele and Kelly, including a delicious ratatouille, baked acorn squash divided in half with the centers scooped out and filled with hot maple syrup, onion soup, deep fried potatoes, and a host of greens.

The room was filled with general merriment. Kelly sat silent at her end of the table, for once being permitted to feed herself. Adele had removed her collar and bracelets and dressed her in one of her nicer skirts and a smooth, beige, silk blouse. The satiny fabric rubbed pleasingly against her bare nipples every time she moved.

All during the meal, Kelly beamed with pride at the happy, extended family the dream man had brought together. Cindy and Natalie were dressed in modest, bright colored, long sleeved blouses and fitted jeans. They sat next to each other, reserved and seemingly somewhat unsure of themselves. But the naïve delight of the young girls from the lab was contagious and soon they were chatting and laughing with everyone else.

Sitting next to her dream man, Kelly could not help but feel her lust build up for him. She reached under the table and stroked his thigh and he turned and smiled at her, sending her a message of caring and comfort.

After dinner, while everyone else cleaned up, Hardings took Ramón for a walk out in the back of the house. There was a brick walkway that circled the vast rear yard and skirted a wide flower bed, the plants dormant for the winter. Hardings had lit a cigar and the two men strolled along the path silently, side by side. Finally, when they had entered a small copse of white birch trees, carefully and artfully placed amidst a broad, wide rock garden, Hardings spoke.

"I built this place for my wife, Emily. She loved flowers and gardening. You should have seen it when she was alive. There were flowers everywhere, blooming almost all year round. She did it all herself. I pay one of the landscaping companies to keep it up. I just can't stand the thought of it all going to brush. After she died, it was really all I had that was truly hers." He took a deep drag of his cigar and let the grayish blue smoke waft away in the slight breeze. The sun had set and there was just a bare residual of light.

The men had stopped walking and a few desiccated leaves danced idly around their feet. "When we lost Natalie, my wife was heartbroken," Hardings continued. "And then when she got sick, I think she just kind of gave up on living. I've been all alone for five long years. It hasn't been easy. And now, all of a sudden, I've got a huge family. I went into the bathroom before and slapped my face to see if it was all real. It's really too good to be true."

The man paused to cover up a surge of emotion. Ramón could feel the echoes of his years of unhappiness well up inside him. He had never encountered a species that had so much love to give their fellow creatures but had so much trouble doing it. What the man, Shabazz, had done to these women was beyond his comprehension, contrary to everything the Whole had taught him. As he felt Hardings' pain, he realized that together with the great capacity of these creatures to feel pleasure came also a great vulnerability to pain. He remembered his second day with his familiar and the distress he felt when he realized he had hurt her more than he intended. It was an aching, empty feeling. How awful it must be to experience this every day for years on end as this man had.

"I'm not very good at talking about these things," Hardings confessed. "It goes against everything I was taught about what a man should be, strong, silently suffering. But I wanted you to know that when I tell you I'm grateful for the happiness you've given me, I really mean it. I don't know who you are or what your real purpose may be. I know you told me about this other 'being', as you called him, and how bad he is. Maybe I believe you and maybe I don't. But I promised you that if you restored my daughter to me, I would give you everything I owned, help you in any way I can, no questions asked. I meant it then and I mean it now. You've given me much more than you promised and I never renege on a deal."

The man stood, his eyes fixed on Ramón's. The dream man could feel his sincerity and honesty flowing from him. Ramón had taken a huge gamble and it looked like it had paid off. Very soon, he would be able to begin his work, subsidized by the business man's riches and access to tools and raw materials. He searched into his human mind for the appropriate response. He knew mere words would be insufficient. He held out his right hand to the man and he took it in his. "Thank you," Ramón told him, shaking it firmly. "Thank you very much."

CHAPTER SIX

By the time they returned home after the party at Hardings', Kelly was burning with lust for the dream man. It was the longest time since the man had enthralled her that she had spent free from her bonds and in the company of people who did not know her secret. She had remained silent throughout the afternoon and early evening, something everyone, including, strangely enough, Hannah's children, had accepted without comment. It had actually been a relief not to have to focus on anything but the presence of her captor and, except for when he had gone outside with Mr. Hardings, she had stayed close to his side.

As usual, Adele disrobed her as soon as she crossed the threshold to the farmhouse and restored her bindings to her. She received them with a new joy. She had not thought it possible for her devotion to the man to grow any deeper, but the sight of all the happy people he had brought together had erased her remaining doubts as to his beneficial purposes. She still had no idea what they were, but was willing to serve him in any way that would help him, was proud of her role in bringing him into existence.

When she had finished readorning her with the symbols of her captivity, Adele gave her a warm kiss and explained that she was going to spend the night at her folks' house so she could be with them Christmas morning. Ramón had stripped as soon as he got into the house and, as she heard Adele's car drive away, he led Kelly into the bedroom. He took his time in pleasuring her, causing her to moan with passion as he gave her enflamed pussy, long, languorous strokes of his cock. He did not bind her hands and she was free to express her lust and love for him with them. After he had come in her once, she urged him to his back and knelt between his outstretched legs. Her hands reveled in the feel of his firm, muscled body as she mouthed him to climax, stroking his strong thighs, cupping his scrotal sack. She took her time, pulling back each time she felt him yearning for release, running her tongue along the underside of his cock's bulbous head, letting her broad tongue wash along its shaft. When he came, she drank joyously at his essence, her pussy pulsing with pleasure.

Kelly had not been alone with Ramon since the day of his appearance in her bed and she relished their time together even though the house seemed somewhat empty without Adele. Ramón had discovered the pleasure of music and they spent a peaceful hour listening to Beethoven piano sonatas ensconced on her couch, Kelly curled up into his lap, his hands stroking and caressing her, sending her his warmth. Afterwards, he bathed her, making her lust burn while he explored every inch of her body with his hands. Before he put her to bed, he made love to her again, her body glowing with the warmth of her bath, her soul captivated by the man's affections for her.

Christmas day was a busy affair. Ramón and Kelly were awakened a little after ten by Adele. She had shucked her clothes at the door, and she lay beside Kelly while Ramón drew from her the mists she had accumulated in her blissful dreams. Afterwards, she took her turn with him as Kelly recovered from the mesmerizing effects of her task.

Later, when they had finished the Spanish omelets Adele had cooked them for Christmas breakfast, she presented them both with gifts, a new, elegant Italian knit shirt for Ramón and a pair of turquoise earrings for Kelly. Hardings came by and dropped off Natalie and Cindy for a visit about noon. Like Adele, they stripped as they entered and then, after giving Kelly and Adele warm kisses and hugs, dragged Ramón into the bedroom. Chandra arrived a little later bearing her gifts, long, silk, flowered scarves for Kelly and Adele and a pair of fine, leather gloves for Ramón. Seeing the growing pile of women's clothes piled by the door, she added hers to it.

It was a little after one when Felicity and Melissa arrived. They brought with them a special gift for Ramón.

Lucy Douglas had been pestering Felicity ever since her interaction with the dream man in Hardings' conference room. She was a couple of years older than Felicity, but had been classmates with Felicity's elder sister in high school. It was a simple thing to do to get her cell phone number. She had had a strange compulsion for the tall, dark man ever since the meeting. She couldn't explain it. She was drawn to him like she had never been drawn to any man before, and there had been a few. Felicity had talked it over at length with Melissa and finally acceded to the older girl's request. They had forced her to swear to double cross your heart and hope you die secrecy and had picked her up at her small apartment, driving her over to Dr. Jameson's house, giggling and teasing her all the way. Lucy took the teasing fairly good naturedly, but, for some reason she could not fathom, she felt a surge of apprehension as they pulled up the gravel driveway to the farmhouse. When the three girls came into the house, she got the shock of her life.

The beautiful, black haired Chandra was sitting on Adele's lap on the couch. They had obviously just broke from a passionate kiss and Adele's hand was buried between the Indian girl's thighs. Cindy and Natalie were sitting crosslegged and naked on the floor on either side of Kelly, whose arms where bound behind her. They were taking turns feeding her Christmas chocolates and kissing and stroking her breasts and thighs. A movie was on the TV, White Christmas with Bing Crosby, and the room was gaily decorated with evergreen garlands, Santa Clause figurines and a host of Holiday knick knacks, providing an incongruous background for the scenes of lust. Adele had purchased a small artificial Christmas tree at Wal-Mart, with bright, thin strips of aluminum standing in for branches and needles and small, multicolored lights which flickered on and off individually at random. Kelly's unanswered Christmas cards from family and friends were hung about the room on long ribbons.

Deep in her heart, Lucy had known something funny was going on between the dark stranger and the females over at Dr. Jameson's lab. It was not based on anything particular, but since her meeting with the man in Mr. Hardings' conference room, she had sensed odd emanations whenever she met the three lab assistants leaving the building at quitting time. But her imaginings had never included wild Sapphic orgies. And on Christmas day at that!

Before Lucy had the chance to bolt, Ramón came walking out from the kitchen. He was naked and carrying a large mug filled with whiskey laced eggnog, a concoction put together by Adele. He liked the warm sensation of the liquor entering his body and this was his second helping. When he saw the startled girl, he froze her in place immediately.

A quick scan of the girl's mind revealed to him what it was all about. It was a complication he had not anticipated but which could be easily dealt with. What was surprising was the initiative the young girls had shown in bringing the girl here. He chided himself for not anticipating their desire to please him by recruiting another stunningly attractive female for him. He would have to alter their instructions to prevent a recurrence. It was not part of his plan to randomly accumulate a bevy of female slaves to serve him. Just the opposite, in fact. He had recruited only those females he found necessary to his goals and had resisted the urge to capture the demure, brown haired young woman now standing before him even after watching her lustful display in Hardings' conference room the other day. He realized he must have unconsciously transmitted his desire for her when he was controlling her and, when he had released her from her spark of passion for her boss, his own natural attraction to her pleasing form and amiable personality must have been left as a residue. The girls had been right to bring her. He couldn't have her wandering around the building pining for him. There was no telling what might result. It was lucky she had spoken to one of his lab assistants about her strange infatuation with him rather than anyone else.

Now that she was here, he needed to decide what to do with her. Felicity and Melissa had merrily discarded their clothes and, once naked, dragged Lucy over to him by her arms gleefully wishing him a Merry Christmas. They had tied a little red ribbon around the pretty girl's neck, terminating in a little bow beneath her chin. His cock stirred at the thought of sampling her flesh.

Adele had come to her feet and she stepped over to where Ramón and the three girls were standing. She took Lucy by the hand and gave her a long, lascivious look.

"Hello, Lucy," she said to the girl. Everybody knew everybody else in Jacksonville. As Lucy had gone to school with Felicity's older sister, Adele had been classmates with Lucy's older brother.

Lucy's eyes, which had been pinioned by Ramón's gaze, drifted over to the tall, naked, blond woman for a moment and then drifted back. Her mind was a jumble of emotions and she could not shake her fascination with the coffee colored man's well formed flesh. After all, it was what she had been wanting and obsessing about for the last few days. She had just thought it would be different, that's all. She had imagined an afternoon of flirtatious exchanges with him culminating in a declaration of passion and a tryst in the back seat of his car when she was able to convince him to give her a ride home.

Adele turned to Ramón. "Well, honey, you've got to shit or get off the pot. Don't just leave her there all nervous and all." The tall, blond woman stepped up to the flustered young girl and put her hand on her cheek. "She's the prettiest Christmas present I've ever seen. I know what I'd do with her." Adele leaned forward and kissed the brown haired girl on her lips. "Ooooooh!" she remarked lustfully. "She tastes sweet. Maybe I can help you make up your mind."

Ramón was constantly surprised at how easily his principal servant read his wants and needs. She had matured quickly over the last few weeks, abandoning her tendency to prattle on and on about nonsense. She had an unshakable and unquestioning dedication to him. This commitment extended to her friend, his familiar, and to the other servants he had recruited. She was his major domo, his executive officer and their mother hen. And now, it appeared, she was preparing to act as his procurer.

Lucy was wearing a short, tight, dark brown, flannel skirt with long, stylish, high heeled, black leather boots that covered her shins to just below her knees. The gap between her skirt and boots showed off her graceful legs, which were enwrapped by a pair of fishnet stockings. Her blouse was a deep maroon and buttoned up to just above the cleavage of her firm breasts. Her long, elegant, brown leather jacket was open and at Adele's signal, Melissa and Felicity urged it off of her shoulders.

Lucy had spent some time decorating her face and her eyelids were beautifully highlighted in light green and outlined with black mascara. Her lashes were long and curled upwards invitingly. Her pert mouth was painted in a deep, dark red that accentuated the color of her tight blouse and her long, finely manicured fingernails had been adorned with a matching color and sprinkled in gold.

Once the jacket was gone, Adele began to slowly

unbutton Lucy's soft, satin blouse. The girl uttered a mild, inconsequential protest as the front of her top was loosened but made no effort to stop it. She licked her lips and her eyes were wide as she continued to stare at the form of the naked, appealing, dream man. Felicity and Melissa had loosened the buttons on her cuffs and were ready to slide the garment from her when Adele freed the last button.

A dainty, white, silk bra was revealed, barely covering the bottoms and tips of her breasts. It was joined by a hook at the front and the man's blond haired acolyte gently released it and pulled the half shells of the garment apart. The young lab assistants pulled it down her graceful arms and chucked it, along with the shiny, maroon blouse into the pile of female clothes near the door.

The partially enthralled young woman now stood half naked in front of the strange man who she had pursued. Her developing lust was readily perceivable by her stiffened nipples and the hardening of her attractive, pale breasts. She had wide, dark areolas encircled by a line of small raised bumps. The high heeled boots pushed the girl's breasts out invitingly. In the small of her back, just above her waist line, was a broad tattoo, a set of blue, interlocking geometric forms intertwined with a flowing vine with little red roses on it. Adele, standing slightly to the side so her lord could watch, took hold of Lucy's nipples with her thumbs and forefingers and began to tease them. She leaned over and spoke softly into the girl's ear.

"Lucy, you have very pretty tits. Did you know that?"

The girl, dazed by the powerful glance of the dream man and befogged by her growing lust, uttered a low, soft affirmation, "Mmmmmmm."

"Did you come here today so Mr. Vazquez could fuck you, Lucy?" she asked teasingly.

This drew a little more of a response from the girl. It was, of course, why she did come, but admitting it in front of all of these naked women was something else. She wanted to explain, to let them know she wasn't a slut, that the idea of physical union with the man had started from a little urge and then had grown and grown until she could think of nothing else. She wanted to apologize for her fantasy of somehow stealing him away, luring him with the promise of the delight she could show him between her young thighs. She saw now that that was not what being with the handsome, alluring Latino man was all about. "I..., I...," was all she could get out of her mouth.

"You have to earn it first, Lucy," Adele told her softly. She had shifted her hands and was now massaging the dazed girl's breasts gently. Lucy's hands, which had been hanging limply at her sides, moved over her hips and began to rub her taut, bare belly and the fronts of her thighs. Her plump lips were parted and her breath had begun to become heavy. There was a faint trace of pink expanding over her chest. She tore her gaze away from the naked man in front of her for a moment and looked at the blond woman quizzically.

"Mr. Vazquez wants you to suck his cock first, Lucy. He wants to come in your pretty, little mouth. Will you do that for him, Lucy? Will you suck Mr. Vazquez's prick for him?"

Lucy looked back at the object of her obsessions. She gazed down at his lengthening prick, which he was idly stroking. "Okay," she said softly. "Okay."

"Why don't you take off your skirt and panties first, Lucy? Let Mr. Vasquez see that you're worth fucking," Adele asked her.

"Okay," Lucy answered distantly.

Every female in the room knew exactly what Lucy was going through and what the consequence of sucking Ramón's prick would be for the dark haired young girl. Kelly was ablaze with passion as she took in her seduction. Part of her wanted to warn the girl away. She had no idea what she was consenting to. But another part of her wanted to see her pretty lips working her lord and master's cock, bringing him to pleasure. She wanted to feel the surges of lust as they filled the room, as they were already passing tantalizingly through her.

Cindy and Natalie were still on both sides of the enraptured scientist. They had all shifted to their knees, the better to watch the girl's developing passion, and their bodies were pressed together, shoulder to shoulder. Their hands were stroking her breasts and belly, enflaming her.

Adele stepped away from the trembling Lucy and took the cup of eggnog from Ramón's hands, placing it aside. For a few moments, the girl just stood there staring at the dream man, but suddenly, as if she remembered what she had been told to do, she reached her hands behind her and undid the hook holding the top of her skirt tightly to her waist and lowered the zipper. She shimmied her hips slightly and, hooking her thumbs into the waistband, drew the short brown garment to her ankles. She was wearing a pair of plain white, bikini panties and the undergarment had been lowered at the same time as the little skirt. She stepped through the leg holes as she carefully pulled the skirt over her shiny, black boots.

Adele motioned to Felicity and Melissa and they fell to their knees to help Lucy remove her boots. They were held tight by small, brass zippers down the backs and the girls pulled the zippers down and eased the boots off. But for her alluring, brown, self supporting, fishnet stockings, Lucy now stood before the dream man completely naked.

Ramón had watched the progress of the girl through her disrobement with tremendous excitement. His human maleness had taken command of his senses as he viewed her fine, round breasts, her graceful hips and her carefully trimmed pussy. The helplessness of the girl as she struggled with her lusts was a powerful aphrodisiac. Her body was beautiful, as he had expected it to be, and he awaited the pleasures of her mouth with fevered anticipation.

The girl stepped closer to him and tentatively put her hands on his muscular, hairless chest, exploring it as if seeing for herself that he was real. She placed her mouth on his nipples, worrying them with her tongue while her hands caressed his sides. Slowly sinking to her knees, she dragged her tongue and lips downwards over his firm belly and to his awaiting loins, her practiced hands caressing the man's strong, solid thighs. His cock was hard now and jutted out proudly. The brown haired girl wrapped her hands around it lovingly and, leaning forward, placed her lips on its tip. She suckled it tenderly for a few moments, teasing the tiny opening with her tongue and then, sliding her hands to its base, took its bulbous head into her mouth.

Lucy slowly made love to the dream man's cock. Kelly, through her own fevered haze, watched with amazement. It was like watching a master at work. The girl gently fluttered her fingers along the upper portion of the cock's stem as she spread her widened tongue along its bottom. She ran her tongue around the underside of the plump helmet as she cupped and massaged his soft stones. She tightened her lips around it and slowly worked her way down until Kelly could see the cock's thick head form a bulge in her throat.

The dream man had his eyes reduced to tiny slits as his body rejoiced in the pleasure the new girl was giving him. His thick thigh muscles were clenched tightly and his back curved back in an arch as the heat of her mouth and the agility of her tongue sent waves of ecstasy through his body. He had his hands on her head, gently coaxing her to her task and sending waves of his will and his lust through the girl. Lucy moaned deeply, her body quivering as she received it.

The man's lusts spread like a radiance throughout the

small room. The other women watched intently, their passions rising steadily. All hands went to their sexes, rubbing furiously, driving their excitement higher and higher. All except Kelly, that is. But her connection to the dream man was so strong, she did not need the use of her bound hands to drive her need. She pressed her thighs together and moaned. It was as if she could feel the young woman's tongue and lips washing the man's prick. As his lust grew higher and higher, so did hers.

Ramón gave a mighty groan when his cock began to throb and spasm in climax. Lucy cried out as she came too, her voice muffled by the hot, jerking meat in her mouth. All of the women experienced their own orgasms at the same time, and the room was awash with the sounds of their moans and cries of pleasure.

When Ramón's orgasm subsided, Lucy slowed her ministrations to his cock, but did not release it. She suckled on it languidly as the dual pleasures of having come and having served the great man flowed through her. She understood everything now and was pleased she had sought the man out, had so persistently lobbied Felicity to let her meet him.

Adele was the first to recover. She had sunk to her own knees beside the young woman while she pleasured Ramón's cock.

"Oh my god," she cried. "That was incredible. Lucy, you're the best!"

She pulled the happy girl from Ramón's loins and hugged her. "You're gonna have to give everybody lessons, sweetie," she told her.

The orgy continued for the rest of the late afternoon and into the evening. Adele had Melissa run into the bedroom and bring out the quilt and, after all the furniture was pulled aside, it was placed in the middle of the living room. The blond woman escorted Lucy to it and laid her on her back while Ramón placed himself between her knees. "Lie back," she told the girl, "you're going to enjoy this."

Ramón brought Lucy to repeated orgasms before he discharged himself into her womb. Kelly was next. Ramón raised her knees to her chest while he fucked her, driving himself deep into her belly, making her cry out with pleasure. While Ramón recharged his forces, the other women took turns in pleasuring each other on the quilt while the rest watched, anxiously anticipating their turns. Later, it was hard to recall exactly who had fucked who, except they all remembered Ramón plunging himself into Melissa's smaller entrance while she knelt crouched down before him, crying out, "Oh god! Oh! Oh! Ohhhhhhh! Ohhhhhhhhh!" as she came.

It was after nine and everyone was lying sprawled around the room either asleep or nearly so, languidly caressing whatever soft flesh was within their reach. When the sound of a car coming up the driveway entered the room, Natalie looked out the window and cried out, "Fuck! It's my father!"

The women tore through the pile of discarded clothes frantically trying to match garments to females. Ramón scurried into the bedroom, a nearly comatose Kelly in tow, and pulled on a pair of jeans and a t-shirt. He slipped on his sneakers without bothering for socks. Leaving Kelly lying on the bed, he came back to the living room. The women were in various stages of dressing, giggling and laughing at their haste and confusion.

Natalie and Cindy ran into the bathroom to brush their hair and wash their cum covered faces while Ramón answered the door. Hardings had knocked several times and he had a bewildered look on his face when the door finally opened. Hannah was with him and she was smirking conspiratorially. Natalie and Cindy kissed everyone goodbye and pushed him out of the house.

Felicity and Melissa left soon thereafter, taking Chandra and a very happy Lucy with them. The three residents of the house took a shower together in the large shower stall. Although they had just recently fucked themselves to exhaustion, the experience of washing Ramón's body was so sensual, Adele and Kelly sank to their knees and took turns sucking the dream man's cock while stroking each other's pussies to pleasure. It was Kelly who received his discharge, both women shuddering to climax when he came. She shared his essence with her loving friend as she gave her a deep, passionate kiss.

Kelly's comforter was too covered with the remnants of countless discharges for use and so Adele took the one off of her bed and the three lovers slept together. Kelly fell asleep sandwiched between the man and her friend, her bindings and gag restored, blissfully looking forward to her dreams.

The day after Christmas, it was back to work. Ramón met with Hardings and provided him with a list of supplies he needed. Adele had set up an interview with a well experienced female engineer, an Asian American woman named Nancy Lee. She had been laid off a few weeks before the Holidays and was eager to find a new job. Bright, in her mid thirties, she had a nice, if somewhat mature, figure, and an intelligent face. Ramón recruited her immediately and Hardings put her on his payroll.

It was on Friday, three days after Christmas that Shabazz showed up. Hardings had alerted his cousin, the County Sheriff, to look out for him. The car with the easily identifiable license plates had been spotted in the parking lot of a local diner. He had brought two muscle boys with him. One was a dark, foreboding looking black man with a shaved head and a golden earring. The other man was white and he had a heavy, black beard. Both men were well over six feet tall and well muscled.

The sheriff waited until they left the diner and had driven a few miles out Route 73 en route to Hardings' house when he pulled them over. He had called for two back up patrol cars and the desperados were confronted by six Caleb County officers. All of the men were relieved of their sidearms and other weapons. They had brought four sets of handcuffs and two gags and these were confiscated. They protested at the illegal roust while they were cuffed and placed in the patrol cars and driven away. The cars turned off the highway onto a little traveled, dirt road, one of the cops driving Shabazz's Caddy behind them. When they pulled to a stop far from the main highway, Hardings and several members of the company softball team were waiting there with baseball bats.

While Shabazz and his compadres watched, the men did a thorough job of destruction of Shabazz's car. They pounded out the headlights, broke the rear and all of the side windows and produced a series of impressive dents all over its shiny, new body. By the time they were done, the formerly clean lines of the luxury car were so distorted, it looked like it had the mumps.

When the ballplayers finally put their bats to rest, Hardings retrieved his double barreled shotgun from the rack in the rear window of his pick up. He walked over to Shabazz, who was standing there handcuffed, screaming and yelling and promising all kinds of retribution to the men. Hardings shoved the shotgun up against his chest and, after pausing to look into the frightened pimp's eyes, pulled the trigger. The force of the gun's discharge blew the black man off of his feet.

When the sheriff's deputies pulled him back to a standing position, there were two large burn marks on the front of his luxurious fur coat and the man was blubbering and crying. Hardings had loaded the shotgun with blanks. Deep down, he would have preferred using live rounds. Discretion had got the better of him. But he definitely wanted to put the fear of God into the despicable man.

When Shabazz was finally able to calm himself, he and his companions were freed from their handcuffs and made to strip to their skivvies. Once they were back in the car, the sheriff leaned into Shabazz's window and gave him a short, but firm speech. "Let me just tell you this, sonny," the heavyset, fiftyish man said in a low, firm voice. "I wouldn't come back here if I were you. But if you do, you'd better bring a lot more guys. Cause if I catch you anywhere in this county, I'm going to shoot first and ask questions later."

One of the deputies had retrieved Shabazz's broad brimmed pimp hat and threw it into the car.

"It's going to be a long, cold drive home," the Sheriff continued. "If I were you, I'd try to get there before the sun goes down."

Shabazz was still too freaked out to drive and it was the other black man who pulled the battered Caddy back onto the main road. One of the patrol cars followed them until they hit the county line.

The work was finished on the new space the week after New Years. Ramón now had his own work area, complete with a lab table, a computer and space for the additional equipment he was designing and which Hardings' people would help build. Hardings had arranged for the expedited installation of the additional 220 volt power lines he needed, although his work would, hopefully, soon make those power sources obsolete. A drafting desk for the engineer he had recruited was also installed. She would be working closely with him on developing the specifications for and installing the other equipment he would need. Her work was the most confidential in the lab and so it made sense to have him work with him, even though it made the other girls jealous. The plain, conservative business suit she had worn in the interview had given way to more stylish and revealing outfits and she had already lost a few of the excess pounds she had brought with her to the job. Her work was efficient and neat and she did not question the strangeness of some of the designs she was working on. The only real problem was, since he liked working in the nude and they spent their days in such close proximity, he had to stop several times a day to grant her sexual release.

One of the new rooms had been specially designed for Kelly, although she didn't know it. Since Christmas, the man's use of her seemed to intensify, although she could not have thought that possible. Her periods of lucidity in the mornings had become briefer and briefer. When Ramón was busy, one of the girls, or Adele, would relieve her of her sexual tensions.

It was her loss of her hold on reality Kelly minded most. Sitting dazed and sexually sated at her desk, her pussy still burning from its latest assault, she sometimes found it hard to recall what day it was, what she had done in the morning, who she had spoken to. For there were still the occasional phone call she had to handle, carefully scripted and made in the presence of her master and his acolyte. Afterwards, blindfolded, gagged and bound, the man's soothing cum seeping into her cells, she would have a hard time remembering who she had talked to and about what.

From time to time, she would recall her project and her research, and protest mentally at the loss of her purpose in life. She was a highly trained scientist, with years of education, and all she did all day was answer a few emails, sign some letters or purchase orders and fuck. But her concern for her work quickly faded each time her captor passed his hand over her head, emitting a warmth and affection that made her pussy burn with lust for him.

New Years, like Christmas Day had been passed in a fog

of sexual bliss as all of the women, this time with the lovely Nancy Lee included, came to the house to celebrate the advent of the new year. The party had actually started the night before and continued, intermittently, until the early evening of the next day. The surprise of the day had been the arrival of Hannah. Ramón was surprised to see her and was somewhat wary of her presence there since she and Hardings had formed a couple. But he could sense her need for him and acceded to her request to pleasure him. He sat in one of the easy chairs in the living room while she knelt between his knees, naked, mouthing him to climax.

Kelly had been just as surprised to see the black woman there. But she was more surprised when she found herself being led by her into the bedroom. They spent about an hour together. The woman's soft body and heartfelt gentleness was soothing to the captured young woman. Her broad, dark lips brought fire to her loins and her breasts while they coupled, and Kelly felt overwhelmed with lust as she lapped her tongue along the older woman's cleft, nestled between her widespread, black thighs. But it was the languid, satisfying periods between their frenetic lovemaking Kelly appreciated best. Suckling leisurely at her plump, mature breasts, Kelly felt almost child like, loved and protected, the black woman's soothing, deep voice giving her motherly encouragement, her strong hands stroking her.

Chandra, who had received holy hell from her parents for staying out all night, moved in with them the next day. Adele welcomed her into her bed and now the beauteous Indian princess assisted her in her management of Kelly's care. The first time Chandra came home from work with them, Kelly had been disconcerted as Adele taught her how to prepare Kelly for the insertion of her vibrator. It thereafter became her daily task. Her love for Kelly was so clearly evident and her handling of her so gentle and respectful, Kelly soon gave up her unhappiness at it. Not that she had lost her dismay each time her passions were placed on automatic and she was left for what seemed to be longer and longer periods to languish blindfolded, gagged and bound in the trembling device's lustful effects.

Each morning, the dark skinned girl also took over the job of preparing Kelly's pussy for the day. Kelly would lie back on the edge of the bed, her thighs split widely, while Chandra happily shaved her pudenda clean and then coaxed her to climax with her tongue and lips. In the evenings, while Kelly knelt naked and bound in the living room at her lord's feet, eagerly waiting for him to break from his work on her laptop to satisfy her lust, Adele would help Chandra with her homework in the kitchen.

On the second Wednesday after New Years, right at lunch time, Kelly's new space was unveiled to her. She was been sitting in one of the visitor's chairs in her office when Adele came in. Ramón had been in his new work room all morning and sweet little Melissa had a short while before stroked her to orgasm. She was lost in a dazed reverie, the afterglow of her climax still upon her. Adele freed her hands from behind the chair and, after helping her to her feet, pulled her knit blouse back down over her breasts and lowered her skirt from around her hips.

"Ramón has a surprise for you today, Kelly," Adele told her as she led her from the sequestered office. She had fastened her hands back behind her and had reinstalled her gag. Kelly, even in her confused, post orgasmic state, balked at being led through the lab by her leash, but Adele was insistent.

To her surprise, the lab was empty. Kelly had expected to see the girls busy at their posts, but instead, she saw their lab coats draped over their stools and their workplaces abandoned.

The new space Ramón had leased from Hardings was separated from the rest of the lab by a strong, steel door. It was secured by heavy, iron hinges and an electronic combination lock. Adele quickly fingered the buttons and the lock snapped open. She pulled the door towards her and led Kelly through. The door led to a small, whitewashed, cinderblock hallway with one door on each side. The door on the left, closest to the wall that separated the space from Hardings' shop was Ramón's new office and workplace. The door on the right led to Kelly's surprise.

The door had another combination lock on it and Kelly stood behind her blond friend as she keyed it in. Kelly was amazed at the work that had been done and its very existence reminded her of the fact that she had lost all control of her laboratory. What was her life becoming, she thought unhappily. She wondered what terrible new development awaited her beyond the imposing steel door. Each time Adele had previously promised her a "surprise" or a "treat" it had turned out to be yet another step in her reduction to a purely sexual being. Kelly felt like her humanity was slipping away. She hated the turmoil it caused her. Why couldn't she just serve the dream man like the others did, happy and unquestioning? If she was to be some kind of community whore, why couldn't he just make her forget everything else?

Adele opened the door and led Kelly through it. The first thing she saw was the bed. It was a wide, king sized mattress without a box spring sitting on a foot high wooden platform. It was positioned with its head to the right as you entered the door and was covered by a taut, smooth aqua sheet. Kelly stared at it long and hard. There was a short, thin chain connected to the headboard. Her heart sank as she realized its purpose. The bed was for her and the chain was for her too. There would be no need to confine her in her office now. The dream man, and anyone else who wanted to, could fuck her right here.

Kelly was so startled by the presence of the bed that, at first, she failed to remark the rest of the room. It was a large room, perhaps 20' x 30'. Its cinderblock walls were painted a light, pastel green, just like her office. Whoever had decorated it had taken a good deal of care and time since there were pretty prints mounted along the walls, a Degas ballet scene, not the same as in her office, but similar, a Van Gogh, the one with the lilies mounted in a lavender vase, a Pizarro landscape and others. There were vases with flowers on a long, polished oak credenza along the wall on the other side of the bed, a small dresser and a nightstand with a crystal glass lamp atop it. The rug was a copy of the one she had in her office. In the corner of the room was a glass enclosed shower, big enough for two and a screened off toilet. The ceiling of the room was high and painted white and along the outside wall, high up, were the room's only windows, slits, really, no more than eight inches wide, just enough to let in some natural light. A ceiling fan hung from a long pole from the ceiling with an array of small lamps in its middle. It cast a circle of light onto the bed, bright in the otherwise dimly lit room.

It was incongruous to see such a beautifully appointed bedroom appurtenant to a place of work. But it was disconcerting to see the girls from the lab and all the other women whom Ramón had entranced, even Lucy Douglas, standing around the foot of the bed expectantly, all eyes on her, all faces alight with beaming smiles.

Ramón was standing there too, his dark, mesmerizing eyes peering at her. The women were all dressed, but he was naked. His cock was hard and jutted out from his loins like a sword. Kelly felt her knees wobble as she took in the sight of him. He was going to fuck her in front of all of these women, she knew that. He was going to make her put on a performance for them, for their delight and their edification.

It would be like a ceremony demarking the dream man's supremacy, a coronation of sorts. And all the women were going to be eager, willing observers, if not participants.

For Kelly, there could have been no greater reminder that the women were Ramón's dedicated slaves. They treated her kindly, almost with reverence, but they served him. She wanted to cry out to them, awaken them from their trances. But aside from being gagged, she knew it would be of no avail. No one could resist the strange visitor she had conjured. He was master of all.

Kelly felt Adele stroke her long, auburn hair that was tied into a ponytail behind her head, reaching down to the middle of her back. "I know it's hard, honey," she said softly, kindly. "But it's important. Everybody here loves you, especially Ramón."

Kelly began to whine behind her gag. Looking at the dream man, she could feel her desire for him rising. She knew she would be unable to resist him. She would put on a show of virulent lust for his adoring servants and she hated the thought of it. She had mated with the man in their presence before, and with most of the women separately, that was true. But this would be different. They would not be coparticipants in her sexual acts, they would be an audience.

Adele's hands went down her back and reached for the zipper of her tiny, soft cotton, beige skirt. Kelly felt it descend and the clasp unhooked. To her dismay, the skirt fell easily to her feet, revealing the tops of her thighs and her hairless sex. Adele then reached around her front and pulled her russet colored sweater blouse up over her head and down her bound arms. Her friend, or the person who had been her friend, unhooked her wrists and slid the sweater free. Kelly tried to pull her arms away to prevent them being bound behind her again, but the blond woman quickly took hold of them.

"Don't fight it, Kelly," Adele told her. "It's what Ramón

wants." She refastened the bracelets on her wrists together. Usually, Adele used the little chain to connect them, giving her arms some play and easing the strain on Kelly's shoulders and back. But this time she connected them directly to each other, pulling her shoulders back, making her naked breasts jut out in presentation to the gallery.

While Adele knelt down to pull her skirt from around her ankles and remove her shoes, Kelly rued her nakedness before all of the clothed women. All eyes were on her and she was shamed. Her teeth clenched tightly on her gag in anguished frustration. Her breasts, which were denied her, swayed slightly on her chest, her nipples hard and pointed, as she lifted her feet one at a time obediently. She was dismally conscious of her hairless slit, displayed for all to see. At the same time, her pussy began to burn with unwanted need and she feared her crevasse was already glistening with her lubrication. Ramón stood in the center of the small crowd of women and she could feel his powers emanating from him towards her.

Kelly was wearing a pair of sheer, mauve stockings to match her now discarded beige skirt. Adele had removed her ankle bracelets and began to roll the stockings down her legs. The feel of the woman's hands on her thighs caused her to shiver with her rising passions. Kelly dolefully lifted one leg and then the other in passive, but disturbed acceptance of her fate as the stocking were removed.

Tears filled her eyes and drifted down her cheeks as Adele led her by her leash to the bed. She climbed upon it dutifully and allowed herself to be pulled to its center. Adele unhooked the leash and her gag and left her kneeling there, facing Ramón and his servants. She remained there, misery and anguish passing through her, for what seemed to be an eternity. Her collar and her bracelets, the symbols of her ownership by the enthralling man were her only adornments.

Why had she been selected for this role as the focus of the stranger's lusts, she thought miserably. Any other of the women would be happy to serve him. She had had independence, a purpose in life. And now she lived like some kind of strange temple whore, the repository of others' lusts. All eyes perused her bare flesh appreciatively, apparently either unconscious or uncaring of the torment her lascivious display caused her. Adele had said everybody loved her. But if they did, would they cooperate in her debasement like this? Enthralled as they were, were they capable of real love?

Ramón had been studying the reactions of his bound familiar. He sensed her unhappiness and turmoil. He couldn't help that. It was the price of her still free mind, a necessity if she was to continue to serve as the receptacle of the essence of the Whole that she drew for him from the other side of the dimensional wall. He had prepared this little ceremony both for her edification and that of his other servants. Their dedication to her protection and her well being would be reinforced. Now that his plans were beginning to advance, she would need to deliver more and more sustenance to him from the other side and would need to be kept in a state of almost constant sexual arousal. These women, his acolytes, would perform those services for him and they needed to be able to deal with his familiar as if she were a revered vessel, a being that had been transformed from being merely human to something else. They would have to ignore her right to self determination as a modern, free thinking woman and yet treat her gently, sympathetic to her plight as a captive of his will.

For the female, she would learn she was bound to obey his servants as she would he, to accept their ministrations to her. He would not have as much time to spend driving and satisfying her lust, an emotion necessary to facilitate her role as a conduit of his life force. She would have to accept their lips and hands and bodies as extensions of his. Her isolation from the world would from now on be near total and would remain so until his mission was complete.

The dream man had held back the radiance of his lusts while the female knelt uncomfortably under the gazes of the other women. Satisfied she had absorbed her lesson, he let the passionate emissions from his psyche to her mind slowly grow. He watched as her eyes and body recorded its delivery, her thighs tightening together, her eyes becoming glazed, her breath rising in tempo and depth. When she was ready, she would come to him.

Kelly felt the man's forces build up inside her. It was what she had feared, had known would happen. She gave a little cry and pressed her lips tightly together. Her breasts were taut with her rising need, her sex yearned for attention. She had been kneeling with her torso erect, as Adele had left her, but the wave of passion that passed through her made her lean forward, lower her head to her knees. She closed her eyes and moaned. Why didn't he come to her, she thought miserably. What did he make her suffer so?

Kelly looked up at the man who held her in his thrall. He was a man and yet, not a man. He was an alien, a specter from the abyss, and he owned her as much as any creature ever owned another. She knew what he wanted. For the past several weeks, her ability to feel his thoughts, his demands, had grown. It was like he was inside her head and, although he did not communicate in words, she understood him, obeyed him. Now he wanted her to pay obeisance to him, to worship him with her mouth so all the other women could see her subservience, her surrender to his needs and pleasure. Her mouth tingled with want for the feel of his plush, hard meat, the salty taste of his flesh, to experience the radiance of his powers.

Kelly knew the only way to assuage her misery was to take hold of the man's rampant cock with her lips. All of her shame and unhappiness at her nakedness before the other women, her regret for her abasement, would wash away in an instant. And the burning lust she felt for him, a lust that permeated her very soul, would be satisfied, her agony turned to bliss.

And yet, she still hesitated. She was required to move to him. She was to confirm his dominance over her by her own volitional act. It would be like an act of confession before the assembled women, proof their blind faith in the man was right. The accomplished scientist, the modern, liberated woman would pay tribute to the man, cast away all other wants and needs. Their belief in her consent to everything that happened to her, everything that they did to her in his name, would find its justification right here.

Overcome with her desires, anxious to put an end to her suffering, Kelly finally began to inch towards the man on her knees. Her gaze was focused on the object of her lust, the man's jutting prick. Out of the corners of her eyes she saw the women come closer to the bed and surround it, all the better to witness her worship of the man's tool. His prick was at the level of her breasts and she had to lean over to address it. Ramón held it still for her with his strong right hand. Tears still flowing down her face, she gave a soft sob and then, parting her trembling lips, took it inside her.

The contact between the hard wand of flesh and her lips brought Kelly immediate relief. She moaned as she pressed her lips down the thick shaft, let the head push along her tongue. Her whole body rejoiced at union with the dream man. She had not noticed the tension in the room while she was lost in her own dismal quandary, but she felt it now even as it dissipated. It was as if the women were sending her their own mental messages of approval, of joy at her compliance with the man's will.

Kelly worked her tongue and lips feverishly over Ramón's

cock, her head bobbing with each stroke of her lips, her breasts swaying freely beneath her. All her worries and fears seemed so unimportant now. It was true the other women had been relieved of the burden of their self will, had subsumed their thoughts and wills to the dream man's, but none of them, she knew, felt what she was feeling now. The man's mind and hers was one. As she suckled at the bulbous tip to his cock, she could feel his pleasure, his thrill.

When she leaned back and teased the tiny opening at its tip with her tongue, the exquisite sensations passed through his mind to hers. As she lowered her pursed lips down the long, rigid shaft, she could feel the warmth of her mouth raise her own lusts as it raised his. What a fool I was to resist, Kelly thought amidst her rising passion. Whatever the man wanted, whatever price she had to pay to feel what she was feeling now, to experience the bliss of mingling her lusts with his, was worth it.

As Kelly felt the man's passion building to its crescendo, she became aware of the minds of all the other women in the room. They had all joined hands and her and her lord's building climaxes were passing through his hands to their bodies. It was like she was looking into them through the man's mind. She felt their honest love and affection for her, could identify all of their distinctive psyches, Adele, Chandra, Felicity and Melissa, Hannah and Lucy, Cindy and Natalie, even the new woman, Nancy. They all had their distinctive tones and flavors. Whatever happened, whatever the man demanded from her, she realized they would help her, be all around her, as they were now.

When Ramón's cock began to throb and spasm inside her mouth, Kelly's pussy exploded with pleasure. She moaned deeply as the man's hot discharge flooded her. Her lips thrilled to feel the pulses of his ejaculations, her mind reeled at the sensations of his pleasure as they were passed on to her.

The other women cried and moaned as they received the blessings of the couple's mingled passions.

The enthralled woman drank at the flow of the man's rewarding essence until its source ran dry. Her mind dizzy with its effects, her body warm with satisfaction, she slowly eased her lips back until the still hard shaft escaped them. Ramón, breaking his contact with the other women, took her head in his hands and kissed her lips, mingling his tongue with hers. Kelly's tears of shame and unhappiness had turned into tears of joy. He dropped his hands to her back and encircled her, his strong arms pressing her body into his. The woman felt her lusts begin to build again. She wanted more from her dream man, all he could give her.

Ramón unfastened Kelly's bound wrists and pushed her body so she was lying on her back on the bed. He pulled her up to its center and knelt between her widespread thighs. His eyes drank in her beauteous, supine form. She looked up at him expectantly. But he would wait for her invitation, the gesture of her subservience.

Kelly desperately wanted the man to pierce her, to fill her with his pleasure giving cock. For a moment, she wondered in her fevered lust why he had paused. And then she remembered. She would have to present herself to him, confess her need, invite his possession of her. Conscious of the watchful eyes of the enthralled women, Kelly spread her legs wide, raised her knees and thrust her hips upwards, proffering her shaven pudenda to its real owner. The shame of the bared flesh was still with her, but her need was great. She watched with lustful anticipation as her captor's eyes were directed towards her hairless slit. Her hands were free to roam her body and, in her lust, she pushed them over her flat belly and along her inner thighs. It had been a long time since she had been able to do so. Her arms were now almost always locked behind her, her personal needs seen to by others. It was strange to be able to feel her own body with her hands. Her own touch seemed almost foreign to her, the touch of a stranger. She resisted the urge to stroke herself, to assuage the fearsome need of her loins, an act forbidden to her.

Kelly rued the fact that the other women were witnesses to the fevered display of her need. She closed her eyes and bit her lip to stop from crying out. Her mind focused on the vision of her proffered sex, the smooth, plump skin, the long, uncamouflaged slit. Fearful she would violate the taboo of touching it, she balled her hands into fists and withdrew them, drawing them in towards the center of her body. Her wrists brushed the bottoms of her breasts and she was reminded of the fact that they, too, were forbidden to her. Her nipples ached with the need for caresses, for the man's pleasure giving hands to seize them. She felt her breasts sway as her body began to writhe, heightening her awareness of them, and she pulled her arms up towards her head, arching her back, offering her soft, engorged globes to her lord and master.

Ramón watched the woman's display with lustful interest. He was pleased at her obedience, a difficult task considering her need. He reached out his hand and stroked her proffered sex gently with his fingers, causing the woman to shudder with pleasure. Proper behavior deserved its reward and he began to caress the gap between her flush labial lips with his thumb. She moaned as he worked it deeper and deeper into her cleft. When he spread her moisture over her hardened clit and began to rub it gently, she gave out a long, deep sigh.

His own lusts were near to bursting. He crept forward and ran his hands over his familiar's pleasing, firm belly and upwards to her breasts. When he seized them, drawing his hands tightly around them, the woman sighed again and then moaned. He massaged them firmly, but gently, sending a message of passion to her from his mind. He took her distended, fat nipples between his fingers and pinched them, lightly, at first, but increased the pressure until he sensed the response of the woman turn from pleasure to an exquisite pain. Her eyes opened and her hands went to his arms, torn between pulling them away and holding them in place.

Ramón held the enthralled woman's nipples captive for several moments, waiting until she seemed ready to cry out. When he released them, she sighed again and her thighs closed around his hips, pulling him towards her. His stiff cock was lying on her belly and the woman seized it with her hand. She arched her back and raised her hips, directing it to her moist gash. When the bulbous head found the entrance, he thrust his hips towards her and his cock slid in easily up to its hilt.

Kelly's mind flooded with pleasure as she felt the man's meat fill her. She surrounded him with her arms and pulled him down onto her. She reveled in the contact of his hot skin with hers. When he began his motion, drawing the thick instrument along the walls of her excited canal, she gripped him tightly, digging her fingers deeply into his flesh. Her lips sought his and, when she found them, she hungrily sucked at his tongue, bringing it inside her mouth. Her legs circled around his thighs and locked him in place while her hips thrust back at him, accenting the scouring of her pussy's walls by his thick manhood.

The enraptured woman and the otherworldly man fucked madly on the bed while the array of appreciative females watched. Hands had wandered to breasts and bellies. Felicity and Melissa had begun to kiss each other passionately. Adele had stepped behind the beautiful Chandra and had pulled her blouse up over her breasts and was caressing them while kissing her neck. The normally reserved and shy Nancy Lee had reached under Lucy's short skirt and pulled her panties to her feet. She was lustfully kissing her while her hand stroked her pussy to pleasure.

Ramón absorbed the developing passion all around him. He fed on it as he gave his familiar long, hard strokes of his cock. He felt her body shudder and begin to squirm under him as she came, her pussy clamping tightly at each spasm around his prick. While she shook and screamed in orgasmic bliss, he did not pause, but continued his frantic thrusts. His testes ached with the need of release and his cock felt electrified as his climax approached. When he came, he emitted a powerful surge of lust throughout the room. The cries and moans of the women acted like an accelerant to his pleasure, overwhelming his human mind. As his discharge flooded his captive's womb, she came again, frantically tightening her embrace of him, calling her ecstasy into his mouth.

The lovers maintained their embrace, letting their passions cool. The after shocks of Kelly's orgasm continued to squeeze the cock that still filled her. Her hands gently stroked the body that had pleased her. Kelly treasured the opportunity to explore the firm, smooth flesh, the rare chance to express with her fingers and palms the love she had for the man who had enthralled her. She let them linger along his strong, broad back, glide across his hips, absorb the warmth of his firm rear globes.

Finally, Ramón eased his cock from her lush crevasse and rose from her. He took her by the arm and brought her to the edge of the bed to sit next to him while the women, recovered from their own sexual releases, filed out the door. Each of them paused to kiss and stroke first Ramón, their lord, and then Kelly, his treasured vessel.

Natalie, Cindy and Adele remained behind. Kelly felt secure and happy as she leaned against the naked form of her captor. Her mind was fogged by the effects of her absorption of his essence. Adele knelt in front of her and caressed the tops of her thighs.

"I'm so proud of you, honey," she said, her voice full of her admiration. "You were wonderful." Kelly could see the affection in her eyes.

"I have something here for you. It's something Ramón has made for you. You need to drink it all up."

The blond woman had taken a tall, wide glass of thick, mocha colored liquid from a table near the door. Kelly looked at it with apprehension. She felt some kind of corner was about to be turned. Why would the man concoct a special drink for her? What was in it? What effect would it have on her? She gave her friend a frown and shied away from the glass. She turned and looked at the dream man. His eyes conveyed his command for her compliance. His hand had been around her back, stroking her, and he lifted it to her head and sent her a strong message of his will. Natalie and Cindy had crawled up on the bed behind her and they took hold of her protesting hands and brought them behind her back. Adele pressed the glass to her lips.

Kelly's happiness at her bout of love with her captor evaporated as her mind resisted her master's will. She started to struggle and turned her face to the side to avoid drinking the suspect liquid. Suddenly, she felt something she had not felt for a long time. The dream man had sent her a punishment for her disobedience. Her insides ached and her body soured as his angry message went through her. She gave a cry of unhappiness. It was as if her whole body had revolted against her.

The inner pain lasted only a few moments. But its effect on the captive young woman was deep and strong. Nothing could have emphasized her status as the man's prisoner more than this. She had almost forgotten how awful he could make her feel with a mere touch. The message of pain had been mild, but it was decisive. Tears filling her eyes, Kelly turned back to the kneeling blond woman and opened her lips. The thick liquid began to spill into her mouth, slowly at first, but then increasing as her head tilted back and her lips widened. It had a mild coffee flavor, but with a sharp, tart edge to it. It slid down her throat and into her belly like a thick milkshake. Although its taste was not unpleasant, Kelly was filled with revulsion at being forced to drink it. The man was leaving her nothing. She was totally his. She feared the drink was filled with some kind of drug that would steal even more of her consciousness away.

Adele had to pause twice to let Kelly swallow and absorb into her stomach the contents of the large glass. As the forlorn woman drank it, Adele kept murmuring to her, "That's a good girl, Kelly. Drink it all down. Drink it up. Good girl. Good girl."

When the glass was empty, Kelly began to cry. Ramon put his arm around her shoulders and hugged her tightly to him, sending her his strong message of warmth and approval. Kelly's discomfort left her. She looked up at him with her starry, blue eyes, her lips trembling. The recollection of her punishment was still fresh in her mind and its effects still reverberated through her body. She was sorry she had displeased the man. She leaned her head onto his shoulder and began to sob. The girls had released her arms and she threw them around the man, pressing her body close to his. She wanted so to be wholly dedicated to him, to please him in every way. Why did it have to be so difficult? He had left her mind free. It would be so easy if he just took it like he had done the others. She couldn't help but resist the things that went against her nature. She couldn't help having fear for her future, of what was to become of her. She was willing to give the man everything, but her mind wouldn't let her. She feared losing him, that some day, she would revolt against his will and he would abandon her. The mere thought of separation from him brought a whole new cascade of tears.

Ramon let the woman release her pent up emotions. He knew her role as his familiar was hard on her. He meant her no harm. But what had to be done had to be done. He stroked her long, bound hair behind her back and sent strong emissions of his affection to her. After a few moments she began to calm. He pushed her head back gently and kissed her lips long and hard. She kissed him back feverishly.

When she finally broke her kiss with the dream man, Kelly felt her arms being drawn back behind her. She looked back as they were clipped together. She saw Natalie and Cindy kneeling on the bed. They had discarded their clothes. Their faces were full of admiration for her. Adele was crouched at her feet, reattaching the bindings around her ankles. When she was done, she presented to her her gag. As she guided it home, she told her, "Cindy and Natalie are going to take care of you, Kelly. They'll be here with you all the time."

Kelly felt her arms being pulled back and the two former ladies of the night guided her to the middle of the bed facing the headboard. They brought her to her knees and had her lean over, her breasts pressed against her thighs. The dream man took up a position behind her. She had come several times during the past hour or so and she felt tired and worn. But when she felt his hands on her soft, round, rear globes, her lust began to rise automatically. When the man's hand dropped below her proffered rear and began to stroke her bare love lips, she felt her energies renewed.

Ramon teased and caressed Kelly's pussy until her lubrication began to flow. He waited until she moaned with passion and then dragged his moisture covered fingers along her perineum until he reached the small star between her rear cheeks. Kelly always felt a wave of shame flow through her when he used her there and this time was no different. When the fingers gently pried the small entrance open and began to rasp along the delicate tissue, she moaned with pleasure despite herself. Adele had climbed on the bed and she placed a sleeping mask over Kelly's eyes, drawing the elastic that held it in place behind her head, plunging the bound woman into darkness.

Kelly protested her blinding with a whine and the shaking of her head. She hated being deprived of her sight. But she soon found the isolation it brought her intensified the sensations she was experiencing in her rear. The man removed his hand from her small ring of flesh and she felt the head of his cock pressing against it. Kelly bit down hard on the thick, penis shaped gag that filled her mouth in mournful anticipation of the pleasure she would feel when it entered her. There was a small tinge of pain as the delicate ring was expanded and then the thick cock slid slowly home.

The man took his time in plowing Kelly's small, rear entrance. Each time he slowly eased the wide, hard member back across the sensitive flesh, a fierce flow of pleasure coursed through her. When he pressed the rigid meat home again, Kelly moaned with growing lust. Bent over and sightless, her body folded compactly, her forehead on the mattress, her bound hands clenched tightly behind her, Kelly surrendered to the man's will.

Whatever the man had given her to drink, it was beginning to have its effect on the prostrate young woman. Her mind became dizzy, her thoughts scattered. The sensation of the man's cock as it scraped across her rear's entrance seemed to reverberate through her. Her body became light and yet full of energy. As the strokes in her rear continued, filling her bowel, everything else fell away. There was nothing else but the enrapturing sensations brought by the man's cock. It radiated lust and the man's power all through her. Kelly moaned long and loud as the feeling drove her pussy into hard, almost painful contractions. Her body shook as she came and her mind reeled. And yet, the merciless cock went on and on.

The first orgasm melded into a second. Each pulse of her pussy's muscles sent the enthralled woman deeper and deeper into a mesmerized state. She came again as the cock's pace across the small circle of tissue increased. The man's body stiffened and he groaned and his manhood began to throb and spasm within her. Kelly could feel his seed flowing into her, being absorbed by her bowels, passing throughout her body. His hot hands were on her hips and Kelly could feel his pleasure passing through them and into her.

His ejaculations having finally ebbed, the man slowly and gently drew his detumescing organ from Kelly's rear. The dazed woman struggled to regain some mental equilibrium, but her ass fucking had sent her mind to a place it had never been before. The echoes of her pleasure resounded in her brain. Her whole body felt aglow. Her heart pounded in her chest and her pussy burned with the memories of her orgasms.

Ramon went to the shower and washed himself. When he emerged, the woman was where he had left her. It had taken him a while to develop the formula Adele had fed her. He had carefully combined some of the enzymes from the female's laboratory with a culture derived from his essence. He had added enhanced vitamins and nutrients along with flavorings to make the substance palatable. It would help maintain the woman's mind in a sort of suspended state, facilitating her lusts, improving her use as a conduit for the power giving mists from across the dimensional barrier. It would clear her body of impurities and strengthen her. He had prepared a modified formula for his servants. The presence of his essence would alleviate the female's physical needs for him while he was busy elsewhere and would help satisfy the lusts of the other women for his seed.

It would still take many weeks before he would be ready to challenge the renegade. He would need to strengthen himself as much as possible beforehand. The female's body was the source of his power. It was unfortunate she would suffer as she felt her abilities to reason give way to her service to him. There was no other way.

Ramon finished drying himself and strode purposefully to the door. He would come back later to drain the mists that would fill his familiar's body during her trance-like state.

Although sightless, Kelly sensed the departure of her captor. Her mind protested briefly his abandonment of her to her mesmerized condition. But it passed quickly as her consciousness drifted off. She felt soft, gentle hands release her wrists behind her back and pull her body forward. She was urged to her back and her hands lifted over her head to be attached to the chain that led from the headboard. Smooth, female flesh lay down on either side of her. She tried to protest as she felt the hands glide across her body. She wanted to come to rest, to stop the whirling in her mind. A mouth seized the nipple of her left breast and a hand descended across her belly and delved itself between her thighs. As a feminine finger traced the gap between her smooth, naked nether lips, she moaned and spread her legs invitingly.

PART FOUR: THE QUEST

CHAPTER SEVEN

From the fourth floor of the Omaha Airport Best Western, Ramon could see nothing but a white wall of heavy, late February snow as it fell to the parking lot below. All flights had been cancelled due to the storm and he was resigned to spending another night away from his familiar. He had called Adele earlier to check up on her and his servant had assured him the woman was dealing with their separation as well as could be expected. She had been fed a dose of his formula a couple of hours before and Melissa and Felicity with her now, comforting her.

It had been a productive two days. His search for the renegade had begun. Before he had made his jump, he had known the approximate arrival point of his quarry some five years before. But everything else had to be done by research and deduction. Like Kelly, the familiar who had drawn the renegade to this side of the dimensional wall would be single, female, somewhere between the ages of 25 and 30 years old, bright and probably successful in her field. She would have disappeared without a trace and there could be expected to have been some publicity.

Over the almost three month period of time since he had been adorned with human form, Ramon had researched through the newspapers of the period around the time the renegade would have arrived. Female disappearances were unfortunately frequent, usually with tragic results. But he was able to discount those cases where the women's lifeless bodies had been recovered or who had turned up days, weeks or months later. The renegade would not have murdered his familiar or let her go. She would still be missing, her case long ago relegated to the unsolved files.

He had narrowed his search to four women who had disappeared within a three month period in the Chicago area. The first one, a pretty, blond, 28 year old artist, was easy to eliminate. On investigation, she had led a quite dissolute life. Her heavy involvement with liquor and drugs made her an improbable candidate for a familiar. Her emissions of passion and her ability to cast them through the dimensional divide would have been severely compromised. Moreover, there was evidence she and her boyfriend had been involved with some rather unscrupulous drug dealers and had received a number of threats from them for unpaid services. The woman and the man disappeared on the same day. Unfortunately for them, their bodies were probably resting in shallow, unmarked graves somewhere.

The second woman he looked at was a 31 year old surgeon. She was the first African American female surgeon to be named as head of the surgery department at Cook County Hospital. She had published numerous articles based on new procedures she had developed for removing lesions from the brain. She was unmarried and, apparently, had no boyfriend or other private life to speak of. When he investigated the circumstances of her disappearance, Ramón found out she had just left a late night seminar at the hospital. Her car was found a few miles away, its doors left open and there had been signs of a struggle. This was not consistent with the means the renegade would have used to convert her. Ramon could not help but morn for the loss of this promising woman and cursed the profligacy of this culture with talent and life. He had been astounded as he perused its history and reviewed its daily news at the amount of violence and harm the humans inflicted on each other. There was apparently a dear price to be paid for their remarkable passions and sensuousness.

That left two women who could qualify as the familiar of

the renegade. One was an aspiring architect. She was 26 years old and had already designed two large skyscrapers. Both were notable for their environmentally friendly design, their comfortable, interesting interiors and their inspiring structural aspects. She was a handsome, shapely, brunette. She had not reported to work for several days and when the police eventually went to her apartment to investigate, she was just gone. Nothing was missing. It was as if she had just disappeared.

But it was the final one that really caught his interest. Professor Diane Lanier had called in sick to work one day and was never seen again. Interviews with her associates at the University of Chicago Biology Department had revealed no reason for her to run away. She was bright, well liked and very successful. She had been only recently hired and it was assumed that in a couple of years she would be a candidate to replace the retiring head of her department. She was only 25 years old, on the lower cusp of the age group Ramón considered likely as the renegade's host, but there were other circumstances that intrigued him. Apparently, all of her cash had been withdrawn from her accounts. There was evidence in the apartment that an unknown man had stayed there for a few days. His fingerprints, unknown to any database, had turned up on glasses and on several items of furniture. Semen stained sheets had been found on her bed and in her laundry basket, in spite of the fact she had not been known to have a boyfriend. And most peculiar of all, her 19 year old sister, Nadine, had gone missing with her.

Ramon had decided he had enough to justify a trip to Chicago to find out more, if he could, about the woman's disappearance. Once there, he had hired a private detective, a female one of course, to search through police files and interview the family. Yesterday, she had hit paydirt.

Two years after the disappearance of the young women,

Nadine had turned up in a raid on a house in East St. Louis. She had been working as one of a stable of whores for a local gangster. He had started out as a pimp and had expanded to drug dealing. The house also served as his headquarters and the police had been given a tip on a major drug delivery. The gangster had objected to the entry of the police into his safe haven and had announced his opposition with shots from his 9 millimeter automatic. He went down in a blaze of bullets.

Three of his girls had been there at the time and normally they would have been processed and released. But the one, a pretty, little brown haired, white girl, had reacted hysterically to the death of her owner. She had screamed and moaned when they tried to drag her away from the body. Nothing had seemed to console her or to calm her down. The other girls didn't know much about her except that she had been wholeheartedly devoted to the gangster, had never complained or argued with him and was wholly compliant with all of his orders no matter how scurrilous or degrading. She had been known by the name of Candy, but had no identification. She had been with the pimp for about two years.

One of the enterprising detectives solved the mystery of her identity. He noticed she spoke with a distinctive, flat, Midwestern accent. He was originally from Nebraska himself. On a hunch, he sent off an inquiry to the Nebraska State Police together with a mug shot. As luck would have it, one of the clerks there had been long friends with the Lanier family and recognized Nadine right away.

For the last three years, Nadine had been resident at St. Catherine's Psychiatric Hospital. She had never recovered from her pining for the dead gangster and was normally kept heavily sedated. The PI, who had come with Ramón to Omaha from Chicago, had learned from Nadine's family the facts surrounding her discovery and Ramon had been granted reluctant permission to see her.

The skies were already heavily clouded with the impending storm when Ramón drove his rental car out to the hospital. It was an aging structure, built sometime in the Fifties and was situate about ten miles outside of Omaha. Nadine was considered a charity patient since her family had long ago exhausted their resources in her care. A nurse at the reception desk was very helpful, after Ramón gave her a little nudge, to arrange for him to see her in a private conference room.

The room was small about five by ten. Ramon was sitting behind an ancient, wooden table on a rickety, wooden chair when Nadine was escorted into the room by one of the attendants. He was a burly, black fellow, genial in appearance and he kept a tight hold on Nadine's arm as he led her into the room. Nadine was dressed in a short, flimsy, faded yellow hospital gown. Her chestnut hair was cut short and in disarray. Her eyes had a glazed look and her hands were confined to her waist by a leather belt with handcuffs on both sides. Her face was gaunt and a speck of drool peaked out from the corner of her mouth. He skin was pale and dry.

"I'll be right outside if you have any trouble," the dark man said helpfully. "She can get a little wild from time to time, but she had a shot about an hour ago and she should be okay for a while."

Ramon nodded to the man as he left the room. A probe of the distracted girl's mind told him all Ramón needed to know. He felt the presence of the renegade at once. He had done much damage to her mind. He reviewed her memories and saw the life of hell he had condemned her to. A well of sorrow flooded him as he perceived the harm done to this life form. Even now, although suppressed by the heavy dose of Thorazine she had been given, he could detect her wrenching need for the presence of the gangster to whom the renegade had enslaved her. He saw the long line of men she had been required to service, the indignities she had suffered. But, most importantly, deep inside her, buried beyond her own conscious memory, he saw the face of the renegade.

Blonde, handsome, with piercing eyes, the image of the man who had enthralled her was burned deep into her subconscious. She knew him as Jonathan. For her, he had no last name. She had no clue as to what happened to him after she had been sold to the pimp. She had never again given him a conscious thought. Neither had she recalled her sister, the enthralled Diane Lanier, or her former life. Her parents had been unrecognizable to her.

The young woman's eyes barely recorded Ramón's presence. His heart went out to her. He was torn as to what to do. He could easily relieve her suffering. But if he unblocked her mind, the memories of what had happened to her would flood her brain like a torrent. She would recall her role in her own sister's enthrallment by the renegade. She would remember each and every depraved act she had been forced into, the years of slavery to the ruthless, conscienceless gangster, her long time as an irrational prisoner at this dreary, hopeless hospital.

On the other hand, could he permit himself to leave her as she was? He had been sent here, in part, to undo the harm caused by the renegade. The ethics of the Whole demanded nothing less. But he would need hours, if not days, of contact with the woman to relieve her suffering, to adjust her mind so she could live with herself. And, there was also the fact that her sudden recovery would be astounding to the doctors and her parents. It would be immediately connected with his visit. He did not want the questions and notoriety that would result.

But he had to do something. He could not, in good conscience, leave her like this. He decided on a middle ground.

The dream man pushed aside the effect of the sedating drugs from the young woman's mind. As her mind stirred, he claimed her, calling her to him. She looked at him for the first time, a spark of life emanating from her eyes. She rose slowly from her chair and stepped around the small table until she was close to him. He took her arms and pulled her to his lap. He put his hand behind her head and drew her into him, circling her with his arms, sending a long, strong message of comfort to her. She began to cry.

Ramon knew he had only a short time to deal with the disconsolate woman. The attendant was just outside. Luckily, the door to the room had no window and he couldn't see in. It would take a long time to explain why he had a nearly naked mental patient sitting on his lap. It was an unjustifiable risk, given the importance of his mission, he knew that. But he did not want to walk away from this hospital knowing he could have helped her and did nothing.

The dream man stroked the petit woman's short, brown hair as she cried on his shoulder. He removed her obsession for the dead pimp. He barred her access to her memories and adjusted her so she would adapt comfortably, for the time being, to her life as a psychiatric patient. He gave her a spark of hope, knowledge of his promise to return and redeem her, to free her from all of her suffering. Finally, he rendered her unable to relate to anyone what had happened between them, to remain silent and distant with only her knowledge of his covenant with her to return to comfort her.

Nadine pulled her head from his shoulder and looked into his eyes. Life had returned to them. There was a look of happiness on her face. Her lips trembled as she whispered to him hoarsely, "Thank you."

Ramon knew he needed to seal the frail, young woman's connection to him. He had touched her lightly and there was always the danger his commands to her would fade. He rubbed his hand over her head and passed a message of lust to her, the first she had experienced for many years. Her eyes widened and she gave him a timid, hopeful smile. He sent another wave of passion to her and she moaned, her thighs tightening, her body shuddering.

The dream man eased Nadine to her knees in front of him. She waited expectantly as he lowered his fly and freed his already hardening cock. He would need to be quick. If the guard chose this moment to come in, he would probably pound the shit out of him before calling the police.

Nadine opened her pale, dry lips and took his cock into her mouth. Her eyes closed with bliss and she moaned lowly as he filled her mind with his radiance. She slowly slid her lips down his shaft, caressing it with her tongue. When her head pulled back, she suckled at the thick helmet of flesh at the end before descending once again.

The experienced former whore quickly picked up her pace. Soon, she had Ramón emitting moans of his own as his fluids rose. He placed his hands on her head, fueling her passion as he came closer and closer to climax. He suppressed his groan of pleasure as best he could as his cock exploded in the kneeling woman's mouth. She moaned too as her pussy recorded and echoed his pleasure.

When his soothing essence had ceased to flow, Ramón raised the dazed woman from her knees. He kissed her and brought her back to her chair. With a caress of his hand, he sent her deeper into her funk, restoring the numbing effects of her Thorazine shot to her brain. She would look to the attendant as she had when she came in. But over the next few days, her mind would slowly spring back to life. Her violent outbursts of desperate yearning for the gangster who had held her in bondage for so long would be gone. She would be childlike in her innocence, with no memory of her life. But deep inside, she would have a source of joy, a kernel of hope the strange man who had changed her would return.

Now, staring out the window of the hotel, Ramon was happy at his choice to relieve the girl of some of her suffering. But he was dismayed at being a prisoner of the storm. He turned towards the large king sized bed behind him. The P.I. who he had retained was sleeping. She was lying on her stomach, her arms beneath the pillow, her face turned away from him. She had short, brown hair, straight and cut into a mop like shape around her head. She had a long back which arched down to her firm, well rounded ass. There had been nothing to do since he returned from the hospital but fuck. He had worn her out.

Having been deprived of the essence of the Whole for two days had weakened him, but the strong lusts of the brown haired woman had helped to sustain him. Her name was Jacqueline Wasalowski, a daughter of Polish immigrants and raised on the streets of the North Side of Chicago. She had a pretty face and small, but pleasing breasts. She also had a strongly sardonic outlook on life and a fierce independent streak, both necessary for and a product of her chosen profession. She referred to herself as Jackie, but most of her close friends and her former associates on the Chicago Metropolitan Police Force knew her as 'Jack', as befitted her tough, tomboy exterior. As usual, Ramon had only altered her mind as much as was necessary and she had been a pleasant, amusing companion on their trip. Between their bouts of pleasure, she had persuaded him to watch a Marx Brothers movie on the cable television, Duck Soup. He had laughed heartily at their antics and their wordplay.

Ramón was becoming quite enamored of his life in this culture. Adele was somewhat of a movie buff and she had introduced him to a number of them. The four of them, Adele, Chandra, himself and his familiar, and anyone else who had stopped by to visit, would sit crowded together on the couch in the living room eating popcorn while the love story, the western or the swashbuckling adventure would play out on the TV screen.

And Adele had become quite an accomplished cook. Chandra contributed her knowledge of Indian cuisine. He had had to begin a program of daily exercises to keep himself trim.

But it was the richness of the varied personalities involved in his existence here that meant the most to him. Each person had their distinctive mental patterns, a kind of flavor. He loved to watch Melissa and Felicity tease each other when they came to visit the little cabin, sessions which would invariably lead to a retreat into Adele's bedroom, sometimes with him and sometimes without. Hardings' and Hannah's pleasure at their new lives with each other was evident in their faces each time he saw them. Hannah showered him with her sweet potato pies and homemade dishes on a regular basis.

The two recovered drug addicts and prostitutes, Cindy and Natalie, had put on some weight and looked now healthy and vibrant. Hardings had arranged for a plastic surgeon to erase the degrading tattoos on their bellies, but the girls had their own ideas about that. Two days after their session with the plastic surgeon, they came into his lab and raised their short skirts giddily. The inscriptions on their lower tummies, just above the waistbands of their pretty, low cut, white, lace panties, now read, "Property of Ramón."

Of all the beings with whom he had made contact, however, the one who had become most precious to him was his familiar. Their bond had become the strongest he had ever formed with another being of any kind. He admired her courage in meeting his needs, treasured her affection for him. Her mind was as beautiful and attractive to him as her body. He had read all about the emotion the humans called love, had seen it in action both with respect to the female's fear and concern for her friend Adele when she learned he was going to convert her and with Hardings and his love for his daughter, for Hannah, and even for the former whore, Cindy, whom he had adopted as if she were one of his own. Was it love that he felt for the female who served as his connection to the other world? His human side longed for her, rejoiced in her touch, cared for her. Even now, he rued his separation from her, both because of the unhappiness and discomfort it caused her, but also because of the need he had for contact with her flesh, the warmth of her presence.

Ramón was startled from his reveries by a timid knock on the door. It was about ten p.m. and the snow was just beginning to taper off. The airline had called to confirm his reservation in the morning. He walked over to the door and opened it. A young, blond haired girl was standing in the hallway dressed in a frilly, pink and white, gingham waitress's uniform. Her long, yellow, gossamer thin hair was pulled behind her head in a ponytail. She had pale, milky skin, almost translucent. The hem of the dress reached down to just below her knees and the bodice was open just enough to expose a small, modest glimpse of her chest. She wore no makeup other than a slight rouge she had applied to her cheeks. She was wearing a pair of high topped, white cross trainers with pink laces and white bobby socks with a lacey fringe at the tops. Her arms were crossed in front of her, cradling her heavy, winter coat and the strap of a small, black, imitation leather pocketbook. She had a nervous, expectant look on her face.

Ramon stepped aside and the young woman walked hesitatingly into the room. She turned to the naked, coffee colored man and said in a sweet, slightly tremulous voice, "We're not really supposed to...."

It was all she got out as Ramon sent her a strong,

mesmerizing message of acceptance. He shut the door behind her and urged her deeper into the room. He took the coat and pocketbook from her and laid them over a chair.

Abigail Lagerkvist came from solid, Norwegian stock. Her forbears had crossed the plains in a Conestoga wagon a hundred and fifty years ago. Her father and mother, together with her older brothers, Michael and Jan, still worked the three thousand acre farm out in North Platte. But 19 year old Abigail, her friends called her Abby, was not made for the bucolic life of a Nebraska farmstead. She had left a little over six months ago and, together with her friend Heloise, had taken an apartment in Omaha while they attended nursing school at the University. The job in the motel coffee shop helped pay the rent while her family subsidized the tuition and some of her living expenses.

The dark, handsome stranger at booth ten had seemed so polite and friendly and Abby was drawn to him naturally. The woman he was with was pretty and sophisticated and spoke with the flat, nasal accents of a Chicago native. Abby felt somewhat jealous of her friendship with the alluring man. When she had served the couple dessert and coffee, she had been pleased when he introduced himself and proffered her his hand. A strange tingle had seemed to climb up her arm and, as the night wore on, her fascination with him had grown obsessive.

Abby's boyfriend was a three sport jock at the University of Nebraska, playing football and baseball in the fall and spring and wrestling in the winter. He was okay as far as Abby was concerned, but he didn't measure up to the maturity and confident good looks of the Latino man. Besides, she knew he cheated on her. Lately, she had felt he was using her as a sexual convenience when any of the other, prettier girls were unavailable. Although Abby had a voluptuous figure, with large, soft breasts, her face was just a little plain and her body just a little too big boned to be considered alluring. Heloise had been after her to dump Ben, but the thing was that she enjoyed, if not the sex, the physical closeness and the warmth of his hard, naked flesh, and she didn't want to be all alone. She was shy and reserved and found it hard to relate to boys in general. Ben was only her second lover. She was sure Ben had spotted these qualities in her and was taking full advantage. But having him over a couple nights a week, even if she had to spend Saturday night alone many times while, as he put it, he was "out with friends," was better than nothing. He was kind and friendly while he was with her and never hit her or was mean.

When her shift was over, Abby had called Heloise and told her she would be staying the night at the motel. When it snowed here, it often snowed hard, and the winds that rolled across the prairie whipped the streams of heavy, white precipitation into a frenzy, obscuring the roads and leaving dangerous, deep snowdrifts. The motel manager let the girls stay in empty rooms on nights like this and so Heloise was not surprised at Abby's call.

Rather than going to the main desk and getting a room, Abby had taken the back elevator to the fourth floor and knocked on the room that corresponded with the room number on the dinner check. Although she felt frightened and somewhat foolish at her presumption that the man wanted her, somehow she was sure it would work out. She had no idea what she would say when he opened the door or if, god forbid, the woman opened it instead. But her compulsion to see the Hispanic man again was so strong, she decided she would think of something if she was asked "what the fuck she wanted."

Abby had been startled to see the man naked when he opened the door. But the sight of him made her heart flutter. After she had entered the room and the man had given her a long, enthralling look, her skittishness had vanished. She was beginning to feel this was going to be one of the most exciting nights of her life.

Ramon could feel the emanations from the girl's psyche and they were as sweet and pure as fresh cream. He detected her inner loneliness and doubts about her beauty. Her spirit was generous and giving and he saw she longed for the company of someone kind and gentle enough to share it with. The dream man was overwhelmed with the goodness of the girl. He was constantly astounded at the capacity of this species for love. As he saw her warm, blue eyes looking up at him, he felt his own eyes brim with tears. He put her arms around her and hugged her, sending her waves of affection. Her body was supple and giving and he could feel her mind welcome him and his embrace. He placed his hands on either side of her head and kissed her, gently at first, brushing her lips with his. When he felt her passion start to rise, he parted her lips with his tongue and touched hers, transferring his desire to her. Her arms circled his back and she pulled him into her, crushing her breasts against his chest and kissing him back. Her yearning for him flowed from her and the dream man stoked her lusts.

When their lips finally broke, Ramón stood back from the panting girl and began to unbutton the front of her dress. When the top was loose, he pulled it from her shoulders and then down over her broad, curvaceous hips, down her thighs and to the floor. She leaned on him with one hand as he helped her step out of it. While on his knees, he loosened the laces to her sneakers and pulled them and her socks from her feet. As he rose again, he ran his hands up the girl's soft thighs, over her hips and to her shoulders. He embraced her once more, enjoying the heat of her thighs and belly as they pressed against him.

Ramon guided the excited, panting girl by her hand to the

bed. The room had come equipped with two double beds and he led her to the empty one. While she stood at his side, clad in her pretty panties and sturdy bra, he pulled the covers down to its foot, leaving a broad, white expanse of crisp clean sheet, and urged her onto it. She sat demurely and patiently on the edge of the mattress while he stepped over to the dark haired woman on the other bed and, placing his hand on her head, deepened her slumber. He then turned off the bright, overhead light and turned on the small lamp on the nightstand casting the room in a soft, soothing light.

Abigail had seen the naked form of the sophisticated older woman when she had come into the room. She had not given her much thought. Whatever this man wanted seemed right to her. Even though making love to a strange man with another woman in the room was not something she thought she would ever do, it didn't bother her. The man was everything. She needed him and didn't care whatever his terms were. She felt safe with him, cared for, like it was supposed to be.

By the time Ramon had come back to the bed, the young girl had removed her bra and panties and was lying on the bed on her side facing him. One of her soft, pale arms was under her pillow and the other was laying along her thighs, her palm rubbing her skin languidly. He got onto the bed next to her and laid his body alongside, pressing his skin against hers. She put her arm around him and offered him her lips. While they kissed, he stroked his hand the length of her plush body, fueling her need.

He made love to the pleasant, happy girl for almost two hours. Her large breasts were sensitive and she moaned with pleasure as he suckled at them. The dream man luxuriated in her soft, smooth, pale flesh. She was not trim and toned, but she was not fat. Lying on her, their legs and arms intertwined, was like swimming in a sea of soft, warm, comforting flesh.

When he passed his hand over her downy sex lips and delved his finger between them, she sighed deeply, spreading her legs to give him access. He made her come twice with his cock before flooding her womb with his essence. When he placed his lips between her thighs, she called out, "Oh, yesssss! Yesssssss! Ohhhhhhhhh!" grabbing his hair tightly in her strong, farm girl hands. Her body shook and writhed with pleasure when she came as he sucked and lapped his tongue at her stiffened bud of pleasure. It was his turn to groan when she reciprocated, drawing her lips tightly around his cock, drinking down his discharge as his cock throbbed and spasmed in ecstasy.

* * * * * * * * * * * * * *

Jonathan Blackthorne was in the dream lab at his New Mexico Fortress when the call came in. It was Bob, his Apache major domo, who had taken it. He told the caller to stand by and immediately phoned his superior. When Blackthorne answered his cell phone, Bob gave him a simple message, "He's here."

The dream lab was a sprawling, windowless, one story building located near the hacienda. It was surrounded by two electrified barbed wire fences and its gate was always manned by two or more armed Apache guards. A tunnel led from the building to the hacienda giving Blackthorne direct access to it. Of all of his projects, it was the one he had had the most hope for.

The interior of the building was simple. The entranceway was a large, steel reinforced door and opened to a small reception area staffed usually by one of the young Apache women who had pledged their allegiance to the Lord of Conquerors. There was a telephone on the desk that led only to the interior phone system of the Fortress and did not carry an outside line. Its purpose was primarily to notify the facility of the arrival of new subjects or so the staff could be reached in case of an emergency.

The rest of the building consisted of a series of offices for staff, a cafeteria and a conference room, a large shower and preparation facility and a long row of small rooms. In each room was a bed, mind scanning equipment and a young, female subject.

The director of the facility was Dr. Sanford Morton, founder and formerly the chief scientist at the Pennington Sleep Disturbances Laboratory in Boston, Massachusetts. Dr. Morton had been recruited several years ago and now lived within the confines of the Fortress in a luxurious mansion that had been constructed for his personal use. He had been enticed away from his research and very profitable sleep disorder clinic two years ago. The money was not really a factor, although it was certainly enticing and generous. The fact that Blackthorne had, during the course of his interview with the doctor, converted three of Morton's pretty nurses to his service right in front of him was certainly persuasive. Watching them disrobe and crouch down on their knees, their foreheads to the floor and their hands obediently crossed behind their backs had been impressive. But the real enticement was the project itself.

Dr. Morton had no doubt about the powers of dreams. He had studied the subject for too long to doubt the mind could cast out forces that could be measured and quantified. That they could pierce a dimensional divide was also no surprise, theoretically, at least. The chance to try and manipulate psychic forces to establish a bridge between dimensions, with unlimited control over his subjects, a virtually unlimited budget and free from the prying, bothersome eyes of government and colleagues who might question his methods was too much to resist.

The doctor had been at Blackthorne's side when he got the call. They were in the room of subject 722. She had proven to be especially promising and Blackthorne had just finished driving her to a series of ecstatic orgasms while filling her mind with gut wrenching fear. She now lay sobbing and moaning on the bed, naked, bound and hooded, ready for the injection of a cocktail of psychedelic drugs that would cause strong emanations from her mind to flow.

Alison Mulvihill, a shapely, twenty-two year old brunette, had been a physics major at Colgate and in her senior year when she had popped into a job fair at the Student Union Building one afternoon. She was with a couple of friends and hadn't intended on going until they coaxed her along. "What the hell," she thought. "Nothing ventured, nothing gained." She had already been accepted for a postgraduate program at MIT, but she was curious at what private industry might offer. She had wandered over to the booth for Marjoram Industries, an up and comer in the technology market. A pretty young woman was at the desk and, after talking to her for a few minutes, Alison agreed to an interview with the company representative in the little office they had set up. She was impressed with the handsome, blond haired man with the deep, entrancing eyes, but didn't remember much else of their meeting.

Two weeks later, Alison was standing on the corner of College Boulevard and Cayuga Street in Utica with a small suitcase in her hands. She really didn't know why. Her bag contained just a few pairs of underwear, her toiletries, two clean t-shirts and all of the cash she had been able to raise from selling her car and closing her bank accounts. She had broken up with her fiancé the week before and withdrawn from all of her classes. She had dropped a short note to her parents in the mailbox just moments ago, explaining her desire to 'see the world' and not to worry about it if they did not hear from her.

A late model Ford Explorer pulled up and she got in the back seat after tossing her suitcase in the rear compartment. There were four other young women in the car, none of whom she recognized. They nodded a greeting to her and the car pulled away from the curb. They made one more stop and a young, black haired, Asian woman got in. She introduced herself as Linda and the car headed for the Interstate.

Alison felt strange riding in the Explorer for hundreds of miles without any clear idea of what she was doing there or where they were going. The other girls were cheerful and amiable and they traded stories about boyfriends, movies, courses they had taken. But none of them shared any other real personal information aside from their first names.

The car made infrequent stops, the girls taking turns driving. It was funny that none of them knew their ultimate destination but always seemed to know just what route to take. They kept on heading south and west, stopping only for gas, convenience food and the bathroom, paying for everything with cash. Only one night, when all the young women were too tired to drive, did they stop for the evening. They rented a double room at a motel some miles off of the Interstate outside of Tulsa and shared the beds. A quick shower and breakfast at McDonald's and they were on their way again.

The women all remarked the beauty of the surrounding country as they entered the Southwestern region of the country. The Tribal Police at the entrance to the Apache Reservation admitted them without question. Driving a considerable distance along a two lane road, they approached a large gate manned by strong looking, dark skinned men in mirrored sunglasses. After passing through, their car was pulled over to the side and all of the women got out. They were ushered into a little hut located some 25 yards or so from the gate.

It was there that Alison began to become really worried about what was going on. The man at the desk knew her name and checked it off on his list. The women were all standing nervously shoulder to shoulder in line when he stood up from the desk and approached them. He had something in his hand. Alison was in the middle of the line and could not see it at first, but she recorded apprehensively the moans and cries of fear that came from the women on her right as he showed it to them one by one. When he stepped in front of her, holding it at his waist and directing her eyes to it, Alison's heart stopped and a feeling of deep despair coursed through her. All at once, she remembered everything.

The tall, muscular and attractive, blond haired man had been friendly and polite when she had entered the interview room. He was sitting on an easy chair with a large bottle of sparkling water and a glass on a small table next to him. The room wasn't really a room, just a set of four dividers that had been set up in the middle of the job fair for privacy. A nice rug had been set down in the middle and there was a comfortable chair for her to sit in. It was almost like being in somebody's living room.

The first few minutes went well enough, although Alison couldn't help but feel the man was somehow assessing her, probing her with his mind. And then it struck. Suddenly, her mind was filled with fear and anxiety. She clutched the arms of her chair as she felt her brain rewired to obedience to the man. He showed her the medallion, the same one the dark skinned, mean looking man was showing to her now. The blond haired man had forced her to pledge her obedience to it, subsume her will to his. Trembling with fear, her eyes full of tears, she had knelt before him, pulling open her blouse and raising her bra so he could see her breasts. She had crept closer to him and, after he pulled his thick, already rampant cock from the slit in the front of his pants, she had taken it in her mouth and sucked him until he discharged a viscous stream of his spunk into her. As it slid down her throat, she felt it corrupting her being, binding her irremediably to him.

The young physics major had been calm and almost blissful when she finally left the interview room. The demonic man had taken the memory of her enslavement from her mind and filled it instead with the subversive instructions that brought her to where she was now. As she stared at the small, rust colored, copper disk, she realized, dismally, she could not resist the man who wielded it.

When the man had finished displaying the infernal device to the now crying, unhappy women, he ordered them to strip and place their clothes in a plastic bag he held out for them. The women all cast off their clothes obediently. They stood there, naked, fearful and docile, as the man circled their waists with thick leather belts that had handcuffs built in at the hips. He bound their hands to their sides and applied shackles to their ankles connected to a thin, foot long chain. The last touch was a large, spongy ball he thrust into their mouths filling it and forcing their jaws wide apart.

Alison cried as she helplessly followed the other women, shuffling out the back door of the small hut to an enclosed area behind it. It was screened off from view by large, wooden panels. A dark blue minivan was waiting there and they were loaded into it. Once seated, the man who had entranced them placed dark hoods over their heads, shutting out all light and then buckled them into their seats.

The women were driven directly to the dream lab where the Apache staff was ready to receive them. Alison whined with fear as she was led into the building, a rough hand holding her arm tightly. She was third in line and had to wait, standing with the other women in the lobby for a long time, hooded, bound and naked until it was her turn. It was a distinctly feminine hand that took her in tow. She was guided down the long hallway and into the preparation room. Once her hood was removed, Alison trembled to see emblazoned on the wall a large imprint of the demonic design from the disk. It sent a wave of fear through her and reminded her of her servitude to the blond haired, dark eyed man who had enslaved her.

There were three dark skinned, black haired women in the room with her. They sat her down in a large, padded chair and strapped her torso and legs into it. The women were wearing long, white laboratory coats. One looked middle aged and had streaks of grey in her hair. She seemed to be the one in charge. The other two women were younger, in their early twenties. They were gentle but firm with her as they tightened the confining straps.

Alison cried and protested through her filled mouth, her eyes affixed to the dreadful and terrifying design on the wall, as the women proceeded to shave off all of her long, dark brown hair. When they were done, her hairless head smooth as a cue ball, they raised her legs in stirrups attached to the chair and removed all of her pubic growth. The girls then took her from the chair and brought her to a shower where, after removing her confines, they washed and scrubbed her body thoroughly. After drying her off, they attached fur lined bracelets to her ankles and then forced her to her knees. Bracelets were attached to her wrists and her arms were locked behind her, wrist to wrist. A long, black leather sleeve was drawn up her bound arms and fastened tightly around them. Alison struggled and moaned with pain, terrified at what dismal fate the women intended for her, as her arms were bent back to her torso so that her wrists were in the middle of her back. The women were strong and apparently practiced at applying the device and her struggles failed to frustrate them. Straps from the end of the sleeve, which was now just below the back of her neck, were draped over her shoulders, between her breasts, around her back and tied off to its base at the points of her painfully bent elbows. A form fitting leather hood was placed over her head and buckled around her neck. There was an opening in the hood for her mouth and it had tabs over the eyes which could be opened to allow the prisoner sight. For now they remained closed.

The sightless and distraught young woman was placed back in the chair and forced to lean back painfully on her imprisoned arms. Her legs were locked back into the stirrups. When a hand removed the large, rubber ball from her mouth, Alison attempted to take the opportunity to scream and protest at her treatment. But one of the women pressed a hard, leather object into it while strong, female hands held her jaws open. It was a long, thick wad of leather that filled her whole mouth. The gag was designed to be affixed to the hood directly by means of small clips and the businesslike attendants connected it so that the new experimental subject could not spit it out.

The mind of the young physics student from Colgate was filled with despair as she felt her body being strapped more tightly into the chair. Already her treatment had been so bizarre and cruel she could not imagine, did not want to imagine, what the remorseless women would do to her next. She strained at her bonds and clamped her teeth down hard on the long, thick, insulting leather that filled her mouth as she felt her stomach washed with a cooling liquid. She identified its smell as alcohol. There was a strange, irritating buzzing noise and, immediately after, a fierce stinging pain to her lower belly, just above her now hairless mons.

The procedure lasted about a half hour. From the hostile noise of the apparatus and the continuous burning on her skin, Alison realized they were inscribing some kind of tattoo on her. Her mind reeled in sorrow at the desecration of her body. She realized she was being made into some form of weird sex slave and was fearful the women were labeling her body with an obscene appellation appropriate to her new status. When the procedure was finished and she was led, crying and moaning behind her hood and gag a short distance away from the chair, the women opened the eyelets to the hood and Alison saw in the long, wall mounted mirror something far worse than what she had imagined. There, amidst the bright red, irritated skin on her lower belly was inscribed in bright, blue ink, the unmistakable form of the dreaded, fear inspiring insignia. Her knees sagged and had she not been held up by the strong arms of the young, dark skinned women, she would have fallen to the floor.

Alison was allowed to take in her grotesquely hooded form for several moments so her new, abject condition could sink in. The female she saw in the mirror possessed her body, her recognizable, large, round breasts, her long, trim legs, but nothing else was familiar. Harsh, black straps crossed her chest and disappeared behind her back. Her plush, wiry bush was gone and in its stead was a clean, smooth set of fleshy lips with a narrow gash between them. Where her face should have been was an expanse of tight, smooth, black leather. Not even her mouth was discernable, only two little holes by her nose for access to air. The eyelets for her eyes were tiny, barely permitting sight, and she could just make out her pupils in the mirror, wide and full of fear.

The older woman came up to the terrified, shocked woman and presented to her her final adornment. It was a narrow, black leather collar. Dangling from a ring in its front was a small, brass medallion. Etched on it, in black, was the number 722. When the collar was circled around her neck and buckled shut in the back, the older women closed the eyelets to Alison's hood and reconnected the chain between her legs. After they had attached a leash to the front of her collar, they led her disconsolate figure from the room.

Experimental Subject No. 722 had proven to be the most promising in a long time. After a series of test protocols recording her dream patterns and her sexual responses, she had been kept in an almost constant hallucinogenic and lustful state. It had been found through trial and error that sensual deprivation played a significant role in increasing the strength and duration of the dreams of the many test subjects that had passed through the lab, and so 722 was kept constantly hooded and bound, confined in her little, windowless room, except for the purposes of cleaning and maintenance. The shaman, who continued to cooperate in the dream experiments, wove his own terrifying and lust inducing spells around her. Once her potentials had been realized, Jonathan tormented and drove the female to a series of wrenching orgasms at least once a day when he was at the Fortress, filling her mouth or her other, fevered orifices with his radiant, enthralling cock and spilling his seed within her. Using his ability to rewire the synapses of her brain, he manipulated her sexual urges to a constant, excruciating need. At other times, the subject's passions were seen to by the lips and hands of the female Apache lab assistants or the stiff, hard pricks of one or more of the male security staff drafted for that purpose.

Dr. Morton felt they were on the verge of a real breakthrough. Jonathan had been able, for the first time, to follow the tendrils of a subject's nightmares to the edge of the dimensional divide. He was sure of it. Of course, identifying the barriers to this dimension and breaking through them was only part of the problem. There were a virtual infinity of universes out there and this female's lustful, fearful emanations would need to be directed to the right one. It was Dr. Morton's hypothesis that once it had been shown the divide had been pierced, the mind of Blackthorne's familiar could be used to direct No. 722's to the precise place necessary to obtain access to the Whole. Jonathan had ordered the intensity and frequency of the subject's torments of fear and pleasure be increased in the hopes she could be pushed over the top. Morton had, initially, demurred, fearing that, like so many others, 722 would be driven into a deep psychosis as a result. But the renegade dream man had been insistent.

Now, as he watched the bound and naked, hooded female squirm and moan with distress on the broad, comfortable bed from the heavy dose of pain and lust he had implanted in her mind, Jonathan felt something he had not experienced since assuming male, human form five years ago: fear. The pursuer was coming, had arrived at long last, and everything he had worked for and accumulated was now at risk.

Blackthorne was a man of action, not of contemplation, and he immediately set into motion. The arrival of the pursuer was not unexpected and he had not been idle all of these years in preparing his defenses. The good news was the fact that the pursuer's arrival would certainly entail the existence of a familiar. If he could capture her, he would kill, so to speak, two birds with one stone. He would eliminate the threat of the pursuer and he would have another possible route of access to the Whole. Also, if he could convert the pursuer's familiar to his own use, Diane, his current source of the Whole's essence, would be available for the continued experiments Dr. Morton wanted to conduct. Any concern his familiar's ability to draw sustenance for him across the dimensional divide would be compromised by the experiments would be assuaged.

Jonathan was pleased his trap for the pursuer had worked. It was he who ratted out the pimp who had taken ownership of the pretty, brown haired girl, Nadine, his familiar's younger sister. He knew that the abrupt deprivation of her reason for life itself, the master he had bound her to, would drive her into a near psychotic state. He had assumed that the pimp would be imprisoned for many years and had been even more pleased to learn he chose to shoot it out with the police rather than face a long jail sentence. Eventually, the police would trace Nadine's origins and her family would have her hospitalized. He had assumed the pursuer would readily be able to discover the identity of his familiar. After all, how many prominent, single women disappeared every year in the Chicago metropolitan area? Once that identity had been revealed, it was a sure, short line to finding Nadine.

The man who called had been in service to Blackthorne for the three years since Nadine had been a patient in St. Catherine's Psychiatric Hospital in Omaha. He had been corrupted in the usual ways, a financial incentive together with a revolving series of abject, devoted sexual slaves to serve as his mistress. Reggie Johnson, a clerk in the administrative offices, had noted the fact that Nadine had had a visitor. Although he would have discovered it anyway eventually by going over the visitor's log, a task he undertook at least once a week, he had been marooned at the hospital by the same storm that kept Ramon and his PI prisoners at their motel. Having nothing better to do, he went down and checked the log book. He assumed the name used was a false one, which it was, but the mere fact a visitor had come at all was important. He placed his call to the number he had been given, initiating a series of portentous events.

A casual questioning of the attendant who had escorted Nadine to and from her meeting with the stranger had resulted in a rough, but adequate description. Blackthorne had 'donated' a security system to the hospital and Reggie was able to obtain copy of the surveillance tape showing the man coming in and out of the hospital. He emailed a copy of it to the security firm Blackthorne had on retainer in Omaha. The storm had been a lucky thing, delaying the pursuer's departure. All bets were that the pursuer would fly out the next morning. A crew of investigators, armed with an outtake from the video and the verbal description, would be waiting there in the morning for the purpose of identifying him and monitoring the flight he took. Once his destination was known, another crew of agents would be ready to pick him up at that airport and follow him to his base of operations.

Blackthorne ordered Bob to have a crew of his best and most ruthless Apache warriors on standby. Once it was known where the pursuer was going, they would be placed on one of Blackthorne's private jets and flown there to make the snatch of the pursuer's familiar. Of course, no plan was foolproof, the pursuer might manage to give the agents the slip. Or the familiar might be too well protected to make the snatch. But no security the pursuer could devise would be flawless and, if it turned out she could not be captured, she, or the pursuer, could always be killed.

Jonathan walked through the underground connection to his hacienda pensively. His whole person was aflame with the thrill of the chase. This had been what he had been waiting for for years. Nothing had tempered his enjoyment of the experiences of this world and his life as a virtual god in it. His plans for national political power were well underway. Senator Grant, who Jonathan had corrupted many years ago, was well poised for success in the primaries next year. Blackthorne would pour ten million dollars into his campaign and influence many others to contribute vast sums. He imagined himself walking into the White House on inauguration day and setting before the new President his personal agenda. The entire nation would dance to his tune. He would be impregnable, even if the Whole sent agent after agent against him.

The tunnel from the dream lab led directly into his private quarters in the basement of the hacienda. It was here that his familiar resided, protected by heavy steel doors to which he alone had the combination. The series of rooms was equipped with all the amenities of life and the female and his three enthusiastic acolytes could subsist down here for weeks on end should he not be able to return to the Fortress for some reason.

The lock to the outer door was keyed to Jonathan's brain patterns and opened easily when he projected his thoughts to it. Each room in his bunker was separated by its own locked steel door. The 'playroom', as he thought of it, was the second door on the right. It had served as the home of his familiar and his three acolytes for the last four years, ever since it was built. Kept constantly naked, they ate their meals there, slept there and existed in a state of almost perpetual sexual arousal. It was large, about 50' long on each side. The walls were of white plaster covering the cinderblock construction. The only decoration in the room was the large replica of his talisman painted on the wall. There was an entertainment system, to occupy the women between their frequent bouts of sex, exercise machines to help maintain their fitness, showers, a bathroom, everything you could want. Their meals were sent in via a conveyer system from the upstairs kitchen. It was like a twentieth century nuclear fallout shelter, designed to sustain them indefinitely.

Blackthorne unlocked the heavy steel door and entered. As usual, the room was a beehive of sexual activity. His servants Darla and Christine had one of the Apache girls who were delegated to him until the next festival out of her cage and lying on the plush, red rug. They had bound the pretty, dark skinned girl's hands to her sides. Christine had her mouth between the young girl's widespread, naked thighs and was mouthing her to pleasure while Darla straddled her head, using her mouth for her own delight. The Apache girl squirmed and writhed under the onslaught of the two fiercely impassioned women, crying out her unwanted pleasure into

Darla's engorged and distended cunt. Yvonne, his black skinned beauty, had his wife, the still aristocratic looking Dolores, on her knees and bent over on the floor and was fucking her from behind with a large, black dildo which was strapped to the black woman's waist. Dolores, her arms locked behind her, was moaning with enforced pleasure, her ample breasts swaying under her madly as Yvonne gave her frantic strokes with the merciless instrument. Jonathan, pleased by the orgy of lust and enjoying the waves of passion emanating from them, sent his servants a mental command to continue as they were.

His familiar was on the large, plush bed, her hands bound to the headboard above her, her head covered with the deer skin pouch the shaman had given him so many years ago. She had been dosed with peyote milk about two hours ago and she was squirming, naked on the bed, in desperate need and full of the life giving essence she had been drawing from the other side during the course of her hallucinogenic dreams. He would collect it in a short while, but first he wanted to lose some of the anxious energy that had built up in him as a result of the news about the pursuer.

The demonic other worlder strode over to the cages that were stationed along one of the walls. Anxious eyes peered out at him from three of them. The two remaining Apache women who had been loaned to him in the name of their tribe watched him warily as he passed them. To their relief, he had no designs on them for the moment. The last cage contained a pale skinned, naked, black haired woman. She was new, hardly even broken in. She had been part of a shipment of Ukrainian women who had been smuggled into the country ostensively to find work. They had been whisked here to the Fortress upon their arrival. The other six were now on their way to one of the sex clubs run under his authority in Dallas, all properly enraptured and enslaved. They would be dutiful, lustful employees and, after they had learned their new trade, would be shipped out to other clubs around the country. This one, a girl named Ulrika, had caught his fancy. After he had enthralled her, he had brought her here to await his pleasure with instructions no one should touch her until her had had his way with her.

The pretty, blue eyes of the black haired girl looked out at him with fear from between the steel bars of her little prison as he approached. She was thin and pale, with a graceful figure and long legs. Her straight, black hair fell to her shoulders, accentuating the paleness of her lustrous skin. Her face was round and well appointed, with large, luscious lips and an elegant, long, strait nose. She did not yet bear the tattoo which would symbolize his ownership on her flesh. He would have it done in the morning. But she had been educated as to the fearful power of the heavy copper disk and, as he showed it to her now, she cringed and fell back as far as she could go in the tiny enclosure. Blackthorne unlocked the gate to the cage and, sending her a strong psychic message of his will, ordered her out.

The thin, pale girl gave a sob and edged her way out of the steel prison. It had been her prison, but also her refuge. At least while she was inside it she was not being abused. She had watched the three devilish women earlier as they tormented the bound woman on the bed and also the three dark skinned girls, each in their turn. They were insatiable. And now the man who had captured her mind, had destroyed her ability to act and think on her own, had compelled her to leave her tiny sanctuary. She could not fathom the mysterious power he had over her and, concluding that he was some form of devil, had spent her lonely hours in her cage awaiting his return bemoaning her fate and praying for divine deliverance.

Jonathan used a mental command to urge the pretty, young girl to kneel outside of her cage and place her hands behind her head. Her round, coffee cup sized breasts stood up proudly and she trembled as she looked up at him anxiously with her tear filled eyes. He crouched down in front of her and seized the firm, pert mounds, circling his powerful hands around them and sending a strong message of lust to the girl. At the same time, staring back at her terrified eyes, he sent her a message of psychic pain and fear. He could feel the mixed emotions emitted from her confused, agonized mind. It flowed through him like ambrosia.

"I'll never get tired of this," the renegade dimension traveler thought to himself as he drew strength from the girl's effusions of emotion. "Pretty, tender breasts in my hands, a beautiful body to explore. I'll never give this up, never!" Blackthorne had lost count long ago of the number of women he had captured and converted to his will. There were thousands of women all across the Untied States, Canada and Mexico who labored under the mandates of his will, slaves to callous masters. And overseas too. Last year they had sealed a deal with a Korean outfit, three pretty, lithesome Asian girls for each Western one. The ruthless gangsters shipped them over by the containerful and delivered them by truck to the Fortress for enslavement. And it was easy to send the Caucasian girls the other way. A few minutes with him and they would arrange their own passports, even buy their own airline tickets, and deliver themselves to their doom. All it took when they arrived was a glance at the little, copper colored medallion and they would obey their new masters energetically and without question until the day they died.

His own lusts upon him, Blackthorne stood and began to disrobe. The Ukrainian girl whined as she anticipated her ravishment. At the same time, her rigid nipples and the engorgement of her breasts and lips bespoke her rising passion.

Once naked, Jonathan ordered her to her hands and knees

and took up a position kneeling next to her. With one hand he fondled her downward pointing breasts while he roamed her long, sensuous back with the other. Her skin was soft and smooth. He ran his hand over her taut, pale rear globes and over the back of her thighs, transmitting waves of lust to her. When he pushed her graceful thighs apart and he captured her still hairy mons with his hand, she moaned.

The passionate sighs and moans of the other women in the room served as a background to the renegade's excitement of the new girl's lust. Her pussy was wet and soft as he stroked it, and the unmistakable aroma of her arousal floated up to him. His cock was hardened and distended and he pressed it up against the distressed woman's thigh as he drove her passion higher and higher. The girl could not help herself as she pushed her heated pussy back against his hand, grinding her svelte hips, crying out her need.

Blackthorne maneuvered himself behind the girl. The tiny brown star between her rear cheeks peeked up at him invitingly. He took a swipe of her pungent moisture from between her dilated pussy's lips and applied it there, pressing his fingers inside it, spreading the tight ring of flesh in preparation to receive his hard, thick cock. He could feel the girl's misery as she realized how she was to be used. It was amusing to him how almost all of the newly enthralled females revolted at the piercing of their small, round rear hole. To him, it was perfectly natural a man would want to take pleasure in the tight opening. It was an act that permeated all of recorded history and was probably the second thing the first man had done after he had discovered the pleasures of fucking.

Having lubricated the entrance, Blackthorne compelled the frightened but impassioned young woman to loosen her rear muscles in anticipation of his penetration. He could feel her torrent of shame as he addressed the head of his thick prick to the hole. He left it there while he increased the frail woman's lusts with his hands, rubbing them over her rear globes. He wanted the girl to impale herself, to accomplish her own degradation.

The distressed woman felt the surge of need the man sent through her body. Its intensity was beyond anything she had ever experienced. Suddenly, her mind could focus on nothing else but her desire to have the man fill her there, to feel the rasping of his cock across the sensitive ring of flesh, to experience the filling of her bowel with his cock. She pushed her rear back slowly, moaning as the large wand of flesh stretched and tore the tender tissues. She gasped as it inched further and further within her. Her eyes were clamped shut, her delicate, bony hands clasped into tiny, little fists. Her heart beat wildly and her breasts ached with the blood engorging them. When she felt the front of the man's thighs against her pale, round rear cheeks, her mind filled with joy.

Once the woman had encased him fully in her bowels, Jonathan began a slow, steady, rhythmic stroke across the enflamed membranes of her anal ring. She cried out at each thrust, her thin, reedy voice filling the room. Her body was awash with the sweat of her lust and her hips welcomed each stroke of his cock. Her pussy tingled and burned. All reticence at this deviant form of intercourse had left her. Her passion built higher and higher towards an inevitable climax.

Jonathan reveled in the feel of the tight ring circling his cock and the hot, murky warmth of her interior. He could feel his fluids rising, electrified signals of pleasure shooting through his body. The woman's lusts flowed from her like a cloud escaping her body and he drank them in, thrilling at their sweet taste. As he felt his lusts cresting, he reached down and took hold of the moaning woman's hair, pulling her head back. He commanded her to open her eyes. There, on the wall in front of her, was the harsh, cruel emblem of her subservience. She cried out with pain and fear as she beheld it.

At that moment, just as her new lord's cock began to pulse and throb within her, her own lusts crested, pushed over the top by the demonic mind that held her in thrall. "Ohhhhhhhhh! Ohhhhhhhhh!" she moaned with pleasure and despair. "Ohhhhhhhhhhhh!" Jonathan filled her ecstatic and terror filled mind with a vision of her dark future, the endless procession of cocks that would fill her, her slavery to her lusts. As his seed was absorbed by her inner pores, she felt its corruption, the permanency of her indenture to the evil symbol that filled her view. "Ahhhhhhhooooooooh! Auughhhhhhhhh! Auughhhhhhhhhh!" she cried out in pleasure and despair.

Jonathan felt a wave of relief and pleasure flow through him. His tenseness and anxiety had left him, replaced by the satisfying absorption of the woman's emissions of terror and unhappiness. It took him a few moments to recover his sensibilities, and when he returned to awareness, he sensed his beautiful, lust filled, black skinned acolyte kneeling at his side expectantly. She had finished, for the moment, with the exhausted, still moaning Dolores, who she had left still kneeling and crouched over, behind her. The shiny, discharge covered black instrument jutted fiercely from Yvonne's loins. Jonathan eased his still hard cock from the distraught, pale skinned women's rear and stroked her flush pussy with his hand, reigniting her lusts for the pleasure and amusement of his favorite acolyte. The thin, elegant, black skinned woman pushed the other woman to her side and then turned her to her back, spreading her thighs. She pushed the head of the black dildo between the young girl's widened pussy lips and entered her, causing her to sigh deeply. Leaning over, Yvonne pressed their breasts together and taking the other woman's lips with hers, began a steady, languorous stroke with her hips. The other woman, filled with Blackthorne's induced need, reached her arms around her and drew her body in.

Still infused with his own lust, Jonathan turned his attentions to his familiar on the bed. He went to the washstand and cleaned himself thoroughly and then stepped over to her. He could sense her desire for him. She was filled with the essence of the Whole, having drawn it into her as her mind whirled in psychedelic dreams. He would drain her now, feed of the life's blood she had accumulated for him.

Diane had sensed the arrival of her lord and master when he entered the room some time ago. After five years, her mind was exquisitely attuned to his psyche and could feel his emanations of dark, brooding lust. Her body yearned to be filled by him and her lust had been primed and accelerated as she received his waves of passion while he copulated with the other woman. Her thighs were spread with her need and her hands twisted and turned in her bonds to gain access to her yearning slit. She sensed him as he approached her and she presented her loins to him lasciviously.

Diane had no idea how long she had been enthralled to the loathsome, evil man. Time had seemed to stand still ever since she had been brought to this place. She had no yardstick to measure the passage of the days, months or years. She knew it had been a long time. And yet she felt like she was in some kind of suspended animation, had entered a weird, sensual Twilight Zone. Her body never tired of its stimulation, even as her mind screamed for its surcease. Every time he entered her, be it her loins, her rear or her mouth, it felt as feverishly pleasurable as the first. Her prior life was a far distant memory, its details misted in fog. Her bouts of sanity were few and far between, and in those rare moments, she would cry and mourn her loss.

Blackthorne saw and felt the turmoil of his familiar. Her resiliency was a happy surprise to him. This race was sturdy and held on to life dearly. He had not rued his choice to remain as one of them for a single moment. He would stay forever if he could.

The renegade dream man knelt on the bed and approached the franticly lustful woman. He captured her writhing legs and caressed the inside of her thighs, fueling her passions to an even higher level. His ears heard her anguished moans and his mind received her mental turmoil. His hands relished her softness and heat. He made a note to increase her exercise regimen, to keep her body better toned.

The captured female's bodily state was carefully monitored, her weight, her blood sugar levels, the rhythm of her heart, everything that could be measured. She was still his only access to continued life and he spared no expense in maintaining her health. She was his strength and his weakness. He had come to despise her, in spite of his need for her. He detested being bound to her, needing her. He tormented her frequently, bringing her mind and body acute pain. He had created this subterranean hell for her to live in, ordered his acolytes to drive her mad with desire, denied her all human warmth. And yet, here she was, opening her pussy to him, begging him to fulfill her slavish needs.

Blackthorne tantalizingly ran his cock along the length of the woman's hairless, dilated slit. He could feel her lusts billowing from her body. She was suffused with the essence of the Whole and he felt drawn to her in spite of his contempt. When he sank his cock into her womb, the vital, psychic substance from the other dimension began to soak into him.

The clinging, hot warmth of the woman's canal sent the renegade into a state of ecstasy. He lost all mental control and fervently began to pump his cock back and forth in the steamy sex. He tore the hood from her head and seized her mouth, thrusting his tongue deeply inside it. She came almost at once, her back arching beneath him, her hips grinding against his. He drank the ethereal substance from her body and could feel his strength being restored.

It did not take long for his own climax to come. He groaned loudly as his cock began to spurt and spasm within her. She came again, her moans and cries reverberating in his mouth. The essence she had gathered flowed to him in a torrent as his mind reveled in his pleasure. He pounded his strong, broad hips into her, causing the whole bed to shake. As his lusts overflowed, his passions spread throughout the room, evoking a cacophony of moans and cries from the other females as their bodies responded with wrenching orgasms of their own. It was his satanic orchestra. Bereft of their souls, which he had stolen, the women's bodies writhed and shook as if overcome by a contagious epileptic fit.

And then it was over. The task of delivering the otherworldly essence to him had exhausted his familiar and she lay beneath him limp and unconscious. His acolytes and the other women emitted soft, languid moans as their bodies reverberated with the aftershocks of their climaxes. He rose from the bed, sated, momentarily.

Blackthorne left his sexual menagerie behind and exited the catacomb like warren beneath his hacienda. The stairs from the basement led into the library on the first floor. He had not bothered to redon his garments. They were confining on his body and he didn't want to disturb the fine sensations of satisfied lust reverberating in every pore.

It was late and the well pleasured renegade did not linger in the well appointed room. He stepped out into the grand entrance hallway and proceeded up the broad, polished oaken staircase leading to the second floor. The house was quiet and dark, the lights having been turned low by his servants. Embonded, naked females stood like silent sentries in various alcoves along the way. As he passed them, they fell to their knees and bowed their heads to the ground fearfully. He had no interest in them tonight. He could read the sense of relief filling them as he spared them from his terrible usage.

His bedroom suite was at the end of the second floor. He opened one of the heavy, wooden double doors and entered it. The sound of a piano echoed through the connected rooms. A lovely, enraptured female sat at the keys to a large, shiny black grand piano. She was wearing a diaphanous, white, silken chemise and her long, brown hair was done in a braid down her back. The light in the room was dim, giving her lithe body a warm, sensual appearance. He approached the woman quietly, not wanting to disturb the graceful, elegantly rendered notes of the Chopin Prelude she was playing.

"She must have sensed me coming," he thought. "She looks lovely tonight."

There was an easy chair located about ten feet from where the young woman played and Jonathan slid into it. A small table next to it held a small snifter of 50 year old cognac, the corked bottle standing next to it in the event he wanted a refill. The Lord of Conquerors sat back in the chair and, taking a small sip from the rich, oaken flavored liquid, closed his eyes and let the comforting notes surround him.

There had been, in the many years since he had been in this dimension, only one female who had enraptured him. She had grown on him slowly after her capture. Her soul had proven so sweet, so fragile, he had decided to preserve it. Cathy, the stepdaughter of his gold digging wife, had proven to have charm and grace and a deep sensuality. He had found himself returning to her use again and again. He had removed the harsh, damning control he had emplaced in her mind and replaced it with a tender, fulfilling love for him. She was like a mate to him, someone he could relax his eternal vigilance with, a flower he nurtured in the midst of his almost universal callousness. If only he could draw his essence through her, he often thought. It would be like a communion of souls. But he refused to have her placed in the insensitive hands of Dr.

Morton for his cruel experimentation. Her delicate psyche was something, the one thing, he never wanted to lose.

He had developed a strong bond with the young woman, now five years older than when he first captured her. It was she who had poured his cognac, knowing he would want it, detecting his approach from far away. When she was finished with the melodious, harmonic piece, Blackthorne opened his eyes and looked at her. She turned from her music momentarily and gave him a warm, affectionate smile, happy to serve him. "Another," he said to her softly. "Play another, the one I like."

Happy to please him, Cathy softly and delicately commenced the Prelude in F Sharp minor, No.8. Her hands floated above the keyboard and her body swayed gently as the notes rose fluidly around her. Jonathan took another drink from his glass, letting the fiery warmth infuse him with peace and tranquility. For this alone he would fight the pursuer with the last breath in his body. His trap for the Whole's agent had worked so far. Tomorrow, he would know better if it would bring the opportunity for victory. He would kill the man if he had to. Jonathan had cast aside almost all of the ethics of the Whole in becoming who he was now. He had little sympathy for the lesser creatures that populated this world. They were like ants under his feet. But to take the existence of a portion of the Whole and snuff it out, that was something else. It was a taboo so engrained in him that doing it was almost unthinkable. But he had thought about it many times. He would lose what was left of his soul, but he would do it if he had to, even if only to preserve this little island of peace.

He had done everything he could to maintain the happiness of the pleasing woman. The chambers where she spent almost all of her time were bedecked in resplendent flowers all around them. He had molded her mind to be content here and had detailed the prettiest and most compliant of the young Apache girls who worked for him to serve her. He had even captured a well known concert pianist to act as her teacher and companion. If she ever became lost to him, he had sworn to rain destruction down on this world Armageddon style. And he could do it too. He had already produced designs for a weapon that would extinguish, in a fiery blaze, almost all of the oxygen on the planet.

Jonathan put these thoughts from his mind as the soothing, delightful piano piece came to an end. He sent the woman a strong message of his affection and need for her. She shuddered as she received it, smiling broadly at him. With easy grace, she rose from her piano bench and stepped over to him, drawing her garment over her head and dropping it to the floor. She sank to her knees before him and spread her long, delicate hands over his thighs.

"How may I serve you, Lord?" she asked, her voice tender and sweet, her soft, round breasts quivering.

"Pleasure me with your mouth," Jonathan answered quietly.

The young woman, her face alight with devotion to him, smiled again and pressed herself forward to gain access to his long, thick cock. It was soft and resting neatly between his thighs. She ran her fingers over it lightly, coaxing a response, until it began to stir. Taking it into her sensitive hands, she brought it to her soft, pliant lips and applied the warmth of her mouth and tongue to its tip. Jonathan moaned as he received her loving attention. He felt it grow thick and hard in response to her attentions and his lust grew.

Cathy, his songbird in a gilded cage, took her time in bringing pleasure to her master. She suckled the bulbous head, running her tongue along the glans, one hand softly stroking the shaft while the other cupped and gently massaged his soft stones. Pressing her head downwards and pursing her lips firmly around his cock's stem, the enthralled woman pushed down its length until he was fully engulfed, breaching the entrance to her throat and holding it there, humming softly. Jonathan's cock radiated his passion back to her as he caressed her head, sending his approval and gratitude to her.

The alluring young woman brought her master and lord to the edge of completion several times. Each time he threatened to peak, she withdrew her mouth until his need had subsided and then began again. Blackthorne's thighs were quivering with lustful need, his brain begging for relief when she finally allowed him to come. His cock exploded in a heavy flow of his essence and sent hard, intense messages of pleasure to his body at each ejaculation. His hands sent the object of his desires a strong command of rewarding passion and the beautiful, young woman's shuddering body recorded each convulsion of her pussy.

When his flow of essence had ceased, the devoted servant continued to stroke his cock with her lips, maintaining its hardness. Jonathan eased her head away from his loins and, standing, guided her to her feet. He circled her small, frail body with his arms, pressing their naked bodies together, and kissed her deeply, letting the fire that still smoldered within him stoke hers. When their lips broke, he separated from her, taking her hand in his. "Let's go to the bedroom," he told her gently.

CHAPTER EIGHT

Ramon woke in the morning with the two delightful, young women's bodies pressed up against him. Jackie had eventually been awakened by Abby's cries of passion and had joined them in the other bed. His body had been rejuvenated by their almost all night bouts of passion, but he sensed the weakening of his powers from lack of access to the essence of the Whole. He needed to get back to Virginia as soon as possible.

Careful not to disturb the women, Ramon stepped into the bathroom and started the shower. It was a little after 5:30 a.m. and the plane was at 8:30. The motel was only a quarter mile from the airport and he was certain he could make it in time.

The flow of the hot water over his body was refreshing and, as he washed himself, the dream man thought forwards to the time when his mission would be complete. If he failed, it would be likely he would have lost his life force and exist no more. It was one of the risks he had assumed in accepting the challenge of neutralizing the renegade. But what would happen if he succeeded? The temptations of this world were great. Just the sensation of the hot water exciting his skin was something he would sorely miss. And the emotional thrill he felt when he bonded with his familiar, the pretty, auburn haired woman he had enthralled, what would ever replace that?

He wondered what the circle of females he had captivated into his service would feel when he was gone. Would they curse him for having used them, stolen their will from them, used their bodies as receptacles for his lust? Or would they decry their loss, the absence of the joyful sense of purpose he had given them?

He knew that, in spite of his use of them, he had done

them some good. Certainly Cindy and Natalie had nothing to complain about. He had freed them from a perverse bondage. Chandra had also been liberated from the constricting influence of her family and was now on the road to becoming her own person, the mistress of her own life. Adele had gone from the somewhat frivolous life she had lived to one of dedication and purpose. She would never be the same. All in all, he believed, the women would live happier, more complete lives as a result of his interventions. But he would miss them.

When Ramón emerged from his shower, the two women, the hard edged, brown haired investigator and the sweet, somewhat naïve, blond haired nursing student, were locked in a passionate embrace. Jackie was on top and she was devouring the blond girl's passionate mouth with her own as she pressed and rubbed her pussy between Abby's widespread thighs. The blond girl's arms were circled around Jackie's body, embracing her tightly. The dream man felt his cock awakening at the lustful sight. He knew that if he joined them there was a chance he would miss his plane.

When the lustful bodies finally came to rest, only after loud, passionate cries of pleasure from them both, the women's gazes turned to him. He was stroking his hardened cock idly, sitting on the bed across from them. He sent them a regretful refusal of their nonverbal proffer of pleasure and urged them to their showers. They scurried into the bathroom holding hands.

While the women were showering, there was a knock on the door. Ramon had ordered breakfast from room service. He had donned his jeans and t-shirt and walked barefoot to the door. A pretty, brown haired girl was standing there with a cart next to her. She looked about 19, and was wearing the same pink and white, gingham uniform Abby had been wearing the night before. She had long, shiny hair tied into a ponytail behind her that went almost all the way down her back. She had bright, brown eyes and a long, pleasant face. Before Ramón could say anything, she had pushed the cart into the room.

While Ramón signed the check, he could see the girl eying the pile of women's clothes in the middle of the room. On top was Abby's waitress uniform. Near them, cast about as if discarded in the middle of a strip tease, were Jackie's jeans, blouse and underwear. The young woman looked up at the Hispanic man with interest. He was a few inches taller than her and his t-shirt accentuated his strong chest and masculine build. His shoulder length, black hair was still shiny and wet from his shower. Ramon remembered what Adele had said when he had first adorned himself with human clothing, that there would be a line of women at their door once they caught sight of him. His strong, inner psyche leaked lustful emanations almost all the time. This girl had caught a whiff of them.

"My name's Karen," the attractive brunette said. "I get off at 1 o'clock."

"That's nice. Karen," Ramón answered. "But I have to catch a plane."

"Oh," the girl said, disappointment evident in her voice. And then her face brightened. "But I'm due my break now. I could stay a little while and...." Her proposal was interrupted by the sight of Jackie and Abby emerging from the bathroom, their naked bodies flushed pink from their shower, long, fluffy towels in their hands. "Oh," she said.

The two naked women giggled at the sight of the enamored brown haired waitress. "Hiya, Karen," Abby said.

"Hi, Abby," Karen replied forlornly. She looked back at Ramón desperately. "Why do I always miss out on everything?" her face conveyed.

Ramon saw Jackie lean over and whisper something in

Abby's ear. Abby giggled and nodded affirmatively. The women dropped their towels and skipped merrily over to the disappointed and somewhat dazed girl. Before Ramon knew what was happening, Abby had guided the brown haired girl to her knees and Jackie had knelt down next to him and had lowered his fly. Her experienced hand captured his flaccid tool and wormed it out of the slit in his underwear.

"Would you like to suck Ramón's prick," Abby asked her friend gaily. "It's really nice."

Karen didn't answer, but edged herself closer to Ramón and took the proffered dick in her hand. In a trice, she had engulfed it with her lips and began to work it assiduously.

Ramon stood in the middle of the room as the girl pleasured him. His mind swooned as she drove her lips down its length and retreated, teasing it with her active tongue. Jackie and Abby had taken positions to either side of her and Abby was caressing her breasts through the bodice of her uniform while Jackie reached below the skirt and was stroking her sex from behind. The girl moaned and squirmed as Ramón's cock sent wave after wave of lust to her. When he came, she cried out, her own climax coursing through her. She made sure she had drained him completely before she brought her head back and released him.

"Oh my god!" she exclaimed. "That was incredible!"

Jackie and Abby laughed and hugged her in response. "We've got to get dressed, sweetie," Jackie told her in her nasal Chicago twang. "Thanks for the room service," she added, laughing.

Karen rose to her feet and, stepping on her tippy toes, reached her face up and kissed Ramon on the lips. "I don't know who you are," she said happily. "But I hope you stay here again next time you come to Omaha."

Everyone laughed as the brown haired girl reluctantly left the room. "Call me," she yelled out to Abby as she closed the door.

Ramon and the two women finished dressing and then devoured quickly the muffins and coffee Ramon had ordered. "You better leave Karen a big tip," Abby said, smiling. This brought another round of mirth.

Before he departed with Jackie for the airport, Ramón embraced the delightful blond waitress and kissed her. While doing so, he adjusted her mind to give her more self confidence and an appreciation of her inner and outer beauty. He slowed slightly her craving for sweets, not to make her an emaciated, weight obsessed model type, but just to help her keep her tendency to heaviness under control. And he convinced her to dump that asshole, Ben.

The airport was crowded with other stranded passengers from the day before. Jackie's flight to Chicago was on the other side of the airport. Outside Ramón's gate, she hugged and kissed him.

"Like the girl said, I don't know who you really are, but if you're ever in Chicago again, look me up," she told him. As she spoke, she caressed his cock through the outside of his pants.

Ramon replied affirmatively and after they parted, he walked up to the metal detector and stepped through it. Finally, he was on his way home.

A short, dark haired man, about 35 years old and dressed in a cheap, off the rack, brown suit followed Ramón through the gate. He flashed a badge at the attendants who waived him through. He followed Ramón down the long hallway until he arrived at the loading area for his flight. He watched as the tall, well built, black haired man boarded. He opened his cell phone and punched the speed dial. "Flight 227 to Dulles," he said. "Arrives at 11:25."

* * * * * * * * * * * * *

The three days of separation from her dream man had been a torment for Kelly. All of the women he had enthralled took turns in comforting her and the potion Ramon had concocted was some relief. Nevertheless, it was only the presence and the flesh of her captor that would satisfy her burning need

After her initiation ceremony in the bedroom at her lab, Kelly's life had descended into a state of virtually continuous mesmerized enthrallment to the man and his will. She never again thought of refusing the dream bringing drink Adele administered to her every afternoon at the lab. While entranced under its influence, she felt herself filling with the mists she had heretofore gathered for her lord-like master only in her dreams at night. Now, every afternoon around three o'clock, he would come to the bedroom and drain her of what she had accumulated for him, leaving her exhausted and limp.

Every morning now, Kelly would spend at most an hour at her desk in the lab signing papers or making obligatory phone calls only she could make. Afterwards, Cindy and Natalie would gather her up and escort her to the bedroom. They would deprive her of her meager clothing and bind her to the bed. Stripping themselves naked, they would join her and jointly bring her to ecstasy.

When not entranced by the drug administered by Adele, Kelly spent her time in the room in a haze of sexual need. The other entranced women would take turns spending time with her, teasing her to wrenching orgasms or just cuddling with her, stroking her body languidly or suckling at her breasts. Ramon insisted she get some exercise to keep her healthy and every day, before she was fed her potion, Natalie and Cindy would lead her on a long walk in the wooded area behind the factory building. There was a large pond there circled by a well worn path and the girls would coax her along it, her arms confined before her and covered by the sleeves of her heavy, winter jacket. The area was surrounded by a tall, barbed wire topped fence and Hardings made sure the three women were constantly monitored by the security system inside the building when they were out there.

To Kelly's surprise, Ramón had given her a gift the morning she had performed lustfully for the other enthralled women. When she had come, her lord's cock throbbing and pulsing in her mouth, all the women had been holding hands, with Ramón at the center. She had felt the psyche of each one of them as they came too. Now, as they made love to her, or she to them, she could sense their inner beings, see into their minds. While she occasionally still fretted over her conversion into a paragon of lust, the fact that she could feel the caring and affection of the women who worshiped her brought a stream of joy to her. Whether abed with Melissa or Felicity, Chandra or Lucy, even the somewhat taciturn, Asian-American engineer, Nancy Lee, she could feel their love flowing through her. Each woman's psyche had its own taste, pleasing, like toasted almonds or butterscotch.

One morning, Kelly had been surprised to see her mother and sister come walking in the door of the handsomely decorated bedroom. She had been permitted short, disjointed telephone conversations with her mother about once every week. Kelly had begged off coming home for the holidays citing the demands of work. Naturally, her mother had detected something was wrong and, strong headed as she was, had determined to fly down without telling her to get to the bottom of it. To everyone's consternation, she and Kelly's younger sister, Terry, had burst in to the lab one morning unannounced and demanding to see her. Ramón had been on the other side of the building meeting with Hardings about some designs and Adele had taken charge, calming the women until he could return. They were sitting in Kelly's office impatiently when he came back. It took only a moment to convert them.

Kelly was lying on the bed naked and swooning after a passionate half hour of making love to Cindy and Natalie when the women, led by Ramón, came in. Her hands were affixed to the head of the bed. It took her a few moments to realize who they were and, when she did, a wave of shame passed through her. She whined into her gag and tried to crunch her body into a little ball to cover her nakedness. Ramon came to her side and stroked and petted her until she calmed. Her mother and sister held her in their arms for a long while, assuring her of their understanding of what had happened to her and their approval. Nothing was more important than serving the dream man.

While Kelly was relieved the dream man did not force her to make love to her own sister and mother, when they left she experienced a wave of unhappiness nonetheless. How easily the man had overcome their wills and made them accept was what, on the face of it, appalling. She was, essentially, the man's sex slave and Terry and her mother had done nothing to help her. She cried disconsolately for a long time until Ramón came back to comfort her. He kissed her and caressed her while sending messages of care and affection to her. It did not take long for Kelly to rediscover her commitment to the other worlder's purposes, whatever they were, and understand that everything that was being done was necessary and important. It was better her mother have an understanding and acceptance of her role as the fulcrum of the dream man's existence than have her worrying about her fate. And as to her nakedness and sexual submission, there was nothing to be ashamed of. She was a special, sacred vessel and was ennobled by her service to the man.

Once Kelly had calmed, Ramón made long, languorous love to her. As he slid his lust giving cock into her moist, welcoming womb, Kelly's mind screamed with joy. When he discharged his essence inside her, her whole being glowed with its soothing, mesmerizing effects.

Kelly was at the lab in the bedroom when Ramón got back from his trip. She felt his presence immediately, even before he had opened the door. Her body was bursting with the energy she had accumulated for him and she had been writhing and twisting on the bed frantically for many hours. Adele had decided to keep her here rather than transport her in her frantic state back and forth to the farmhouse. Last night, about one in the morning, she had given her a shot of Demoral to grant her some surcease from her agony. She had slept for several hours dreamlessly. But when she awoke at about 6 o'clock this morning, she declined to give her another one, knowing Ramón would be back soon. She had given Kelly another draught of Ramón's potion and since then had held and soothed her piteous friend, her heart breaking at her suffering.

When Ramon saw the sight of the agony of his familiar, he almost broke into tears. He stripped quickly and climbed up on the bed. He caressed her twisting, shuddering body with his comfort giving hands. He could feel her mind pleading with him for relief as he lay himself on top of her. Her sex was wet and expectant and he entered her easily. Their mouths conjoined in a fevered, passionate kiss. Adele had freed her hands and she grasped at his body with relief and desperation as she circled his thighs with her legs and pressed him deeply inside her.

Kelly's mind exploded with happiness as he she felt the man's cock take possession of her hungry cleft. She sucked at his hot tongue eagerly. Almost instantly, she felt the flow of the mists that had filled her to bursting begin to release to him. She came at once, screaming and moaning into his mouth, slapping her hips hard against his, embracing him with all of her might. When he came, her pussy massaged his cock with her intense contractions of pleasure. His seed seeped into her, soothing her, assuaging her need.

After the dream man's second explosion of lust inside her, the two lay quietly in each others arms. Kelly soon drifted off, the exertion of transmitting the essence of the Whole to her captor having drained her of energy. When she awoke an hour later, she was still in his arms. They made love again languidly.

The rest of the afternoon, the other women came to Kelly, one by one, to express their happiness of her release from her ordeal. Adele withheld the administration of her daily potion until everyone had a chance to spend some time with her. Poor, little Chandra was so upset at what she had gone through that Kelly made her lie down on the bed and, holding her hands above her head, kissed her mouth and breasts while stroking the brown skinned girl to orgasm with her free hand. Chandra, her legs splayed widely, shuddered and moaned as her climax ran through her. Afterwards, she hugged and kissed Kelly tearfully.

Ramón had gone back to work almost immediately. The equipment he would need in combating the renegade was ready. Hardings had fulfilled his word and given him every assistance he could. He used his connections to obtain vital raw materials and helped manufacture the tools and materials Ramón needed.

One thing Ramón had needed was more power. He required tremendous energy to fuse the specially fabricated substances together. He had designed what was essentially a small fusion reactor and a source of enriched uranium was essential for its completion. They say money can buy anything, but this was one exception. Enriched uranium was probably the tightest controlled substance on earth. Ramón needed only a few grains and the private eye Hardings had used to track Natalie quickly found a prospective source of the substance.

Commander Desiré Watkins had worked at the Newport Naval Yard for fifteen years. A graduate of Annapolis's nuclear engineering program, her current duties were supervising the crew servicing the nuclear fueled destroyers that came into the base for refitting and maintenance. She was a loner and lived by herself in a condo overlooking the confluence of the James River with the bay. At night, she could watch from her veranda the naval vessels pulling in and out of the base, heading home or out to the open sea. Years ago, one would have said she was 'married' to her career. But, it was just that she had no affinity for men. Because of her high security clearance and her career in the Navy, she had never explored the other possibility for sexual fulfillment. "Don't ask, don't tell," was official military policy, but she knew better. She would be out of the nuclear program on her ear in a New York minute if there was even the suggestion she was swinging lefty.

Hardings' PI was a resourceful man, a veteran of the Navy himself. He was unquestionably loyal to Hardings, whom he had known for 45 years. All Hardings had to tell him was that he couldn't tell him why he needed the uranium and that he had to trust him, for him to trust him.

In a democratic society, scads of information which would be considered secret by a more closed system are available to those who know where to find it. Roger Billingsly, Hardings' PI, consulted the navy lists and the newsletter put out by the base to announce promotions and job assignments. Billingsly scoured them for an appropriate candidate. He was told to look for a female who might have access to nuclear materials. He knew he struck gold when he saw Commander Desiré Watkins' name next to her job function. To make things even easier, the December 1999 edition of the Newport Navy News, as the journal called itself, had a picture of her in her dress whites as she received a meritorious service award.

Desiré was what is sometimes politely called a handsome woman. Her features were plain and neat. Her calf length dress skirt showed off thick shins and her hips were a mite broad. Her expression was all business and Billingsly thought to himself that she would be a hard nut to crack. He wondered whether he would be spending his prospective retirement in federal prison.

Making contact with the Commander was not easy. She did most of her shopping at the PX and usually drove directly from the base to her condo. She had no social life Billingsly could detect. Their chance came when he saw the base was conducting an 'open house' for the public as part of its public relations efforts.

Ramon was nervous about going on the military installation. He had obtained false i.d.'s, but didn't know how well they would stand up to close scrutiny. He had a limited ability to influence males and he would probably be able to distract whoever was examining identification at the gate from taking a close look at them. They were all valid on their face, a driver's license, even a passport. But if for some reason he got picked up by security and they took the time to check him out, there might be a problem. The fact was that Ramón Vasquez was a common enough name, but he himself had no real pedigree. His social security number was real but had no history. He had no school records, no health history and a birth certificate for a birth that never occurred.

Nonetheless, he took his chance as the need for the nuclear material was acute. It helped that Billingsly had his old military card to show the M.P.'s and was given a welcome greeting as a returning vet. Since Ramón was with him, he benefited from the good will.

Commander Watkins' assignment that day was to give a limited guided tour on one of the nuclear destroyers.

Billingsly spotted her first. She was on the forward deck, directing a group of tourists around the six inch guns. Billingsly introduced himself as a former navy man and, in turn, introduced his friend, Ramón. When Commander Watkins shook his hand, a light seemed to go on in her eyes. The contact between the flesh of their hands lasted about thirty seconds with the woman's eyes glued to Ramón's. When she finally let go, she cleared her throat and asked the tourists if they would excuse her for a few minutes while she showed the new visitors where the head was below decks. Dressed in her crisp, dress blue uniform, her heavy, black low heeled shoes, and her blue and white officer's cap with her short, curly brown hair peaking out, the Commander led the two men into the body of the ship. Once inside, they followed her down a steep ladder to below decks and then halfway down a narrow passageway.

Commander Watkins turned to Billingsly and politely but firmly asked him to, "Please remain here, sir," and then, taking Ramón's hand, guided him down the passageway and into a cabin. The door slid shut behind them.

A minute or so later, Billingsly could hear the distinct sounds of a woman in passion. Muffled by the closed door, he could still make out her shouts of, "Oh, god! Oh yeah! Oh! Oh! Oh!" It lasted about three minutes and then there was silence. After a few minutes more, the door slid open and a flushed Navy Commander, her cap askew, stepped out with a satisfied looking Ramón behind her. Watkins led them back to the stairs and, before guiding them back up, grabbed Ramón and gave him a long, sensuous kiss. She straightened her cap and smoothed her skirt before they went back out on deck, shaking hands with them both politely as they stepped back onto the dock.

Ramón knew he would not be able to direct the woman to the necessary task by means of a quickie in the officer's ward room. When she had closed the door, the prim, 37 year old officer had proceeded to immediately kick off her shiny, black uniform shoes and then pull her regulation pantyhose down to her ankles and off of her feet. Her simple, white cotton panties had been next. Ramon had lifted her up onto the ward room table and pulled his hardened cock from his pants. He pushed her blue uniform skirt up around her waist and, spreading her thighs, placed his cock at the portal to her moss covered slit.

Commander Watkins was no virgin. She had tried male/female sex once on leave from the Academy. But her cleft had not been penetrated for many years and Ramón took his time in easing his cock into the lubricated space. Once he had probed it to its depths, and the engorged flesh had become loose and pliant, he began to roger her with gusto. The woman began to call out almost immediately and continued to shout out exclamations of passion until he sprayed her womb with his discharge. She gripped him tightly as she came, clutching his arms and burying her face in his shoulder to muffle her screams. When they were done and the woman lay against him, sated and relaxed, he gave her directions to meet him later at a motel some 30 miles inland down Route 67.

It took a long time to fully convert the naval officer. It was a delicate procedure to convince her to commit what was essentially treason, certainly an act that could end her career, if not land her in Portsmouth Naval Prison for twenty years. And she was, as befitted her military status, extremely committed to the service and a devoted patriot. Ramon spent a good three hours with her at the motel, filling her with his seed several times and rewiring her brain before instilling his command into her. Naked and on her knees, his cock in her mouth, he compelled her into his service. Two weeks later, at the same motel, she delivered 2 milligrams of fissionable material to him in a small, leaded box. He brought her to pleasure four times as a reward. Before she left, he insured that the memories of their copulation and the task she had performed for him would fade in her mind over the next couple of days, leaving a renewed residual curiosity about male/female sexual relations.

The afternoon of his return from his trip to Omaha, Ramon took the time to recheck the functioning of the weapons he had developed for dealing with the renegade. The six inch long filament with a series of three inch long, flexible, extending arms had been forged in the kiln he had built, powered by the small fusion reactor he had created. The metals, a combination of platinum, silver and aluminum, had been treated and coated with the special chemical formulas he had refined. Hardings' access to several top secret military processes and substances had been crucial. The other piece of his unlikely looking weaponry was a simple, marble sized, ceramic ball. It was made from a combination of crystals Ramón had the girls in the lab grow from organic materials and the coating used on the B-1 bomber developed to reduce the electronic signature of the plane. It had taken several attempts to get the right combinations, and it too, had been processed in the nuclear kiln. Its weight and size disguised its mass, a compression of substances 100 times that found naturally on earth. Ramon had developed a process to remove the gravitational properties of the substances so the ball, which should have weighed about 75 pounds, came in at only a little more than an ounce.

Since the hunt for the renegade had begun in earnest, Ramon would now carry his weaponry with him at all times. He put the marble in his pants pocket, and slid the filament into a slim pocket he had had sewn into the waistband of his pants.

Kelly had been dosed with her special dream formula late

in the afternoon. It was now after 6 P.M. and the dream man was ready to call it a day. He had told Adele he wanted to be alone with his familiar tonight and that she and Chandra should sleep at her apartment, which she still maintained although rarely used.

The enthralled woman was lying almost comatose of the bed in the special room he had had built for her. Natalie and Cindy were with her, lying naked on either side of her on the bed. They had been lightly caressing her and stroking her head softly while she drew in the essence of the Whole through her dazed dreams. Rather than take the time to draw the vital mists from her, Ramon ordered the two young women to dress Kelly so he could take her home. One of the security men would take the girls to Hardings' house, where they were living. There was always the chance Shabazz had not learned his lesson and would be lurking about.

Once Kelly had been dressed and adorned with her winter jacket, Ramon fastened her wrist bracelets together in front of her and led the swaying, barely conscious woman from the lab. He had become quite an adept driver over the last few weeks and he was quite capable of navigating Kelly's silver Sentra back to the farmhouse.

Kelly sat dazed in the front seat of the car as they sped their way home. Traffic was light, it being after rush hour, and they made it home within twenty minutes. As soon as they got back into the house, Ramon undressed her and, after binding her arms behind her, brought her to her bed. Before laying her down, he made her drink another draught of his potion.

Ramon sensed his familiar's dismay as she drank down a tall glass of the dream making liquid. She was already suffused with the mists of the other dimension, but the process of finding and neutralizing the renegade was in progress and his need for an increased flow of power was acute. When the glass was empty, he gave her a strong message of reassurance and affection and laid her naked body down. He was sorry to make her suffer, but there was little choice. Before leaving the room, he placed the blindfold she wore every evening over her eyes and connected her bound wrists and ankles together. He went into the lonely, quiet kitchen and made himself a cup of tea.

* * * * * * * * * * * * * *

Jonathan received the news that his agents had successfully followed the pursuer to his destination with glee. It was just a matter of time now. The Apache crew had already arrived at the Dulles airport and were preparing for their mission at a safe house a few miles from the industrial building to which the pursuer had been followed.

From his agents' reports, the building looked like a hard nut to crack. There were security guards and plenty of people around. There was no assurance the pursuer's familiar was inside. He might have her stashed somewhere else entirely. It would not do to capture him and lose his familiar. Blackthorne wanted to sweep the board, win all of the marbles. He ordered his men to wait until nightfall. If the pursuer didn't leave the building by 3 A.M., the Apaches would storm it. If he did leave, one of the agents would follow him and see if he led him to the valuable, enthralled woman.

In the meantime, Jonathan had a new toy to play with, one who had already given him much valuable information.

When Jackie had parted from Ramon at the airport, she had been walking on air. Needless to say, she had never met a man like that before. Ramon's delicate reshaping of her mind had left her unquestioning about the unusual nature of his powers and the dedication with which she had served him. His control of her would fade over the next few days and she would not recall much more than the fact she had enjoyed a good fuck with him. Ramon had not seen much need to make any significant refinements to the mind of the capable, well adjusted, liberated woman. But everyone could use a little boost in their confidence and self image and he had given her that.

As she was waiting to board her flight to Chicago, two security officers accompanied by a hard looking man in a cheap suit and narrow tie had approached her. He flashed a badge and asked her if she would mind coming with them to answer some questions. She was made to understand that having posed the issue in the form of a request was a polite formality and her compliance was mandatory. Since 9/11, any kind of disturbance at an airport was considered a serious offense and Jackie didn't want any legal hassles from trumped up 'resisting' charges or 'assault on an officer', the two tags cops gave you after they smacked you around and cuffed you, so she obliged them. She wasn't about to answer any questions about her business in Omaha. Ramon had given her strict commands about that. Name, rank and serial number was all they would get.

When they entered the security offices, Jackie was made to remove her down filled, winter jacket at a metal detector and was then led down a long hallway and into a small, windowless room. The only furnishings were a cheap, Formica covered table and some wooden chairs. She was about to turn around and protest at being held incommunicado and to demand an attorney when she felt her arms being gathered behind her back. Cold, steel handcuffs were slapped on her wrists. When she tried to struggle in protest, she felt a jab in her arm and then an intense, agonizing jolt that made her body go liquid. She had been Tasered!

Two men took hold of her arms to prevent her from

falling to the floor and a third slapped a wide piece of heavy tape across her mouth. A hood was pulled over her head and cinched tight around her neck. In a trice, she was dragged out the door of the little room, down the hall and out the rear door. A car was waiting for her there and she was shoved into the back seat. The door slammed and it pulled away.

Jackie regained her equilibrium slowly. She knew she was in car and it was moving fast. A large, bulky man sat on either side of her. Her instinct to fight took over immediately and she began to kick her legs and squirm her body frantically while screaming out behind the tape over her lips. The men grabbed her arms and held her fast to the back seat and she felt a sharp, painful jab to her solar plexus, driving all of the breath out of her. Her body went limp and her mind fogged over as she moaned and her chest heaved for air.

Before the frightened PI had time to recover, the car skidded to a halt. The doors flew open and she felt herself being dragged from the car into the 20 degree Nebraska air. She was clad in only her faded and worn, brown and red, Chicago Bears Superbowl XX t-shirt, her tight, bright blue denim jeans and a pair of Khaki work boots she had brought because of the impending wintry weather. The cold struck her fiercely with its icy hand. She was pulled up a steep set of metal stairs and through a doorway. She could hear the loud whine of a jet engine. Her body was thrown into a cushioned seat and a buckle came across her chest. Her feet were manacled to the legs. She heard a large, metal door slammed shut. A few, long, agonizing minutes passed and then she had the sensation of movement. The whining got louder and louder until it seemed to become a roar in her ears.

She was in a plane, she knew it. She had been kidnapped and was being flown somewhere. It had to have something to do with the man who had hired her and the girl at the psychiatric hospital. She had crossed some unknown line. Her shoulders ached from her confined arms behind her and her body still felt sickened from the dose of electrical charge she had been given. Was the man here too? Had he gotten away? How long would it be before somebody knew she was missing? Where were they taking her and what would they do with her when they got her there? All these things ran through her panicked mind. She struggled in her bonds and cried out from behind her taped lips until a hard hand cuffed her head and told her to 'shut the fuck up!" in an angry, coarse voice. The plane's motion had stopped for a few minutes and then, suddenly, it began to rush down the runway. As she felt it lift off into the air, a terrible knot formed in her stomach. She began to pray.

It was an hour and a half flight from Omaha to the New Mexico panhandle. Jackie had a long time to experience the gnawing terror of being kidnapped. The men who were with her on the plane were mostly silent. The rare voices she heard spoke in a strange, guttural language and the sounds of a foreign tongue made her apprehension all the more keen. Her unhappy reverie was disturbed only once when she was unhooked from her seat and a strong, vice-like grip on her arm led her to the cramped bathroom. Hooded, her tight blue jeans and panties pulled to her ankles by unseen hands, she gratefully released her bursting bladder.

A hand roughly wiped her pussy clean and then frog marched her back to her chair, her jeans and panties still around her ankles. Jackie unhappily sensed the staring eyes of the men in the plane on her half naked body as she shuffled down the aisle between the seats, hooded and bound. She was pushed back down callously into her chair and strapped back in. Jackie struggled futilely and yelled through her taped mouth as her heavy work boots and socks were removed and the jeans and panties pulled free of her feet. It took two men to do it, and she could hear them laughing over her muffled protests. Their arms were strong and forceful and her resistance was easily quelled. She spent the rest of the flight clad only in her t-shirt and bra with her legs manacled wide to the feet of the chair. Her mind was distraught with apprehension and focused on her exposed and vulnerable sex.

Surprised, but happy she had not been further molested on the flight, Jackie's heart sank as she felt the plane slowing and circling to land. When it rolled to a stop, she was pulled from her seat and led down a metal stairway onto the tarmac. Wherever she was, it was warmer than Omaha, although the air was still crisp. She did not have long to suffer the cold air on her exposed lower body. She was pulled into a car which sped her away. About fifteen minutes later, she was dragged out of the car and led into a building. Two strong men held her bound arms as she was led across a polished, hardwood floor and brought into a room. She could hear the door opening and shutting as she passed through it. The room was warm and there was a plush rug under her naked feet.

The frightened PI was made to stand, half naked, hooded and her hands still bound behind her, for about ten minutes before she heard the door opening and shutting again. Her heart beat wildly in her chest and her throat was constricted and tight with fear. The deep voices of the unknown men who held her prisoner had been chuckling and chatting amiably in their strange language. She resented being the object of their apparent derision. Now she sensed the men in the room coming to attention and she knew she would soon learn the purpose of her abduction.

Jackie had imagined all kinds of things on her terrifying trip. She had first thought that some secret government organization had taken her prisoner. But the unfamiliar language of her captors had put paid to that idea. If the men were government agents, they would have been speaking English. There had not been an American voice in the crowd.

She moved on to the idea she had been captured by terrorists. But she had been brought through the airport security office. It was doubtful that terrorism was so powerful and rife in Omaha, Nebraska that they would control the airport security offices. Was the government in league with some foreign power that Ramón had somehow angered?

As she stood in the middle of the unknown room, in the unknown house, which for all she knew be anywhere in the United States or even Canada or Mexico, she knew she was about to be interrogated. Jackie was well versed in interrogation techniques and she was aware that one of the purposes of keeping her body exposed was to increase her mental vulnerability. She resolved to tell them nothing. She was an American citizen, after all. She wasn't some Arab terrorist that could be held incommunicado indefinitely. They had to let her go eventually. And when they did, she would create a whole world of shit for them. She knew plenty of cops and reporters, even some FBI guys. She could almost imagine the headlines in the Chicago Tribune.

But it did not turn out at all like Jackie expected. Whoever had come in took a few minutes to examine her. Darkness all around her, she felt his eyes assaulting her half nude body. The other men had all turned quiet. And then, she felt a probing of her mind. It started out as a small tingle in her brain, something she thought she was imagining in her fear. Then, it became all too real. It was like someone was inside there, rifling through her memories. She tried to twist away and scream, but her body would not obey her. She was rooted in place, unable to move a single muscle, incapable of making a sound. The mind that was probing hers announced itself. She could feel its malignant intent towards her and its immense power. A wave of dreadful unhappiness flowed through her as if she had been injected with some poisonous fluid. It was like a hand had seized her brain and was squeezing it. She cringed in abysmal fright.

Jonathan was enjoying his capture of the half naked, brown haired young woman. As soon as he had learned she was at the airport with the pursuer, he had ordered her to be picked up and brought to him. Although he had been provided with his physical description and a grainy outtake from the security video at the hospital, he wanted to steal from her mind the actual visage of the man who had come across the dimensional divide to confront him. As she shivered in fear before him, clad only in the now ridiculous, faded, football t-shirt, he saw the dark face of the pursuer, his long, black hair, his broad, handsome face. And he felt more than that. He sensed his identity.

While individuality was not a preeminent feature of the aspects of the Whole, they did enjoy a degree of personality, otherwise he would not be here, would not have developed the yearning for expression and freedom from its confining, and in his mind, cloying, blanket of community. The girl, in her thoughts, referred to the strong, brown skinned man who had seduced her as Ramón, but he recognized the personality at once. Raijamoon! He had always known it would be him. He was the most experienced jumper, the strongest. He had taught the fledgling Jnthrn the fundamentals of dimension jumping, had coaxed him through his fears.

Raijamoon was a formidable adversary. A slight tremor of fear went through him as he thought of their impending confrontation. But then, why should he fear him? He had had five years to build his powers. It was doubtful Raijamoon had been here for more than a few months. Jonathan, as he preferred to think of himself, had an army to protect him. And he had the element of surprise. Even as he stood here in the large, sumptuously decorated reception room of his immense hacienda, the pursuer was being trailed to his base and his crew of Apaches was readying itself to capture or kill him.

The brown haired former private investigator had pleasing, long legs and a curly, furry bush between her thighs. Her thighs were well toned and she had boyish, narrow hips. He wanted to see the rest of her. He ordered one of the dark skinned, heavy set Apache guards to release her from her bonds and to remove her hood.

Jackie quailed with fear as her hood was removed and the gagging tape ripped from her face. She sensed she would be presented with the form of some monster, a shriveled, old, demon of a man with fiery eyes and drooling, perverted lips. She was surprised when she saw the handsome, blond haired man, tall and strong, dressed in a flowing off-white, short sleeved cotton shirt and loose, sharply creased white pants. He was wearing hand tooled, snakeskin boots. He had a devilish, self-satisfied smile on his face. He didn't look like a demon, but she had felt him take possession of her mind and there was nothing benign about him. His blue eyes were like fiery sapphires and they pierced her mercilessly.

She had known all along she was being controlled by Ramón. She had fought it at first, but his mind had conveyed such a feeling of goodness and warmth to her she had eventually happily succumbed. She had detected his beneficent purposes, had enjoyed the pleasure he had brought her, was comfortable in serving him. But this man was nothing like Ramón. His evil purposes were blatant. She could feel no comfort in his control of her. He had stolen all of her thoughts, her memories. Her resolve not to talk, to protect the mission of the dream man was vitiated by this man's powers to invade her mind and take what he wanted. And now that he had everything her mind could give, she feared what else he would want.

The room seemed to spin around the distraught young woman. She could see the dark skinned men who had brought her here lolling around the expansive room. It was decorated in dark, heavy wood paneling, with light beige, cloth covered couches and easy chairs. Heavy, wooden beams crossed the low ceiling and there were colorful Indian shields mounted on the walls, covered with feathers and painted with the strange, hieroglyphic-like designs typical of the American Southwestern natives. The light brown rug was plush and her feet sank into it as she stood there nervously, ashamed at her displayed sex and thighs.

Jackie felt the strange, evil man's mind take firmer control over her. Her body seemed to sicken as she received his command to remove her thin, cotton t-shirt. She didn't want to, but her hands obeyed him, drawing the fabric up over her belly and breasts and then over her head. After she had tossed it aside, she drew her hands behind her back and unhooked the clasps of her seamless, comfortable sports bra. As she dropped it to the floor, her stomach began to churn with hopeless dread. She could feel her knees wobbling and the sweat pouring down her frame. Her mouth had gone dry and her small, dainty nipples had stiffened with fear.

The man sent her a compelling, irresistible command to approach him. At the same time, she felt her lusts begin to rise. The man was a god, she could see that, an evil, powerful god, and her body yearned to be filled by him. Overcome with despair, knowing she was sealing her own fate, that her days now would be filled with obedience to him and his desires, whatever they were, she slowly sank to her knees before him. She was inches away from his knees and she reached up and lowered the zipper to his pants. She wanted his cock, needed it like she had never needed anything before. She pulled the thickening meat free of his pants. It burned in her hand, sending a pulse of passion through her. She closed her eyes, opened her lips and surrounded the forbidding yet tantalizing thick wand of flesh, its heat alighting the sensors of her mouth and her tongue. Its radiance filled her and she had no thoughts but of bringing it pleasure.

Jonathan felt the lips and mouth encompass him and he gave a low sigh as the warmth spread up his cock and though his body. He placed his hands on the woman's head and sent her a vicious message of pain and fear. He felt her mind reel at the unhappiness that pierced it. The kneeling female groaned and gave out a muffled sob, even as she continued to energetically pleasure his steel hard cock with her lips and tongue.

With each downward stroke of her pursed lips, Jackie felt more and more of her soul melt away. The hot cock filled her mouth and touched on the edge of her throat each time she descended over it. She was crying, something she I't done since childhood. She realized she was lost, a helpless prisoner and slave of Ramón's deadly enemy. And yet the sensation of the rigid but soft skinned meat that scraped across her lips, the heat and taste it gave off, sent her passions higher and higher. She could feel the burning of her loins, the aching of her breasts. She squeezed her bare thighs together in an effort to slow the building lust between them, but her need continued to grow and grow. She knew that the other men, ruthless, callous men she would probably have to serve in their turn, were staring at her, enjoying her lascivious display of enforced lust, but she did not care. All that mattered was the cock in her mouth and the will of the hard, evil man who owned it.

When the lust giving prick began to throb and pulse in her mouth, Jackie gave out a deep, soulful moan. She felt the man's essence pouring into her, sealing the man's control over her. Her pussy began to convulse and throb with her own, unwanted pleasure as her lips gripped the offensive pole and her tongue slithered around it. Her hands grasped its base as if to life itself.

Jonathan waited until his last pleasurable spasm subsided before releasing the forlorn woman from his mind's irresistible grip. He grabbed her chin with his hand and turned her face upwards, making her gaze into his eyes. Her eyes were flooded with tears, red rimmed and puffy. He could feel the despair flowing from her and drank of it joyfully. The controls of the pursuer, the man she called Ramón, had been washed away and replaced with his own. He had detected the gentle, affectionate, delicate commands his pursuer had given her. To him it was a sign of the other being's weakness, his inability to break free of the dictates of the Whole to take full command of the inferior creature.

Blackthorne despised the man's loyalty to the Whole, his spineless obeisance to its rule. He particularly enjoyed possessing a creature whose mind the other dimensional traveler had touched, blasting away the loyalty and affection he had placed there. There would be others the pursuer had converted to his service. He saw in the mind of the newly enthralled woman kneeling before him the fleshy, voluptuous, young, blond girl he had mated with in the motel just yesterday, the pretty, brown haired girl who had pleased him with her mouth this morning.

After he had defeated the pursuer, he would send his men for them. He would collect all of the pursuer's servants and place them in a special hell where, from time to time, he could savor his victory over the Whole by tormenting and abusing them. He would leave them the memories of their beloved master and make them rue the day they had met him, the Lord of Conquerors. Blackthorne especially enjoyed the prospect of capturing the other being's familiar. He could just about taste the sweet flavor of her terror and unhappiness as he bent her to his will. The brown haired girl he had just enthralled had not met her, had no vision of her in her mind. But, if all went well, he would meet her soon, mere hours from now.

There was time before there would be more news. He had
put aside all other business of the day. He decided he would
spend it visiting more torment and abuse upon the body and
mind of the abject prisoner on her knees before him. He sent
her an order to stand and place her hands behind her back,
crossed together as if held there by an invisible bond. She
followed, trotting dolefully behind him, as he strode
purposefully and confidently from the reception room.

* * * * * * * * * * * * * *

Ramon was still sitting at the kitchen table when he heard the
knock on the door. He had been engrossed in his thoughts
and had not discerned the car that had brought his visitor. He
looked into the bedroom as he passed it. The female was lying
there quietly, still lost in the dreams his potion had induced.
He crossed the living room and opened the door.

He had felt the emanations from the young girl as soon as
she had knocked on the door. It was the lovely Lucy Douglas.
All of the other girls had been told to stay away tonight so he
could be alone with his familiar, but apparently, the word had
not gotten to the file clerk from Hardings' factory or she had
ignored it. Her youthful, expectant face peered up at him as
she stood on the porch begging admission.

"C-can I come in?" the bashful, brown haired girl asked
tentatively. She had not been bashful when he had met her,
but his captivation of her had brought out a whole new side of
her personality. It was dark outside and her body was framed
by the light that was released when Ramón opened the door.
She was wearing a rose colored, plump, down jacket zipped to
her chin. Her bare legs descended from her tiny, green and
white, pleated miniskirt and she was wearing a pair of very
dark green high heels. It was about 25 degrees outside, and he

didn't want to make her stand in the cold. To his dismay, the car that had brought her had pulled from the driveway and was already making its way down the road.

"Okay, Lucy," Ramón replied. "But you can't stay. You'll have to get someone to pick you up."

Lucy stepped through the door and Ramón closed it behind her. She drew off her heavy jacket to reveal a light green, short sleeved, cotton top that had a round, deep neckline covered by a lacy, white border. The tops of her breasts were displayed enticingly and Ramon felt a stirring in his loins knowing they were available for his loving attentions. When she started to pull her blouse up over her stomach prefatory to removing it, Ramón stopped her. "Not tonight, Lucy," he told her. "Come into the kitchen and have a cup of tea. Then we'll call somebody to come and get you."

"Okay," Lucy relied mournfully.

He had her sit down at the table and he placed a bag of Earl Grey tea in a cup with some water and put it in the microwave. He stood silently next to it for the three minutes he had given it to heat. Lucy sat quietly at the table, looking up at him with her large, limped, brown eyes, her thighs pressed together demurely, her arms crossed in front of her, under her breasts. The only sound in the room was the humming of the microwave as it performed its electronic chore. When the bell rang, Ramon brought the steaming cup to the polished, wooden kitchen table. There was a plastic squeeze bottle of honey there in the shape of a bear, and he offered it to the nervous looking girl. She nodded and he gave her a long, thick squirt. Once he had brought her a spoon, he sat at the table catty-corned from her.

"So what's this all about, Lucy?" he asked her. She had taken a small sip from the misty cup and placed it back down in front of her.

"I, I don't know," the girl replied.

Ramon could read the girl's mind like a book and so he knew the answers to his questions, but he often found it useful to utilize actual speech to his servants. Frankly, it made him feel more human and he liked that.

"Didn't Felicity tell you I wanted to be alone with Dr. Jameson tonight?" Ramón asked her, knowing full well the answer.

"Yes," Lucy replied. Her face was pretty and her lips were luscious. Her braless breasts stirred with each movement. He saw in her mind that she had come without underwear in the hopes of getting lucky.

"Then why did you come?" Ramon returned.

"I, I …," she started. The girl was having a hard time getting it out.

"Is there something you want to tell me, Lucy?" Ramón asked.

A tear started forming in the girl's pretty right eye. The edges of the girl's eyes were delicately mascaraed and she had a light green coloring applied to her eyelids. Her lips had been painted a pale reddish orange. Ramon could feel her desire for him growing. His body was reciprocating.

"It's just that I had this bad feeling. I've had it all day. I was worried about you, about Dr. Jameson. I just had to come."

Lucy had always believed she had ESP. Years ago, she had had a dream about a terrible car accident and the next day two of her friends had been killed by a drunk driver out on Route 256. The night before her parents announced their decision to divorce, she had dreamed of them both sailing away on separate ships. She seemed just to know certain things before they happened. It didn't work all the time and sometimes, like now, she just had a severe sense of dread.

"Something's going to happen, I just know it!" the girl blurted out. "I'm scared!"

Ramon pushed his chair back and opened his arms. Lucy had started to all out cry and she rose and paced herself on the dream man's lap. "I don't want anything to happen to you or Dr. Jameson!" she said between sobs. "Please tell me you won't go away! Please!"

The dream man circled Lucy's body with his arms and pulled her tight to him. He let her sob herself out for a while before replying.

"You know I can't stay forever, Lucy, don't you?" he asked her in a tender, soft voice. "Someday I'll have to go away."

Lucy's crying became louder. "But I don't want you to go away! I couldn't stand it! If you go, I want to go with you!"

Ramon hugged the girl tighter. He stroked her plush hair and kissed her on the shoulder, just below her neck. Her skin was salty and sweet.

"You're going to be fine, Lucy," Ramón told the distraught girl. "I can't take you with me. I'm sorry. But you'll be happy, I promise you. There are lots of wonderful things that will happen to you in your life. This is just the beginning."

Lucy tightened her grip around Ramón's neck, her breasts pressed against his chest. "I love you, Ramón!" she told him. "We all do. You can't just leave us!"

The girl pulled her head back and sought connection between her lips and Ramón's. Finding them, she opened her mouth and slid her tongue into his, mingling their heat. She moaned as she kissed him hard and deep, bringing a sigh of arousal from the man. Ramón could feel lust and affection flowing from her and he returned it twofold. He placed his hand on her curvaceous hip. It was too late to send the girl back home tonight. He knew it.

Just then, the living room door flew open.

Bob Cloud and his specially trained team of Apaches had been waiting patiently outside for about twenty minutes. They had been just about to crawl over the stubbled field surrounding the house and storm it when the car had pulled up and disgorged the pretty, young woman. They had waited awhile in the hopes she would leave. Bob didn't want any complications. An extra female to snatch was a definite complication. She would be missed and questions would be asked. Not that it wasn't something that couldn't be handled. It was just, messy, and this operation was too important.

After about ten minutes, Bob gave up waiting. They needed to get the pursuer and his woman and get them on a plane back to New Mexico. That had been the boss's order and that was what would be done. Bob thought it silly not to put a .45 in the man's brainpan while they had the chance. One shot and all their worries would go away. Jonathan had let him and a few key advisors know about the importance of the pursuer and how he would be intent on bringing about their leader's destruction. One shot and that would be all over. It was stupid to let him live a moment longer than necessary. But Blackthorne was the boss and if he wanted him alive for some reason, that's what he would get.

There was one out though. Blackthorne had instructed him that if things got too hairy, if it looked like the pursuer was going to put up a resistance or get away, he had authority to terminate him. Bob was itching for the excuse to exercise that option. Just let the man give him a reason and all their problems would be solved.

The skilled Native Americans crawled silently up to the decrepit looking structure. The man could be seen through the kitchen window with the pretty girl on his lap. One of the Apaches gave the man to his side an elbow and a knowing grin. Blackthorn's propensity for fucking was well known. Apparently, this guy was not much different.

To Bob's surprise, the door was unlocked. He swung it open and he and five of his dark skinned, black clad men came streaming in. He went directly to the kitchen where their principal quarry was. The man looked up at him, an expression of mild disdain and surprise on his face. The girl who had been kissing him jumped up and screamed. One of Bob's men shot a Taser wire out at her and it stuck in her right breast. Her body jerked and seemed to leap into the air and then she crashed to the floor.

The quarry had risen to his feet and he made a motion to move to protect the now squirming and convulsing girl on the floor, but then, looking Bob square in the eyes, stopped himself. Slowly, deliberately, a look of scorn on his face, he lifted his hands into the air. While Bob held his .45 steady and aimed at his heart, one of his men circled the kitchen table and locked the man's hands behind his back with steel handcuffs while another placed a long strip of tape across his lips and pulled a black bag over his head. When done, they pushed the unresisting man back into his chair.

Kelly had been snapped out of her dream filled reverie by Lucy's scream. Fear ran through her and her heart began to pump rapidly. She was defenseless, naked, bound and blindfolded on her bed. Strong, ruthless hands grabbed her arms and she felt the chain linking her fastened wrists and ankles being loosened. She screamed in terror through her gag as she was pulled up from the bed. As she was dragged from the bedroom and into the living room, her mind called out for her dream man to save her.

Something was going dreadfully wrong! She knew her captor had a vital, secret task to perform, something that justified his use of her and of all the other females he had captured. She had sensed it was fraught with danger, but always believed the dream man would protect them. Now that danger had become all too real! What was happening? Her mind reeled at the thought of being separated from the man who had become her whole life, to whom she was connected to like the Moon revolved around the Earth. Her stomach roiled at the thought of losing him.

Bob watched as his men bound the arms of the supine and moaning, pretty brown haired girl in the kitchen behind her and connected her ankles with a short chain. While they completed her bindings by taping her mouth and hooding her, he went into the living room to inspect the grand prize, the woman who Jonathan Blackthorne desired above all others. The raid was a complete success. The pursuer had conveniently stripped and bound her for them and he admired her naked form. She was moaning, her body limp, and if two of his men had not been holding her arms tightly, she would have fallen to the floor. He ordered them to turn her around so he could see the rest of her. She had fine, plump breasts and a taut belly. Blackthorne would be pleased.

When the pursuer had gone to the laboratory after his flight from Omaha, Blackthorne's men had found out all they could about the facility. When they learned that a young, female medical researcher owned it, Blackthorne had Googled her. Her description fit the profile of a familiar to a 'T' and he had provided his men with a picture obtained over the Internet. This woman standing moaning and distraught before Bob now was the spitting image. Her hair was the real giveaway, dark, burnt orange tresses, just like in the picture. Bob ordered his men to remove the gag and eye mask just to make sure. The terrified, blue eyes that stared back at him frighteningly were a perfect match. This was her all right. Mission accomplished.

Kelly quailed as she looked at the intense, pleased eyes of the formidable, dark skinned man. Something terrible was going to happen to her, she just knew it. She saw it in the demonic look in the man's face as he appreciated her naked form. What frightened her most was the fact that the man seemed to recognize her. Someone had pointed her out to him for abduction and he was pleased he had found the right woman.

The men dragged the struggling and squealing Lucy and the docile Ramón into the living room. Kelly recognized the young girl and her heart went out to her. But she was astonished at the unresisting form of her dream lover. Why wasn't he fighting? Why didn't he do something? If he was powerless to oppose these men, where did that leave her? Her body shook with fearful panic as her gag and blinding eye mask were reinstalled.

Bob instructed his men to turn off all of the lights in the house. He then went to the door and blinked his flashlight twice. A few moments later, a dark van trundled up the driveway, its lights dimmed. At Bob's command, the prisoners were marched out the door of the house, down the steps of the porch and thrown into the back. The Apache men joined them. The door slammed shut and the van backed away from the house.

* * * * * * * * * * * * * * *

Jonathan was in his bedroom when Bob's call came in. It was a clean sweep! In four hours, his nemesis would be here, in his power. It had been remarkably simple, almost too much to hope for. Within hours, he would be safe. If he defeated the pursuer, he doubted the Whole would send another jumper. There would be no reason to believe another aspect of the Whole could succeed where this one, the best and most experienced, had failed. Even if they did, by the time the scientists of the Whole located another familiar and sent another aspect across the dimensional divide, it would be years hence. No one would be able to get near him. A virtual eternity of paradise spread out before him. Even if he could not transfer to a new body, this one could last hundreds of years.

The thin, brown haired girl he had enthralled earlier today lay sprawled across the bed. He had brought her several shattering orgasms amidst gut wrenching fear and psychic pain. He was exhilarated from the absorption of her terrible lust and the prospect of his confrontation with Raijamoon. He decided he would turn the meeting between him and the other worlder into a demonstration of his power for his Apache allies.

He got up from the bed and called the number he used to communicate with the old, wizened shaman who had facilitated the creation of the Fortress and so much of what had followed the ceremony five years ago in which he had been anointed as Lord of Conquerors. He left a message with one of the shaman's aides. They would all meet in the reception room on the first floor of the hacienda. He would have his familiar brought there as well as his acolytes and all the Apache leadership. Afterwards, there would be a huge celebration. There was a shipment of newly converted women waiting for assignment down at the security center next to the Apache barracks. He would adjust their minds and distribute them among his loyal subjects.

Although the former private investigator and servant of his enemy was limp from exhaustion from her ordeal, his lusts were not yet sated. He ordered the trembling young woman to her knees, her forehead touching the mattress as he got back onto the plush, large bed. Her wrinkled brown star presented itself to him. She moaned with lust and unhappiness as he spread his large, powerful hands over her back, filling her with passion and pain. His cock was as hard as steel and he presented it to the small opening which he had already plowed twice in the last two hours.

The Chicago PI had been at his mercy the entire time he was waiting for word from his team as to the capture of the pursuer. He had left her here briefly, giving her a rest from her torments, while he had visited his familiar and drained her of the life maintaining essence she had gathered for him. He would bring the girl down there later, a present for his most devoted and longstanding servants. She had a strong, independent personality and her abhorrence at being converted to a willless slave gave her emotional emissions a particularly piquant taste. He had not taken her memories from her, nor her power to rebel mentally at her treatment. Her mind screamed with shame and despair each time he made her come.

As he sank into her tight, rear opening, Jonathan could feel her revulsion at the pleasure his thick cock sent her as it rasped across the delicate entrance to her bowels. He reveled at the feel of the tight flesh around his prick. After he had sank within her to the hilt, he started a steady, long, stroke. His cock sent her an irresistible pulse of passion. She cried out miserably as her pussy began to spasm with pleasure.

CHAPTER NINE

Bob kept a close eye on his prisoners during the long flight out to New Mexico. It had been a simple matter, due to Blackthorne's connections, to breeze through airport security and load them onto the plane. The man stayed quiet and docile, strapped into his chair. The young girl kept crying and struggling with her bonds. Although she had a delectable body, he kept his men away from her. Blackthorne would want first dibs. The naked Dr. Kelly Jameson writhed and moaned in her chair between periods of fitful sleep. He kept the women far away from the man, knowing Blackthorne's powers and assuming he was just as capable of influencing the women. As far as he was concerned, they could drop him out from 15,000 feet anywhere over the Midwest, but orders were orders.

Ramón concentrated his mind on his familiar. He knew she was suffering both from the mists she had absorbed for him while at the lab and back at the house, and because of their prospective separation. He tried to calm her into sleep. Their bond was very strong, and even though they were separated by the length of the interior of the aircraft, he could reach into her mind.

His stomach churned at the prospect of his upcoming confrontation with the renegade. He would be very powerful, having had such a long time to develop. Ramón feared for the fates of his female servants back in Virginia. He knew if he failed the renegade would want to wipe out every trace of his existence and that the next mission for the brutal men who had kidnapped him would be to return and retrieve the women so their new lord could convert them to his own use.

The thought of them serving such an evil master caused him great pain. He had shown them joy and happiness while they served him, but the renegade would show them only pain and misery. He remembered the fate of the girl Nadine, her years of service to the pimp, her destroyed mind and wounded body. Poor Natalie and Cindy had just escaped from a life of degradation and Melissa and Felicity were such good natured, affectionate girls. And then there was happy, innocent Chandra, just coming out of her shell. And Adele. She had served him so well, so faithfully, it would be a poor reward for her to become the renegade's sexual slave.

It was of some relief the men hadn't killed him outright. But then, killing an aspect of the Whole would be as base a crime as any part of the Whole could commit. It was unthinkable, like killing a part of yourself. That the renegade had not crossed the line meant he was not totally lost to the Whole. There was something to save, but it would take more than talking to convince the renegade to go back. Ramon still had his weapons. The men had not searched him other than a rather perfunctory patdown. The marble was still in his pants pocket and the filament was still inside the waistband of his jeans. If only the renegade let the men release his hands, he would have access to his instruments and have a chance of victory.

Kelly, when awake, was filled with dread. She knew that if the enemies of her dream man were successful, all her sacrifice for him would have been in vain. She loved him so much that she didn't really care about her own fate. She would give her life for him if given the chance. But she doubted she would be capable of any volitional concerted action by the time they got to wherever they were going. Her mind was befogged with acute physical need for the man. She felt herself bursting with the essence she had drawn for him from his world. Her pussy burned with desire for him, her breasts ached. She wanted to beg the men who had taken them to allow her to be near him, to let her caress him, feel his body next to hers. But, even if she had not been gagged, she was barely conscious enough to form words when she was conscious at all.

The frantic woman could feel Ramon's mind as he made contact with her. She sighed with temporary relief when she felt his calming energies. But it did not last long. Moments later, she would be fierce in her need, her mind ajumble with both her lust for him and her fear. And then, mercifully, she would pass out.

But even sleeping was a mixed blessing. Her mind would go to that flowered field where she had first seen the dream man. The mist would come, and, although her body was already suffused with the energized fog, it would surround her and enter her, belying her belief she could absorb no more.

When the plane touched down, the prisoners were hustled off of the plane and into three separate awaiting SUV's. They were driven directly to the hacienda and brought into the reception room. Kelly had to be held up by the men who escorted her. Her body was too weak to walk.

A crowd of Apaches were awaiting them when they were escorted into the large room. Ramón could hear them murmuring in their strange tongue as he stood there awaiting the arrival of his adversary. He could detect the being's presence in the minds of some of the women in the room, women who had been tormented and ruled by him for many years. And he sensed the renegade's familiar, Diane.

Ramón had never visited such a tortured mind, even when he had gone to see her sister, Nadine. He saw how the renegade had driven her to agonized, mental pain, had abused her unmercifully. This would be the fate of his familiar. His heart came close to breaking as he thought of her at the renegade's mercy. This was love, he knew it now. He was in love with her and he could not bear the thought of her suffering. He had to win, he just had to. It went beyond his ethical obligation to ameliorate the vast suffering the erstwhile agent of the Whole had caused. Anger rose up in him and he twisted his confined arms behind his back. He had to get free! He just had to!

The room fell into a hush when Blackthorne entered. He was followed by the cowed and terrified female he had converted, Jackie. Ramon sensed them both as they walked through the doors. He was revolted at what the renegade had done to her. At the same time, he felt the other being's extreme power and confidence. It did not bode well for him at all.

Jonathan had donned the white ceremonial garb that denoted his assumption of the role of Jitendra, Lord of Conquerors. The heavy, feathered bearskin cap was on his head and he was dressed all in white deerskin. He walked quietly and confidently over the soft rug in his white moccasins. He sensed the mind of the pursuer reaching out to him. As he had predicted, his mind was weak and as yet untrained as compared to his. He realized he had nothing to fear. This was going to be fun.

Blackthorne stepped up on a platform in the front of the room. All eyes in the crowded room were on him. The shaman, draped in his ceremonial robes, was seated in his ceremonial throne on his right. Standing to his left was the woman, Barbara Feathers, the high priestess of the tribe. She was also dressed in her sacred garb, a long, tasseled, white deerskin sheath bedecked with multicolored beads and feathers. His familiar, Diane was kneeling in front of the platform to its right. She looked haggard and tired. He had not been down to her subterranean prison to drain her of her mists for a while and Jonathan could feel her fullness. He had instructed his acolytes, who were kneeling obediently next to her, to dose her with the hallucinogenic peyote mixture several hours ago so he could reenergize himself, if necessary, after his engagement with the pursuer. He sensed he would not need it, but he would enjoy draining her in the presence of his subjects as part of his victory celebration.

The tension in the room was palpable as the three bound and hooded prisoners stood before the crowd of expectant men and women. Some of the female 'nurses' from the dream lab were there along with Dr. Morton, who had a more than academic interest in the proceedings. There were fifteen or so of the tough, muscular Apache security guards around the room, men who, like a modern Praetorian Guard, had sworn to protect and serve the god-like white man. There were household servants there and those members of the Tribal Council who could get there at short notice, dressed in their workaday business attire.

Altogether, there were somewhat over a hundred spectators in the large, sumptuously decorated room, sufficient to spread the news of his power and the vanquishing of his foe. Blackthorne felt as he believed Julius Caesar must have felt when he forced the defeated, mighty King of the Gauls, Vercingetorix, to strip and bow before him in front of his legions. Caesar's struggles to conquer Gaul had lasted six years; his wait for the opportunity to defeat his nemesis had lasted five. The result would be the same, the winning and securing of a vast empire ruled by the dictates of a single man.

Blackthorne raised his hands to draw the attention of the crowd which had been peering inquisitively at the three prisoners. He spoke to them in their native tongue.

"Five years ago, I came among you with a promise to bring the Apache people power and honor. I have kept my promise. Today, men and women of your tribe sit in places of responsibility in some of the richest corporations of America. Wealth flows into the reservation like a mighty river. I have built schools for your young, houses for your people to live in, medical facilities for the sick. And I have supplied you with the service of my many captives, young, beautiful women to serve the needs of the young men and to act as servants to your women. The Americans and the Mexicans, your ancient enemies, no longer threaten you or steal your children to be slaves to their lusts, poison them with their powders and their liquor. The Apache nation stands again on the verge of greatness.

There was only one thing that stood as a threat to the renewal of Apache power, to the defeat of its enemies. It was prophesied a man would come, a pursuer, who would seek to defeat me, to take me away from you. Now, he has come. But I have captured him and he stands before you this day as my prisoner. I have called you together to watch as I defeat him. I will send him back to the ghost world from which he came, or, if he will not go, I will destroy him here in front of you. Nothing will stand in the way of Apache greatness and our path to power."

For a moment, the audience was silent. Then, from the back of the room came a loud, fierce warrior's whoop. The crowd broke into a cacophony of celebration. Blackthorne smiled as he absorbed the adulation of the small crowd. These were his people, his allies, the soldiers of his coming empire. After today, he would reach out to the other Apache tribes, the Mescaleros, the Lipan, the Jicarilla and others. From there, they would branch out and recruit other surviving Native American groups, the Comanche, the Arapahoe, the Sioux.

Like the Mongols of old, his 'barbarians' would sweep the land and claim all of the positions of power. But his conquest would not be made by force of battle. He would use his ability to corrupt the weak culture and his technical knowledge to dominate their economy, to install his loyal servants in positions of power. By the time anyone knew what was going on, it would be too late to stop it. It might take a hundred years to complete, but he had plenty of time now.

Ramon could not understand the words his enemy spoke, but he could read his mind. It was clear Jnthrn was mad. Here was positive proof. The sickness that had made him turn renegade had become a megalomania. He would bring down the entire planet in an ever increasing obsession to rule and control it. Like the twentieth century madman, Adolph Hitler, he would initiate a chain of destruction that would result in a world-wide conflagration. Ramon did not know how he would gain access to his weapons, but it was essential he did.

The Whole would be devastated by the harm it had unintentionally brought to this world. It would be such a shock to its core it might precipitate a fatal decline, a loss of will to exist. More than the lives and welfare of his familiar and his servants were at stake. He twisted and turned his wrists in the steel confinements that encircled them. He could feel his skin burning as he tried to draw his hands free. But the manacles had been drawn too tight. He could not free himself. Fate would somehow have to intervene. His mind searched the room for an ally. It was difficult to isolate the individual minds of the females in the room due to the intermingling of all of the excited psyches. But then he felt it. One person, one sole doubter existed. All would depend on her.

Jonathan, feeling the time for the entertainment to begin ordered the bound and hooded, brown haired girl, Lucy, be brought to him first. Lucy was shivering with fear as she heard the man speak in the odd, guttural language. She had no idea where she had been brought, but knew something very bad was going to happen to her. She yearned for the protection of Ramón and had been trying to find him with her mind. When she felt strong, masculine hands grab her arms and drag her to the center of the crowd, she wanted to scream and plead for mercy.

The terrorized girl was made to face the excited crowd. A cheer went up from them in anticipation of the prospective demonstration of their demi-god's power. Lucy felt her hands being released as well as the chain that had connected her ankles. At the same time, her hood was removed and someone brutally ripped the tape that had covered her lips free from her face. She cried out at the pain of her torn skin, placing her now freed hands over her mouth. And then she lifted her tear filled eyes and took in the throng of feverish onlookers. It was a sea of dark, unfriendly faces. She tried to make a dash for the door, but the way was blocked and she was pushed back into the middle of the room. She tried it again and again, until she finally fell to her knees and began to sob uncontrollably. Her graceful, bare legs lay beneath her and her little skirt rode up on her thighs. "Pleeeease!" she yelled. "Pleeeease let me go! Pleeeease!"

The crowd of foreign looking people laughed and mimicked her frantic pleas. She had not noticed the bound and hooded forms of Ramon and Dr. Jameson, and the sight of them now drove her deeper into despair. She leaned over, placing her head between her thighs and began to sob.

Jonathan had enjoyed the little show put on by the distressed, young woman. He felt he should complement his pursuer's taste. She was a delightful creature, one he would be pleased to torment and abuse. Her levels of unhappy emotions was quite high and he enjoyed the sampling of them. But her display of grief at her predicament was getting boring. It was time to act. He raised his hands to silence the crowd again.

"This white woman belongs to my enemy. He has made her his slave. But here, he has no power. Watch while I take her from him."

The intrusion of the evil dream man's mind into hers felt like a knife had been shoved into Lucy's brain. She had not even been aware of his presence. But she was now as he filled her mind with his terrible will. She grabbed her head and screamed "Noooooooooo!" as she felt her connections to Ramón slipping away. The dread she had felt all the previous day was becoming reality. Her mind protested when she was given the command by her new, demonic master to stand. But her body obeyed it.

The crowd was quiet now and she felt all eyes on her as she rose to her feet and turned to look at the man who was enslaving her. When she looked into his hard, cold, blue eyes, she shivered with fear. She knew she could not resist him. She groaned with agony as she felt him fill her with a terrible lust for him. She needed him, needed to obey him, craved for contact with his flesh. She stepped slowly up to the platform where he was standing and her hands unconsciously reached for the hem of her light green, cotton blouse and pulled it over her head. She cast it aside and then reached behind her to loosen her skirt. She unzipped it and let it fall to her feet. Rueful now that she had dressed so provocatively for Ramón, the curvaceous and appealing young woman now stood before the callous crowd and her new master naked.

Jonathan watched the girl struggle with her entrancement. She had fine, full breasts that swayed and shook when she moved. The bow of her belly was sweet and inviting. His cock was hardening from just looking at her. He could taste her fear. He sent her another command.

The pretty, distraught young woman stepped closer to her new lord. She fell to her knees before him and bowed her head to the ground, her long, brown hair falling around her face. She felt the words the man had ordered her to say and she was helpless to resist him. "Command me, Lord of Conquerors. I am yours," she shouted out, her voice tremulous, her mind full of revulsion at her abject surrender.

The crowd gave a great cheer at the demonstration of the white man's power. But there was more. Lucy brought herself erect and spread her graceful thighs. She arched her back, presenting her beauteous breasts to her captor. He had filled her with irresistible lust. Her body burned with it and her sex yearned to be stroked to completion. Her nipples ached with their hardness. She ran her hands over her engorged, plump breasts and then lowered them over her taut belly. When they found her sensitized lower lips, she gently pried them apart and dipped the fingers of one hand inside. Her fevered crevasse was lush with her arousal. Her fingers felt like they were filled with electricity and every part of her she touched glowed with heat. Leaving one hand buried in her cleft, she spread her moisture to her stiffened bud of pleasure and began to stroke it, slowly at first, and then harder and harder as she felt her passions rise.

Lucy was shamed at her lascivious display before the crowd of strange, dark people. She had been wild before she became committed to Ramón, but had never caressed herself before anyone before. It was private, something she did alone and in the comfort of her bed. Now she was frigging herself madly, wanting only to please her lord, knowing the dark places he would take her. She could feel the man's psyche driving her lusts higher and higher and filling her brain with dismal, unhappy messages of his will. Her body was afire and she felt her orgasm building to crescendo. She wanted desperately to stop, wanted to run and hide from this monster who had possessed her, but she knew she couldn't.

Finally, her lust drove all thoughts away but the powerful buildup of orgasmic forces. "Oh! Oh! Oh! Oh!" she yelled as it came closer and closer. She gave up on fighting it and let the pleasure flow through her body. When her pussy's spasms began, she moaned loudly and her body shook. "Oh! Ohhhhhhhhh! Ohhhhhhhhhhh!" she called out. Every nerve in her body was overwhelmed with the pleasure her throbbing sex was sending her. "Ohhhhhhhh! Ohhhhhhhhhhh!"

Blackthorne watched the girl perform for him. His lusts were high. Her pretty breasts shook and danced as she stroked herself. Her face was a mask of agonized pleasure as her climax tore through her. He drank in her passions hungrily.

When the newly enslaved girl's pussy's pulses subsided, she collapsed to the floor. The crowd of his loyal followers stood mesmerized by her autoerotic performance. Suddenly, as if awoken from a trance, they began to hoot and shout with lustful approval. Jonathan knew that the tale of the pursuer's coming had been widespread among the Apaches and they had lived with the fear he would come and steal their lord away. He had proven his power over the other being from the 'ghost world', as they called it, and he could feel their relief. Now he would get down to the real task ahead of him. First he would take possession of the pursuer's familiar. Then he would deal with him.

"Bring me the dream woman!" Jonathan commanded.

Kelly had been swooning, held on her feet by the vice like grips of two of the Apache men on either side of her. She knew Ramón was close by and her mind yearned desperately for physical contact with him. She was conscious, barely, of the crowd around her. She heard them cheer and howl and the voice of the man who seemed to be their leader. She was ashamed to be naked in front of them, but more worried as to her fate and that of her lover. From time to time, she felt his soothing psychic messages, but they only served to make more frightening the goings on around her.

When she felt herself being led across the room, Kelly's heart began to pound with fear. Her eye mask was removed and she saw the costumed form of the group's leader, his blue eyes piercing her, his long, blond hair flowing down to his shoulders. She felt his mind probing her. She felt its evil and its strength and she knew the man intended to claim her as his own. How right, she felt, it was for her dream man to oppose him. He was a paragon of corruption, a powerful force of vile purpose. Her body turned cold and she felt her stomach tighten. She yearned to scream out her terror, but her sealed lips emitted only a loud, high pitched moan. She struggled in the arms of the men who held her as she watched the man coming closer to her and experienced his psyche pierce her brain.

Jonathan reveled in the beauty of his enemy's familiar. Her mind was pure and honest, a sweet contrast to his own dark and devilish one. He seized her heavy, round breasts in his hands and sent the female an intensely painful surge of his ill will towards her. He showed her what her life would be like with him, demonstrated the abject misery which would henceforth be her lot. She squirmed and called out from behind her sealed lips, her eyes full of tears and worry.

Jonathan knew he could not just convert the woman's mind as he had the other slave's. He needed her mental patterns to remain stable so as to not to risk breaking the connection she had established there with the Whole. But he could drive her to passion, increase her lusts, make her perform for his audience.

He ordered the men who were holding her up to bring her to the platform. Once atop it, he stood behind her and, reaching his hands around her graceful, desirable torso, seized her breasts. He sent waves of lust through her while stroking them, squeezing them tightly and playing with the stiffened nipples at their tips. The woman shuddered and moaned as he caressed her plush mounds and he could feel her fear and revulsion at his touch. He pressed his body against her back, rubbing his hardened cock along the valley between her rear cheeks. The costume he wore consisted of leggings that tied off at the tops of his thighs and the only thing hiding his manhood from view was the breechcloth that lay across the belt that he wore around his waist.

Blackthorne felt the flood of the Whole's essence that pervaded the woman's body. He would drain her of it later, in front of the crowd, claiming her as his own, but not until her had vanquished his foe. He wanted the other to watch, however, as he made her dance with lust for him, cried out her passions, passions induced by his mind, his hands, and not the other's.

He drew his hands down her pleasing torso and began to caress the insides of her pale, tender thighs. The woman tried to close her legs, to deny him access to her loins, but the men who held her placed their legs around hers and drew her legs open. When Jonathan began to caress the hairless mound of her sex, sending irresistible waves of lust through her, the woman moaned and cried, twisting and turning in the arms of the men who held her. He placed his fingers on the firm, engorged nub at the apex of her smooth, engorged sex lips and caressed it, rubbing it in small circles, letting his fingers drive her to the edge of climax.

Kelly's knees buckled when the fingers of her tormentor touched her bud of pleasure. She strained to free herself and to avoid the hated caress. But the finger kept on pushing her lusts higher and higher. She felt her blood begin to boil and her need become extreme. She didn't want to orgasm for this man, didn't want to confirm his mastery over her flesh, but she had no choice, her body had a will of its own, would not obey her efforts to suppress its desires.

Jonathan didn't want the woman to come just yet. Satisfied that he had proven his mastery over her to his servants, he withdrew his fingers and ordered his men to place her on the side of the platform on her knees. When she was forced to her knees, her bound arms still behind her, her mouth sealed, her body still quivering with need, he turned to the pursuer. The moment of confrontation had come.

"Remove the hood of my enemy!" he called out to his

followers. "Let him see I have claimed his whore!"

Ramon knew Kelly was in the hands of the renegade. He could feel her distress and fear from across the room. He cursed himself for his powerlessness. His arms were held tightly by the men on either side of him and it was impossible for him to do anything. He tried to influence their minds, but their loyalty to the renegade was to strong for him to be able to induce them to do anything that would be contrary to their duty to obey and protect him. Time was running out, he knew that. His confrontation with the madman was only moments away.

When his hood was removed and his body dragged to the middle of the room, Ramon took in the physical form of his enemy for the first time. He had seen the man in the mind of the girl, Nadine, just yesterday and his appearance was no surprise. He stared into the other's eyes, hatred and anger emanating from the human, male part of his mind. He tried to fight it back. He needed his rational self, needed all his other worldly powers. Human emotions were useless in the upcoming battle of wills.

Jonathan looked back at the face of his nemesis. It was odd to be in the presence of one of his own kind after so many years. On the other side of the dimensional wall they had met many times, although their corporal forms were different then. They did not have bodies as we knew it, but were, rather, more like centers of consciousness. It was too bad, really, that he could not make the other being an ally. It would be useful to have another mind available to help in his tasks. Jonathan knew though he could never trust him, that Raijamoon would refuse to cross the line necessary to dominate this race, to secure his power. No, the dimensional traveler would have to go. He could either voluntarily cross the dimensional divide, back to their universe, or perish here, right where he stood.

"Remove his clothes!" Jonathan ordered. The Apache men jumped to comply and within a few moments had dragged Ramón's trousers from his body and had ripped apart his shirt, rendering it into rags and tearing it from him. One of the men brought the remnants of his coverings to the renegade who looked at them briefly and then waved them away. They were thrown on the floor in front of the bedecked shaman. Ramon looked at his discarded pants forlornly. His last hope of defeating the renegade was gone. His weapons were beyond his reach. If only he could somehow get to them.

When Ramón looked up, he saw the beady eyes of the shaman looking at him, almost in recognition. The old man had seen Ramón's reaction to the loss of his trousers and his longing gaze at them. He whispered something to the dark skinned man beside him and the man picked them up and gave them to him. Ramon watched disconsolately as he saw the old man pull the tiny ball from the pocket of the pants and look at it. As the old man began to feel through the pants to see what else was there, Ramón's attention was drawn back to his enemy.

The renegade spoke to him through his mind.

"Here we are at last, Raijamoon. Did you really think you could defeat me?"

Raijamoon received the renegade's taunt. He wanted to strike back in anger, to communicate his rage at the man's abuses. But he knew better. He waited a moment until a calm descended over him. His human nature put aside, he felt his native psyche take command of his mind.

"Greetings, Jnthrn," he replied calmly. "I am not here to defeat you. I am here to heal you."

Jonathan gave out a loud, raucous laugh. "Heal me? You don't have to heal me. I've healed myself. I've cured myself of the sickness of our race, its lack of personhood, its lack of emotions. You are the ones who are sick."

"You're wrong, Jnthrn," Raijamoon replied. "Our race has its own ways. There is peace and harmony in the Whole. We are all one. Let me heal you so that you can be one of us again."

Jnthrn looked back at his enemy coldly. "I'll not debate with you, Raijamoon. I'm not going back. But you are. I could have had you destroyed yesterday when my men found you, but I had no enmity towards you. If you do not go back, I will terminate your life force. You will no longer exist. I will sorrow at your loss, but I am determined to stay in this form and in this world."

"You will destroy this world, Jnthrn. You have visited much harm on these beings. The Whole cries out from your crimes."

"These beings will destroy themselves sooner or later, Raijamoon. Do you see how they treat each other? Have you read their histories? They are puny of mind and think only of their pleasures. It was so easy to corrupt them. The universe would be better off without them."

"You are wrong, Jnthrn," Ramón answered. "I have felt their love for each other. There is much goodness in them. Every race has its dark side. You know that from the studies that have been done. But their love for each other is greater than their faults. You have no right to pervert them and to lead them to a horrible end."

For a moment, Jonathan thought of the feelings he had developed for the beautiful Cathy in whose arms he had spent the night before. She was upstairs now waiting lovingly, patiently for him whenever he should return to her. He knew that her attentions to him, her devotion, was not love. He had placed that there. But did he love her? Was that what he felt? If it was, it was a weakness. He resolved to terminate the 'relationship' between them as soon as possible. He would send her to the meanest whorehouse he could find, to live out her days as a scrofulous receptacle of lust. He did not need love. He rejected it. How like the demands of the Whole it was, cloying, suffocating. He had nothing to give. He needed all of himself.

Looking at his enemy, Jonathan decided enough was enough. The pursuer would leave or die. He cast his will at the mind of the dark skinned, human male that stood before him. His mind was so much stronger and he felt the other's give way at once. He pressed on it harder and harder. He would make the pursuer go back! He would force him to dissolve his physical presence in this world and return to the Whole.

Ramón felt the psychic powers of the renegade begin to overwhelm him. He steeled his mind in resistance to it, but his powers were much weaker than his foe's. He felt himself slipping away slowly, his mind beginning to crumble at the edges, his human side dispersing. "It cannot happen!" he thought. "I must fight it! I must survive!"

Suddenly, a female voice cried out in the room. "Stop! Stop, I say! Stop!"

The crowd had been astonished at the mental battle being fought before them by the two god-like figures. No words had been spoken between the two men, but their struggle was evident. Their bodies glowed with their power and the life force given out by the new man, the enemy of their lord, was fading, his skin becoming pale. The strong, authoritative woman's voice startled them and brought the battle between the two ghost men to a halt.

Jonathan looked up. What female had dared to interrupt his crushing of his enemy? He would strike her down like an insect and then finish his task of sending the pursuer back to his own world. It was Barbara Feathers, the High Priestess. What did she think she was doing? He reached out his mind to seize hers. To his surprise, her mind resisted him. It was like his powers had just bounced off of her. Something was wrong!

The tall, broadly formed, middle aged woman looked at the demonic blond haired man. "Do not try and capture me, Jitandra, Lord of Conquerors!" she shouted at him in Apache. "I too have my powers and you cannot conquer me. I have prayed for this day, when the other ghost would drive you from our midst! Too long have you deceived the people with your evil ways!" The angry, determined women looked over at the shaman. He was holding in his hands Ramón's weapons, the tiny, marble sized ball and the six inch long, silver filament he had found in the dark skinned man's pants.

"Do you see what you hold, you old fool?" she asked him, her voice dripping with venom. "What of your dream now?"

The shaman looked back at the woman guiltily. He was holding the long, thin filament in one hand and the marble in the other. Suddenly, it was like a light went off in his head. He threw the ceremonial robes from his body and stood. "Seize him!" he yelled.

For a moment, no one did anything. Jonathan stared at him perplexed. "What is going on?" he thought, panicked. "This can't be happening!"

The old man shouted again, "Seize him!" This time he pointed at Blackthorne. Four of the Apache men leaped onto the platform and took Jonathan by the arms.

"No! No! You don't know what you're doing!" Jonathan yelled. "Let me go! Let me finish him!"

The priestess pointed at Ramón. "Free his hands!" Two men rushed to Ramón and unfastened the cuffs that had held his hands behind him. It was hard for him to believe he was still here. He had felt himself slipping away. But there was no time to delay. He needed to act while the renegade was distracted.

He looked at the old man who was holding his devices in

his hands. "Give them to me!" Ramon shouted in English. "Now! Hurry!"

The shaman handed the filament and the marble to one of the other men who rushed it over to Ramón. Ramón took them in his hands, the filament in his right hand, held upwards, its small arms extended, and the marble in the palm of his left. He closed his eyes and reached his mind out for that of his familiar. She was frightened, cowering on her knees from what she had experienced from the blond haired demon and at the force she had felt being directed at her dream man, her lover.

When Kelly felt his mind joined with hers, she rejoiced. She felt his love and affection for her, his need for her. From across the room, she experienced his yearning for the essences she had been gathering for him, the mists that had filled her every pore. All at once, she understood her purpose. All that he had done to her and with her had been in preparation for this moment. She was delirious at the prospect of serving him, of giving him everything that was hers. She was overwhelmed with love for the man who had possessed her, captivated her, made her his bondwoman. She opened her mind and let everything flow to him over the connection they had built up between their minds over these many, long weeks. Her body vibrated with pleasure as she felt the forces that had built up in her pour from her body to his.

Ramón almost swooned as he felt the woman's energies filling him transferring the essences of the Whole she had gathered and refined with her love. The forces flowed through his body and up to his right hand, causing the filament, held upwards now like a bright, silvery feather, to begin to reverberate. The device concentrated the pure, unblemished energy he sent to it and transmitted it to his other hand. The marble like orb began to glow, lightly at first, and then became brighter and brighter. Soon its light filled the room. It was like he held a miniature sun in his hand.

The shaman stared at the dark skinned man with awe. This was his dream! A feather in one hand and the sun in the other, that was what the man in the dream held! The prophesy was coming true!

Blackthorne felt the light from the pursuer's hand wash over him. His body seemed to melt from its effects. He felt himself growing weaker, his mind fading. "No!" he screamed. "No! No!" This couldn't be happening! All that he had worked for, all his dreams were slipping away. And then suddenly, like a revelation, he saw the righteousness of the Whole. All of his crimes, all of his demonic acts flowed through his mind. It was painful to see the evil he had done. It was right that he should go. His mind yearned for communion with the Whole, for its forgiveness, its acceptance. Only one thing held him back. Cathy! His mind pictured her sweet face, her loving eyes. His heart ached at the thought of leaving her. "Cathy!" he cried desperately. "Cathy! Cathy!" And then, surrendering himself to the force of the light, he fell to his knees, bent himself into a crouch, his head to the floor, and disappeared.

CHAPTER TEN

The men who had been holding the blond haired white man stood back in awe as he vanished before their eyes. All that was left was the clump of ceremonial clothing he had been wearing. The crowd of people just stared in silence. One minute they had been cheering their dark leader and the next minute he was gone. What could it mean?

Ramón, weakened by his efforts, sank to his knees on the floor. The light went out from the marble in his hand and the feather-like filament ceased to quiver. He had done it. The renegade's illness had been cured by the light and he had gone back to The Whole. It was a close run thing, but all had gone according to plan.

When Ramón had gone to visit Nadine at the psychiatric hospital, it had all seemed too neat and convenient. If it had been he that was the renegade, he would have made sure the girl would never have been found. The fact that she had conveniently been identified after being arrested following the pimp's shootout with the police was too good to be true. Ramón had assumed the renegade was watching her, that she had been set out as bait for him to find. He knew that as soon as he appeared there, word would go out to the renegade that his pursuer had arrived and he would be followed back to Virginia. And so Ramón had set his own trap. He had been unhappy when the earnest and loving young woman, Lucy, had appeared. He knew she would suffer at the hands of the renegade or of his servants. But it was too late to send her away. He knew the men were outside and it might have tipped his hand.

Ramón knew the problem was really not how to find the renegade. He would be conspicuous enough. He had already developed a list of suspects from his research over the internet and he had narrowed it down to about four or five men. Jonathan Blackthorne, with his meteoric rise to wealth and his subsequent reclusiveness, had topped the list.

No, the real problem was how to confront him. He knew Jnthrn would have developed considerable strength and power over the years. He would be protected by an efficient and ruthless bodyguard. So how was he to get access to the fugitive? He couldn't just go up and ring his bell and announce himself. "Hi. Remember me, Raijamoon? I'm here to take you back." That approach would have resulted in quick failure. And he needed to have his familiar present when he confronted him. Ramón's hunch was if he let Jnthrn capture him and his familiar, somehow he would end up in the same room with them at the same time. He I't worked out how he would get the opportunity to have access to his weapons, but he felt somehow he would. The intervention of the priestess was just the kind of 'lucky' intercession he needed.

On the night of his capture by Jnthrn's men, he had agonized at the risk he was taking. But he felt he had no other choice. If he waited too long, the renegade might discover him anyway at a time when he was more vulnerable. Also, the renegade's powers grew daily and the evil he was perpetrating was ongoing. Ramón had to act, even though he was putting his familiar in dire jeopardy. He could have been wrong about there being a kernel of decency left in the renegade. The Apaches who had come for him might just as well as killed him outright, as he knew their leader, Bob Cloud, had wanted to do.

But, all had worked out. Now, if the disappointed and still stunned Apache crowd didn't tear him to pieces for destroying their source of power, their golden goose, everything would be fine.

The priestess, Barbara Cloud, mounted the platform. She raised her arms and spoke to the bewildered people.

"Jinthra, the Lord of Conquerors, has returned to his ghost world. His work with us was done. When he came, our people were suffering. Our children were deserting us for the white man's world, losing themselves in the evils of their culture. We were poor, powerless. Now, our children have come back to the old ways. We are a people once more. It is time for the war on the white man and the Mexicans to come to an end. Nanteeka, the Lord of Light, has come among us and will show us the way of peace and prosperity. Go to your homes. We will assemble at the ceremonial grounds in three days. At that time, Nanteeka will give us his laws and tell us how to live."

As the dazed, confused people shuffled out of the large room, Ramón crept over to his still bound familiar. All of her energy had been drawn out of her. He took her in his arms and hugged her, suffusing her with his love. She raised her head and he slowly removed the gag that had covered her lips. He kissed her deeply, grateful for the love she had shown him, happy her times of turmoil and sacrifice were over. Tired as he was, his lust stirred as he felt her tongue intermingle with his. Recalling her bound arms, he reached around and freed them. She circled his body with them and returned his embrace.

Kelly was joyous at her liberation. She had pleased her dream man and played a vital, essential role in his defeat of the evil blond man. She understood now the reasons for her confinements, the limits on her speech, the development of her sexual energies. It had all been truly crucial to her dream man's mission. Happy that she had trusted him, still enraptured by his flesh, she brought her lips back to his, murmuring, "I love you, Ramón. I love you."

When he sensed Kelly had calmed, he turned to see what was going on in the room. Barbara Feathers was sitting on the end of the platform waiting for him. She had taken a huge wad of chewing tobacco from a pouch in the pocket of her ceremonial dress and had stuffed into her mouth. She was smiling at him, a large bulge in her cheek.

"Well, you took your sweet time getting here," she told him.

Ramón was startled by her directness, not to mention the sight of her jaw working the tobacco in her mouth. "What?" he said.

"You were supposed to be here two years ago. What took you so long?" she asked. She spoke with a heavy country twang. She was bent over, her elbows on her spread knees like she was sitting on the stoop at a country store. All she was missing was the straw hat.

"Well," Ramón answered her, "these things take time."

"I guess the hell they do," Barbara replied. She looked down at Ramón's cock which had sprung to attention and laughed. "I see you've got some work to do."

Ramón, for the first time since becoming human, became self conscious at his state of arousal. There was something about the woman's frank manner and her obliviousness to his charm that was disarming. But she was right. He was weak and he needed to refresh himself with the essence of the Whole. Kelly was drained and would need to sleep. She was leaning on him, almost comatose from her exertions.

"I think this one's about to pop," the heavy set, merry, Apache woman said. She was referring to Diane, Jonathan's former familiar, who was kneeling where she had been left at the start of the confrontation between him and the Lord of Conquerors. He could sense her pain and unhappiness. Although Blackthorne was gone, her need for him still tormented her. He would have to remove her attachment to him. At the same time, he would relieve her of the mists she had gathered.

"There's a bedroom upstairs you can use," the priestess said. "We'll talk some more later. Mrs. Blackthorne and three of our young girls are locked up in the basement. The lock was keyed to Blackthorne's mind and so we'll need your help in opening it. They'll be okay for a while, but not too long, okay?"

Ramón nodded his assent. This was not the ending he had anticipated.

He looked over at the three women who had been Blackthorne's acolytes. They were cowering fearfully, anticipating his wrath.

The priestess spoke like she was reading his mind. "You can take care of them later. In fact, there's a whole lot of stuff for you to do. But for now, just go upstairs and enjoy yourself. You earned it."

The shaman was sitting in his ceremonial chair, dejected. This was not how he thought things would work out either. However, the person who was really upset was Bob. He had been Blackthorne's right hand man. He had been correct about throwing the black haired man out of the plane. Blackthorne, like most demented megalomaniacs, had brought about his own downfall. But, he thought to himself, maybe that wasn't a bad thing. There was something about the new ghost man that was special. The light he had emitted had seemed to change something in Bob. He wasn't sure what it was yet, but what the priestess had said to the people had made a lot of sense. They had been at war with the white world and wars weren't supposed to last forever. What happened, he wondered, to the warriors when the war was over? He had done some terrible things. What would happen to him?

After relieving the startled and still fearful Lucy and Jackie from their distress and granting them sleep, Ramón led Kelly and Denise up the broad, polished oak staircase to the second floor. When he entered the suite of rooms that had been Blackthorne's, he met the pretty, young woman named Cathy.

After all the harm he had done, the minds he had stolen, Jnthrn's last thoughts had been for the love he had for the beautiful, ethereal woman. Probing her mind, he could see why. She had a pure, innocent soul. Blackthorn had suppressed all other parts of her personality but her strongest traits, her loving and giving nature. Ramón could feel her mind searching for her master, wondering who this new man was. The dream man sent her a wave of assurance and put her to sleep. He would deal with her later.

The bed in Jnthrn's private bedroom was large and sumptuous. Ramón guided the two naked women to it and laid them down. Kelly fell immediately into slumber, a smile of satisfaction and contentedness on her face.

While she slept on his left, Ramón turned to the shuddering, frightened woman on his right. He could see the fear in her eyes. He probed her mind and found the ravages of her many years as the renegade's slave. In spite of her torment at his hands, or rather, from his mind, she still had a deep, insatiable need for his flesh, the feel of his cock, the effusion of his seed inside her. It would take a lot of work to restore her to sanity. Like Kelly, she had not been captured by Jnthrn in the same way as he captured other women. It had been far worse for her, her mind essentially free, but a slave to her emotional and physical need for the evil man. Ramón knew it would take time to bring her peace. He would take the time and there was no time to start like now.

Diane was still a beautiful woman with a pleasing, shapely body. Ramón ran his hand down her shoulder and along her arm, conveying his beneficial purposes to her. With his mind, he began to suppress her need for the renegade and replace it, for now, with a need for him. He couldn't just remove her dependency. That would be too much of a shock to her system. Besides, he needed her to be open to him, to deliver to him the mists from The Whole she had garnered. It was impossible to just take them. If Jnthrn had won their battle, he would have forced Kelly through fear and pain to give up her vital essences to him. Ramón would take another path. Jnthrn's former familiar would surrender her harvest to him from desire.

Diane had been afraid when her master had taken her from the subterranean prison in which she had lived for so long. She had been suffering through a drug induced dream when she had been awoken and was filled with the fog she had collected for him. She wanted release and was unhappy when she was blindfolded and bound and led from the basement prison. She had knelt wordlessly, suffering from her need during the strange ceremony that had taken place. She I't understood anything of what had happened. But she felt the strong, frightful emanations of her master's will as he fought another man in the room. Then, the battle had ceased and, after a few moments, she sensed a strong, energizing ray pass through her. It was like nothing she had ever felt. It was warm and pleasant and, for a short while, made her forget her torment, her need for release.

Then, she heard her master yell. There was a surge of his will, a seeming last gasp of his powers, and suddenly, he was not there. It was like one of those bubbles children make from a wand dipped in a soapy fluid. One minute it was there and then, bursting, it was gone.

Diane sobbed in misery when she felt the evaporation of her master's persona. Who would grant her relief now, she thought miserably. It was a literal hell to be the evil man's captive, he had tortured her beyond tolerance. But she needed him, a need that was buried deep in her cells like some horrific drug. When she felt the mind of the black haired man reach into hers, grant her a respite from her misery, she began to hope. Now, lying next to him, his hands caressing her flesh, she saw she had been saved.

Warmth and comfort flowed from the man's mind into hers. Diane circled her arms around the man and hugged him tightly to her body and began to cry. It was over. Her torment was over. She could not believe it. She would do anything for this man who had rescued her from the depths of hell. As their bodies met, she absorbed his heat and her lust began to build. She craved union with him, wanted his cock inside her. She would give him the essences she had absorbed, feed him, sustain him.

Overcome with passion, Diane pushed the man over onto his back. She climbed upon him, circling his cock with her hand. She felt its radiance and power. Her slit was moist and dilated and she rubbed the tip of the man's hot pole along its length twice, relishing the energy it sent her before pushing her self down upon it, encompassing it in her fevered canal. She moaned as it filled her. It was like paradise. The man, she still didn't know who he was, not that, at this moment, she really cared, placed his pleasure giving hands on her breasts and squeezed them gently. A wave of passion flowed through her and she moaned loudly. She looked down at him. He had kind, gentle eyes, a strong, noble face, luxurious, brown skin. His lips were parted as he recorded his pleasure. She wanted them, wanted to possess his mouth with her tongue. She wanted to grant him the boon of the mists she had gathered.

Diane leaned forwards. As she slowly began to rock her hips, causing the man's meat to scrape across her hardened clit, she slid her hands over his strong, hairless chest. Just before kissing him, she spoke for the first time in a long, long while. "I've got something for you," she whispered mischievously. And then she pressed her lips against his, entered his hot mouth with her tongue. Her body and mind filled with bliss as she felt the mists flowing from her and entering him.

It did not take long for the woman's pussy to explode into

climax. Ramón reviled in its spasms around his hard, needy cock. Their mouths were still joined in a feverish kiss and she moaned into his mouth, her arms circled tightly around his neck. When he came, she came again, this time riding his cock wildly, caressing it with the walls of her throbbing canal. He filled her twice with his seed and drained her of the essence of the Whole she had accumulated.

When she finally collapsed in exhaustion, he let her body rest down on the bed and wandered from the suite of rooms to see what was going on downstairs. His clothes had been left in the reception room and he walked down the halls naked. Several of Jnthrn's enraptured women stood sentry, naked and trembling as he passed. He stopped at each one and relieved them of their fear.

Barbara was waiting for him and led him to the basement. He was able to use his psychic powers to open the locks and he saw Blackthorne's wife and the three young Apache girls in their cages. At the end, in the last cage, was a cowering white woman, the unhappy Ukrainian woman Blackthorne had captured and tormented less than twenty four hours ago. One by one, Ramón freed the women from their fears. He pushed aside Blackthorne's controls and installed ones of his own. He did not know yet what he would do with all of these women, but he didn't want them running around free until he had a plan of action. It would draw undue attention to the Fortress and Blackthorne's operations, and therefore to himself, for hundreds of young women to suddenly awake from their entrancement and appear at their former homes, even if he had erased their memories of their captivity. Questions would be asked which would eventually lead to the Apache reservation.

He took his greatest care in reforming the mind of Blackthorne's former wife, Dolores. He was not happy keeping her a prisoner after all she had been through, but her mind was heavily damaged from her torments and he wanted to delicately restore her to happiness. Now that Blackthorne was gone, she would be back in control of her fortune which had expanded many times over under the renegade's directions. Ramón wanted to maintain the status quo until he thought things out. For now, being free of her fear of the devilish man who had held her enthralled would have to do. To the delight of the other freed women, Ramón coaxed Dolores into bringing him to climax with her mouth, granting her several of her own orgasms as a reward. His seed would help seal their connection. Barbara stood by watching, amused, and said in a saucy voice when he was done, "That looked like fun, dream man. When you have the time, you'll have to give me a taste."

When he got back upstairs, leaving the women in Barbara's care, Ramón gave Adele a call. It was late in the afternoon on the day following his kidnapping and he knew she and the other women would be fraught with worry. She started to cry when she heard his voice on the telephone. He made arrangements for all of the women, except Hannah of course, to fly out the next morning. He missed them and wanted to spend some time with them. He had been afraid for them while he had been the renegade's captive and he needed their physical presence to assuage his guilt at putting them at risk.

Back in Jnthrn's former bedroom, Kelly and Diane had made acquaintance. When he came in, Kelly was holding the other woman in her arms. They had both been crying. He sensed his familiar's empathy for the other woman and her sorrow for her travails.

His auburn haired lover reached out to him when she saw he had returned. "Diane needs you," she said. It was strange to hear her voice after so many weeks of silence. She had spoken to him earlier and he had been pleased to hear her words. There was no need for her silence any more. His mission was accomplished.

Kelly kissed him and then made him lie down on the bed. Diane gleefully took hold of his cock and subsumed it in her mouth. She took her time in pleasuring him, suckling on the bulbous head of his manhood, licking its shaft, caressing his soft stones, while his lover lay next to him, caressing his chest and face, kissing him tenderly. When Diane finally let him come, he groaned his pleasure and then Kelly took her turn while Diane switched positions with her. Cathy had awoken and was kneeling at the foot of the bed watching the display of lust. Kelly decided she needed his help too. While he was passionately plowing the pale, thin young girl's hot, tight sex, he relieved her mind of the controls Blackthorne had placed there and claimed her for his own. Jackie and Lucy were brought up to the room by Barbara and he spent some time 'helping' them.

When the three Apache girls who had been Blackthorne's servants came up with trays of food and jugs of tis-win, the Apache corn beer, they too clamored for attention. In fact, the rest of the afternoon and well into the night was a continuous fuck fest. Barbara kept on sneaking in, one by one, and sometimes in twos and threes, Blackthorne's enthralled women for him to 'treat'.

It had been a grand party. When not seeking his sexual attentions, the women sought pleasure in each other's arms. Cathy played the piano, and not the soothing, cerebral tones she had played for Blackthorne. Deep down, the delicate young woman was a rock and roller and she really let it all hang out. The happy, naked women danced and laughed, spilling food and beer all over the fine floors. Ramón danced too, a first for him.

The jugs of high proof beer, bitter to taste and carrying an extreme wallop, kept coming. Ramón, although he had learned to enjoy the effects of liquor in moderate amounts, had never consumed enough to get drunk. But by the end of the night, he was so toasted he had to crawl back to the bed.

In the morning, Ramón awoke with Kelly and Diane ensconced on the bed with him. Naked, snoring women were spread out all over the floor. Quietly, so as to not initiate another round of orgiastic mayhem, he woke and then, to his and their enjoyment, drained the two women of the mists they had gathered during the night. His head had been pounding from the effects of the beer, but when he was finished and refreshed by the vital substance, two happy, exhausted, comely women sleeping in the bed next to him, he felt much better.

The three pretty, black haired and dark skinned Apache girls awoke when he went to the bathroom to shower and they insisted on washing him. One thing led to another and they ended by taking turns sucking at his prick until he came once for each of them.

When Ramón returned to the bedroom, he took a moment to relish the memory of the night's festivities. It had been a joyful evening. He I't realized how much the burden of his task had weighed down on him. He felt relieved, reinvigorated.

"What a world this is," Ramón thought for perhaps the hundredth time. The happiness and affection of the women last night had been wondrous. He pitied the renegade who had missed the best things this world had to offer. Why conquer the world when you could conquer hearts? He would miss this world. He looked over at the sleeping Kelly and realized leaving her would be the hardest thing he had ever done. He owed her so much and had given her so little. Would his heart ache when he returned to the Whole, he wondered. Of course, in his native form he did not have a heart. But he would always remember having had one and the pain he felt at the loss of human love.

It was late morning. The desert sun had reached a midpoint in the sky. There was a large veranda just off the bedroom and he walked outside to take in the beauteous vista. It was cold and he was naked, but he did not mind. The smell of the clean air filled him with pleasure. Off in the distance, high in the sky, was an eagle, looping in wide circles, searching for prey. Its graceful flight reminded him of his first morning in this universe. He had watched a hawk coasting an air current high above the Virginia landscape. He remembered his delight at his bath in the brook, the first apple he ate, the taste of the orange juice he had drank. All this would soon be gone. It made him sad to think of it.

Ramón heard a sound behind him and when he turned he saw the ample figure of Barbara Cloud, the High Priestess standing there. For some reason, being naked in front of her was always disconcerting to him. She must have read his mind since she told him, "Don't worry, Nanteeka, Blackthorne was a real clothes horse and you look like you're just about his size."

Ramón smiled. The heavyset woman was wearing a bright red house dress with wide, vertical, golden stripes that descended down to just above her ankles. Her oversized breasts stood out like mountains. She had a pair of dark brown, leather sandals on her feet. Yesterday, her long black hair was tied up in a braid behind her head, but today she had let it all hang out and her hair fell down around her shoulders and back loosely. She stepped up next to him and looked out over the rough, awe inspiring terrain. "Kinda pretty, ain't it," she said.

"Yes, it's beautiful," Ramón replied wistfully.

"Blackthorne used to stand right where you are now and look out over it. Somehow, I don't believe he appreciated it as much as you."

"Well, that was his loss," Ramón answered. "He was mad, you know, before he ever got here. If we had known…"

"Never mind all that, Nanteeka," the woman replied. "Everything has a purpose."

"Why do you call me that?" Ramón asked. "I'm not a god. Far from it. I'm not even really a man."

"No, you're not a god. I know that. I know more about you than you may think. I've been probing what we call the spirit world for almost 40 years and I've done some traveling myself. Ghosts like you have been here before. Many times. Some have wreaked havoc like your friend. Some have done good. Mostly good though."

The pair of dimensional travelers stood quietly enjoying the view of the craggy mountains and the sun brightened semi-arid desert that stretched for miles between them. After a while, Barbara spoke again.

"We've got to talk. Why don't you put on some duds and come on downstairs? I'll have some breakfast set up in the study."

The long, polished wood table in the study was covered with a huge, colorful bowl filled with fresh fruit salad, muffins, a steaming plate of flapjacks and plump, flakey, fresh baked croissants. Blackthorne's clothes had fit him fine. He was wearing a white, cotton, peasant style shirt with delicate, embroidered flowers over it and a pair of crisp, bright blue jeans. The renegade's sandals were just a little big for him and so he had come down barefoot. Barbara Cloud was waiting for him. Two places were set at the table at either side of a corner.

The priestess proceeded to fill her plate with a stack of flapjacks and lather it with a generous dollop of butter. As she poured a flood of maple syrup over it, she smiled at the dream man. "Help yourself. I'm starved. My daughters keep on telling me I should watch my weight, but I tell 'em, 'What for?' I've had my share of strapping young bucks in my day. Not that I wouldn't enjoy a tumble now and again. But the guy I'd be lookin' for would be built for comfort, not for speed."

Ramón had decided he liked the matronly Apache woman. She had a homey style to her speech and lacked pretensions. Her face was round and full and her smile expanded her mouth all across her face.

"Well, I'm famished," Ramón told her, "so, if you'll pass the flapjacks, I'll join you."

The other worlder wolfed down two stacks of the delicious, round pancakes and then filled a small bowl with fruit salad. One of Blackthorne's enthralled women came in, a tall, lithesome, young woman with high cheekbones and widespread, warm, brown eyes. She was naked and Ramón took notice of her pert, firm breasts and her flat, smooth belly. She wore Blackthorne's demonic emblem tattooed on her loins, just above her long, hairless slit. Her blond hair was straight and long and fell down her back to just above her waist. Ramón thought he recognized her from the debauchery of the night before, but he wasn't sure. She smiled at him and poured him a cup of steaming hot coffee, brushing the tip of her breast on his arm as she did so. Ramón remembered her. He probed her mind and found she had a happy memory of their lustful encounter. His cock rose of its own will as his body relived the memory. He smiled back. "Maybe later..." he thought.

"Mary Ellen," Barbara remonstrated with the young woman, "Ramón's got a busy day. Put your name on the list I started in the kitchen and we'll try and fit you in."

"Yes, Mrs. Cloud," the girl said, gleefully. She left the pot on the table and quickly exited, but not before flashing the dream man another smile.

"You're gonna hafta ration your self, big boy," Barbara

said, laughing. "There's a dozen or so women down at the guest motel, fifteen or so over at the security barracks and ten down at the dream lab you need to take care of. And that's just for starters. I got about half of the house staff in last night. And then there's your girls. I imagine you'll want to spend some time with them."

"Adele..." Ramón thought out loud. "When do they get here?"

"Oh, they're here already. I had them wait until we started our little powwow together. I need to talk to you and once they hook up with you, you'll be tied up, I guess, for most of the day. They'll be upstairs in the bedroom when we get finished."

Ramón was pleased the women had arrived. He took a drink of the hot, strong coffee, which he liked taking black with a teaspoon of sugar.

"Okay," he said after putting the cup down, "what do you want to talk about?"

"The future, obviously," the priestess replied. She poured herself a cup of coffee from the pot which she diluted with a little milk and two heaping teaspoons of sugar.

"I don't have a future in this world," Ramón answered her. "I have my duty. I can't stay."

"But who's going to fix this mess your friend made?" Barbara asked. "Are you going to leave all those women out there to live their lives as sex slaves? And what about us, if it gets out what Blackthorne did, there'll be hell to pay. You'll set us back a hundred years."

"Not me, I won't be setting you back. It's what you did. No one forced you to ally yourselves with Blackthorne."

"That's true. But you have to take the long view about these things. Blackthorne set things up pretty good. This is a perfect base of operations and he had amassed a huge fortune, had control of dozens of powerful companies. It'd be a shame to let that all go to waste."

"Maybe," Ramón answered. "But that's not something I can get involved in."

Barbara paused. She looked directly at Ramón and took a deep breath.

"Let me put all my cards on the table, Ramón," she said. "You have a unique opportunity to have an important influence on this tired old world of ours. Our civilization is sick, bent on self destruction. Only a dramatic change in the direction it's going can save us. And I think you're the one to do it."

"Me?"

"Yes, you," Barbara answered.

"Tell me how," Ramón demanded.

"Well, for one thing, that little trick you did with the fireball in your hand had a powerful influence on a lot of folks yesterday. I've been getting calls all morning asking when you're going to do it again. It made people feel pretty good."

"It should," Ramón replied. "It was the essence of the Whole. If Jnthrn I't been mad, it would have blessed the lives of those he had touched as well."

"You see what I mean?" Barbara insisted.

"I can't go around zapping people wherever I go. Besides, unless reinforced, it's just temporary."

"True enough," Barbara answered. "But it's a start. And there's something you can do that would be more permanent."

"And what would that be?" Ramón asked, impatiently.

"You've heard of Genghis Khan, haven't you?"

"Of course. But are you suggesting I conquer the world? That was Jnthrn's madness. It can lead only to destruction, even if it could be done."

"Jnthrn, as you call him, had the right idea. He just went about it wrong. You see, somewhere along the line human beings took a wrong turn. There's a sickness inside us, and that sickness causes most of the world's misery. If you want to change the world, you have to change man. And that's something you can do."

"Change man? How can I change man?" Ramón asked.

"Did you know Genghis Khan is said to have had 20,000 children?"

"No, I didn't know that. That's a lot of kids. He must have fucked all day long, every day of the week."

"Just like someone we know," Barbara rejoined, laughing.

Ramón was beginning to see where the priestess was going. 20,000 kids? That would make for a very expensive Christmas, what with all those toys to buy, he thought. The idea of it made him smile.

"They say one out every twelve Asian men carry DNA from the Mongol invaders," Barbara added.

"You're telling me you want me to have 20,000 kids to spread around my DNA? Is that what you're getting at?"

"20,000 would be a good start."

"You're out of your mind," Ramón responded. He tried to imagine it. Where would he put them all?

"No, I'm not." Barbara answered. She sat staring at the dark haired dream man. There was a long pause between them.

Ramón considered it. This planet was headed to hell in a handbasket. He could see that even in the short time he had been here. And he had seen the basic goodness in most people, people who had not been corrupted or who weren't mad like Jnthrn. Could it be done? How long would it take?

Staying beyond the completion of his task would make him a renegade. But wasn't this what the Whole was all about? Wasn't harmony and peace the purpose of his culture? What good did it do to study other cultures and not give something to them? No one knew how long the Whole had been in existence. It went back beyond any recorded memory.

Should this race have to last millions of years before it saw the benefits of loving one another?

Humans could not be converted to the culture of the Whole in all respects. They would not tolerate the loss of self it required. But that did not mean they couldn't be nudged a little closer. It would be like planting thousands of seeds across the earth and letting them bloom.

Ramón had been staring at his plate. He looked back up at the expectant priestess. "And how would the Apaches fit into all this?" he asked, suspiciously.

"You've studied Indian culture, I'm sure. Our religions all teach communion with the earth and the world around us. Peace is at the heart of all Indian faiths. If you united us, we could be a beacon to the world. While you were changing bodies, we could be changing minds. It has been a long tradition for Apaches and other Indians to adopt other peoples into their tribes. We would be adopting the whole world."

"And Blackthorne's financial empire?"

"Most of that is still in Dolores's name. Blackthorne wanted to make sure if the government ever really challenged him the stocks and properties would be securely tied to a real person. It wouldn't be difficult to keep that together. You'll need it."

"Just tell me this." Ramón demanded, leaning over, his eyes studying Barbara's face for an honest answer. "If you knew Blackthorne was so evil, why didn't you get rid of him? He was just a man. One bullet, the slip of a blade, that was all it would have taken. Why didn't you just kill him and put an end to his madness?"

Barbra paused before answering. "Do you remember what I told you earlier up on the balcony to your room? It's an ill wind that does not blow some good. Everything happens for a purpose. If we had gotten rid of Blackthorne, then you wouldn't be sitting here today. It's as simple as that."

* * * * * * * * * * * * * *

Kelly put down the telephone and smiled. Ramón would be here by 5 o'clock. It had been two months since she had seen him and five years since the dramatic events at the Fortress on the Chiracahua Reservation back in New Mexico. A lot had happened since then.

The girls had all been ecstatic to see him when he came into the upstairs bedroom of the hacienda. Adele had cried as she hugged him. They spent the next twenty four hours in a celebration of his victory. When he told them of Barbara Feather's plan, they had all agreed, happy he had decided to stay, and that Kelly should be first. Ramón was able to convince her mind to cause her to ovulate and the next day, having made his sperm motile, impregnated her. Adele insisted she be next, followed by Melissa and Felicity. Only Jackie opted out, for the time being. She came back to the Fortress a year later and he gave her a child too.

The Apache ceremony had been a grand affair. The whole tribe had assembled. Diane and Kelly agreed to spend the day in preparation absorbing the essence of The Whole during dreams induced by Ramón's potion which Adele had taken with her just in case. There was dancing and singing and, when darkness came, Nanteeka performed the ceremony of the light with his metallic feather and the marble like orb while his two familiars discharged the mists they had gathered while bound and hooded throughout the day. The glow from Nanteeka's hand lit up the night and sent waves of warmth and peace to the whole crowd. There were no doubters after that.

All the girls went back to Virginia the next day except for Kelly, Natalie and Cindy. The two young women insisted in staying with Ramón, flashing the tattoos on their bellies and declaring they, "belonged to him." Ramón still needed Kelly, although Diane, who recovered quickly from her ordeal, supplemented her efforts.

Dr. Morton had been right about Alison. The dream experiments continued at Barbara's insistence, although Dr. Morton's methods were reigned in and, in the future, it was understood he would work only with volunteers. Ramón had removed the fears and pain being suffered by the young women and replaced them with his strong messages of affection and caring. To Dr. Morton's surprise, the results improved dramatically. It was Diane who led Alison the way through the dimensional divide to the Whole. After that, there were breakthroughs with three other women.

It had saddened Kelly, in a way, to give up her role as the sole source of sustenance for the dream man. On the other hand, now that she was not spending her days entranced, she was anxious to get back to her lab and work on her project. Ramón had made much progress on it based on Kelly's earlier research. In fact, the final formula was based on the potion he had concocted for Kelly, but in a much modified form. He had been supplying the modified formula to his other servants and Kelly found it had made dramatic improvements to their immune systems. The best thing of all was that the final product did not have to be licensed as a drug. It was being marketed now as a health drink for women called Mother's Milk, and was a resounding success. The profits made from it in the States were used to subsidize its availability in the Third World.

Kelly cried when she left for Virginia. Her intense, physical need for the presence of her captor had subsided, but they had been through so much together and she loved him so much that it was difficult to part. She knew Ramón had much work to do and comforted herself that it was all for the better.

Ramón promised to come and see her as soon as he could, and his visits over the years were long, frequent and welcome. When the first baby was born, a boy they called Adam, for obvious reasons, Kelly had the baby in the Fortress infirmary and spent the first three months of the baby's life nursing him at the hacienda. Sad at being parted again from Ramón, she went back to Virginia and to her work.

The fact that all of the women who worked at Kelly's lab had become pregnant at the same time had been the talk of Jacksonville. But people soon got over it. Melissa and Felicity had gone back to school and obtained certificates in child care and ran a day care center in town. They lived together as lovers with their four children by Ramón. Chandra had changed her major to study fashion and Ramón had set her up with a major fabric design company in Los Angeles. She had named her daughter Kelly and she now lived with her husband and her son by him outside L.A. The dream man had kept his promise to Nadine and had gone to Omaha to finish the cure he had started. She and Diane still lived at the Fortress with their babies. Nadine had had two, a boy and a girl and Diane was expecting again and due in a few months. Cindy and Natalie still lived there too, but came East often to visit with Hannah and Natalie's dad and show them his grandchildren.

Adele had returned to the lab and continued to live and work with Kelly for about two years. She had given birth to a delightful baby boy. The women continued to be passionate lovers, although Adele had moved to Richmond to get a business degree. In June, she would be graduating and planned to move out to New Mexico to work with Ramón and have a "passel" of babies with him.

Poor, brave Lucy Douglas had been killed in a car accident out on Route 256 a year after she gave birth to twins, a girl and a boy. They had been adopted by Hannah and Phil

Hardings. Ramón had attended the funeral and it was the only time Kelly had ever seen him cry.

Ramón had gradually released most of the women who had been enslaved by Blackthorne. Almost all of them were 'convinced' to spend a year or so at the Fortress while the babies Ramón had given them gestated. Some, unfortunately, like the women who had been sent abroad, they were unable to find. But Ramón had insisted the search continue and even five years later they kept trickling in.

The women who had been enslaved to the various executives and scientists Blackthorne had corrupted had almost uniformly gotten divorces. Many of them, after meeting Ramón and partaking of his gentle, loving attentions, opted to accept his child. The men were made to understand that their crimes would go unpunished as long as they kept their mouths shut and kept doing their jobs. There were, unfortunately, some retaliatory killings by enraged former wives or girl friends, but with lawyers hired by the battered women's legal defense fund set up as one of Marjoram Industries' charities, and certain political influence exercised by Ramón, the punishments were light.

As to Blackthorne's demonic symbol, Ramón had wanted to erase its memory from the women's minds, but it was Barbara Feathers who derived a better solution for it. The pentagram was converted to a symbol of hope and love. It had been very close to one of the Apache totemic symbols anyway. While not mandatory, most of the prospective mothers chose to have the mark affixed to them as a sign of their commitment to the Project and to a new way of life for the world. The sight of it would comfort them and reinforce their bond to the Project's goals. Kelly and all of his former servants now wore one happily.

Ramón had convinced Barbara that a target of 20,000 offspring was a little ambitious, at least in the short term.

Even for a human with Ramón's stamina it was a bit much. They agreed on an initial goal of 500 a year, although now, five years later, Barbara had convinced Ramón to raise it to 750. Each of the tribes that had joined the Genghis Khan Project, as Barbara called it, contributed three volunteers a year. That alone accounted for 100 babies the first year. And the women coming in from their various enslavements around the country, after they had been cured and made healthy with the help of Kelly and Ramón's formula, helped them more than make quota easily in the first two years.

After that, word just seemed to spread somehow. A formal, confidential and underground application process was developed and Barbara and Ramón would go over them every month to select candidates. Careful consideration was given to ethnic diversity and a steady stream of women of all races and colors made their way to the Fortress. Bob and his agents continued to troll the streets of the inner cities for women who had lost their souls to addictions or lives of degradation. Once recruited and cured of the sicknesses of their bodies and minds, they would be incorporated into the Project. Recently, Barbara had begun recruiting abroad and Asian, African and European women were pouring in.

Careful track was kept of Ramón's many offspring. Liberal subsidies were provided together with comprehensive health plans. Some of the women formed what Barbara referred to as colonies, choosing to live and raise their children together. When in their cities, Ramón would stay with them and satisfy any of the women's demands for 'seconds'.

Barbara had insisted, and Ramón agreed, that the process of impregnating the women should not disintegrate into a fucking factory. Once a woman was selected, and her day had come, she would be pampered and catered to by Ramón's servants. A ritual bath and beautification ceremony would take place and the nervous but eager woman would be adorned with an alluring, delicate chemise or nightgown and introduced to Ramón in a specially reserved room decorated with flowers and bathed in a soft, comforting light. She would get to spend an hour with the dream man, during which he would claim her as one of his servants, mold her mind to assure her happiness in her new role and bring her to several earth moving orgasms.

Usually, the women stayed on at the Fortress for a time, sharing their newly liberated minds and bodies with their newfound sisters. Although he had mated with hundreds of women, Ramón never tied of exploring their natures, tasting of their personalities and appreciating their capacity for love.

Ramón was able to keep Marjoram Industries on the forefront of technological innovation and the company could well afford the costs of underwriting the Project. Dolores, Blackthorne's former tortured wife, was one of its directors and she insisted that job training, advanced education and job placement for the mothers be a part of it.

The dream man also took his 'light show', as he called it, on the road. Small but well attended ceremonies were conducted in parks, private homes and rented VFW and volunteer firehouse halls around the country. The gatherings were not advertised and were by invitation only. Publicity was resisted and more than one reporter found his story killed by his editor when he tried to relate what he perceived as the beginnings of a mass movement.

Now, five years later, as Kelly sat at her desk at the lab waiting for 5 o'clock to arrive, she tried to shake herself out of her reverie of reminiscence. She had to go over her checklist one last time. It was about a quarter to five and Ramón would be there soon. She gasped as she felt her new baby kick inside her. She had been depressed for a while at her separation from the dream man, but the presence of his child in her womb soon began to provide her a feeling of warmth and comfort, almost as if a piece of him were inside her. The other girls all said the same thing. Adam had more than a little of Ramón's personality and gifts for love and affection in him. The little boy seemed to glow at times and, whenever Kelly felt low because she was missing her former master, all she had to do was hold the child in her arms and it would seem like the tall, black haired man was there with her.

Kelly had decided Adam needed a brother or sister and that it was time for her to turn the lab over to someone else so she could spend more time with Ramón. The Fortress was overrun with happy, healthy children now and Kelly wanted to help set up a school there. It was a great place to raise kids. Also, she wanted to act as Ramón's familiar again after the baby was born, at least for a while. She missed the closeness she had developed with him and the experience of being fucked by him into insensibility every morning.

Her love for Ramón had not faded and neither had his love for her. Kelly was proud of the man she had concocted from her dreams. He was on his way to making a profound change in the world and she was happy to have been the catalyst for it. Barbara referred to her as "First Mother", a title Kelly relished.

Tonight she and Ramón would spend at the farmhouse where it all began. Adam was staying with his "aunts", Melissa and Felicity, for the night. It would be Kelly's last night there and while she was excited at the prospect of living with Ramón, the event was filled with melancholy. She wanted the night to be special. She was about three weeks away from delivery and her doctor had given her strict instructions on abstaining from sex. But it just didn't seem right not to have the small house reverberating with moans of passion.

Ramón arrived at 5 o'clock sharp. Kelly rushed to him as quickly as her expanded form would allow and gave him a firm hug and a deep, loving kiss. Linda Roberts, the attractive, new lab director, came over to greet him and Kelly made the introductions. As she shook hands with the dream man, a tingle spread up her arm and her eyes widened. Smiling affectionately, Kelly invited her over for dinner.

The End